Forging Divinity

By Andrew Rowe

DEDICATION

For my parents, Bruce Rowe and Christine Rowe, for helping me live my dreams.

CONTENTS

ACKNOWLEDGEMENTS

First off, I'd like to thank my editor, Jessica Richards. Her support throughout numerous revisions of this project has been invaluable.

Thank you to Daniel Kamarudin for really going the extra mile and making me some amazing cover art.

I'd also like to thank my beta readers, Caitlin Bates, Danielle Collins, Rachel Judd, Rachel Noel, Bruce Rowe, Aaron Rowe, and Jennifer Williamson for their excellent notes, feedback, and support.

I owe sincere thanks to Micky Neilson for many years of mentorship and guidance.

Jesse Heinig has earned my thanks for providing me with tons of support when I was struggling to find my way in the gaming industry. I really appreciate all his help and support.

Mallory Reaves has provided support with building this world since its very inception, and Kieran Brewer was instrumental in giving life to the character of Lydia.

CHAPTER I – A MISPLACED WEAPON OF LEGEND

Taelien's jail cell was surprisingly well-furnished. A table of lacquered cedar encompassed much of the center, topped with books, scrolls, and an ostentatious gold-framed mirror. A padded chair sat beside it, unattended, much like the four-posted bed near to the barred window. None of these luxuries were accessible from the position where the dark-haired man was chained to the darkest, coldest wall.

At first, Taelien had guessed that the fine trappings were intended to be a temptation. Perhaps the intent was to imply that cooperation would lead to the reward of a more comfortable imprisonment. Disturbingly, when the questions had come, no such reward was offered. Now he suspected that his captors simply had a demented sense of irony.

His suspicions were supported by the sound of knocking upon the chamber's heavy iron-lined door. *Maybe the headsman will ask me politely before bringing down the axe.*

"Come in," Taelien said, a smirk stretching across his lips.

The sound of a key turning in the lock was jarring. Perhaps some part of him had forgotten that the door was locked – after all, such a measure was largely superfluous, given the extent to which the chains bound his body. He was clothed in them, which was perhaps reassuring, as he was clothed in little else.

As the door opened, an unfamiliar figure stepped into the privacy of his cage. She wore thin spectacles over a freckled face, her hair the red-orange of firelight constrained into a single neat bun. Her loose violet robes, cinched at the waist by a scabbarded belt, emphasized the slenderness of her frame. At a glance, she looked younger than he – perhaps only twenty years of age.

Interesting, Taelien considered. *She is the first female they've sent to see me. Perhaps they think I'll respond better to more delicate persuasion, since force has proven worthless.* After a moment of consideration, he reassessed that idea. *No, the violet robes mean she's more than likely a sorceress.* He noted three silver pins on the collar of her robe, each with the stylized insignia of a spear etched into their surface. *Three pins means she's pretty high ranking, assuming they use a similar ranking system to the one at home. She's less likely here to seduce, more likely here to try to wrest secrets directly from my mind.*

The young woman looked him over for a moment, grimaced, and turned to close the door behind her. He didn't see a key in her hand, nor did he hear the sound of someone else relocking the door from the outside. For an instant, it seemed almost an opportunity, but common sense told him that the woman would be ready for any attempt he made at escape. *Be patient,* he told himself. *You can probably talk your way out of this. It hasn't even been a day yet.*

The sorceress reached upward with her left hand, straightened her glasses, and spoke in a clear tone. "I've been told that you have not been cooperative."

Taelien quirked his left eyebrow. "Hard to do that when no one has told me what I've been accused of."

"You have committed an act of blasphemy against the noble gods of Orlyn." The woman began to pace around the room as she spoke, wearing a disinterested expression. "I am Lydia Scryer, court sorceress. I have been sent here to provide you with legal advice, and to gather details about the incident."

"You can call me Taelien. I'm surprised to hear that I am being offered any sort of representation," Taelien said dubiously, offering her the same name he had given to the other guards.

She glanced toward him at the sound of his name, pursing her lips. After a moment, she shook her head in a dismissive motion. "I may not have been clear. I am not an attorney. My job is to ensure that a confession is extracted from you in a timely fashion."

"Ah, that's much clearer," Taelien replied, a hint of disappointment penetrating through his attempt at cynicism.

"Before we continue our discussion, I must perform a cursory examination," the sorceress continued. She approached him without hesitation, and though Taelien felt an urge to stretch forward to test her response, he kept that impulse at bay.

Lydia came to within arm's reach of him — a mistake, from his perspective, but he did not yet know her own capabilities. His eyes scanned her for any weapons beyond the obvious sword at her side, but found none. The weapon did not frighten him, but her unknown sorcery could pose a threat.

"Dominion of Knowledge, I invoke you," the woman began, reaching out to touch Taelien's arm. His jaw clenched in response, but he made no move to intervene. Lashing out at the sorceress was unlikely to earn him anything other than harsher treatment and more impediments to his attempts to escape.

There was no tangible sensation as the spell took effect, no flash of light, no hiss of sound. He felt only the warmth of her fingers pressing against his bicep. In truth, he had no way of knowing if any spell had been cast at all.

Knowledge sorcery sounded relatively innocuous, but Taelien knew from experience that it could be utilized to devastating effect. He had no talent for the Dominion himself, but his adoptive mother had been an expert. She had taught him that the Dominion of Knowledge could identify weaknesses or fears, even peer into recent memories. He had no defense against it; simply thinking about other subjects would provide no distraction, and any effort to close his mind entirely would be obvious to the sorceress.

Lydia's incantation gave little hint as to what information she was divining. She closed her eyes, seemingly concentrating. After a moment, he realized that her eyes were moving rapidly beneath their lids, almost as if she was dreaming. *That's sort of creepy. Can she learn my goals from a simple touch and a few hastily spoken words? Can she reach into my memories?*

The woman withdrew her hand a few moments later, her expression grim. The sorceress folded her arms across her chest, the fingers of her right hand dancing dangerously close to the hilt of a sheathed saber. Her eyes narrowed, scrutinizing something, or perhaps sorting through whatever information she had just harvested from his mind.

"You are a metal sorcerer," she said matter-of-factly. "Though your connection with the dominion is distinct from others I have analyzed in the past."

Taelien nodded once. He felt the muscles in his shoulders tense. *If she can identify dominions, that might pose some problems.*

The young woman's hand moved away from the hilt of her sword, allowing Taelien to take a breath of relief. "If you cooperate, I may be able to answer some of your questions. Demonstrate your ability to use the Dominion of Metal."

A daring request, he considered, *and a potential trap. Still, I have little choice.*

Taelien had no need for words. His eyes sealed themselves shut, though in truth, such a step was hardly necessary. He could already sense each piece of metal roughly abrading his bare skin – and with a minimal amount of effort, he could extend that sense further into the interlocking rings.

It would have been a simple thing to make a subtle change, weakening the iron bonds at the point where they met with the larger iron rings embedded into the wall. Taelien thrived on complexity. He sought out the weakest points in each link, formulating a map in his mind that highlighted each of these flaws.

Degrade, he told the chains, focusing his mind on key locations in the web of metal that enshrouded his form. As he compelled the metal, Taelien stretched his arms outward. There was only the faintest hint of resistance as each piece of metal tore apart, his silent spell expanding existing weaknesses even as he exploited them. The motion may have looked to an outsider as if he was tearing through the bonds using brute force; in reality, nothing could have been further from the truth. The Dominion of Metal performed feats that his arms could have never achieved.

The chains, shattered by a casual motion and an unspoken word, clattered noisily to the floor.

To her credit, Lydia hardly blinked. Free of the metal, Taelien was suddenly aware that he wore nothing beyond his underclothes. He stretched, yawning intentionally, but the effort had drained him more than his performance confessed. Using any form of sorcery had a cost on the body.

Using flame sorcery would steal his body heat, and he had heard that using water sorcery would consume water from the blood. Metal sorcery was a more obscure art, and the effects on the body abstruse. Whenever he overused the Dominion of Metal he found himself exhausted and profoundly hungry, but he suspected those were side effects of a cause he did not understand.

After a moment of pause, Lydia said quietly, "I was hoping for something subtler. Someone could have heard that."

Taelien shrugged casually, trying to hide his disappointment in Lydia's uninspired reply. "You could have been clearer. In any case, I doubt anyone heard me. Nothing happened last time."

Lydia took a step back, her face betraying a hint of surprise for the first time. "You've broken the chains before?"

"Of course," Taelien reclined against the wall, a crooked smirk favoring the right side of his mouth. "Putting them back on is significantly more difficult, but I would have been insane not to test my most effective method of escape."

The sorceress reached up and pushed her glasses back further on her nose. "You could have been caught."

Taelien held his hands up in a gesture of helplessness. "To be fair, I was already caught. Imprisoning me further would be redundant, would it not?" He paused a moment, and then noted, "That rhymed, I think."

Lydia folded her arms again and tilted her head slightly to the side. "If you could have escaped at any time, why are you still here?"

"Courtesy?" he tried.

She shook her head. "Unlikely. You must have some incentive to remain here. Perhaps you are biding your time, waiting for an ally to rescue you?"

He sighed, holding his hands up in a gesture of helplessness. *She thinks I'm some kind of criminal mastermind. That's kind of flattering, but I should probably set her straight. And if honesty doesn't get me anywhere, I can always fight my way out if I have to.*

"Nothing like that. I'm here alone, not as part of any sort of grand conspiracy." He paused, knowing this conversation could quickly maneuver a saber into his body.

"A few reasons I haven't broken out. First, the last guy who visited me – Veruden, I think – was pretty friendly. I was hoping I could eventually talk my way out. Second, even if I could get out of this room easily enough, I'd have to harm innocent people to get all the way out. Third, I don't know where any of my belongings are, and I'd really like them back. If I fought my way out, I might never see them again."

Lydia furrowed her brow, silent for several long moments. "What is your connection to the gods of the Tae'os Pantheon?"

Taelien briefly glanced downward at the chains piled around his feet. "I'd love to have a good answer to that myself."

"And the sword you carried into this city?" Lydia asked, her right hand drifting toward her own weapon as she spoke. He did not tense for an attack; her motion looked incidental, not hostile.

Taelien's thoughts went to his missing weapon, the object that had presumably been the cause of his arrest.

This sword is your inheritance, his adoptive mother had told him. *The Paladins of Tae'os may cause you trouble — they consider it sacred. They call it the Taelien, "the sword that gives".*

He had learned later that the full name of the sword was Sae'kes Taelien, and he had taken the latter word as his own title and surname. He knew some people would find that arrogant, but humility had never been his greatest strength. The weapon's winged hilt and jeweled pommel were quite distinctive, especially given that the Paladins of Tae'os wore tabards with the sword featured prominently upon it.

"Nothing but trouble, I assure you." He stretched again, and then began to rub at the spots on his arms where the chains had abused his skin the most severely. Fortunately, the chafing was his only current injury. His arrest had been smooth and methodical once he had surrendered his sword, and his captors had not resorted to physical torture. If they had treated him poorly, he would have attempted an escape immediately. "I had no idea that symbols of the Tae'os Pantheon were illegal here."

The young woman stood, unfaltering, seeming to carefully measure each word. "How did you acquire the weapon?"

"I was found with it as a child," he explained, still nursing his bruised flesh. "My parents — that is, the people who took me in — assured me that it was my birthright. Seems less than plausible, really, but I have thus far failed to find a more satisfactory explanation. Would you happen to have any ideas?"

"Several," she said simply. Taelien assumed she was bluffing, but her tone didn't give anything away. "What is your business in Orlyn?"

Taelien pressed his hands against his back, and then flexed backward, applying pressure with his hands. He felt a familiar crack along his spine and his muscles beginning to relax. "I was told to meet someone here. Erik Tarren."

Lydia tilted her head downward and leaned forward toward him, a gesture that was somehow more intimidating than the threat of her blade. In spite of her delicate frame, her green eyes burned with dangerous intensity. "The scholar," she said more than asked.

He nodded, appraising her as he did so. Her stance was not well suited toward initiating combat, but the tightness of her jaw showed the potential for violence. He knew nothing of her capabilities, save that she claimed to be a sorceress. Her spell could have been faked, but given that her assessment afterward had been accurate, it seemed more plausible that it had been real. He was not concerned with her weapon, but antagonizing a sorceress while he was unarmed was an unwise prospect. "I was given a note to deliver to him, but it was confiscated along with my sword and supplies."

Effective, he considered. *The combination of my limited knowledge of her sorcerous capabilities and her threatening body language is making me far more nervous than the guards did. As a result, I'm talking more to her than I did to them. She might not have any offensive sorcery at all, but she doesn't think I'll call her bluff.*

"Don't move," she instructed him, unfolding her arms.

Taelien waited quietly as she reached down to her sword belt – and unfastened it, slowly lowering it to the floor. She bent her knees carefully as she let it down, never letting her gaze leave him. Her gaze glowed with distrust.

After removing the belt, which carried both a scabbarded blade and a large pouch on the opposite end, she grabbed the bottom of her violet robes and began to lift them off of her body.

Taelien found himself at a loss for words, which was a remarkably rare event.

As Lydia removed her robes, it became apparent that the sorceress' motives had nothing to do with seduction. Beneath the violet cloth he discovered a second, identical robe. He found that both comical and somewhat disappointing.

As she concluded pulling the robe over her head, she cast it toward him. He caught it deftly, his expression perplexed. Lydia reached down and hastily donned her belt, her eyes only briefly abandoning him this time.

Taelien examined the soft fabric in his hand for a moment, momentarily perplexed.

"Put it on," she commanded, adjusting her belt with her lips flattened in a self-conscious expression.

Taelien quirked a brow, but wordlessly complied. The inside of the robe was warm from Lydia's body heat. It had fit her loosely, which allowed for just enough room for his arms to fit inside the sleeves without tearing them off. After a moment of confusion at the presence of a protruding bit of cloth in front of his face, Taelien realized he had put the robe on backwards.

The swordsman slipped his arms out of the sleeves, turned it around, and settled into the garment. Lydia shook her head silently, opening a pouch on her waist without shifting her eyes.

"You will put this on and follow me. Once we leave this chamber, do not speak unless you are addressed directly or if I prompt you to do so. If you need to speak, speak in a deep monotone voice. You are to call yourself Istavan, a court sorcerer in service of Queen Regent Tylan," she instructed him, digging through the pouch.

Lydia removed a featureless white leather mask, unfolded it, and tossed it at him. It didn't make it quite far enough, so he lunged forward to catch it, bringing himself a couple steps closer to Lydia in the process. She stepped back immediately, her hand again flashing to the hilt of her weapon.

Good instincts, he considered. He smiled warmly and nodded to her, finding the leather strap on the back of the mask that he would need to use to fasten it into place. The mask smelled like freshly dyed leather – which meant it most likely hadn't been worn much or at all. He knew from experience that leather masks tended to collect sweat quickly, and the smell of a well-used mask was very obvious.

"Keep your hands in the pockets of your robes," Lydia instructed. "Istavan's skin is much darker than yours."

"Are you rescuing me, or are you just capturing me a second time for a different faction?" he inquired, donning the mask. She hadn't asked him to put the hood on to cover his hair, but he did so instinctively.

"You may assume I am doing at least one of those things," she replied coolly.

"May I ask why?" he asked, cracking his knuckles unconsciously.

"You can ask," she said, adjusting her glasses, "But you won't get any answers until we're clear of this place. If things go poorly, I will need to let you be recaptured, and I can't risk telling you much."

"I understand," he replied, disappointed. "Now," he said, deepening his voice. "Does this sound like Istavan?"

Her lips twisted slightly in consideration. "Too deep, actually. That sounded pretentious."

Taelien sighed, lowering his gaze in disappointment. He liked his malevolent monotone sorcerer voice. "Very well," he said, making a second effort. "I must insist that we retrieve my sword before leaving."

"That was a better impress-" she paused. "Your sword? That won't be possible."

He shook his head, continuing to speak in his Istavan voice, "I won't be leaving with you, then. I can't take the risk that the weapon will be transported to a location I can't reach after I leave."

"Who is to say it hasn't been already?" she asked, flexing her fingers. "Never mind. I know where it is," she added in a frustrated tone. "You will follow my instructions exactly. No exceptions. Understood?"

He nodded gratefully.

"Let us go, then," Lydia said, turning toward the door.

"Wait," he replied. "One moment."

Lydia spun back around, folding her arms and glaring at Taelien.

He waved his hands in front of him, trying to defuse her. "My lack of shoes is obvious, since the robe is short on me. Just give me a moment."

Lydia regained her composure in an instant, reaching up to straighten her glasses again. "Very well."

Taelien slipped over to the bed, casting off the heavy blanket atop it and finding a thin sheet beneath. He was loath to damage a part of such a comfortable bed, but the necessity was pressing. He grasped the corner of one of the sheets and pulled it free, then began to tear the sheet into strips. The cloth was surprisingly resistant, but after a minute or so of effort, he managed to pull away a few pieces.

Taelien wrapped his feet and ankles in the cloth, layering it as heavily as possible, and then stepped over to the pile of chains on the floor. He reached down, grabbing a handful of rings, and concentrated. "*Flatten*," he told them. The rings of metal shifted in his hand, merging together into a single thin, malleable sheet. He wrapped the piece around his right ankle, folding it so the metal overlapped with itself. "*Merge*," he told the iron, fusing the ends together, forging a thin metal cylinder around his lower leg.

He repeated the process with his opposite leg, creating a similar metal casing. Finally, he picked up a third handful of rings and flattened them around his left arm. Feeling the weight of the sorcery on his body, he stopped there, turning to Lydia. "Istavan is a name from the Teris-Guard region. This might look like their style of training without boots. Maybe."

Lydia's eyes narrowed, but she nodded thoughtfully. "Sabatons might have been better," she offered.

"Too complex for me to make under these conditions," he explained. He intentionally avoided saying that he would have had a hard time making something that complex under any conditions. "Even real greaves would be too difficult. These are just flat sheets of metal. They wouldn't offer much real protection, but they look like armor."

"It will do," she conceded. "We need to go."

Taelien nodded and followed as Lydia turned and opened the door.

Lydia led the way into a carpeted hallway. Not a single guard stood outside the room, leaving Taelien feeling oddly disappointed by the lack of security. He had envisioned dozens of guards prowling the halls, specifically dedicated to preventing his escape. Fighting such a large group would be difficult – especially without killing anyone – but he had enjoyed the idea of the challenge.

The sorceress pulled the door shut with her left hand, whispering as she held her right hand open. "Dominion of Protection, form the key to this door."

A shimmering glow enveloped Lydia's right hand, and she moved it toward the lock, turning her hand. Taelien heard the familiar shifting of tumblers and the click of the lock.

Clever trick. I've never seen protection sorcery used like that before. I suppose that means she doesn't have the real key.

Lydia strode with purpose toward a stairway on the right. Taelien followed awkwardly behind, his fabricated greaves proving even less hospitable for his skin than the chains had been. *I really shouldn't make anything to wear in the future without practice*, he considered. *Apparently, my legs aren't perfectly cylindrical. Who knew?*

He considered pausing to try to adjust the dimensions of the greaves, but he decided that the cost on his body from performing additional sorcery was not worth the comfort. He was already starting to feel lightheaded from using his previous spells.

As Lydia continued to guide Taelien, they made their way up two flights of stairs. He held his head high, confidently, like he imagined a sorcerer who likes to wear a mask might do. It wasn't all that different from how he was used to behaving in a courtly setting, anyway. They passed a few people in the halls – a couple of people in servant's garb, and a single patrolling guard. No one paid them any significant attention. The guard actually gave him a salute, to which he nodded silently in reply.

As they walked, Taelien observed the trappings on the walls. There were tapestries, paintings, and even mounted weapons and armor. The paintings were in a style he wasn't familiar with, favoring colorful landscapes that didn't seem quite real. He wondered briefly who might have painted them, but a glance at the weapons jarred him back into the moment.

If any guards catch on to us, I can grab one of those decorative weapons, fix the balance on it, and fight my way to where my sword is being held, he considered. If he had been more proficient at Dominion Sorcery, he could have called raw material in the shape of a weapon directly from the Dominion of Metal. His manipulation of metal was a type of Core Sorcery, which allowed him to manipulate the properties of metal objects that he was in contact with.

Using Core Sorcery, Taelien could freely shift the distribution of the material within the metal, allowing him to sharpen edges or alter the weight in favorable ways. With greater effort, he had discovered that he could change some of the characteristics of the metal by commanding it to take on properties of a different type of metal – but this did not extend to appearance, which prevented him from changing iron to gold and making a fortune. He suspected that altering the inherent properties of the metal required drawing from his own body's dominions to make the alteration, but he had never found anyone who could teach him more about metal sorcerous theory. Metal was a relatively obscure dominion, and Core Sorcery was not taught as widely as Dominion Sorcery.

Learning how to conjure or manipulate each dominion was a unique challenge, and thus far, Taelien had only managed to demonstrate any degree of control over two dominions.

Taelien glanced at Lydia, who was walking with a similar air of superiority to his own. *I'm sure she doesn't wear an extra pair of robes and carry a duplicate of this Istavan's mask everywhere. She planned to rescue me from the outset, or at least considered it. Either that or this is all part of some kind of extremely complicated trap.*

The swordsman grinned at the idea of someone setting up a convoluted trap for him – it seemed a ridiculous notion, given how he had peacefully surrendered, but anything was possible.

They reached a large wooden door without passing more than a half dozen people. He contemplated the possibility that Lydia had timed the rescue during a lull in palace activity – after most people had gone to sleep, perhaps, or during some important meeting.

"It should be in here," Lydia said vaguely, indicating the door with a gesture. She reached down and turned the knob tentatively. The door was apparently unlocked and it began to slide open.

A single figure stood inside, examining Taelien's sheathed blade. He stood behind a wooden desk littered with weapons, his body clad in robes, and his face concealed behind a familiar mask. Familiar, in that it was identical to the one Taelien was wearing.

Istavan. Great. Definitely a trap.

Taelien improvised. Surging forward, he shook his left wrist free of the robe, revealing his makeshift plate bracer. *Sharpen*, he told it, creating a thin blade that protruded from the metal cylinder. His initial plan was to grab Lydia from behind and hold the blade to her throat, holding her hostage against the real Istavan. For perhaps the first time in his life, Taelien moved too slowly.

Istavan raised a single hand and thrust it toward Taelien. "Ignite," he said simply, a surge of burning light issuing forth from his hand. Lydia stepped sideways, directly into the path of the blast.

Taelien froze in place as the burst of sorcerous power slammed into the red-haired woman's body. He had seen a similar spell before – and he had seen it kill with ruthless efficiency.

Lydia recoiled from the assault, nearly stepping into Taelien. He caught her as she staggered, ashamed of his aborted effort to hold her hostage, and observed as smoke rose from the front of her body.

His eyes shifted downward for just an instant, registering that a circular section of her robe a few inches in diameter had been incinerated, but her flesh looked unaffected.

Lydia shook free from his grasp and lunged forward, while her attacker dropped Taelien's weapon and retreated in apparent surprise.

Looks like she's helping me after all. Taelien grasped the metal encasing his left wrist, focusing for an instant. *Unfold*, he told it, causing the seam that held the cylinder together to separate. *Ball*, he continued, reshaping the metal into a tiny sphere.

Istavan grabbed a dagger from a nearby table and hurled it at Lydia as she advanced. Taelien's metal ball intercepted the dagger in mid-flight, sending both weapons to the floor. Lydia didn't spare a glance back at Taelien as she advanced, her right hand sitting menacingly on the hilt of her weapon.

Lydia's masked opponent pulled a naked longsword from a nearby table, holding it in front of him defensively. "I suspected we had a traitor among us, I didn't think it'd be you, Lydia." Taelien winced. His earlier impression of the man hadn't been very good.

The red-haired woman bent her forward knee as she approached the range of Istavan's longsword, keeping her weapon in the sheath. Taelien had never seen such an impractical stance – and he wasn't ready to watch his rescuer be butchered. Taelien followed behind her, rushing to the table that contained his own weapon, among others.

Istavan raised his longsword and swung it downward heavily, attempting to utilize his reach advantage. Lydia's cut came diagonally upward – not aimed at her opponent's torso or weapon, but at her attacker's wrist. She twisted the blade at the last instant, slapping his arm with the flat of the blade rather than the edge. The jarring force of the strike sent Istavan's own attack awry and forced him to take another step backward, directly into a chair. To his credit, Istavan both retained his grip on the weapon and his balance, growling audibly as he kicked the chair aside.

Lydia flourished her blade silently, pointing it directly at Istavan's chest. Taelien snatched up a random sword from the table, not daring to draw his own weapon in a place like this. The risks were too great.

Before Taelien could move to flank their opponent, Istavan jabbed his palm in Taelien's direction. "Burn," the man said viciously, a flickering sphere of orange flame surging in Taelien's direction. Lydia moved to intercept the spell, but the table blocked her path. This time, however, Taelien was ready.

Taelien's blade flashed twice. *Disperse*, he told the flame as it met with iron, and the incendiary globe obeyed his command. Flame was the second of the two dominions he could shape using Core Sorcery, but his mastery over it was feeble by comparison. Rather than setting him aflame, the ball split further apart each time his weapon struck, washing harmlessly over him in a wave of warmth.

Istavan lashed out at Lydia again with a slash aimed at her midsection. Lydia caught the horizontal strike on her hilt and pushed his sword toward the floor, stepping in and tapping him on the face with her off hand. "Sleep," she said.

Istavan collapsed unceremoniously, colliding with the chair and knocking it over as he fell.

"Effective," Taelien mused, staring at Lydia and furrowing his brow. *Either thought or dream sorcery*, he considered. *Both extremely difficult to perform, both among the most dangerous types of sorcery to fight against.*

"Efficient," she replied. She leaned down to Istavan, pressing a hand to his forehead again. "Dominion of Knowledge, shatter his last memories into fragments," she said. There was no visible effect. Afterward, she leaned down further and whispered another phrase in the downed sorcerer's ear.

Memory erasure? I was led to believe that was impossible, Taelien considered. He said nothing. Either the woman in front of him was proficient in a type of sorcery he was unfamiliar with, or she was trying to trick him into thinking she could do something that she couldn't. In the latter case – and possibly the former – he was better off pretending he believed her.

Lydia stood up and gave him an incredulous look. "Did you bisect his fireball?"

"No," Taelien replied in his ominous emulated sorcerer tone, "I cut it into quarters. Halves might still have hurt."

Lydia quirked her eyebrow. "You're going to have to tell me how you did that later."

"Trade secret," he replied, grinning broadly.

Without any further hesitation, Taelien abandoned the ordinary blade he had acquired and retrieved his own sword from the table. The ornate weapon was still in its unique scabbard, and that scabbard was still on his belt. He fastened the belt on his waist, immediately feeling a sense of comfort at the presence of the weapon that had accompanied him through every memory he possessed.

Lydia glanced at the sword, narrowing her eyes. "We need to wrap that up in a bundle of cloth or something, it's too obvious," she explained.

Taelien nodded. The sword was about as conspicuous as any weapon could be. The hilt consisted of a pair of silver wings, outstretched as if in flight. Between the wings sat a single sapphire, glowing perpetually with sorcerous light. The hilt held a similar, larger sapphire, grasped within four claw-like prongs. The blade – once unsheathed – was even more distinctive.

Ordinary, he told the sword with a pang of regret. He found his eyes momentarily closing as the spell drew from him, and he shook his head to dismiss the feeling of exhaustion. When his eyes reopened, the weapon's guard had been replaced by a simple cross. The pommel appeared to be a ball of metal.

"What have you done?" Lydia asked, her voice tinged with an unfamiliar note of panic.

"Nothing of significance," Taelien replied calmly, raising an eyebrow at her outburst. "I simply reshaped the metal, covering the gems-"

"That is a *sacred* weapon," Lydia said desperately, wringing her hands in the air. "Assuming, of course, that it isn't a counterfeit," she added in a more typical, analytical tone.

"It is most certainly genuine," Taelien replied with a chuckle. "What's the problem? I thought you were Edonian, not a Tae'os follower. Why would you care?"

"Your observations do you credit, but your assumptions are flawed. We need to leave," Lydia insisted vehemently, "and then we have a talk. A long talk," she assured him, taking an audible breath.

"By all means," Taelien said, adjusting the familiar sword on his waist. "Lead the way."

CHAPTER II – A CONTEMPLATION OF CONSTANT COMPLICATIONS

Twelve Hours Earlier

Lydia woke to the sound of a gentle rapping at her door. This was unusual, as few dared to interrupt the sorceress during the early hours of the morning; it was well known that her work often kept her awake past the rising of the dawnfire.

Lydia rolled out of her bed and to her feet, taking her sheathed sabre from beneath the sheets along the way. After a moment of debate, she set the weapon beside her dresser and withdrew a set of her uniform robes from within. She didn't like the idea of keeping whoever was at the door waiting long, but appearances were important.

Once she had donned her robes, the sorceress retrieved her spectacles from the pages of an open book that sat on the chair next to her bed. She put the glasses on, glanced at the mirror near her dresser, and cringed. Vanity was not among her flaws, but even she could discern that her hair was in dire need of aid.

Retrieving her weapon, Lydia strode to the door, carrying the sheathed saber in her off hand rather than belting it on. It was a conscious decision, intended to draw attention to the sword and away from her perilous lack of grooming. She swung the door wide.

A young man stood before her, his demeanor modest, his pose timid. Lydia somehow managed to look downward at him, slanting her eyes, though the man was at least her own height.

"F-forgive me for the intrusion, sorceress," he began.

At least he knows he's bothering me, she considered. *This must be important.*

22

Why don't I recognize him? She quickly noted that he wore a single earring shaped like a harp – the symbol of the queen - on his left ear, that he had a small but noticeable facial scar under his right eye, and that his stance favored his right leg. She found that identifying distinctive characteristics helped her recall individuals more easily, which was useful in her line of work.

"Yes?" Lydia inquired, lowering her left arm to rest the saber against the ground. Though the movement was the opposite of hostile, her action would serve to attract even more attention to the weapon's presence.

"A meeting of the court's sorcerers has been called," the man explained, standing up a little straighter.

"For when?" she asked.

"Right now," he said in an apologetic tone, wincing slightly.

"Resh," she cursed lightly, using a popular expletive that literally meant 'raw garbage'. "All right, I'll be there. In the Cobalt Room?"

"Yes, I'm to take you there-"

Lydia scowled, leaning forward just a fraction, "I believe I am more than capable of walking up a flight of stairs on my own." She felt bad for the lad – she had been a timid youth herself, and intimidating others did not come naturally to her. But her present role, "Lydia Scryer", required meeting certain expectations. Lydia Hastings might have been gentle or compassionate, but Lydia Scryer most certainly was not.

"Of course. Forgive me," the man replied, folding his right arm across his chest and bowing slightly at the waist before retreating. The gesture was slightly odd – in the local culture, one only bowed using the right arm when addressing a member of the nobility. Perhaps she was being mocked, or this man held the court sorcerers in particularly great awe. She had seen similar behavior before, but most of the palace servants were acclimated to the presence of sorcerers.

At the moment, that bit of minutia was too insignificant for Lydia to waste her time on pondering it. She shut her door the instant the messenger departed and rushed to prepare for the meeting.

What could be important enough for a meeting at this hour? She pondered possibilities. An invasion. An assassination attempt on the queen. Perhaps Edon, the leader of the local gods, had laid down a new edict.

The worst possibility occurred to her as well – her identity could have been discovered.

It didn't seem likely, since her head was still firmly attached to her shoulders, but it was possible.

After swiftly maneuvering her hair into a workable bun, Lydia belted on her sword and a small leather pouch. She glanced at her writing table, a handful of books stacked atop it near dozens of smaller scrolls and pieces of parchment. When attending a meeting with her fellow sorcerers, she always did her best to be – or at least look – prepared.

Her eyes briefly lingered on *The Nature of Worlds* by Erik Tarren, the first book she had ever owned. It had been a gift from her actual father – not the man she had grown up with thinking was her father – to her mother. Her mother had never taken an interest in it, but Lydia had found the contents fascinating.

The tome described the various Dominions as physical locations – which the author sometimes called "Planes" – and claimed that inhabitable areas existed on these other "Planes". The world Lydia lived on was said to reside within the "Core Plane", and it was speculated to be one of many. The term Core Sorcery, now commonly used among sorcerers, was named in reference to this planar theory.

Dismissing her errant thoughts, Lydia retrieved a scroll at random from the pile, knowing it was almost certainly unrelated to the discussion at hand, and headed toward the meeting chamber.

As she walked down familiar halls, Lydia pondered the possibilities for the meeting. *They could want us to interview a new potential apprentice, or someone to serve in the Queensguard. Selyr might have sent another ambassador, since things with the last one didn't go anywhere. Or maybe someone has finally identified the assassins that were discovered in the palace a few months ago?*

Two months before, a group of armed men had been found near the chambers of the crown prince. They had been noticed, but most of the men had managed to evade capture. Rialla, one of the local gods, had personally interrogated the man who had been captured. Whatever she discovered had caused the prince's coronation to be delayed, and the new date for the crowning ceremony was currently three weeks away.

Lydia rubbed at her eyes as she approached the door to the meeting room. *Gods, I hate mornings. Maybe I should have sent that hugely conspicuous servant to get me some breakfast.*

The Cobalt Room was named after Corrigan Cobalt, one of the city's founders. While most of the rooms in the palace had colorful names – literally in some cases, figuratively in others – the Cobalt Room was utterly plain in appearance. The nondescript gray walls completely lacked adornment, which Lydia had quickly realized was a security measure. Sorcerers tended to find ways to turn mundane objects into tools, and practically any item could hold hidden danger.

The lone wooden table in the center showed many years of use, though the chairs around it were plush and comfortable. There were no windows, and the room only had a single entrance.

"Close up the room, we're all here," said Sethridge, one of the three sorcerers seated at the table. Lydia nodded and shut the door behind her as she entered, moving to take her place in the single vacant seat.

Lydia glanced at her colleagues, noting who was present. Sethridge had spoken first and, if his usual behavior patterns held, he would do his best to speak last. He was senior among all those present, having served the queen regent for more than fifteen years. His face was lined with light wrinkles, not from mirth, but the deep creases of worry.

While Sethridge wore three pins on his collar just as most of the others did, he unofficially functioned as the group's leader and primary organizer. This meeting had most likely been his idea; the majority of the other sorcerers tended to avoid each other unless they needed something specific. Aside from coordinating the sorcerers, Sethridge spent most of his time politicking with the city's nobility. The city's nobles commanded comparatively less influence to what Lydia had seen in Velthryn and other cities – the queen regent commanded virtually absolute power, at least in theory. This was, at least in part, because Queen Regent Tylan was also considered one of the four local gods.

To Sethridge's left sat Veruden, a younger man with skin bronzed by the dawnfire's rays. With only two pins, he was the lowest ranking of the sorcerers present, but apparently senior enough that whoever organized the meeting wanted him there. Apprentices wore a single pin, and apparently none of them had been invited.

Veruden was the only one among them who spoke openly of his past, often telling stories about his father's farm, which he supposedly still visited. Sorcerers from the lower classes were rare, if only because few could afford the education required to hone their skills. Veruden had been fortunate enough to find a wealthy sponsor, though Lydia did not know the details of their arrangement. It must have been a pleasant one, since he wore a smile like a second set of robes.

Veruden had a series of bandages wrapped around his right hand.

They looked pure white, which meant that they must have been freshly applied. *Recent injury*, Lydia noted, filing the information away for later.

To Sethridge's right was Morella, a woman Lydia guessed to be a few years older than herself. She was a genius at Memory Sorcery, one of the most difficult types of sorcery to master. Lydia had long considered Morella for lessons, but they rarely spent any extended time in the same location. Morella's talents made her incredibly potent at finding criminals and she was frequently utilized for that purpose. Her presence was peculiar, indicating that a crime was most likely involved.

"You heard anything yet?" Veruden asked Lydia, leaning against the table with both arms. In spite of many years in the queen regent's service, he had never learned appropriate courtly manners. Lydia had a soft spot for him – he reminded her of Keras, one of the boys – now men, she supposed – that she had trained with.

"No," Lydia replied, shaking her head.

Almost all of us are here, she considered. *Peculiar.*

Lydia had heard that Istavan, the last of the five full sorcerers in the queen regent's service, had been assigned to a diplomatic mission outside of the city. She had heard that it had something to do with Prince Byron's upcoming coronation, but she didn't have any details. She presumed it involved attempting to track down the potential assassins that had been discovered near Byron's chambers. Regardless of his agenda, she did not expect to hear from him for weeks.

Odd that the queen regent always sends Istavan on long-distance assignments, rather than Veruden. I'd think that she'd want Istavan here – he's familiar with multiple types of battle sorcery – and Veruden only knows travel sorcery, as far as I know. Maybe she just trusts Istavan more. Veruden is a bit impulsive.

In the many years since Orlyn had been freed from Xixian rule, sorcery had retained a degree of mysticism amongst the general populace. For centuries, sorcery had been the tool that was used by the most powerful Xixian nobility to keep their slaves in check. While slavery was illegal in modern Orlyn, sorcery was still considered an endeavor reserved for society's elite. Sorcerous training was passed on directly from experienced practitioners to a small number of apprentices.

The other major cities on the continent handled sorcery differently. Liadra and Selyr tested children for inherent talent at a young age, drafting them into mandatory training and military service if they demonstrated a significant degree of potential.

In Velthryn, sorcery was largely controlled by the burgeoning merchant class, with sorcerous academies selling educations of varying degrees of quality to those wealthy enough to afford the privilege. Some degree of elitism remained among the highest degrees of Velthryn's nobility, who proudly attributed their training directly to the city's greatest masters.

As a result of these cultural differences, Lydia estimated that the sorcerers in Orlyn numbered in the low hundreds, and the three who sat with her now were among the most influential. By contrast, in the city of Velthryn, there were hundreds of sorcerous students in academies and thousands of trained sorcerers in the city as a whole.

"We have an invasion to plan for," Sethridge said without any hint of emotion, his hands folded in his lap.

Veruden shot Sethridge an uncharacteristic look of dismay. "We don't know that for certain."

"What's this about a potential invasion?" Lydia asked.

"Those worthless zealots in Velthryn seem to be feeling the itch to expand their territory again." Sethridge scowled, and Veruden raised his hands defensively in response.

"Leaping at a conclusion there, Sethridge. He doesn't even look like he's from Velthryn." Veruden leaned back in his chair, shaking his head.

Morella ignored Veruden and Sethridge's argument, looking straight to Lydia. "This morning, the city guard brought in a man for carrying a symbol of the Tae'os Pantheon."

Lydia nodded and the two men ceased their banter, turning to listen to Morella's explanation.

"Normally, this would be a minor issue. I don't think you've had to deal with any cases like that yet, but we typically don't even arrest people for Tae'os worship, even though it has been outlawed for over a century. We estimate at least a fiftieth of the population still worship the older gods, in spite of everything," Morella continued. Lydia knew much of that already, though her estimate of Tae'os worshippers in the city would have been much lower.

"The few arrests that have been made in the past usually result in the culprit apologizing, promising to never worship the old gods again, and being set free after paying a minor fine. This case cannot be so easily dismissed. The man was carrying a sword that resembles the sacred weapon of the Tae'os religion, realistic enough to appear authentic,"

Morella concluded.

A replica of the Sae'kes Taelien? Lydia's mind hit several possibilities immediately. A wealthy noble that worshipped the Tae'os Pantheon could have been making a statement, hoping that his trial would reverse the laws against Tae'os worship. This would be an ineffective tactic, but it was plausible. More likely, a noble had bought the replica in another city, thinking it was a beautiful design and not realizing the significance. Even more likely, however, was that the sword-bearer was sent from the city of Velthryn to provoke the people of Orlyn into taking action against him. If Orlyn took an overt action against the man, it might be significant enough to convince Velthryn to declare a holy war.

Lydia concluded that her colleagues had been discussing the third scenario in her absence. *It couldn't possibly be authentic, could it?*

"We believe it is possible the sword is authentic," Sethridge declared, leaning back slightly as he spoke.

Lydia considered her actions carefully. Revealing her level of knowledge about the weapon in question would potentially lead toward unraveling one of her best kept secrets – as such, she decided to keep her inquiries brief and her statements briefer.

"Why do you believe it may be authentic?" Lydia asked.

Sethridge unclasped his hands, putting his right on top of the table. "One," he said, extending his pointer finger. "The man gave no resistance when he was taken in. He claimed confusion and ignorance of the law. I know this may not seem relevant yet, but bear with me."

"Two," he said, extending his middle finger. "He proved extremely reluctant to part with the weapon, far more so than to surrender any other possessions – or to surrender himself into custody."

"Three," he continued, counting with the next finger. "The city watch members who confiscated the weapon were unable to draw the sword from its sheath. They found no bond, latch, or other mechanism to keep the sword in place."

"Four," he said, extending his pinky. "The man had black hair and blue eyes."

Lydia knew those traits immediately – they were associated with the mortal appearance of Aendaryn, the leader of the Tae'os Pantheon. She said nothing to give any indication that she understood the significance of this, save perhaps with a blink of her eyes. Neither black hair nor blue eyes were individually uncommon, but they rarely appeared together. *Of course, alchemy can be used to dye hair*, Lydia considered. *And someone with Rethri blood might exhibit a rare combination of hair and eye colors naturally.*

"Five," Veruden added, interrupting. "We haven't been able to get the reshing thing out of the scabbard, either. It's up in the armory. Maybe you'll have better luck."

Lydia quirked a brow with that. "All of you have tried and failed?"

"I wouldn't go near the thing," Morella explained. "Veruden tried to teleport the sword out of the scabbard. When he touched it to cast the spell, a flare of blue sparks seared his hand."

Veruden lifted up his right hand with a grimace, displaying the bandages that Lydia had noticed earlier. She crossed that mystery item off her mental checklist, nodding to him.

"Has anyone attempted any sort of identification spells on it?" Lydia asked. "It could simply be an ordinary weapon with some sort of protective sorcery on it."

"That's part of why we woke you up," Sethridge explained. "Veruden and I have no expertise at that sort of sorcery, and Morella won't touch it. Istavan isn't here, so that leaves you. We need information, fast. Chances are we won't get another opportunity to look at it after Myros arrives."

Lydia could not contain her concern at that last statement. "Myros is coming here?"

Myros was one of the four local gods. He represented battle, strategy, and protection. Unlike in any other kingdom Lydia had ever heard of, the gods of Orlyn took part in the affairs of their land, walking among mortals undisguised. To most, this meant that Orlyn's gods cared about their people. To Lydia, it meant several completely different things – not the least of which was that these "gods" were more than likely not gods at all.

Still, they were formidable, and wielded more political power than anyone. She did not relish having to deal with the supposed god of battle for any reason – and this was one of the worst reasons possible.

Myros carried the Heartlance, an artifact that served as a symbol of the gods of Orlyn. Edon, the leader of the local pantheon, had held the spear until Myros had ascended to the position of god of battle. Any blood drawn by the weapon was said to strengthen the wielder.

Faithful of Myros would volunteer to cut their hands on the Heartlance's blade, supposedly contributing to the god's strength.

Wounds inflicted by the weapon were rumored to bleed indefinitely, and thus, Myros would supposedly bless the wounds of his faithful himself, reversing the artifact's effect and showing his appreciation for their dedication.

"How does he know?" Lydia asked, folding her hands in her lap, intentionally mirroring Sethridge's earlier gesture. She frequently modeled her body language after his, as Sethridge was typically considered the leader among them, and any similarity in their behavior would help to cause others to consider her to be of similar importance.

"Protocol," Veruden explained. "I sent him a messenger as soon as we ran our first tests and determined the sword was dominion bonded. Even if it is not the real Sae'kes, someone went to the trouble of dominion bonding a weapon. That costs, and someone would need a good reason to spend that kind of coin."

Resh. Last I checked, Myros was in Torlan. That's only a week's ride from here.

"Such as keeping four court sorcerers busy while they do something unrelated?" Morella suggested.

"An excellent point," Sethridge conceded, frowning. "Well, since you have decided not to be useful in investigating the weapon, you can go try to discover whatever this other scheme might be." His tone was bitter enough to border on outright hostility.

Lydia frowned as well, but she wasn't mirroring Sethridge intentionally this time. She found that the possibilities were growing ever more disturbing.

"I don't need your permission to be here or to leave," Morella pointed out in a neutral tone, leaning forward slightly as she spoke. "But I do have better things to do." She stood, nodding at Veruden and Lydia, and departed from the chamber.

"That was a bit cold," Veruden pointed out after the woman had closed the door behind her.

"I believe she may be involved," Sethridge explained, drawing a shocked glance from Veruden. Lydia managed to keep her own expression neutral. "A spark triggered by defensive sorcery is not a sufficient reason for her to avoid casting a non-invasive spell on the weapon to identify its properties. She is an expert. If nothing else, she could simply wear a pair of gloves."

"That does not necessarily mean she's hiding any sort of involvement," Lydia pointed out. "She could, for example, be going to go inspect the weapon right now, while the three of us are in here debating, and then keep the knowledge to herself."

Veruden turned his shocked look toward Lydia. "Am I the only one here who believes in honesty and trust?"

"Yes," Sethridge said without hesitation.

"Pretty much," Lydia conceded, nodding. "Though, to be clear, I was not stating that I thought what she was doing was inappropriate. She may have a good reason for wanting to gather information and keep it to herself."

"Oh? Such as?" Sethridge asked.

"If she suspects the weapon is real – and finds confirmation that it is – she may want to gather enough information to try to figure out how the dominion marks on the weapon work. According to legend, the Sae'kes has at least seven dominion marks on the blade. Dominion marks are impossible to replicate in modern sorcery. Knowing how to replicate that technique would be incredibly valuable information, especially if only she had it," Lydia asked.

What she hadn't said – but that the others almost certainly knew, save perhaps Veruden – was that dominion marks were only found on the ancient objects imbued with powerful sorcery, colloquially called "artifacts". Artifacts were thought to have been forged by the gods themselves in the earliest days of the world, and many sorcerers actively hunted for artifacts for prestige – or in hopes of learning to weave the sorcery used to create them.

"And what is to stop you or Istavan from learning the same details after she does?" Sethridge inquired, sounding genuinely intrigued by this line of discussion.

"Well, she could replace the weapon with a copy – tricky, given the limited time. More likely, she simply expects that Istavan and I are not as good at analyzing sorcerous characteristics of objects as she is. She would most likely be correct if she made that assumption. But this is pure speculation, and it remains more likely that she is both unconnected to this whole incident and that she is not going to go inspect it right now. I was simply giving an example of an alternate motive behind why she may not have wanted to look at it earlier."

Sethridge nodded. "Your point has been made. Well, regardless, it is best if you take a look at the weapon soon – in case Morella is trying to do something to keep the secrets to herself. Also, we should take turns speaking to the prisoner."

"I already have, actually. He seems nice," Veruden said. Seeing stares the other two sorcerers gave him in response, Veruden continued, "What? I wanted to get a good image of him in my head, in case he escapes later. Too often, we waste time on discussion, not acting until it's too late. He may have escaped by now, for all we know."

"I doubt that," Sethridge said. "They did put him in the Adellan Room, after all."

The Adellan Room was named after Prince Adellan, a legendary prince who had been captured in battle when Orlyn was still a part of the Xixian Empire. The Xixians had promised during a parlay with Adellan's father to keep him in a chamber filled with "all the amenities entitled to a prince" while the other kingdom bargained for Adellan's release.

Adellan had died chained to the wall of a pretty room, just out of reach of his precious "amenities". The Xixians had held true to the word of their bargain, just as they had always been famous for.

A lesser known quality of the Adellan Room was that it was located near the palace's barracks, allowing the palace's guards to keep watch on the room with minimal effort.

The proximity to the barracks means anyone visiting the prisoner will be likely be noticed. Captain Randall probably carries the key, which means several people could find out if I go ask for it. That's less than ideal.

Veruden raised a hand and rubbed his forehead. "Who ordered for him to be put in the Adellan room, anyway? That seems a little harsh."

Sethridge turned to Veruden, offering him an exhausted shrug. "Captain Randall. I assume his orders came down from the prince."

A prince ordering someone to be held in the Adellan room. That's rather ironic.

"Well," Lydia said, "I suppose I'd better go take a look at that sword."

"If you find anything of interest, please let us know," Veruden implored her.

"Of course," Lydia replied. She planned to do nothing of the kind.

Lydia took hasty steps as she headed to the palace's armory. Her heart wanted to run, and her mind quickly outpaced even that. *Is this man an agent of the gods? If so, will my involvement interfere with their plans? No, more likely he is some sort of spy. But if so, from who? Would Velthryn be foolish enough to be so overt? What could they possibly gain?*

Her mind sorted through other options as she walked, trying to maintain some measure of composure. *Either Morella is right and he's a distraction, or he's an agent of a third party. The Kesites, maybe, or the Rethri. The Kesites have the best incentive; a war between Orlyn and Velthryn could leave both cities vulnerable to conquest.*

She noticed her arrival at the armory door as her hand moved to lift key to lock.

I need to focus, she told herself, turning the key.

Inside were assorted weapons, pieces of armor, and seemingly random trinkets. Her eyes caught the unmistakable hilt of the sole object that resembled a legendary sword. Her heart still racing, Lydia hesitated not out of fear, but out of reverence.

Gods, if by your grace you have chosen to guide me to this weapon, please give me the wisdom to know how to deal with it.

With that prayer in mind and a grim expression, Lydia stepped inside and shut the door. While she knew intellectually that prayers had never been proven to elicit direct results, and she doubted the gods had any method for hearing the errant thoughts of their followers, prayer had been drilled into her at such a young age that she engaged in it unconsciously as a matter of habit.

She did not bother to lock the door to the room; it would delay any potential rescuers if she injured herself by triggering a more powerful defensive spell than Veruden had.

Her eyes scanned from side to side. Lydia noted no one else to observe her actions – but that did not mean no one was watching. She desperately wanted to speak aloud, to declare her allegiance to the weapon. Her faith was one reason, but practicality was the greater of the two. The spells on the blade might allow a true believer in the Tae'os Pantheon to draw it from the scabbard.

With the utmost hesitation, Lydia grasped the leather grip of the weapon with her right and the scabbard with her left. Silently, she pulled on the hilt, attempting to separate the two.

The scabbard remained firmly in place.

Some childish fragment of hope in Lydia's mind was shattered, but her natural inclination toward problem solving filled the gap. A scabbard stuck in place did not imply the gods did not want her to have the weapon. It simply meant that there was some force keeping the sword in place – a force she had not yet identified. She had a spell for that.

"Dominion of Knowledge, I invoke you," Lydia said aloud, knowing that unlike a declaration of faith, this would not arouse any suspicion if overheard.

Her vision momentarily blackened as the spell took hold. Letters flashed in her mind's vision, showing her fragments of a broken thought. *Eru ...n de... ..laris, kor. ...s o..n .. taris. D...ni.. ..at e..s ../ o. ...a...n...*

Every knowledge sorcerer experienced using the Dominion Analysis spell slightly differently, from what Lydia had been told. Some saw images, like memories stolen from other eyes. Others said they heard a voice whispering the answers they sought. Still others claimed that after casting the spell they simply knew the answer – as if they always had.

Lydia found herself sitting on the stone floor with no memory of how she had gotten there. The sword lay across her lap, still contained in its scabbard. Lydia narrowed her eyes at the weapon. Knowledge sorcery would extract a fragment of her own knowledge as a cost each time she used it – but she had never experienced a blackout from casting it. Any memories the spells had stolen in her past had been subtle.

Lydia's spell had always presented her with text; that was no surprise. Books and scrolls were her greatest friends and the only loyal ones. She had never before been betrayed with mere fragments of an answer.

Her legs felt weak, but she managed to wobble to her feet. *What in the resh was that? More defensive sorcery, like what Veruden mentioned?*

She did not dismiss that possibility entirely, but she shoved it aside in favor of other options. *Perhaps the spell failed, or I cast it improperly. Or,* she considered with some hesitation, *perhaps the weapon is so powerful I can't even understand what I just experienced.*

The last option she considered only for the sake of completeness; assuming the weapon's dominion marks were beyond her comprehension would be unproductive.

More likely, she continued to consider, *I came in contact with multiple dominions at once. The spell is made to identify a single dominion. If the sword carries several dominion marks – as in legends – perhaps my spell was simply unable to translate that information. I may need to develop a new spell to try to analyze this further.*

Lydia nodded, finding that explanation acceptable for the moment, and returned to her focus on a completely different series of problems.

The sorceress returned the weapon to its position on the table with some reluctance, and then used the table to support her weight. She was still feeling dizzy, which was not a good sign.

Focusing as best she could, Lydia examined the weapon. At a glance, the weapon fit the description she had always heard – a hilt long enough for two hands to fit comfortably, a long and elegant blade, and a metal that shined with greater luster than any silver she had ever before witnessed. She carefully lifted the sword a few inches, trying to peer inside the scabbard to see if she could get a look at the runes that should have been visible on the surface, but the sheath was flush against the blade.

The scabbard itself was an oddity; it was wrapped in white leather (a color used to demonstrate affluence), but with metal plating along the sides and covering the entire tip. It struck a beautiful image, but so much metal on a scabbard had to be impractical. Not that the god of swords would have been inconvenienced much by such a thing, she mused, but he was supposed to be a pragmatic deity.

That's the first thing I've noted that's out-of-place, she considered. *And, now that I think about it, the scabbard isn't in Aendaryn's colors. He wears silver, black, and blue. This is white and...iron, I suppose.*

It was not much evidence of the sword being a fake, but little else provided her with a clue.

Lifting the weapon again, she moved into a combat stance. Raising the weapon into position felt easy, fluid – even with the scabbard on the weapon. The weight of the sword was negligible. She could feel it, but the weight only seemed to be enough to remind her that the weapon was in her hand. The blade felt heavier from the presence of the scabbard, but only slightly.

I could take it, Lydia considered. *I could do more experiments in my room, or just flee the city with it entirely. If this really is the Sae'kes, it could change everything in Velthryn in an instant. If I could learn how the marks work, it could usher in a new era for sorcery. And even if I failed to do that, the mere presence of the sword could save numerous lives. If stories of the weapon's power are true, a proper wielder could turn aside entire armies.*

She dismissed the idea almost as quickly as it came to her. She could get permission to take the sword to her chambers later – just walking off with it now would be a needless complication.

Attempting to get back to Velthryn with the sword would be considerably more difficult. The weapon's absence would be noticed within hours. With Morella's detection spells and Veruden's teleportation, it was likely they could catch up to her.

More importantly, returning to Velthryn now would require abandoning her mission. Her responsibility was to gather information on the most prominent local sorcerers, as well as the supposed gods of the city. She delivered her reports during the infrequent opportunities her position gave her the excuse to travel to Velthryn's territory, and she had no such excuse right now. Her mission had no set end date – she would be dismissed when her superiors felt she had done sufficient work, or if her cover had been significantly jeopardized.

The Sae'kes was most likely worth abandoning her mission – but the prisoner who had carried it was potentially even more important.

I need answers. Conclusive answers. And for that, I need to meet with the prisoner directly.

Lydia returned to her chamber, making preparations and strategizing for contingencies. And then, after preparing an extra set of robes and putting a mask matching that of another sorcerer in her pouch, Lydia initiated the first stage of her plan.

Since Lydia lived in the palace, passing by the Adellan room a few times throughout the day – hours apart – didn't attract any undue attention. Each time she ensured she had an unrelated agenda nearby, just in case she was asked.

It was on the third pass that she deemed the halls sufficiently clear. While there were always at least a few guards on rotation, she knew from experience that there were lulls, especially during meals. It was supper hour, and most likely her best chance to avoid being noticed.

The sorceress pressed her hand against the door's lock, speaking in a whisper.

"Dominion of Knowledge, show me the structure within."

The Structural Analysis spell functioned differently from most of her other spells, presenting her with a series of images rather than text. She could see the interior of the lock, the positions of the tumblers, and the amount of open space inside the keyhole.

Taking a breath, Lydia flexed the fingers on her right hand and formed an image of the necessary key in her mind. "Dominion of Protection, form a key to this door."

The shimmering construct in her hand wouldn't last long, but she took a moment to knock lightly on the door. There was no one in the hallways nearby to hear her, and now she needed to focus on making a first impression on the prisoner within. She wanted to be polite, but firm, and ultimately sympathetic if she decided to help him.

She turned the sorcerous key in the lock, hiding her uncertainty beneath a veneer of stoicism.

Shortly thereafter, Lydia knelt over Istavan's fallen body, whispering a spell into his ear.

"Dominion of Dreams, ravage his mind with nightmares of different versions of this confrontation." She shuddered involuntarily in the aftermath of the spell – it was a horrible thing to do to a person, but better than slitting his throat.

Lady of Destiny, forgive me for abusing the gifts you gave me in your great kindness.

Using dream sorcery too frequently would wreak havoc on her ability to concentrate, but she had practiced frequently enough to be able to handle the use of two spells in a day without significant side effects.

She had faked casting the knowledge spell that would supposedly erase Istavan's memories – she didn't have any spells with that exact function, and most people didn't have a high opinion of sorcery that caused nightmares. She didn't want Taelien to formulate a poor opinion of her; especially now that it was looking more plausible he really might be an agent of the gods.

The nightmare spell wouldn't have any lasting negative effects on Istavan, but she hoped it would sufficiently disturb his memories of the event to prevent him from reporting her as a traitor. And, even if he did report her, she could point out that he had been affected by dream sorcery – making his testimony unreliable.

Taelien and Lydia stripped Istavan of his robes and boots. While Taelien put the boots on in place of his absurd makeshift greaves, Lydia switched out Istavan's robes for her own. His robes were slightly large, but she had no way of repairing the hole he had made in her robe with his incendiary spell. The damaged robes would have aroused suspicion on their way out, but oversized robes would not. Their formal uniform tunics were carefully tailored to fit each sorcerer, but the colorful robes they wore during daily business were much more varied in size and shape.

Why was Istavan here in the first place? Lydia adjusted her newly-acquired robes and belted her sword back into place. *He's not supposed to be due back for weeks. Moreover, if he is back, why wasn't I informed? Someone must have told him about the sword – otherwise he would have had no reason to be in the armory. There's nothing else being stored here that has value to a sorcerer...is there?*

Lydia quickly glanced around the room. "Dominion of Knowledge, illuminate that which is touched by your cousins," she said, raising a hand to her forehead as she spoke. A flash of green in the corner of her eye drew Lydia to look toward Taelien, and she nearly blinded herself when her eyes settled upon the sheathed weapon he was holding. *Gods around us*, she considered, *nothing should shine like that.*

Her illumination spell was designed to be subtle – a quick indication of anything present with a detectable sorcerous aura. The power of the sorcery should have been irrelevant; the spell was not designed to display that. *What could be causing that? Another defensive reaction? Several overlapping dominions, like I speculated about before?*

Lydia turned her eyes away, ignoring the bright after-image from the weapon's unexpected illumination. She saw no indication of any other objects in the room with a sorcerous aura. She did a quick scan over Istavan's fallen body and found nothing on him, either. This particular spell would not detect his ability to use sorcery, or anyone else's – it was only designed for finding objects. Similarly, it wouldn't pick up the nightmare spell's effect. She had other spells designed for tracking and identifying sorcerers and active spells.

"We should get moving," Lydia said, blinking to end the effects of her detection spell. She knew that supper would keep the palace staff relatively busy for the next hour or more, but she didn't need any additional complications.

"Ready when you are." Taelien belted the sheathed Sae'kes around his waist and headed for the door. Lydia followed closely behind him, and then took the lead after they stepped outside.

The sorceress lifted a finger to her lips in the universal gesture for silence, and then began to lead the way toward the palace's first floor. Once there, she knew they would begin to encounter more guards and palace workers.

Istavan could have been told about the prisoner by someone other than the other sorcerers, Lydia considered as she walked. *If he hasn't seen any of them yet, perhaps he thought he could get to the weapon first and do something with it. That would explain why he was not aware of the plan, and why I wasn't warned.*

Or, alternatively, Morella could have told Istavan about the sword. She didn't seem to want to deal with the rest of us for some reason — maybe she's hiding something.

Intriguing possibilities, but all bothersome, she concluded.

Taelien had fallen into position behind her and to the right, which Lydia noted to be an excellent position for him to protect her flank, given that most of the hallways that branched off from the main hall were on that side. It could have easily been a coincidence, but it was also plausible that he was familiar with the layout of the palace and taking his position for strategic purposes.

For a time, their footsteps were the only noticeable sound, until they came near enough to the banquet hall to hear the sounds of supper. Several of the nobles who lived within the palace walls indulged in the late night meal, but Lydia had never had the stomach for anything past dinner. She rarely even ate breakfast. *Taelien is probably starving,* she realized with a pang of guilt. *There's no sense in risking a stop right now, but I'll need to find him something to eat later.*

She could see a steady line of servants making their way to and from the banquet hall as they approached, as well as the two guards posted at the doors. She nodded to the guards as she approached and they returned her gesture with a simple salute, bringing their right hands across their chest to their left shoulder. No further communication was required.

The pair passed the banquet hall without further incident, turning left to make their way toward the entrance to the main hall. A patrolling pair of soldiers passed them, engrossed in conversation. Lydia ignored them and they responded in kind.

She found herself holding her breath as they made their way through the final hall toward the palace's entrance. Three of the door guards sat on the carpeted floor next to the closed door playing a dice game, while one other leaned over them, looking bored. Lydia mentally chastised them for their lack of discipline, but she knew that comings and goings at this hour were rare.

"Good evening," Lydia addressed them as she approached. The guards immediately straightened their posture, looking up at her. One of the sitting guards scrambled to his feet, but the others didn't make the effort.

"Evening, court sorceress," the guard who had stood up said. "How can we help ye?"

"Istavan and I are heading out for the evening. Can you unlock the door?" she said, indicating the massive double doors with a gesture.

"Course, ma'am." The guard replied, moving over to the door. "Up, boys. Help me out here."

The door was barred by an iron-framed wooden beam, designed to prevent it from being opened from the outside. Taelien was eyeing the beam with a contemplative expression, which Lydia judged to be a sign that he was analyzing if he could manipulate the metal around from outside the door. The door itself was equally heavy and several inches thick. During the Xixian rule, the palace had been designed for a siege. Now, most of the defenses had been long abandoned, but the heavy palace door had been maintained.

The guards struggled for a few moments to lift the beam, setting it aside, and shoved against the heavy doors. Lydia felt the night air wash over her skin as the door opened. "Thank you," she said, stepping past the guards and into the city. Taelien followed closely behind.

Lydia took hasty steps across the cobblestone road out of the palace, even as the guards struggled to shut the doors behind the pair.

"Impressive," Taelien said. "There were fewer complications than I expected."

The sorceress clenched her hands shut. "We're not done yet. We still need to find you a safe place to stay."

"Any inn should suffice, wouldn't it?" Taelien replied.

Lydia shook her head, still walking swiftly. They passed between twin lines of flowers that lined the palace road and beneath the stone archway that led into the Noble's District.

Her original plan was to take him to the Miner's District, one of the poorer parts of the city. As the night chill washed across her skin, that plan grew less appealing by the minute. She also reminded herself that while the poorer parts of the city would have fewer guards, their robes of office would also stand out much more. "Nothing close by. Guards will start sweeping the city as soon as they discover your absence. And, once Istavan has been found, your disguise will no longer be usable."

"Could we find a tailor, maybe?" Taelien inquired, his footsteps echoing just behind her. She couldn't tell from his tone if he was being sarcastic.

"Not at this late of an hour. Perhaps I should have carried an additional change of clothing for each of us, but carrying that much baggage would have stood out." Lydia led the way silently for a time, considering other destinations. A brothel would still be taking customers at this hour, and would more than likely be willing to sell them some other clothing. Unfortunately, she didn't know of any brothels nearby, and the parts of town more likely to have brothels would be less than safe at this hour. She didn't find it likely that anyone would try to rob a pair of court sorcerers, but she had heard stranger stories, and she didn't need any more trouble.

As she considered where to find a high quality inn on the edge of the Noble's District that would be discreet enough to serve their purposes, Lydia heard her footsteps fall into a gradual rhythm along with Taelien's.

That was when she noticed the additional rhythm of a third set of footsteps behind them, near-perfectly matching their own.

Lydia spun, drawing her hand across the air. "Dominion of Knowledge, illuminate the hidden!"

A flash of green light momentarily silhouetted a young man trailing a few feet behind them, unarmed and dressed in a simple tunic and pants. A look of shock crossed his features as he flailed his hands and stumbled backward, disappearing near-instantly thereafter, but not before Taelien had closed the distance between the two and grasped the man's shirt.

Lydia drew her sword as Taelien pulled the invisible man forward. As Lydia approached, she saw Taelien's other arm reach upward and grab at the invisible figure at neck level.

"Stop! Wait!" came a choking voice from the nothingness. Taelien shoved forward and Lydia heard the other figure collide hard against the cobblestones.

A foolish move, Lydia considered. *Taelien should have kept him pinned.* Even as Lydia chastised the former prisoner in her mind, however, Taelien advanced on the invisible figure and knelt, opening his hands and bringing them down until they apparently connected with something.

"You should start talking," Taelien said in his Istavan voice. Lydia was momentarily startled, having forgotten that Taelien was still supposed to be playing that role. "I prefer my prisoners alive. My companion, on the other hand..."

He wants me to play the antagonist? Fine, I can do that. Lydia approached, leveling her sword near where Taelien had made contact with the invisible figure. She couldn't make out where the invisible figure was lying – his spell must have been potent, to keep him invisible even after he had been seen and assaulted. She could have revealed him again with another spell, but she decided to wait. Taelien seemed to be physically overpowering the man without difficulty, and every spell had a cost. "We don't talk to assassins, Istavan. We eliminate them."

"I'm not an assassin! Wait!"

The man appeared abruptly, holding up his hands in a warding gesture.

Taelien's hands were encircling the smaller man's wrists. How Taelien had managed to find the invisible man's arms was a mystery, but she reassessed her earlier idea that he had been reckless. Apparently, once he had detected their pursuer, Taelien had some way of tracking the man.

"Talk," Taelien repeated, maintaining his ominous tone.

"I know you're not Istavan," the man said. Lydia raised her sword, causing the man's eyes to widen in horror. "No, no, stop. I'm here to help. Please!"

"Help?" Lydia asked, examining the fallen man. He was olive skinned, with short brown hair and a couple days of weak stubble. His glasses were thick enough to speak of some wealth, but his clothes were simple village fare, his tunic and pants a common brown in tone. There was a belt pouch on his right hip, but no sign of weapons.

"I saw you escaping – I was going to help you. I know a place where you'll be safe," the fallen man explained. "Please, I'm on your side."

My side. How do you even know what my – oh, you're on Taelien's side. That makes sense. "Do you know him?" Lydia asked Taelien, intentionally omitting his name.

"No," Taelien replied. To his credit, he maintained his Istavan voice. While the newcomer appeared to know that the sorcerer was an imposter, any confirmation would have been unwise. "Who sent you?"

Saved me that question, she considered.

"I, uh," the man said nervously, struggling weakly against Taelien's grip, "I should tell you my employer under more controlled circumstances."

"Up," Taelien said, standing, and wrenching the other man to his feet in the process.

"I'm not sure this is wise," Lydia offered, leveling her sword at the newcomer. "There are good odds he's leading us into a trap."

"I know," Taelien said, letting go of the other man. "The sooner I walk into this particular trap, the sooner I can eliminate whoever set it."

Lydia narrowed her eyes. *That sounded insane. It could just be extreme confidence, but insanity is more probable.*

"It's not a trap," the now-visible newcomer said. "Just a place where other people won't overhear us so easily. The name is Jonan, by the way. Sorry to meet you under these circumstances."

CHAPTER III – DEFINITELY NOT A TRAP

Jonan rubbed at his sore wrists as he took the first steps into his borrowed home. *That man has hands like iron manacles,* the scholar considered. *Best to feed him a few relevant lies before they end up around my neck.*

The house was large by Jonan's standards, but somehow he had managed to clutter the place almost immediately upon moving in. He stepped between a pair of tables near the entrance, attempting to put a bit of distance between himself and his would-be allies without looking too conspicuous about it.

"Stay within reach," the woman in the sorceress robes instructed him. "If you have assassins in one of the other rooms waiting for us, I want to have time to execute you before they're on us."

So much for that, Jonan considered with a grimace. "No assassins, I assure you." But he slowed his steps regardless, gesturing broadly within the building. "Please, make yourselves comfortable. There's food in the cabinet over there," he said, pointing to a cupboard near the opposite end of a distant room. "Feel free to help yourselves."

"While I'm grateful for your hospitality," the brutally strong man said to him, "I'd really rather know who you are."

Jonan sighed dramatically. "Have a seat, then." He found his way to the kitchen table, which was covered with bits of metal, panes of glass, and tools. Afterward, he pulled a pair of chairs over for his guests. "Sorry, I wasn't expecting multiple guests. I would have made more room."

The other man seized one of the two seats that Jonan had offered, pulled it back a bit, and sat. The sorceress continued to stand, watching

Jonan closely. Jonan nervously turned away from her gaze, finally sitting in the second chair himself and turning to face the swordsman.

"Tell us who you work for," the woman demanded, leaning toward him just slightly.

Jonan turned his head back toward her, playing through possible answers in his head, finishing the debate that had raged in his mind since they had discovered him. "I am but a humble scholar, and when I happened to-"

"That's a bunch of resh. Start over," the red-haired woman demanded, tapping the hilt of her sword meaningfully.

Now that his first lie had been so easily dispelled, Jonan began the next. "No need for that sword, I assure you. I'm a friend. I believe I work for the same people that you do, but if you have the same instructions that I do, you would know that we have orders not to confirm that or interact with one another."

The sorceress' hand drifted away from her sword.

Interesting, Jonan thought.

"Interesting," the woman replied. "And almost plausible. But, given that we have already come into contact, it's too late for that sort of behavior. We should share what resources we have available, if you are, in fact, working for the same people that I am."

"Would either of you tell me who you're talking about?" the masked man asked them. He was still using an outrageously deep voice. Jonan found it adorably pretentious.

"No," the sorceress replied.

"Not really," Jonan said, shaking his head.

When Jonan had been given his assignment, he had been told that there was a single other person affiliated with his organization in the city. His instructions had been to communicate with this contact by trading information through anonymous notes, but he had explicit orders not to determine his contact's identity.

For that reason, he had started looking for his contact's identity immediately, but thus far he hadn't had any luck. When he had discovered that the bearer of the Sae'kes had been imprisoned, he had immediately reported that information to his contact. The sorceress' actions implied that she might be acting on the information he had provided. He considered asking her questions based on the notes he had sent to his contact, but he decided that might be playing his hand too quickly.

Jonan turned back to the masked man. "Sorry, friend, but you haven't even told me your real name."

The masked man scoffed. "Any names we give one another are pointless until a level of trust is established."

Jonan put a hand over his chest, trying to look wounded by the point. "You do not trust me? I have guided you to the safety of my home, at great personal risk."

"We seem to be at an impasse." The woman leaned back against one of the tables behind her, pushing an unfinished mirror on top of it aside to make herself comfortable. "Fine. I'm not in the mood for riddles and games. I am Lydia, and I am a court sorcerer for Queen Regent Tylan. This man," she said, gesturing to Taelien, "Is Volar, my apprentice."

"Let me stop you there," Jonan said, turning to sit side-ways in his chair to address Lydia. "I already know that this man is a prisoner, and that you're helping him escape. I was planning to break him out myself, but you got to him first."

Lydia pushed her glasses up further on her nose. "That is quite an accusation you've made."

"Again, there's no need for these pretenses. I will hide you until morning, at which point you can safely escape the city." He gestured to the next room, which contained the staircase, though it was currently obscured from his sight by a half-closed door. "I regret that I only purchased male clothing, as I did not anticipate your involvement."

Lydia glanced at her masked companion, and then back to Jonan. "How did you discover us?"

"I am a practitioner of sight sorcery," Jonan admitted. "As I'm certain you noted from my attempt to follow you invisibly. I have been monitoring the comings and goings at the palace as best I could. When I saw the bearer of the sacred blade captured, I could not stand idly by and allow him to be harmed."

Jonan glanced back at the masked figure, but the other man just stared at him, his expression unreadable with the mask. It was somewhat disconcerting.

"All right," Lydia said. "Stand up. We're going to take a look around this place and make sure you don't have any friends listening in on us. When I'm satisfied we're alone, we'll talk further."

The ensuing tour of the house took a few tense minutes. He never could have afforded such a home on his own. The entrance chamber was cluttered with tables where he worked on various glasswork projects, such as mirrors, windows, and spectacles. The kitchen was directly across from the entrance, the majority of its brown wooden cabinets empty, but a few of them contained useful food or other more obscure supplies.

On the right side of the main room, beyond a practical wall of junk, Jonan led them to the reading room. A single bookshelf held a dozen books on subjects ranging from local history to esoteric sorcerous theory. They represented the bulk of his personal collection, and the most valuable of all of his possessions.

Beyond the reading room was his own bedroom, which he showed them hurriedly, explaining that he was embarrassed by the mess. Lydia maintained her usual dubious expression, but he didn't think she detected any of the irregularities that the room hid.

Opposite the reading room was a stairway leading to the upper floor. The two upstairs doors led to the "private room" – which contained a bath and chamber pot – and the guest bedroom.

The sorceress paused in each room to mutter a brief incantation, which Jonan assumed was a knowledge sorcery spell similar to the one she had used earlier. Afterward, Lydia still appeared nervous, but satisfied that there was no one else to eavesdrop.

Nothing on her garb to identify any affiliations aside from her current cover, Jonan considered. *She's cautious enough to be one of ours, though.*

With the tour concluded, each of them returned to the front room, taking seats. In the absence of a third chair, Lydia sat on the table across from the two men, still looking like she might draw her blade and murder either or both of them at any moment.

"All right. If we're satisfied, I believe it's time for some honest discussion," Jonan offered, gesturing magnanimously with both hands.

The masked man glanced at Lydia one last time, to which she responded with a curt nod. With that, he pulled down his hood and removed his mask, revealing a surprisingly young man with dark hair and bright eyes.

"You can call me Taelien," the unmasked youth said in a new voice, still somewhat deep, but much smoother in tone. "I came here to meet someone. My arrest was, so far as I can tell, a simple misunderstanding."

Jonan laughed for just a moment before shaking his head to stop himself. "Sorry, sorry. A misunderstanding. Ah, my friend, you are far too kind to the people of this city."

"What do you mean?" Taelien asked, furrowing his brow and leaning forward on his knees. Without the mask and the intimidating voice, he seemed a completely different person, almost child-like.

Is he just playing another character now? Jonan wondered, but it was too soon to tell.

"Jonan is right," Lydia began before Jonan had a chance to explain. "Following the Tae'os Pantheon is illegal, but it's such a minor crime that it's almost never talked about. Typically, they're just given a small fine and sent on their way. You carried a sacred relic into the city. The court sorcerers believed this was an intentional act of aggression from Velthryn, a provocation meant to trigger an action on Orlyn's part. I'm not sure I disagree."

Taelien shook his head. "I had no idea about the law. I'm not a spy, nor would I be interested in starting any sort of conflict."

"No, but what about whoever sent you?" Jonan asked.

The dark-haired man reeled back as if he had been struck. "My parents? They would have no motive for that. I don't think they've ever even been here."

"That would explain their lack of knowledge of the law," Lydia said. "But your average civilian doesn't just carry around a weapon like that."

Taelien nodded. "I apologize for inconveniencing you. I will be more careful about disguising the weapon in the future."

Jonan quirked an eyebrow. "You're missing the point, friend. Even if your parents didn't have any idea about the law, it sounds as if someone set you up. Perhaps whoever you were sent to meet in the city."

"Erik Tarren?" Taelien mused aloud.

"The scholar," Jonan said incredulously.

Lydia glanced at Jonan, offering him a wry grin. "That's what I said, too."

Ah, she can be amused. Progress.

"Okay, so your parents told you to come to the city to meet a famous scholar, and I assume they gave you the most conspicuous object on the continent to bring along. Did they happen to give a reason why?" Jonan asked.

"To learn about my heritage," Taelien explained, shaking his head. "My parents, well, they are not my real parents. They just took me in when I was a child, you see. They were given instructions to give me the sword when I came of age. I've been practicing with it for several years now, and my parents felt I was ready to come to try to discover where I came from."

"You can use the sword?" Lydia recoiled, eyes widening slightly.

"Only in the loosest sense of the word 'use'," Taelien replied, sounding oddly embarrassed.

"Wait, who gave your parents these instructions?" Jonan asked.

"Erik Tarren did. He's the one who left me and the sword with them. He said that I should come find him when I'm old enough."

"This is quickly turning into an interrogation," Lydia pointed out. "Taelien, you don't have to be so quick to volunteer information. In fact, I'd advise against it."

Jonan gave Lydia a pouty expression for spoiling his fun.

"It's fine," Taelien said. "I have nothing to hide. I'm sure you two are both thinking about using me – and this information – to your political advantage. I don't really care. Telling you what I know is probably the fastest way to reach my own goals."

"That makes things much easier, then." Jonan flipped his dour expression into a grin. "So. Does your family have any enemies?"

Taelien shook his head. "None that I am aware of, and certainly none in this city. I suspect you're overthinking this. My parents, not knowing the law, send me to find information. I, not knowing the law, blunder my way into an arrest. The sorcerers see a conspiracy, but I see little more than a coincidence."

"Perhaps," Jonan replied dubiously. "There is only one way to find out with any certainty, however."

"Find Erik Tarren?" Lydia mused, folding her arms. "That's doubtful, at best. The man stopped publishing books more than fifteen years ago. In all likelihood, that's because he's dead. He was over a hundred years old. Even a powerful sorcerer can only extend his life for so long."

"You're awfully quick to discard our only source of information," Jonan wagged a finger at Lydia for emphasis.

"First, we haven't even established that we're actually on the same side. And second, searching for a presumably dead man while hiding a fugitive who is carrying one of the most valuable relics in the world is somewhat absurd, don't you think?" Lydia countered, staring back at Jonan.

"Sounds like fun to me," Jonan said, looking over at Taelien. "What do you think?"

Please be as impressionable and foolish as you look.

"That does sound pretty exciting," Taelien said, nodding lightly.

Thank you.

Lydia shook her head fervently. "Look, I can't just go running around the city with a fugitive. He needs to be out of the city, and then I can pursue this Erik Tarren business – if there's anything to be pursued – without having to worry about having Taelien recaptured. Taelien, I'd be glad to bring Erik Tarren to meet you somewhere outside the city if I can find him," she offered, a pleading expression on her face.

"Assuming, of course, that you work for someone we can trust. You've already clearly betrayed the government of Orlyn – who's to say you wouldn't just kill this Erik Tarren if you find him, or turn him in to your own people to steal his secrets?" Jonan leaned forward in his chair, narrowing his eyes. He was making a rough gamble and he knew it. He had to hope that Taelien's lack of trust for Lydia was sufficient to put Taelien on his side.

Taelien, unfortunately, remained silent. He scratched at his chin, looking to Lydia, apparently seeking her guidance. *Resh.*

"All right," Lydia said. "You tell me who you work for and why you're here, and I'll tell you who I work for and why I'm here," she offered Jonan. "Do we have a deal?"

Jonan nodded without hesitating. *This should be interesting, if nothing else.*

"You first, then," Lydia said.

Oh, come on. I didn't expect that?

"Very well," Jonan said. "I am a humble servant of the priesthood of his majesty Vaelien, the King of Thorns."

Lydia's eyes narrowed.

That can't be good. Jonan tried to subtly reach for one of the pouches at his side, but it was too far away at his current angle.

"You're a Kesite?" Lydia asked, tilting her head to the side.

Jonan nodded. "Yes, of sorts."

"Bad luck for you, I'm afraid." She gave him an apologetic look, standing up. "I'm Lydia Hastings of the Paladins of Sytira, and you are my prisoner."

All things considered, Lydia was a fairly courteous captor. She had bound Jonan's wrists with some of his own hemp rope – which he had "graciously" provided to her – and ordered Taelien to keep an eye on him.

A gods-curst paladin. Really? I couldn't have been fairly expected to guess that.

Lydia apparently worshiped Sytira, one of the seven gods of the Tae'os Pantheon. Sytira was particularly associated with the acquisition and distribution of information, which made Lydia's usage of knowledge sorcery unsurprising within that context. More surprising was that she was a paladin – essentially a warrior dedicated to enforcing the tenets of her religion. Paladins of Sytira were usually assigned to finding and stopping abuses of sorcery – he had never heard of one being utilized as a long-term spy.

Jonan, on the other hand, was a follower of Vaelien, a solitary deity with many demigods – known as the Vae'kes – in his service. The two religions were often at odds, and many legends depicted the leader of the Tae'os Pantheon as Vaelien's personal rival. At present, the followers of the two religions were not engaged in any open hostilities with one another, but they tended to keep their distance. For Lydia, Jonan knew that the sword would be a symbol of the strength and love of her gods. For Jonan, it was a bargaining chip – the weapon of Vaelien's legendary opponent.

Deciding to steal a Tae'os artifact is probably a bit above my level of authority, Jonan considered. *But it's awfully tempting. Using the wielder of the Sae'kes as a tool, however, fits perfectly within my mission parameters. It even cleanly deflects blame away from Vaelien. The Tae'os Pantheon would look responsible.*

"You can still help yourselves to the food," Jonan offered weakly.

"It's probably poisoned," Lydia replied dryly. She hadn't drawn her sword, thankfully, but now she was watching him with twice the intensity she had been before. This was impressive, seeing as she had already looked like she could burrow straight through a wall with her eyes.

"It's not poisoned. It's food. I eat it. Here, bring me some bread. I'll take the first bite," Jonan offered.

"You're probably immune to your own poison." Lydia shifted in her seat.

"That's absurd. Look, I admitted I work for the priesthood of Vaelien. I'm not a priest myself, and even if I was, that wouldn't make me some sort of assassin," he offered.

"No, working for the priesthood and not being a priest is what makes you an assassin, or at very least a spy," Lydia replied.

She's not entirely wrong, Jonan admitted silently. They did have other branches to the organization, but he was a field agent, not a civilian or even a member of their own pseudo-military. He had never killed anyone, but he was certainly a spy.

"Right, yes, I'm clearly a spy," Jonan said in a deadpan tone. Lydia tilted her head to the side inquisitively. "No more or less than you are, if you'll forgive me for saying so. And I doubt you poison the contents of your cupboard, just for the contingency that you might be having guests that you need to murder."

Lydia nodded slowly. "You're right. That would be a needlessly extreme measure, as well as careless. Taelien, you can bring us some of his food."

The dark-haired youth turned his head to her. "I appreciate your permission, but it's not necessary. I don't work for you," he noted in a bemused tone. He paused for a moment, and then stood and added. "But I am very hungry."

Ah, the lad has some autonomy after all. That's good, that could work to my advantage later.

Lydia sighed as Taelien started walking to the kitchen. "Sorry to presume, Taelien. Please bring us all some food to eat. It's been a long day for both of us."

Jonan watched Taelien go to the cupboard, nodding silently in response to Lydia.

Good move, paladin. Remind him you're human and smooth things over. Keep your game piece friendly.

"Look, we don't need to be at odds about any of this. While I recognize that our religions don't always get along-"

"And occasionally engage in holy wars against one another-," Lydia added, folding her arms and smirking.

"-We can still find common ground on these issues. Neither of us wants the Sae'kes in the hands of the local gods. Neither of us wants anything of importance in the hands of the local gods." Jonan gestured to the ceiling with his bound wrists.

"True," Lydia confessed. "But I find the idea of the Sae'kes in Vaelien's hands...or worse, his son's, to be far more disturbing than losing it here."

Jonan deliberately kept his expression as neutral as he could, but the mention of Vaelien's son sent a torrent of painful memories through his mind. *A teenaged girl with a manic grin, the blood on her right hand illuminated by a globe of flame hovering above it. Oppressing heat everywhere, smoke thick enough to crush his lungs. The screams of the dying reverberating around him, while he hid, useless, praying that he would not be seen.*

No, he considered grimly, *his son is not the one you need to worry about.*

"Well, while I am quite certain that I would be rewarded – immensely, in fact – for securing that weapon, you've made it more than evident that I will not succeed in doing so. Moreover, our good friend Taelien," he gestured to Taelien, who was returning carrying a plate with a loaf of bread and a carving knife, "would likely be averse to either of us taking charge of the sword he carries."

"The sword stays with me," Taelien said simply, setting down the bread plate on the nearby table with a loud 'clack'.

"Right," Jonan said with a faint hint of laughter in his voice. "So, since that is settled, we can feel free to cooperate on other matters."

Lydia glanced at the bread that was now seated next to her, and then back to Jonan. Taelien began to cut the bread into smaller slices.

"I see little else we could cooperate on. I appreciate you providing a place for us to stay for the evening. We will keep watches to ensure you do not try to kill us – or take the sword – while we rest. In the morning, if you have not betrayed us, I can escort Taelien out of the city." Lydia shifted her gaze between the two men, scrutinizing.

"I'd like to hear his proposal, actually," Taelien said.

Lydia frowned, turning to glance at Taelien. "You don't know these Kesites. They can't be trusted. Think back to the beginning of our conversation with him – he tried to mislead us twice before admitting who he worked for."

"What, you mean sort of like you dressing up like a court sorceress and helping a prisoner escape?" Jonan shot back.

"I am a court sorceress," Lydia growled. "I was hired legitimately."

Jonan nodded, putting on an impressed face. "So you actually infiltrated the government of a nation, rather than just putting on a costume. Well, that's certainly a step up in scale."

Lydia glowered at him. "Yes, I'm capable of deception as well. Taelien doesn't have to trust me, either. The distinction is that I've already helped him escape a prison, so he knows that unless that was some sort of absurdly long-term plan, I am legitimately trying to help him. You, on the other hand, just happened to be tracking us on the way out."

A good point, and one I don't have a very strong counter to. Still, I've planted a few sprouts of doubt in Taelien's head, at least.

"Peace," Jonan said. "I concede that. You are clearly trying to help him." That wasn't really true, it was plausible this really was a longer term plan on her part, but he didn't need to antagonize the Paladin any more. "Let me help you both. Not out of goodness, as you would never believe such a motive, but out of self-interest. I didn't come to this city for the sword, just as you didn't. We are both working against Orlyn in different ways. Allow me to assist you."

Lydia swept up a piece of bread with her left hand, bit into it, and put her hand back down without ever looking away from Jonan. He blinked in response.

"All right," Lydia said. "Let's hear why you're in the city, and what you have to offer."

"Excellent," Jonan replied, grinning slightly. When her eyes narrowed in response, he knew he had just made his pleasure a tad too overt, but he continued regardless. "One of Orlyn's 'gods' is called Edon. He appears to be human, but he has presided over the city for fourteen years with no signs of growing older. Much as you pointed out when we discussed Erik Tarren, slowing the aging process is difficult, and every sorcerer that I have studied has eventually run into limitations. Baron Edrick Theas is perhaps the oldest human alive, but even he appears to be ancient and withered – he will eventually die. This Edon apparently looks younger than when he first appeared – which could be an illusion, or it could be that he's found some way to reverse the aging process."

"Certainly, I've met the man myself," Lydia said. "He only looks to be about thirty or thirty-five. The people of Orlyn say he is a god. Do you have a reason to believe otherwise?"

"Oh, yes," Jonan said, grinning and folding the fingers of his bound hands together. "I have discovered who he once was."

Lydia adjusted her glasses again, her gaze shifting to the side for the first time. Nervousness, perhaps? Jonan couldn't quite tell.

"What have you found?" Lydia asked, her tone sounding more suspicious, rather than curious. She looked back to Jonan, pressing her lips together.

Perhaps I stumbled upon a line of conversation I should have avoided, but it's too late now.

"We believe Edon was once Redeemer Donovan Tailor," Jonan said.

"A former Priest of Sytira of some repute," Lydia added, speaking to Taelien, and then turning back toward Jonan. "Go on."

"We believe he is preserving his life by stealing the lives of others."

Lydia folded her arms across her chest. While she was trying to look taciturn, Jonan thought he caught a flicker of something – concern, perhaps? – in her eyes. "And what led you to that conclusion?"

Careful, now. Too late to back out, but if she discovers too much, I might end up eating a yard of steel instead of that delicious bread.

Jonan took a deep breath, considering where to begin.

"About twenty years ago, Donovan Tailor was expelled from the priesthood of Sytira for heresy. As a Sytiran, I'm sure you've heard about it," Jonan offered, gesticulating dismissively with one of his bound hands.

"Certainly," Lydia said. "He claimed that because our gods were once mortals, our priests should aspire to achieve godhood themselves. The viewpoint gained some popularity among his contemporaries, and his superiors in the priesthood most likely saw it as a threat to their control. He published an essay on the subject, and he was excommunicated shortly thereafter."

Jonan raised an eyebrow. He had been expecting more religious fervor.

The spectacled man shook his head to clear his thoughts. "Yes, precisely," he said. "Excommunication robbed Donovan of many of his friends, allies, and resources. He left Velthryn and traveled for a handful of years, eventually making his way to Keldris. That was where the priesthood of Vaelien took note of him."

Taelien looked up from nibbling on his bread, gave Jonan a brief quizzical look, and then went back to eating.

"Donovan Tailor was in Keldris to beg for a meeting with the city's ruler, King Haldariel. Tailor sent word that he had discovered something of vast import. Knowing that Donovan was a former priest, Haldariel wisely invited one of our priests to the meeting to help evaluate Donovan's claims."

Lydia nodded. "I take it Donovan was insulted?"

Jonan shrugged. "I assume he was, but the meeting didn't end explosively. From our priest's report, Donovan claimed he had discovered the source of the power of the gods. He planned to make himself a god, and he offered godhood to Haldariel in exchange for protection until he could complete the process."

Taelien nodded along, looking interested in the tale, while Lydia's expression began to darken.

"And what did Haldariel say?" Taelien asked.

"He refused, naturally," Jonan replied. "The claim sounded preposterous. Our priest assumed that Donovan was attempting to hide from Sytiran assassins and hoping that the king's protection would deter them."

"The paladins of Sytira don't have assassins." Lydia grimaced in distaste.

Jonan shook his head. "Regardless, Tailor was clearly afraid of someone. If not from the priesthood, perhaps he had made other enemies. Power rarely comes without conflict," he noted, pausing to invite her to dispute his point.

Lydia simply half-nodded thoughtfully, brushing a stray hair away from her eyes. "Continue."

"Donovan pleaded at first, but when it was clear the rejection was final, he departed from the city. Over the next several days, a half dozen Rethri were reported missing. No bodies were found, no ransoms demanded. By the time someone thought to connect the disappearances with Donovan Tailor, his trail had long vanished. Those Rethri were never found," Jonan explained.

The Rethri were a people with no sclera – or white portion - in their eyes. It was commonly debated among scholars whether or not Rethri and humans were the same species. While their eyes were the only way to reliably tell a Rethri apart from a human on sight, Rethri biology had some other distinctions. The most well-known of these is that each Rethri had a strong connection to a single dominion, and that this connection was reinforced during a secret coming of age ritual.

Rethri were as common as humans in Liadra, where Jonan spent most of his life, but he had never seen one of their coming of age rituals.

"And you believe that Tailor took these Rethri to use in some sort of sacrificial sorcery?" Lydia inquired.

Jonan nodded. "Yes, but only because of recent events. Let me explain."

"Go on," Taelien urged him, picking up another slice of bread to eat. There was an odd gleam in the swordsman's blue eyes, a hint of interest that had been absent when the conversation started. Jonan took a mental note of that, wondering what had aroused the man's attention.

"It was about two years later that Orlyn, which had never previously been affiliated with any of the major religions, proclaimed that the city had a new official religion. King Osric claimed that he had been visited by a new god, Edon, and that he would be the city's patron deity. When Osric passed away, the then-Queen Tylan – became the queen regent. Osric and Tylan had a son, Byron, but he was just a baby – he couldn't legally take the throne. The city has been always strictly patriarchal, so even with Tylan ostensibly ruling, Edon's influence has grown steadily over time," Jonan explained.

"And Edon's new religion espoused a belief in 'ascension through worship', that anyone could become a god through sufficient service," Lydia added, "Similar to what Donovan was attempting to encourage as a priest. I've seen the connections drawn between the Edonate religion and Donovan's treatises before. It's not an uncommon subject of discussion. The key difference lies in that Donovan claimed that people should seize their own path to divinity, whereas Edon's religion was more about him offering godhood directly to people who pleased him."

"A better business model, to be certain," Jonan said with a grin. "We believe that Donovan eventually came to the conclusion that he could use his discovery – whatever it was – as powerful leverage. King Osric most likely accepted the offer that King Haldariel refused – or maybe Tylan did, and had her husband killed. After all, now she is worshipped as one of the four 'gods' of Orlyn."

Taelien finished a piece of bread and rubbed his fingers together over the plate, ridding them of crumbs. "That makes some sense, but why are you investigating this now? It sounds like your priesthood had this information years ago."

Jonan nodded. "About seven months ago, Edon paid a diplomatic visit to the city of Selyr – another city in Rethri territory."

"I've been there," Taelien said with a nod, drawing a dubious look from Lydia. "What happened during the visit?"

"Edon visiting any other city was unusual enough in itself to warrant attention. Part of the key to Edon's claim that he deserves worship is that he actively watches over his people, tending to the sick and performing miracles. For that reason, he rarely leaves Orlyn – at least not publicly, or for extended periods of time," Jonan began.

"Edon offered to extend his protection to the city, claiming that he would assign Myros, his god of battle, to be their patron if they adopted his faith. The city council refused, their ties to Vaelien running far too deep. Edon left shortly thereafter, but not alone."

Lydia tapped her fingers against the table. "There were Rethri disappearances again," she surmised aloud.

"Precisely. And more of them this time – nearly twenty citizens disappeared. Obviously, this could no longer be a coincidence, and a thorough investigation was launched. As I'm certain you know, the priests of Vaelien have a military branch, which we call the Thornguard. Among the Thornguard, there are specialists in many types of sorcery, including tracking and information gathering. They found no evidence of kidnapping. Rather, it appeared that these Rethri picked up and left the city without telling a single body. They were, of course, headed for Orlyn."

"So, this Edon was recruiting followers among the Rethri, then?" Taelien asked.

"Possibly, but not by simply talking to them. The Thornguard managed to catch some of the Rethri on the road before they reached Orlyn. The people the Thornguard talked to refused to give their reasons for heading to Orlyn, claiming it was personal business. The Thornguard checked for signs of thought sorcery, but they didn't find any. Edon wasn't traveling with the Rethri, and there were no signs of any kind of conflict having occurred, so the Thornguard went back to Selyr to report," Jonan explained.

"The Thornguard simply let the Rethri go to Orlyn?" Taelien asked.

Jonan nodded. "There was no evidence that they were being coerced, and the Thornguard had no legal authority to act outside of Kesite lands, anyway."

"Did the Rethri travelers show any indications of new wealth?" Lydia asked.

Jonan furrowed his brow thoughtfully. "I don't recall anything about that in the report. It's a good question, though. I doubt they were just being paid to go to Orlyn. Their families seemed universally unaware of the spontaneous traveling, with the exception of a couple cases where family members were traveling together. If it was just about money, there would be no reason for such secrecy."

"Interesting," Lydia mused. "Very interesting."

"It gets better still. After the Thornguard returned, we sent a diplomatic party to Orlyn. The city of Orlyn claimed that none of the Rethri we listed had been registered as citizens in the city. One of our ambassadors tried to arrange for a meeting with Edon, but he was turned away," Jonan explained.

Lydia nodded. "I remember hearing about an ambassador from Selyr being in the city, and I wondered why, but he left in such a hurry that I never had a chance to meet him myself."

"And so," Jonan said, folding his still-bound hands together in front of him, "I have been sent to investigate these disappearances. We have no conclusive evidence that the Rethri are being sacrificed, but it seems to be an answer that provides a unified answer to multiple questions."

"Does it, though?" Lydia asked. "People have been trying to research methods of achieving immortality for centuries. At least five other sorcerers in our time have found ways to extend their lifespans, although the two members of House Theas may be using the same method."

Lydia paused, grimacing. "Frankly, as gruesome as it sounds, sacrificing lives to fuel your own is one of the most obvious things to attempt. The priests of Lysandri have a tradition of asking a sorcerer to try to transfer their remaining life to another when they are dying, for example. Numerous methods have been attempted, and none of them have produced any measurable results."

Manipulating scholars of sorcery is so much harder than dealing with civilians, Jonan considered, measuring his words carefully. "Certainly, I agree with you. I am not claiming this is the only possible answer, merely one probable one. Consider the possibility that Donovan discovered a method of transferring life, but it is simply very inefficient. Perhaps it only extends his life a single year for each person he sacrifices. It may also require Rethri, specifically, since they live much longer than humans."

Lydia shrugged. "That's not outside the dominion of possibility," she admitted. "But you still have several key gaps in your information. You have established that Edon and Donovan have similar, but not identical, ideologies. Rethri disappeared both when Donovan visited Keldris and when Edon visited Selyr – those are strong similarities of circumstance, but they do not confirm that these two are the same person. Perhaps Donovan shared his secrets with this Edon, and Edon either helped him or stole whatever methods Donovan taught him."

Jonan cracked his knuckles. "That is absolutely possible. Since they are both male, and appeared to be of similar ages when Edon first appeared, it simply seems easier to assume they are the same person until we find evidence otherwise. We have no records of Donovan Tailor being anywhere else after Edon appeared – do you?"

Lydia shrugged. "I can't say for certain without consulting our records. I don't have quite everything memorized."

Jonan chuckled, assuming Lydia was being hyperbolic, but she didn't join him in his laughter. After a moment of awkward silence, Jonan blinked and righted his thoughts. "Of...course. Well, if you do have a chance to check any records that would be most helpful in the investigation."

"I have not precisely agreed to help you yet," Lydia reminded him.

Taelien glanced at her. "You would consider abandoning these missing Rethri to whatever fate Edon has in store for them?"

Jonan mentally thanked Taelien for his innocence.

Lydia sighed pointedly, looking back toward Taelien. "You can't take everything this man is saying as god-spoken." She turned to Jonan. "No offense intended."

"Of course," Jonan said, waving his bound hands dismissively. "By all means, confirm my claims on your own. In fact, I'd prefer it. I always try to do the same myself."

"I wouldn't even know where to begin," Taelien admitted, his hand floating to the hilt of his sword. It didn't seem to be a hostile gesture, or even a conscious one. Jonan surmised that it was a nervous gesture, and the weapon comforted him.

"I have contacts and records I can consult, Taelien," Lydia offered, adjusting her glasses. "Your priority should still be to exit the city as quickly as possible without detection."

Taelien shook his head. "I will not bend on this matter. I need to find Erik Tarren before I leave the city. Perhaps he can even provide us with more information on this Edon – he is, as you have both noted, a renowned scholar. Now that I have disguised the weapon, I should be much less conspicuous."

"Actually," Jonan said, "I'd really rather you not bring anyone else into this. If you want to find your scholar, that's great – but if you do find him, please don't consult him unless I ask you to. I'm entrusting you with very sensitive information here. If Edon discovered that I was looking into his method of obtaining his power, it could easily get me killed." Jonan gave Lydia a meaningful look.

"I have no intention of turning you in, at least not immediately," Lydia said. "If your motive is truly to investigate disappearing civilians, I have no objections to cooperating with you for the time being. Your investigation, however, is not my primary concern."

She turned to look at Taelien. "If you insist on staying in the city, we will have to find you some new clothes and make you a cover identity."

Jonan scratched at his chin. "You know, Lydia, you keep mentioning that Taelien should be leaving the city. Aren't you at even greater risk? If you just broke him out of prison, people are probably looking for both of you, and you'll be more easily recognized."

Lydia shook her head. "The people in the palace would have just seen me walking around with Istavan, which is perfectly normal. Istavan himself is a bit of a risk, but I've taken some precautions with him. He's always been reclusive – I don't think he'll go to the city guard or the sorcerers even if he suspects I was involved in the prison break. The evidence in the jail cell will look like Taelien broke his chains, which wouldn't require an accomplice. And I never had the key to his cell."

Jonan briefly pondered how she had gotten into the cell without a key, but it wasn't really relevant at the moment.

"It's a risk, you're right, but it's necessary. I'm not going to leave Taelien alone here."

Taelien frowned. "You don't have to take any risks for my sake. Now that I'm aware of the situation, I can take care of myself."

She gave Taelien a conciliatory glance. "I'm sure you're a very competent swordsman, but you have to understand that the sword you're carrying is the single most important object to my faith. Leaving you alone in the city with the Sae'kes would be unforgivable. Especially considering Myros is going to be looking for you."

Jonan's eyes widened at that. "Myros? What, why?"

"One of the sorcerers called him in. He should be here within a few days."

"Um, I don't like saying this, but you probably should both just leave in that case," Jonan mumbled. *Vaelien curse it, why can't things ever be simple? Myros getting his hands on that Sae'kes would be colossally bad.*

"Why are you so concerned? Is Myros known for some sort of divine tracking capabilities or something similar?" Taelien stretched his neck from side to side.

Lydia shook her head. "No, he's the local god of battle. It's not that he's known for any particular type of sorcery. If Myros arrives and you haven't already been caught, he's going to throw the entire city's resources at finding you. I might be able to slow that process down somewhat, but Jonan is right – we'd be smarter to leave before he arrives."

Taelien tightened his jaw. "Fine. I don't like it, but we can plan to leave before Myros arrives. In the meantime, we can help Jonan and look for Erik Tarren."

"You'll still need a way to avoid notice in the meantime. The house we're staying in belongs to a man about your size," Jonan offered. "You can probably fit into some of his clothes."

"Are those really yours to offer?" Taelien inquired dubiously.

Jonan nodded. "Yes, everything here is at my disposal."

"Very well, then," Taelien said. "I suppose we should free your hands."

"I'll do it," Lydia said, surprising Jonan. He had not expected her to agree. She moved gracefully over to him and began fidgeting with the knots.

"You can just cut them," Jonan offered. "I have other rope."

"No need to be wasteful," Lydia insisted, continuing to work at the main knot.

"Just to be clear," Jonan asked, "Do you both agree to keep what I've just explained to you a secret?"

"Sure," Taelien said. "I can keep a secret."

"For the time being," Lydia agreed. "If I think I can gather more information by revealing a portion of it, I may need to do that."

Lovely. My head is going to be on a pike by this time next week.

"I can avoid telling people that you are the source of the information, if that would ease your mind," Lydia offered.

Jonan nodded hastily. "That would be preferable. Who are you planning to talk to?"

"The other court sorcerers may have information on Edon's rise to power. Some of them have been here many years longer than I have," she explained.

Jonan turned his head to the side inquisitively. "You're still planning to deal with the other court sorcerers? Shouldn't you be avoiding them as much as possible?"

"Let me worry about that," she said, flashing a grin, pulling on the end of a rope and undoing the last of the knots all at once. The ropes came free into her hand. Jonan flexed his wrists gratefully.

Jonan locked the door to his bedroom. He had instructed his guests on where they could find everything they might need for the evening, and to knock loudly if they needed him.

Sighing in exhaustion, Jonan walked over to his bed, pulling down the covers. He sat on the bed, adjusted the pillows, and lied down for a few moments before standing back up.

Shaking his head, he walked around to the other side of the bed and adjusted the sheets further. After a moment of examination, he walked away contented, tapping a finger on the mirror on the table beside his bed.

With that done, Jonan stepped back to the middle of the room, lifting a heavy rug that covered a section of the wooden floor. He couldn't see the trap door that he had just uncovered, but he knew the location of the invisible latch from months of practice.

He flipped the latch and opened the door, stepping down onto the stairs to the room below. On his way down, he grabbed the corner of the rug and the handle on the top of the trap door, dragging them back into position as he advanced downward.

With the trap door closed, the chamber was pitch black. He tapped the right side of his head with a finger. The gesture was all he needed to cast a familiar spell, enabling him to see perfectly in the dark room.

His sight restored, Jonan locked the trap door and headed down into his real bedroom. The room was about the same size as his false bedroom above, but barely tall enough to stand in, and far more cluttered. A dozen tall mirrors lined the walls, and a smaller bed, as well as a writing desk and chair, took up much of the remainder of the chamber.

Jonan walked to a mirror on the right side of the new bed first, tapping a finger against the surface. His reflection vanished, the mirror showing instead an image of the room above – the vision of the mirror's twin. He gazed into the image for a moment to determine if the mirror was still sitting at a good angle to display the entire chamber, nodding in satisfaction as he concluded that it was.

He briefly scanned each of the other mirrors, checking to see if anything significant had changed. Of the twelve mirrors, nine were currently active. Five were used to communicate with contacts that he had established since coming to the city. Only one of these contacts was affiliated with the Order of Vaelien in any way, and he didn't even know where they fell in the organization's web of members and mercenaries.

The Order of Vaelien itself consisted of priests of Vaelien, but like most of the largest religions on the continent, they had several other organizations in their service. The Thornguard was their military branch, and comparable to the Paladins of Tae'os in function. Each of the Vae'kes also had their own servants, some of whom were formally employed by the priesthood.

The two most famous of the Vae'kes were Aayara, the Lady of Thieves, and Jacinth, the Blackstone Assassin. Legends depicted the pair as both rivals and lovers, always seeking an advantage in contests that lasted for centuries. As a child, Jonan had found these stories entertaining, even romantic. Now, with personal experience as a piece on their game board, he found nothing compelling about contests waged atop a field of corpses.

It was an open secret that the order also employed a branch of spies and assassins, who were informally referred to as 'Blackstones', named after the title that Jacinth used. Finally, the order also employed numerous uncategorized workers – everything from stonemasons to build temples, to blacksmiths, to scribes. Ostensibly, Jonan fell into this last category, employed as a glassblower. In reality, he was just a somewhat better concealed spy for the Thornguard. He suspected his contact in the city was probably similar – someone who wouldn't be found on the rolls for the Thornguard, but was in their pay and service.

His other contacts in the city were numerous. Only the most significant warranted mirrors for constant communication. These included a palace guard in the High Palace – the location where the Queen Regent herself resided – as well as two information brokers that often provided conflicting information, a former apprentice to one of the court sorcerers, and a woman who claimed to be an officer in a local guild of thieves.

He privately suspected that one of the two information brokers was actually the real thieves guild representative, and that the "guild member" he was speaking to was in the broker's employ, but he could afford to pay them both and let them play their games. Vaelien's coffers were in no danger of running dry.

Tired, he considered, *but I have a letter to write.*

Jonan sat at the writing desk, picking up a fresh piece of parchment and dipping a quill in one of the nearby inkwells. After a moment of consideration, he drafted a simple message.

I have the prisoner. Establishing trust. Identity still uncertain. Paladins of Tae'os involved.

He kept the letter brief. Jonan liked to sound mysterious.

Half-smirking in amusement, Jonan moved the quill and picked up the parchment, blowing on the ink softly in an effort to dry it faster. After a few impatient moments, he picked up the message and placed it directly against the surface of the mirror directly to the left of his bed.

He stepped out of the mirror's sight – his contact could not know his identity – and tapped the surface of the mirror.

There was no visible sign that his spell had taken effect, and as always, he waited a few moments before tapping the surface again. The delay was unnecessary; the image of the letter had been sent the instant he had touched the glass, and the image would remain frozen in the twin mirror now that he had disabled the spell. He just liked to wait a few seconds. It made him feel more comfortable that the sorcery was going to work, since he had no way of visually discerning if it had done anything at all.

With the message sent, Jonan picked up the letter, carefully tearing away the portion on which he had written the text. He hated wasting good parchment – it had been a rare luxury when he was a child, and he had never broken the habit of reusing the pieces of the paper that had not been written on. Putting the blank piece on the table, Jonan tore the inked portion to shreds. He would burn the pieces later to be thorough, but it was important to dispose of his communications immediately, just in case he was somehow discovered.

Vaelien, sometimes I really wish you'd give me simpler assignments.

The majority of what Jonan had told Lydia was true, but he had deliberately omitted the specifics of his actual mission. The missing Rethri were the catalyst for his assignment, but not the goal. Edon and his religion were a growing problem. Jonan's responsibilities were discovering how Edon was faking his godhood and then solving the Edon problem by whatever means were necessary.

I'm not an assassin, his own words echoed in his mind. *Though by the end of this, I very well might have to be.*

He wiped his ink-stained fingers on a well-used rag and retreated to his bed, exhausted. His vision had been reduced to a blur by his rapid uses of sight sorcery, but it hardly mattered. With a tap against the left side of his head, Jonan's vision went black, and he crawled his way beneath the covers to sleep.

CHAPTER IV – AN ATTEMPT AT TEAMWORK

Taelien woke to find Lydia sitting in a chair near the door of their guest bedroom. She had a book sitting on her lap, but she had turned toward him seemingly instantly when his eyes blinked open.

There was already sunlight creeping in the window to his right, indicating that he had slept too long.

"Mm," he mumbled, sitting up. "You could have woken me."

Lydia nodded sleepily. "I could've, but it looked like you needed the sleep more."

And you probably still don't trust Jonan not to slit your throat in your sleep.

Taelien grabbed his sheathed weapon from within the sheets and pushed himself out of the bed, walking over to the nearby dresser. Jonan had indicated the clothes inside would most likely fit him, so he set the sword atop the dresser and began to search for something to wear. "I can take over watch as soon as I'm dressed," he said without glancing back toward Lydia.

"That won't be necessary," she replied. "As soon as we've had a chance to speak to Jonan about our plan of action, I'll head back to the palace and sleep in my own room."

The swordsman frowned. Lydia's constant suspicion and distrust about everything was starting to get frustrating.

He found a suitable pair of trousers and a light brown tunic, pulling them on. The trousers were a little bit short, but still a considerable improvement over wearing the robes Lydia had given him.

After another minute, he also managed to find some clean socks, slipping those on as well. His legs were still a bit sore from the "greaves" he had worn the previous day, and he resolved himself not to make any more clothing out of metal until he was better at making complex shapes.

Fastening his belt around his waist, he turned toward Lydia. "How do I look?" he inquired, striking what he thought was a dashing pose.

"Like a peasant wearing a sword three times too expensive for him to own," Lydia said dryly, "But still an improvement."

Taelien scoffed. "I doubt anyone will be paying me too much scrutiny, now that the sword looks ordinary."

"It doesn't look precisely ordinary. The pommel is far too large, and the scabbard stands out considerably as well. Why is it lined with metal?" the sorceress asked.

Taelien grinned. "That's a trade secret."

Lydia rolled her eyes in response. "Very well, but it would be best if I'm well versed in your capabilities if you expect me to continue to protect you."

Taelien folded his arms across his chest. "I'm grateful for your help, but I don't need protection. I'm fairly well trained with a sword. If you want to work together to investigate Donovan, that's great, but I-"

"I don't think you're taking this seriously." Lydia narrowed her eyes. "I didn't just mean protecting you physically. Not every problem can be handled by a sword. You're going to need help if you want to find answers before you need to leave the city."

The swordsman grimaced, opening his hands and closing them again. "Fine. I'll answer some questions, as long as they're not about the sword."

Lydia quirked a brow at that. "Why won't you answer questions about the Sae'kes?"

"Well, for one thing, because you refer to it by a proper name. My knowledge about that sword is what makes me worth anything to you. If you think you know all my secrets, that makes me expendable."

Lydia shook her head vehemently. "Absolutely not. If you have the sword, there's probably a good reason for it. If what you told me before was true, and you've had the sword for many years, I refuse to believe that the gods would have allowed it to remain with you unless it was intended for your hands."

Taelien blinked. That was a stronger reaction than he had expected. He had known she was religious – she was a paladin, after all – but he didn't anticipate that she would have incorporated him into that viewpoint so quickly. He briefly debated arguing that the sword had been taken away from him easily enough, but he quickly realized that the argument would only serve to weaken his potential leverage over her.

"That's...how can you know? How can you believe your gods had a hand in anything, without any evidence?"

Lydia brushed a lock of hair away from her eyes. "Most paladins would say something about faith. I've never found that quite sufficient – the gods can't be everywhere or do everything. But that sword is both a symbol and a powerful tool – they have a vested interest in keeping track of it, and saying they have significant resources would be an understatement. I don't have direct evidence, but I can still reason out that it's terribly improbable that they don't know you have it."

"Okay," he managed, still somewhat stunned. "Why do you think I'm supposed to have it?"

"There are numerous possibilities. I haven't had an opportunity to narrow them down yet. The sword was historically wielded by Aendaryn, the leader of our pantheon. Members of the Tae'os Pantheon rarely appear in person – they often act through intermediaries. Perhaps you are one of his descendants, or just a chosen mortal intended to serve as an example to his followers. It's also possible you were selected because you have a high potential for martial prowess, and Aendaryn has a particular task in mind for you."

Taelien nodded absently. He had heard the same hypotheses before – and considered them himself. He found it considerably more likely that his biological parents had simply obtained the sword on their own and decided to give it to him for some reason. The idea that his real parents had something in mind for his future was far more palatable than being a game piece for a deity he had never met.

"That's exactly my problem. There are too many possibilities. And how do I learn what might be the plans of the gods themselves?" He sighed. "Maybe they know I have it and just haven't decided to do anything about it yet. You said yourself that your gods rarely appear in person. Why is that, by the way?"

Lydia contorted her lips, apparently considering her response. "The Tae'os Pantheon may have ceased taking a direct role in mortal affairs, but that doesn't mean they would ignore something as significant as who is holding a sacred artifact. If they didn't want to come claim the sword themselves, they could send a paladin or a priest. I've never heard the voices of the gods, but some of my fellows claim to have."

She paused for a moment, taking a breath. "As for why the gods don't appear in person, there are a few reasons for that. The Tae'os Pantheon are not the first generation of gods. They were mortals once, like you and me. Unless you're very well-read, you probably haven't even heard the names of the older gods – except for Vaelien, of course."

"If the histories are true, the older gods took a much more active role in the world. Their reward? Delsen was killed by his own children when he attempted to stop them from warring against one another. Caerdanel sacrificed herself to save a mortal city from a foreign god. Records on the others are scarce, but it's fair to say that they either fled or died."

Lydia looked down, shaking her head in frustration. "We can't be trusted to deal with the gods directly. Time and time again, mortals betray the gods that serve them. The Tae'os Pantheon has taken a safer path – they guide us from a distance, and give us the strength to protect ourselves in the form of sorcery. Vaelien's followers call it cowardice. I consider it a good long-term strategy."

Taelien scratched at his chin. "Didn't sorcery exist before the Tae'os Pantheon?"

"Of course, but it wasn't anywhere near as prevalent. We don't know exactly how the gods work, but each god appears to be able to grant particular types of sorcery to mortals who were born without any talent for it. This is colloquially referred to as being given the 'gifts of the gods'. Some gifted humans demonstrate sorcerous abilities that are beyond what a traditional sorcerer is capable of. One of my mentors has a gift from Sytira that allows him to completely nullify sorcery in a specific area."

That's pretty impressive. "That makes some sense. I can see why people would want their gods to be physically present, though, which must be why the local religion is so appealing."

"Of course. Who wouldn't want to meet the deity they worship? It's an appealing idea from our perspective, but from the perspective of the true gods, it would not be worth the risk. Even Vaelien, the oldest and most powerful deity still living, rarely appears without an entourage. And history has recorded more than one failed attempt to assassinate Vaelien – at least one of which was by one of his own children."

"All right, I can see why your gods might not be making any big public demonstrations, then. But how am I supposed to know what they want me to do without any guidance?" Taelien shook his head. "I need to find this Erik Tarren. My parents were insistent that he could help."

"I understand your desire to learn. I'm a Sytiran, after all. But please, be patient. If I ask you to leave the city for your own safety, I need you to listen. I want to know about your connection to the sword, too – it could be one of the most important discoveries for my religion in a hundred years. I will look for Tarren even if you have to leave." Her expression was soft, her eyes pleading. Taelien turned his head aside.

"Fine," he conceded. "I'll leave if it looks like Myros is going to arrive."

"Thank you," she beamed a smile at him. "Now, where'd you learn how to cut through fire with a sword?"

"Oh, that? I grew up near Selyr. When I was ten, I was sent for sorcerous aptitude testing. My parents wanted me to deliberately fail, but I was too proud. My performance earned me six years of mandatory military training. Since my proficiency was with metal sorcery, most of my training involved learning how to use spells to augment my sword work."

"The practice of taking children away from home like that is barbaric. Your parents must have been furious. How old were you?"

Taelien shrugged. "I was ten. Honestly, it wasn't so bad. My parents were upset, sure, but they had gone through the same thing when they were young. I hated it for the first couple years, but I learned skills I never would have back home."

Never thought I'd be thankful for all those hours of running, climbing, and sparring.

"About four years in, they transferred me to a Thornguard facility for more advanced training. Most of the students there were older, and it was pretty much a foregone conclusion that the majority of us would end up as Thornguard. I finally had a chance to pit myself against some stronger opponents."

"One of my fellow trainees was a talented flame sorcerer named Nerys. She had a spell that surrounded her with a whirlwind of fire. During our training matches, I couldn't even get close enough to swing a sword at her. After losing a couple humiliating bouts, I developed a strategy."

He raised the Sae'kes and ran a finger along the metal rim of the scabbard. "I already could manipulate metal that was touching other metal, and I had a minor talent for flame sorcery. I spent months practicing trying to sense and move a fire just by touching it with metal. Eventually, I succeeded. Nerys still throttled me in our next match, but at least I managed to startle her."

The swordsman gave a deep laugh, raising a hand to his lips. "That girl was a beast. Anyway, I loved the fighting, but I hated the philosophy the Thornguard were always drilling into us."

'That's interesting," Lydia perked up a bit. "You didn't like the Thornguard's philosophy? What about it?"

"My parents had raised me on stories of heroes working together to accomplish things they couldn't on their own, or sacrificing themselves to save their allies. The Thornguard drilled it into us to focus on getting the job done. We had training exercises designed to get us to learn to leave wounded allies behind. It made me sick."

The sorceress smiled. "I can understand why you'd have an objection to that. The Tae'os philosophy emphasizes preserving life."

"I know. My parents are Tae'os worshippers. I assume that's why Erik brought me to them specifically – Rethri followers of the Tae'os pantheon are rare."

"I don't think you mentioned before that you were raised by Rethri." Lydia quirked an eyebrow.

"Didn't I?" he shrugged. "Well, it didn't really matter to me that they were Rethri, or matter to them that I'm not. In any case, the worst part about the Thornguard training was that it worked. I knew what the exercises were designed to do, but I went along with them anyway. It took one of my friends being seriously injured to get me to stop and reassess the situation. Even then, I had to stay until my six years were up. My commander tried to convince me to stay, but I couldn't stomach any more of it."

"Of course, just because I was 'finished' with my mandatory service didn't mean I was completely out yet. I was in the reserves for another four years, going back periodically for more training. They tried to recruit me permanently every time I visited."

A knock sounded on the door. Lydia's hand immediately dropped to her sword, but Taelien just glanced toward the room's entrance. "Good morning," he said. "We're both awake, you can come in."

The knob turned, but the door didn't open. "It's locked," Jonan's voice said. Lydia took a deep breath, relaxing her grip on her weapon and moving to flip the lock a moment later.

As the door opened, Lydia stood up, nodding to Jonan. He looked exhausted. His hair was disheveled, and he looked to be wearing a much thicker pair of glasses. Normally, Taelien wouldn't have paid much attention to the spectacles, but these were both broader in frame and thicker in the glass to such an extent that they dominated the appearance of his face.

"Mornin'," Jonan said. "Care for some food? It's the non-poisoned kind," he said with a wink at Lydia.

Taelien put a hand over his stomach and grinned. "Sounds tasty."

Lydia nodded. "Yes, thank you. We can discuss business while we eat."

Jonan shrugged mildly at that, turning and leading the way down the stairs to where they had held him captive the previous night. He had apparently moved a few things around while Taelien was sleeping, and now three chairs sat next to a table that was no longer cluttered with panes of glass.

Taelien took a seat immediately, but Lydia remained standing a few feet away while Jonan retrieved plates and food from his cupboard nearby. It was simple fare — dried meat, cheese, and more of the same bread from the previous evening. Even so, Taelien was grateful for anything to eat after several days on the road and much of a day in the Adellan Room.

"Thank you for feeding us," Taelien offered as he began to fill his plate. Lydia sat awkwardly a few moments later, looking like she had judged that the plates were not currently planning to assassinate her.

"You're welcome," Jonan said, fetching a set of wooden mugs and a large clay jug of liquid. "It's water," Jonan said meaningfully to Lydia, and she gave him a curt nod in reply.

While Taelien began to eat, Jonan retrieved one last thing — a large swath of parchment — and unrolled it in the center of the table. It didn't quite reach where he was sitting, but Taelien glanced at the parchment and realized it was a map of the city with several locations circled.

Taelien examined the map, but he wasn't familiar enough with the city to recognize most of the circled locations.

The city map was divided into six sections. The "Old City" was a roughly triangular section that stretched from the southern city wall to near the city's current center. There were multiple circled buildings here, including the "Low Palace" and the "Grand Temple of the Spear".

Near the top of the triangle was the entrance to the Noble's District, an hourglass shaped section with a large circled structure – the "High Palace" – north of the center of the hourglass shape.

The Merchant's District encompassed a large portion of the north east side of the map, starting from around the center of the hourglass. Taelien noted several circled structures in that area, but none of them were labeled.

The Craftsman's District was roughly opposite of the Merchant's District, but considerably larger, and the buildings appeared to be more densely packed together. Taelien took that to mean that "Craftsmen" were considered lower class than "Merchants" within this particular city. He guessed that the distinction involved craftsmen making products directly, whereas merchants more than likely were involved in selling finished goods.

South of the Craftsman's district was the Mining District, a smaller area that was similarly densely packed. There were no circled buildings in that area.

Below the Merchant's District was the Worker's District, which encompassed the largest portion of the city. The city gate where Taelien had entered was located in the Worker's District, although he noted other gates in the Old City and the Noble's District. He kept those locations in mind in case he had to flee the city.

From the layout of the city, he guessed that he had been imprisoned in the "Low Palace", and then headed north with Lydia into the Noble's District.

"What's the relationship between these circled locations?" Taelien asked.

"These are places that I suspect the Rethri might be held. I started with a much larger list, and I have been narrowing it down over the last several months," Jonan explained.

Lydia quirked an eyebrow at Jonan. "You've been spying at these places for months without getting caught?"

Jonan shrugged. "I haven't actually managed to get inside everywhere personally. Mostly, I've been gathering information through other sources."

"If that's the case, what is your degree of confidence that the places you've already disqualified are not holding the Rethri?" Lydia asked, a hard tone of disapproval in her voice.

"I, uh, am fairly confident. My informants are very good at their work, and if anything was particularly suspicious, I inspected it as best I could. Admittedly, there have been some locations I have not been able to access extensively, which is why they remain circled here," Jonan explained.

"So, you need our help," Taelien concluded.

Jonan put a hand to his chin, leaning on it against the table. "Your help would, well, be helpful. In the fullness of time, I suspect I could get access to all these places by hiring more assistance. I believe we might be running out of time, however, if we haven't already. Hiring trustworthy people for subterfuge is tricky business. I've had to be very careful, preferring contacts that have worked with my priesthood before."

"I'd like to help you," Lydia said in a conciliatory tone, "But I have other things I need to be investigating, and I've already jeopardized my cover by helping Taelien escape. I'm willing to do some of my own research, but I can't be caught working with you."

Lydia ran a finger across the map, tracing a path between the various circled locations. It was obvious she was thinking, so neither of the men interrupted her.

"What was your methodology for selecting these locations?" Lydia asked.

Jonan nodded as if confirming some thought in his own mind, or perhaps acknowledging Lydia in some way. "I started by researching the areas in the city with the highest degree of security. The two palaces, the high temple, the prisons, some of the universities, and some of the manors of the wealthiest nobles. That was a long list, more than thirty locations, so I consulted with multiple contacts about each of them. I didn't provide a full list of everywhere I was investigating to any one person, nor did I provide them with what I was looking for – I just asked which places would be good or bad to hide a large object of high value."

Jonan took a breath, and then continued. "If multiple contacts agreed that a location was badly suited toward hiding something – and I agreed with them – I cut it off the list. In most cases, these locations were disqualified because they were too public. I was only able to cut a few items off the list that way, but it was a start. From there, I began to hire established contacts that our priesthood has used in the past to investigate specific locations. I asked them to find any areas that looked like they had restricted access – places warded with obvious sorcery, for example – and report that back to me."

"Over the course of months, these contacts investigated all of the locations to the best of their ability. I visited many of them myself, crossing off false leads." He hesitated a bit, his expression darkening slightly.

"Debating how much to tell us?" Lydia asked.

Jonan sighed deliberately, giving her a pointed look. "You're still a court sorceress here. Even with what I've already told you, I'm sure you could dismantle my plans with ease – and you might have to, in order to preserve your own cover. The more I tell you, the more vulnerable I make myself."

Lydia smiled, pushing her glasses further up her nose. "I could sabotage you, yes, but I don't plan to – as long as you're telling me the truth about your goals. Your cooperation helps you in a couple ways. First, it helps convince me of your competence and sincerity. Second, if I do decide I need to get rid of you to cover for myself, it makes it more likely I'll be able to finish your work without you."

Jonan sighed, lifting up his hands in a gesture of surrender. "When you put it like that, ah, I suppose I don't have much of a real choice."

Taelien glanced at Lydia, keeping his expression neutral. *Would she really even consider turning someone in to protect herself? I didn't think the paladins of Sytira did things like that. Maybe I'm just being naïve, though. She's not like a story-book paladin in most respects.*

"I have a cover identity," Jonan admitted. "This house belongs to a member of our priesthood, and I'm using the identity of his son, Travis Case. I pretend to be on the lower rung of nobility, selling expensive glassware as my way of expanding the family's fortunes." He gestured at a corner where he had stacked some of the slabs of glass that had lain on the table the night before. "I have some little minor actual experience at working glass, and the family name has been sufficient to help me sell a few pieces here and there."

Lydia looked over at the glass and then back to Jonan, a look of surprise crossing her features. "You're dominion bonding the glass," she realized aloud.

Taelien gave Jonan an appraising look, considering that. Dominion bonding was a notoriously difficult process. It involved saturating something with a dominion, permanently changing or augmenting the target's properties. From what he had heard, something could only be safely bonded to one dominion at a time.

Rethri were well-known for being born with a kind of bond to a specific dominion. They strengthened this bond during a coming of age ritual, and that somehow drastically slowed their aging process. He wasn't familiar with the details. He had been told that dominion bonds did not work on most humans — something about their bodies prevented the bonds from taking hold.

Ancient artifacts — his sword included among them — sometimes had runes on their surface called dominion marks. Each mark appeared to contain a bond to a dominion, and different marks bestowed different effects. Through the use of these runes, artifacts could be bonded to multiple dominions at the same time, allowing for more complex and powerful effects. His mother had spent years trying to decipher how the marks on the Sae'kes had been made, but she claimed to have had little success.

Taelien guessed that his weapon carried multiple marks tied to the Dominion of Metal — at least one to make it sharper, and one to make it more resilient to damage. He had memorized the appearance of each of the marks, but while he had found pictures of the runes in several texts, none of them had ever been able to explain their exact functions.

Only the gods still hold the secret of forging dominion marks, his mother had told him. *The last sorcerers with that knowledge perished long ago.*

"How does that work?" Taelien asked. "I've never seen a dominion bond created."

"There are a few different ways to do it," Jonan explained. "It depends on what you're trying to accomplish, and what you want to bond. In my case, I've found a way to mix dominion essence of sight with ink. It's very time consuming, but eventually, I can make ink that's sufficiently saturated to make a weak bond. Once I do that, I write my signature on part of the object with the ink — the pedestal, or the backing of the mirror frame, or that sort of thing."

Sight. Of course — that's what Lydia must have realized before. We already saw that Jonan could make himself invisible — he can do a lot of other spy work with that kind of sorcery.

"Very impressive," Lydia admitted. "I've never heard of dominion essence of sight being successfully held in a liquid state." Her second statement sounded more skeptical, but she shook her head wearily. She was looking more exhausted by the moment. "All right. I'm satisfied with the explanation of your basic methodology for now."

"Excellent," Jonan said. "The palaces," he said, pointing at the low palace, "Have had far too many guards for me to get access to most of their secrets. As a court sorceress, however, you should have largely unrestricted access."

Lydia nodded. "If there were a bunch of Rethri being held prisoner in the low palace, I'd probably have noticed by now. But I'll certainly take another look, and I haven't spent as much time in the high palace."

"And you'll let me know if you find anything?" Jonan inquired hopefully.

"I'll consider it," Lydia said, tilting her head as if to look downward at him, even though he was slightly taller than she was.

Jonan gave the slightest look of irritation, and then straightened himself. "Mm, very well, then." He glanced at Taelien. "Would you be willing to help me take a look at one of the more heavily guarded facilities?"

Taelien considered that. He wanted to help, but his only experience with stealth was in a forest environment, not an urban one. He didn't know the local culture or customs, which had already proven to be nearly disastrous. "Which one would you want me to help you with?" he asked noncommittally.

Jonan pointed at a particular spot on the map instantly, not far to the right of their current location. "This one. Talior and Castle Depository".

Taelien nodded. "You think this 'Talior' family is just a 'Tailor' with a slight change to make it less obvious?"

"That sounds a little too clumsy," Lydia interjected. "Changing a couple letters is hardly a cover."

Jonan shrugged. "From what we've gathered, Donovan Tailor wasn't a very subtle man. He was arrogant and egocentric. Tailor might not even be a change to cover the identity of the family – they just might have changed it when they rose to nobility to avoid sounding like merchant-class citizens. It's not uncommon – my own family name, 'Kestrian', is based on the word 'Equestrian'. The family changed it when they were successful enough to move into other business."

Taelien nodded at that. "Why do you need my help?"

"Ah, that's the fun part," Jonan said with a grin. "I managed to get inside. It's not a very big facility, at least compared to the palaces. I found a dominion bonded door."

Lydia perked up at that. "That's fairly unusual, but it could just be where they store their valuables."

Jonan nodded. "It might be, but the room seemed too big for that. From the position of the door and the location of the surrounding rooms, I'd say it was the size of a large bedroom. But that isn't the only suspicious part – I've seen dominion bonded doors before. I have a spell to see through walls. When I see that type of thing, I just look through the adjacent walls. It didn't work – in fact, I was temporarily blinded."

"What would cause that?" Taelien asked.

"They must have bonded the walls inside the room, too," Lydia explained. "And with a type of dominion bond expressly designed for preventing spells like yours," she said to Jonan. "You're right, that is suspicious."

Jonan nodded. "I was hoping you could cut through the lock," he said to Taelien.

"What makes you think I could do something like that?" Taelien asked.

"Well, with the sacred sword -," Jonan began, gesturing at the sword on Taelien's hip. "Huh. What'd you do with it?"

Did Jonan somehow not notice what the sword looked like this last night? It's looked like this since before we met him. Which means...

"What makes you think he's carrying the Sae'kes?" Lydia asked, folding her arms.

"He probably saw me when they first brought me in," Taelien offered. Jonan nodded in agreement. "There was a pretty big crowd that came to watch when they escorted me over."

Or he can see through the scabbard, Taelien considered. *If he can see the runes on the blade, altering the hilt design is almost irrelevant.*

Lydia clenched her jaw, looking dissatisfied by the answer, but she didn't say anything.

"I have no experience at hiding in an urban environment," Taelien admitted. "But if you explain your plan and it sounds plausible, I will do what I can to help you."

And hope this isn't all just some kind of cover to steal something valuable out of a heavily protected room.

Lydia stood up suddenly, a hard expression her face. "Very well, then. With that decision made, I need to report back to the palace and make some excuses."

"Shall we meet back here in the evening, then?" Jonan asked.

"No promises," Lydia said. "I need to protect my identity, first and foremost. If I can slip out tonight, I will. If not, it may be another day or more before we can converse again."

Jonan nodded. "Very well. Good luck," he said.

Lydia looked slightly rankled, but she nodded curtly to him, and then turned to Taelien. "Don't get caught. I don't think I can protect you a second time."

Taelien nodded. "Don't worry. We'll be careful."

This is going to be a mess, Taelien realized. He stood with Jonan across the street from their target building, a solid looking two-story structure of grey stone. A broad sign proclaimed it to be "Talior and Castle Depository". The building was located in a residential area – not exactly where Taelien expected anyone to hold a group of Rethri prisoners. He was not, however, an expert on the subject.

He was beginning to doubt that Jonan was an expert, too.

The dawnfire still shined brightly overhead, which seemed to be precisely the wrong time to infiltrate a building, and Jonan hadn't given Taelien any hints about their plan yet. He assumed it involved trying the same invisibility spell that Jonan had been using to follow him earlier – but Lydia had been able to counter that, and another sorcerer with similar skills could do the same.

Here and there, a few civilians walked by, heading into one or two story houses of hardwood and stone. Further down the street, a small group of children were playing some kind of game involving sticks and a ball. The image put a smile on Taelien's face, faintly reminding him of home. *I wonder how Fal is holding up without me?*

Most of the homes they passed were painted a light brown, giving the area a woodland tone that only enhanced his homesickness. In the few moments that they stood near their destination Taelien didn't see anyone enter or exit it, but that was hardly surprising. It was the only business on a street that was mostly residential.

"Remember, you're James Haven, and I'm Travis Case," Jonan pointed out.

"I've got it, Travis," Taelien assured him.

"This way," Jonan said, leading Taelien past the building. Taelien followed, glancing from side to side. *We really should have talked this out in more detail before leaving the house. We can't talk here – too many civilians around.*

A few blocks beyond the building they reached a street lined with shops, some encompassing full structures of their own, others simply booths on the sides of the road. Jonan led them to the only closed door on the street and rapped twice on it. Taelien looked up at the sign above the door, which read, "The Golden Needle". *Hrm. A tailor.*

A few moments later, the door opened. A balding man, his beard showing more gray than brown, stood in the doorway. The man tilted his head to the side inquisitively when he saw Jonan, a hint of irritation showing in his eyes. "Ugh, what is it now?"

"Just a moment of your time, good sir," Jonan pleaded. "Can we come in?"

The older man sighed. "Fine, fine, just make it quick." He stepped out of the way, giving Taelien only the briefest sidelong glance as the pair stepped inside.

The gray-bearded man slammed the door shut, folding his arms. "You nearly ruined me last time, you reshing con. Give me three reasons not to call the guards on you right now."

Taelien frowned and took a step back toward the door, but Jonan just rolled his eyes and reached into a pouch at his side. He withdrew three silver royals – the largest denomination of silver coinage used in areas near Velthryn. With a deep breath, Jonan dropped the coins in the older man's waiting hand.

The balding man scowled. "That'll hardly pay for the damage you caused last time, but I'm listening."

"Nothing scandalous this time, I promise you. I just need two passable tail coats, for my friend here and myself," he said, indicating Taelien with a gesture. "Just for a few hours. And a place to change and leave our things," he hastily added.

The older man sighed, shaking his head. "That sounds reasonable enough. But you sounded perfectly reasonable last time, too."

"We won't be any trouble, I assure you," Jonan implored him.

He lies as easily as he breathes, Taelien considered, drawing his hand into a fist. Not for the first time, Taelien considered turning back. Rescuing a group of Rethri sounded like a noble goal – and if it was true, he'd be glad to help – but an itching in his mind told him that it was terribly improbable that Jonan was telling him the whole truth.

Unfortunately, Lydia – his only other contact in the city – wasn't much better. She had already proven to be at least similarly adept at deception.

"You say that every time, Travis. Feh," the older man said.

"I'll put in a good word with the wife for you. I'll tell her to give you a discount," Jonan offered.

Wife? Taelien wondered, quirking a brow at Jonan. Jonan didn't even acknowledge him.

The older man scratched his chin. "How much of a discount?"

Jonan shrugged. "That's up to her. I'll still pay you for the rentals, of course."

"Fine, fine. Just don't tell me what you're doing with the suits. And if there's blood, clean it off before you get them back to me. I don't want to see it," the older man insisted.

"Of course, Elor. No need to worry about that," Jonan insisted.

A few more coins changed hands, and a mystified Taelien found himself dressed in a dapper black coat suit a few short minutes later. There were no shoes to match it available, but the ones he had borrowed from Jonan looked passable with it.

The sleeves of the coat and the pant legs were both a little bit too short, but not enough to be particularly noticeable. He briefly considered asking the tailor to make some adjustments, but a glance at Elor's expression told him that it was an unwise idea to press the man further.

Taelien's sword still sat at his left hip – he had insisted on keeping it with him – but he left his other borrowed garb with the tailor. He glanced in his changing room's mirror and appraised himself to look like a professional – if only a professional bodyguard, or perhaps a military advisor.

Jonan emerged from his own changing room a few minutes later, looking about five years older and about two social classes higher. His hair had been pulled back into a long tail cinched with a tiny silver harp, the symbol of the queen regent. He wore silver-framed glasses with thinner lenses and a gray coat with steel buttons that looked tailored to fit him. *Maybe it was tailored to fit him – the owner clearly has a history with 'Travis' here.*

With their new clothes in place, Jonan drew Taelien into his changing room and closed the door.

"And now the plan," Jonan said.

Taelien raised an eyebrow, adjusting one of the cuffs on his coat. "You could have told me more about this before we left."

Jonan grinned. "Nonsense. You weren't committed when we left. Now you are."

Taelien shifted his stance uneasily. *He's probably right. It's amazing how such a small measure of effort can make me feel like it's too late to turn back from something.*

"Not until I agree to what you propose," Taelien said, for his own benefit as much as Jonan's.

"It's actually quite simple. I have a storage unit in the depository. I'm going to ask to visit it. The box is located underground, only a few doors away from the locked room. You are going to go investigate while I fiddle with the contents of the box."

Taelien leaned back against the wall of the changing room. "Don't they have guards?"

"Ah, certainly, but the guards will see you in the room with me, not where you truly are," Jonan explained.

"And if I find the Rethri?" Taelien asked.

"We don't try to rescue them right now. We don't have to. Just get inside that door and see what you can find. We can discuss it afterward," Jonan instructed him.

"You want me to cut through a door and then leave without the contents, with the expectation of coming back later?" Taelien inquired, quirking a brow.

"I, er, can cover the damage up with an illusion. As long as you make clean cuts. Don't take the whole door off if you can avoid it. You just need to cut the lock," he said, sounding a bit nervous.

What aren't you telling me? Planning to leave me behind? Or do you know someone on the inside of the storage facility to cover for us?

Taelien shook his head.

"Let's get this over with."

"Welcome to Talior and Castle. How may we be of service?" a tall woman asked from behind a counter.

"Yes, hello, I'm Travis Case. I have a box below, I'd like to go dig through it to try to find something," Jonan said, withdrawing a key and displaying it to the woman.

"Very good, wait here, I'll fetch someone to escort you," the woman said.

Their escort arrived a few moments later – a pair of big men in grey suits, not dissimilar from the one Jonan was wearing. They had batons on their hips.

"You'll have to leave that up here," one of the guards said, indicating Taelien's sword.

Taelien nodded silently, reaching to unbuckle his belt. *How did I think I could get into the equivalent of a bank vault while wearing a sword?*

Jonan grabbed the belt and sword away from Taelien casually and put a hand on the scabbard as if to remove it from the belt. As Taelien watched, Jonan shifted his hand down the belt in a dragging motion, but the scabbard remained in place. "Can we just leave it here?" Jonan asked, walking over to a doorway.

"Sure," the guard said. "Just can't take it downstairs."

Jonan nodded, making a gesture as if he was leaning something up against the wall, and then handed the belt – sword and all – back to Taelien. "Thank you," Jonan said to the guard.

The guard nodded as Taelien belted his weapon back on, seeming oblivious to the sword's presence. *Fascinating. The guards must see the sword as being in that corner. The illusion probably isn't solid – that's why Jonan didn't want to hand it directly to the guards. How is he making illusions that they see, but I can't? Did he cast something on me earlier to exclude me from the effects?*

Taelien considered Jonan's capabilities with growing suspicion. The Kesite was apparently trained in the Liadran style of sorcery, which involved gestures or directly touching the target, rather than using words. It was the same style that Taelien had learned, but Taelien could only affect things he was in contact with – either directly or through an object he was touching. Jonan's ability to wordlessly cast spells that impacted vision – or perhaps even thoughts – demonstrated a drastically higher degree of proficiency.

I can never trust my eyes around Jonan, Taelien realized. *And he hasn't told me he can influence other senses.*

The other guard inserted a key into the door and opened it, revealing a small room with a pair of stairways, leading up and down. The guards headed to the stairway going downward, and Jonan and Taelien followed.

"Do you know the number of your box, or do you need me to check?" the other guard asked.

"It's number forty-four," Jonan replied.

The guards led them past three small rooms on each side before stopping at the fourth door on the left side. One of the guards turned the key and opened the door, gesturing politely for the pair to step inside.

Jonan nudged Taelien and waved a hand almost casually down the hall. The gesture was conspicuous since Taelien knew to look for it, but the guards didn't seem to notice. Jonan stepped into the room, and one of the guards went in with him. The other guard closed and locked the door from the outside, leaving Taelien standing in the hall.

The remaining guard was looking right in his direction, but seemed to have no idea he was there.

Taelien lifted a hand. He could see himself clearly, and glancing back, he could still see his own shadow as well. Would the guard notice his shadow? He didn't know if the illusion masking his presence would cover the shadow or not – shadow sorcery was a different type of spell casting, but that didn't mean an image couldn't conceal a shadow.

Tentatively, Taelien took a step forward. The guard didn't react – in fact, he looked sort of bored. He leaned against the wall next to the door, shaking his head. After a minute or so passed of Taelien inching forward, the guard took out a book and sat down.

Taelien resisted the urge to sigh with relief, stepping forward slightly after the guard had settled into place. *How long ago did Jonan purchase this storage unit? How long has he been planning this mission?* Taelien wondered, glancing back at the guard every few moments. *How did he get this far by himself last time he was here?*

Taelien slowed himself after passing three more doors, realizing he wasn't sure which one Jonan wanted him to investigate. Thus far, they all looked identical, save the numbers atop. Each door, he realized, must have led to another hall that contained several storage units. Was the warded area in this hall, or one of the ones beyond the doors?

Fortunately, a few steps later he found his answer – the wall on his right was bare, missing a door to match the left side. As he continued walking, he passed two more doors on his left before finally reaching one on the right – a broad door of steel, at least twice as wide as the wooden doors elsewhere in the hall.

Well, that's conspicuous.

Taelien tentatively reached out a hand to touch the metal. He thought he felt a slight tingling sensation, but he dismissed it as being his imagination. His thoughts surged into the metal, picturing the door as if it was an extension of his body. He found three redundant locks, as well as pins to anchor the door directly into the stone walls of the building. It was, Taelien considered, probably a very effective defense against most threats.

Metal sorcery made that defense a triviality.

Taelien glanced back toward the guard, finding the man to be still reading. A glance to his other side showed no signs of any other guards.

He thought he heard movement to his right, so he swung a hand out at the open air, but it didn't catch anything. Gritting his teeth, he put his hand back on the door and concentrated.

Open, he told the door. Rather than causing the door to swing outward, he simply opened a Taelien-sized section in the center of it and stepped through. The hole remained open behind him. While dominion sorcery spells typically produced temporary effects, Taelien's core sorcery manipulated metal permanently unless he chose to deliberately reverse it.

Inside the room, he saw intricate runes written on the inside of the door – as well as the walls – in a language he did not understand.

The left side of the room had two tables sat end-to-end against each other, lined with metallic objects. *Weapons,* he thought at first, but a moment later he recognized the shapes with greater specificity. *No, torture implements,* he realized, taking in the wicked curves of tiny blades and the elegantly arrayed lines of needles. Glass bottles containing colorful fluids sat beside the tools, but there were no labels to espouse their functions.

More importantly, however, he also saw a figure sitting in the center of a web of runic markings about twenty feet away. The runes flickered with purple light, causing reflections to play across the sitting figure's thick obsidian-like scales. Even in a sitting position, the figure's head was nearly level with Taelien's. A thick spinal ridge of similar material to the scales marked the creature as male. Taelien could see that the figure's eyes were closed, but that it drew slow breaths into its lungs.

The figure within the weave of sigils was not a Rethri, like Taelien had been searching for. He was an Esharen, the fabled race native to the Xixian Empire. The last bastions of the empire had been swept away decades ago, and Taelien had been raised to believe the Esharen had been all but wiped out.

Gods, Taelien cursed in his mind. His hand instinctively drifted to the sword at his side, but he forced the hand back away when he realized what he was doing. He would not kill a helpless opponent, even if that was almost certainly what the Esharen would do to him.

Years of his schooling flooded his mind. The Xixian Empire had once spanned most of Mythralis, using humans and Rethri as slaves. He had been told that the Rethri had rebelled, overthrowing their Xixian masters, and freeing their human brethren as well. Of course, since Taelien was raised in a Rethri city, he knew their account would be somewhat biased.

He did not expect them to be wrong about the species being eradicated, however.

Was this just a single remnant, the last of a defeated race? It was possible — but it seemed infinitely more likely that there was a darker explanation. The city of Orlyn was once a Xixian city — could some of the empire have survived here? Were they working in secret somehow?

Taelien turned around and touched the door again.

Close, he told it. The door reverted to its previous state.

He needed time to think.

Aside from the Esharen, the tables, and the runes, the room appeared to be completely bare. *Not even a chair — the torturer must like to stand.* The floors, walls, and ceiling were all the same nondescript grey stone. Taelien saw no other entrances or exits, nor any obvious traps.

He had to have answers.

Taking a deep breath, he stepped away from the door to get a closer look at the Xixian. It still did not respond to his presence, but he kept himself outside of the boundary of the runic pattern, not knowing if the Esharen was faking unconsciousness or what the functions of the runes were.

As he approached, he noted that the Esharen's breathing was rough, wheezing, like a man with a damaged lung. Its blackened scales were marred with cracks, especially along its chest and neck. A single large pattern of damage showed at the back of the creature's head. Though he knew little about Esharen physiology, the patterns were fairly obvious — the creature had been smashed with some kind of heavy bludgeoning object. If the tales were true, no ordinary weapon could pierce an Esharen's scales — but perhaps a heavy enough weapon could crack it. There was no blood near the apparent injuries; just a dry white powder of some kind.

He walked to the table next, inspecting the implements laid out there. The blades of each of the cutting implements looked clean, but he noted a scalpel that appeared to be bent out of shape. Touching the metal handle, he extended his senses into it. He felt the flaws that had formed near the blade, where the surface had been distorted by jarring force. *Someone tried to jam this into the Esharen, but it bent against the creature's scales,* he deduced.

In a moment of obsessive neatness, he bent the object back into its proper shape and set it back down. He went down the line of objects until he found the likely culprit for the Esharen's missing scales – a medium-sized hammer with a pick on the opposite side of the hammer head. Scratches on the hammer head confirmed that it had been used, but there was no sign of the white powder he had noticed on the Esharen's body on the surface of the metal. *It's been cleaned,* he considered. *If that white powder is dried Esharen blood, perhaps they're testing its alchemical properties in one of these vials. Or maybe the powder is some kind of poison, and they're applying it to the Esharen to keep it weak.*

Setting the hammer back down, Taelien took a cautious step toward the Esharen. A quick glance at the floor told him that the runes – much like the ones on the wall – were indecipherable to him. This was intriguing, since he could read and write in both Velthryn and Liadran, and he could recognize several other languages, including Xixian. This was nothing he could remember seeing before – except in one place.

The runes on the blade of his weapon.

In moments, he picked out two of the seven symbols on his sword. He did not find any of the others, but the ones he found were identical to his sword's markings. No scholar or sorcerer he had met could tell him what the origin of those runes were – merely that they represented the gods of the Tae'osian faith.

If these symbols represent gods, well, this Esharen is surrounded by an awful lot of gods.

If he had carried paper, Taelien would have taken the time to write down the symbols before doing anything else. He hadn't, however, and this find was too significant to leave alone. If this room was some kind of holding cell, it was plausible the Rethri had already been held here and transferred elsewhere – and that the same could happen to the Esharen if he left.

Not only did he need to know what the Esharen knew, he could not justify leaving it to whatever fate awaited it at the hands of the sorcerers that bound it here. *No creature, not even a creature of Xixis, deserves this.*

"Esharen," Taelien said, "Can you hear me?"

Jonan appeared at Taelien's side an instant later. "What are you doing? Don't talk to it!"

Taelien took a step back away from Jonan, startled by his sudden appearance, and put his hand on the hilt of his sword.

"What are you doing here? Aren't you supposed to be investigating your box?" Taelien asked.

"An image of me is," Jonan explained. "I never went in there. I was going to warn you that I was following you, but I couldn't think of a way to do it without alerting the guards."

"You changed the plan," Taelien muttered bitterly. "Wait. How do I know who I am speaking to? Perhaps that Esharen is invading my mind."

He glanced warily at the Esharen. Its eyes still appeared to be closed.

"Well, if I was the Esharen, I'd probably want you to free me. I, Jonan, want you to get out of this room. Right now," Jonan replied.

"We can't just leave him here," Taelien said, glancing back at the Esharen. "Whoever captured those Rethri probably took him prisoner, too."

Jonan shook his head, reaching into a coat pocket and removing a mirror. Taelien glanced at the mirror dubiously. "You're not going to leave that here, are you?"

"No need," Jonan said, waving the mirror around for a moment and then putting it back in his coat. He removed a second mirror, held it up to reflect the image of the Esharen, and then tapped the surface of the glass. Looking satisfied, he put that mirror away as well.

Taelien took a step closer to Jonan, gritting his teeth. "You are beginning to try my patience, 'Jonan'. Explain yourself."

Jonan took a step back, a look of surprise crossing his face. "Um, hold, there's no need to be aggressive," he said, backing away further. "Look, I can use the mirrors to send images to other mirrors, like I explained before. If I leave one here, that's the best, since I can watch it constantly. I just cast a spell to send an image of what the mirror saw — just an image — back to another mirror I have. So we can study these runes later."

Taelien nodded, but his jaw was still set tightly. "For the future, I would appreciate it if you disclose your plans to me further in advance." After a moment, he waved his left hand toward the Esharen. "Accurate plans."

"I didn't know this thing was here, I mean that," Jonan said.

Taelien nodded. "But you told me you'd be in your vault. You followed me instead."

"And you were supposed to take a look and leave, not talk to the – never mind. We don't have time for this," Jonan said.

"You're right," Taelien said. He ducked down, grabbing the hilt of his sword and scraping the metal-lined scabbard across a line of the glowing runes on the floor. The runes sparked as the metal impacted against their surface, and then faded out. "We will use our time to get answers."

Jonan's eyes widened and he stumbled back several steps, running into the stone wall of the room. "No, no, you didn't," he stammered.

The Esharen's eyes fluttered open, revealing yellow irises with thick red pupils. Aside from that, it made no obvious movements.

Taelien walked back to the metal door and hovered a hand near it. "I'm opening the door. Leave, and I'll follow you when I am done here."

Jonan rushed to the door. "We both need to leave. Please. These things can kill entire squads of soldiers by themselves," Jonan pleaded, putting a hand on Taelien's arm.

"Stand outside, then, and be ready to make me invisible as soon as I step out. I may have the Esharen with me, if he's cooperative."

Taelien pressed his palm against the door. *Open.*

"You're insane," Jonan whispered, slipping outside.

Close.

The door slammed shut, and Taelien turned to see the Esharen's torso directly in front of his face.

The creature's hand – more accurately a claw – was around his neck before he had a chance to react. It lifted him off the floor with seemingly no effort, pressing him against the metal door.

"Ashavan kor de sahu mes," the creature said, pressing him harder against the wall.

Taelien lifted his hands to grasp the creature's arm, knowing his neck could not support his entire body's weight. He didn't understand a word the creature had said, which was unsurprising. He only knew a few words in Xixian. "Stop. Peace," he said, trying to remember something relevant. When the pressure failed to ease, Taelien released his right hand and slammed his open palm into one of the damaged sections in the Esharen scales. He felt the scales cave further as his hand connected, pressing the stone-like plates into something softer beneath. The creature released him instantly, stumbling back a step, its hand reaching down to clutch at the injured area.

Taelien looked up toward the massive creature, seeing something that looked like disbelief in the Esharen's eyes. The expression lasted only an instant before being replaced by fury, and with a growl, the creature swung its other claw straight at Taelien's head.

He was ready this time, ducking beneath the swipe. A sharp whine erupted as the Esharen's claws ripped into the metal of the door. Taelien slammed another palm into the other side of the creature's chest and then sidestepped to the right, trying to avoid being boxed in against the wall.

The Esharen stepped back, surprising Taelien, and spoke again. "Your sorcery has failed you, human," it spoke in a deep, reverberating tone.

"No," Taelien said, "Hold on, I just freed you. I am not working with your captors."

The Esharen tilted its head to the side, bending its knees and assuming a catlike pose, its claws scraping against the ground. "Indeed?" It glanced back toward where it had been bound, coughing deeply for several moments before spitting a mouth full of white powder on the floor to its side. "And why would you help me?"

"It looked like you were being tortured," Taelien stammered. The creature's eyes narrowed at him, and Taelien took another step back. *Wrong tactic. It doesn't believe I'd do this for moral reasons.* "I also wanted information. What are the runes that were binding you here? Who captured you?"

"Ah," the creature said, nodding. "You share one of my enemies, and you think this makes you a friend."

The Esharen pounced, and Taelien was forced to fall backward to avoid a swing at his chest. He kicked at its face with his left leg, but it grabbed his foot en route.

"You were mistaken," the Esharen pulled him across the ground by his foot, bringing a claw down to disembowel him, but Taelien grabbed the creature's arm with his left hand. The Esharen pushed downward, but Taelien held the huge arm in place. Remembering the creature's difficulty with breathing, he slammed his right palm into a cracked section of the creature's neck. It held tight this time, but began coughing even more fiercely than before.

"Please, I don't want to hurt you," Taelien pleaded. The Esharen released Taelien's foot, swiping its claws up Taelien's leg, tearing through pants and flesh. Taelien tried to roll away, but the claws dug deeply before he managed to tumble aside. He found himself on the floor a few feet away from where the creature was still coughing fiercely.

Taelien tried to push himself to his feet, favoring his wounded left leg, and fell back down almost instantly. The Esharen began to rise, finally seeming to recover from its coughing fit, and Taelien's right hand went to his sword.

No, he told himself. *I won't kill a prisoner I failed to free.*

The Esharen dove for him again, but Taelien reacted faster this time, rolling out of its path and smashing a closed fist into the damaged section at the back of the creature's skull. Brittle fractions of scales caved beneath his fist and the Esharen crumpled, unmoving, to the floor.

Gods curse it. Still on the ground, Taelien unbuckled his belt and removed his sword and scabbard, using the sheathed weapon as a cane to push himself to his feet.

He took a moment to breathe and inspect his leg injury. Blood was flowing freely from where three of the Esharen's claws had rent his skin, from the top of his left foot up to nearly his knee. He had nothing aside from clothing to bind it with, so he removed his coat and tore off a wide swath of his shirt, pressing it against the bleeding wounds. As he watched the blood seeping into the shirt, he noticed the rhythmic rising and falling in the chest of the unconscious Esharen next to him.

I'm going to regret this, he told himself, but he had already made his choice. He couldn't stand the idea of leaving a torture victim behind to face certain death.

After staring at the creature for a moment, Taelien refastened his sword on his belt, took a deep breath, and bent down to the fallen creature. It was over seven feet tall, and its stony hide undoubtedly made it weigh several times more than a human of similar size. Gritting his teeth, Taelien wrapped his arms around the creature's chest and lifted its body over his shoulders.

It was only a couple steps to the door, but the pain from each of them nearly sent him back to the floor. When he reached the door, he brushed up against it, unable to free up his hands to use them directly. *Open,* he told it, nearly falling through as the window opened in the metal to comply with his demand.

Jonan stood on the other side, an incredulous expression on his face. The sorcerer took a step back as Taelien lurched through the doorway, Esharen still atop his shoulders, and turned to nudge the metal with his skin and shut it tight.

The sight sorcerer down the hall, and then back to Taelien. "Put that back."

Taelien shook his head, whispering. "No, we need to take him with us."

Jonan tightened his jaw, raising a hand to cover his eyes. "How exactly do you plan to keep that thing – never mind. We can't talk here. Just follow me."

Jonan made a gesture at him and the Esharen, and then turned to walk back toward the building's entrance. Taelien hoped the gesture was refreshing whatever invisibility spell Jonan had used before. He didn't know if his invisibility had ever worn off – perhaps the Esharen could have seen him through its unusual eyes – but it was the wrong time to ask Jonan about it.

The guard near the door was still reading a book when Jonan walked by. Each step took Taelien several times longer, and he was fairly confident he was leaving a trail of blood behind him, but he pushed himself on regardless. As he neared the exit, Taelien fell to his knees.

Resh. His injured leg had gone almost completely numb, but Jonan was there a moment later, wordlessly stepping in to help him lift the Esharen and stand once again.

With Jonan's help, the climb up the stairs was almost tolerable. They were forced to pause when they discovered the door to the main entrance locked, and Taelien took the moment to adjust how he was carrying the Esharen. A couple minutes later, Taelien saw the pair of guards approaching. Jonan put a finger to his lips in the universal gesture for quiet and waved his other hand – revealing to Taelien what the guards must have been seeing all along.

A perfectly uninjured – and unarmed – Taelien, following behind a much less frustrated Jonan, trailing the pair of guards.

As the guards reached the door, Taelien shifted out of their way, gritting his teeth at the continued strain on his leg and back. When the door opened, Jonan surged through immediately, not waiting for his illusionary duplicate. Taelien followed suit, ducking awkwardly to shift the Esharen through the door. He nearly fell again, but managed to slip to the side instead, merely stumbling into the main room of the bank.

Jonan shifted his stance until he was nearly overlapping with his illusionary double, and then Taelien watched as the illusion faded.

"Thank you, gentlemen," Jonan said calmly to the guards.

"You have a nice day," one of them said with some pretense at warmth, but with a slightly irritated tone.

And with that, Jonan led Taelien out of the building.

It only took a few more agonizing moments to slip around the side of the structure and find an area with no civilians visible.

"Let me look at that," Jonan said, kneeling by Taelien's leg. "Resh it, that's bad. You need to -," he started looking up at the Esharen, "I can't believe you just did that."

"Help me carry him?" Taelien asked weakly, trying at a smile.

"Fine," Jonan said, rolling his eyes. "You're still insane."

CHAPTER V – AN INTRODUCTION TO SORCEROUS THEORY

Lydia awoke in darkness. She rubbed blearily at her eyes, waiting several moments before rising to find her discarded glasses.

Seems I slept a while, she mused, stumbling toward her wall. A brush of her hands displaced the heavy drapes concealing her window, bringing the shimmering light of the nightfrost into her chambers. Even that scant light was enough to force her to blink for several moments as she mumbled to herself and found her way to her closet.

The nightfrost's presence signaled the temporary dominance of the dominion of ice over the dominion of heat – two of the many opposing dominions that influenced the world. While earlier cultures had associated the dawnfire and nightfrost with living entities, modern sorcerers thought them to be inanimate satellites that circled the world. The methods of their creation – and their ultimate purpose – were broadly debated.

After precisely zero moments of deliberation, Lydia picked out the first tunic and pants she came across, setting them out on her bed. She didn't have any formal meetings on the agenda, so she didn't need to wear her robes of office – at least for the moment. Eating was currently much higher on her list of priorities.

Dressing herself in what turned out to be a white tunic and dark brown pants, Lydia belted on her saber and lazily grabbed three silver pins to set on her collar. The pins were typically worn with her robes, but strictly speaking she could wear them with any outfit to identify her rank. At the moment, she didn't foresee needing them, but it helped her feel ready to challenge the world.

Her return to the palace had been uneventful. The guards didn't ask her any questions on her way back in, nor did they show any signs of suspicion. That didn't mean that no one suspected her, but apparently no one had given orders to arrest her on sight. She had sealed her door and window with protection sorcery before going to sleep.

As she finished preparing to leave, Lydia noticed a note on the floor – apparently, someone had slipped it under the door while she slept. *Someone slipped something inside without me noticing? I must be getting soft in my old age,* Lydia chided herself.

Shaking her head, Lydia picked up the letter, inspecting the wax seal on the back – a stylized letter "M". *Morella. Huh.*

Lydia's mind pushed itself further toward wakefulness as she processed the significance of the note. Morella had always been something of an enigma – she had always come across as extremely loyal to the interests of the city, but she rarely wanted to work with others. *And Sethridge thinks she's involved with Taelien somehow,* she reminded herself.

Lydia broke the seal, sitting back down on her bed to read the letter.

Court Sorceress Scryer,

I have pertinent information for you, as well as questions. Meet me at my chambers at your soonest convenience.

-Morella

Lydia considered the content of the note, folding it and setting it down on a nearby table. It was odd that Morella was referring to her by her title. The contents were vague, too, but that was a good precaution in case the note was intercepted somehow.

Maybe I need to make some preparations of my own, Lydia considered. *Jonan could be watching me through the walls right now, invisible, and I would be completely unaware. And he's probably not working alone.*

Lydia remembered that Jonan claimed to use mirrors for most of his reconnaissance, but that didn't mean that it was the only way he could use his sorcery. If he could mark mirrors, there was nothing saying he couldn't do the same to any glass or crystalline structure – like any one of the numerous windows or statues in the palace.

Time for a quick test to see if I'm being watched. Lydia walked to the mirror by the side of her bed, subconsciously lifting a hand to adjust her glasses. "Dominion of Knowledge, illuminate that which is touched by your cousins."

There was no change in the surface of her mirror, nor did she see a telltale aura on the glass of her window. On a hunch, Lydia glanced at the note Morella sent her, but she did not detect any signs of sorcery on that, either.

Well, I suppose sometimes a note is just a note. Something still nagged at the back of her mind, telling her she was missing something important, but she couldn't quite place what it was.

While Lydia continued to ponder the note, she left her room, locking it on the way out. The halls were near to empty, indicating it was even later than she had expected – but the noise from the dining hall told her that she had not yet missed the tail end of dinner.

With her rank, Lydia was able to skip to the head of the small dinner line that remained, retrieving a helping of boiled beef and seasoned potatoes. She could have easily ordered something to be cooked for her, but she never liked to make people go out of their way. She went to the kitchen next, setting down her tray of food, and brewed her tea herself – partly to save the cooks the trouble, and partly because she preferred to make it to her own tastes.

As she finally settled down to eat at a small table in the dining hall, Veruden sat down next to her with a plate and mug of his own. Lydia tensed for just a moment before turning to send a polite half-smile at him. "Veruden," she acknowledged. "How's your hand?"

"Doin' better now, thanks," he said, displaying his bandaged hand and opening and closing it. Presumably, he was displaying that he had regained some movement in his fingers, but she didn't know how bad it had been before. "I'm not bothering you, am I?"

Well, actually–

"No, not at all," Lydia said, taking a sip of her tea. She winced at the heat of the liquid, but she forced herself to swallow it.

"You ever figure out anything about the sword, or the prisoner?"

Time to see how much he knows. "Not much. I tried testing the sword with a basic identification spell, but it nearly knocked me out. After that, I ran into Istavan and spent some time catching up with him."

Veruden blinked. "Istavan's back? Bugger never tells me anything," he lamented, poking his fork into the top of an ambitious stack of potatoes that strove toward the skies. "I'm always the last one to hear anything. But you know Istavan. He likes to keep us guessing."

Okay, good. Istavan didn't talk to Veruden yet, at least. Lydia adjusted her glasses, thinking. "If it makes you feel any better, I didn't realize he was back until I ran into him."

"Huh. Maybe he's on some kind of secret assignment. I guess he could be doing something for Edon or M--," he started, but Lydia raised a finger in a silencing gesture.

"Public," she said meaningfully. Veruden sat up straighter suddenly, startled.

"Oh, sorry," he said hastily, "I lose track sometimes. Guess we can talk more about this stuff later, then," he said, grinning fiercely.

"Yeah," Lydia said, forcing a slightly more genuine smile than she had presented before. *He seems sincere in his concern, at least. I wonder if he's lying about not knowing Istavan is back in the city. I wish I had a spell for detecting lies...But different people have different tells. Maybe I could start with my Illuminate Hidden spell and add a Deception Key and a Stability Key to make a persistent effect that detects the use of the Dominion of Deception...But would a simple lie be enough to trigger it?*

They ate a while longer in silence, eventually dipping back into small talk until Lydia finished her meal and excused herself. She wanted to pry for more information, but caution was a greater concern for the moment. Too many lives depended on her proper handling of this situation.

If I take a step in the wrong direction now, I may end up starting the war I came here to prevent, Lydia realized.

She went toward Morella's chambers next, still considering the vague contents and oddly inconsistent formality of the note.

As she approached Morella's door, Lydia paused, still feeling an itching at the back of her mind that something was very wrong. Can't be too careful, she told herself. "Dominion of Protection, fold against my skin and teach me the secrets of the dominions that assault you."

Lydia felt a chill as the spell completed, a translucent barrier flickering against her flesh for a moment before fading into invisibility. The Comprehensive Barrier spell was her own creation. It was a combination of a standard Protective Barrier spell and Key based on a famous Dominion of Knowledge spell, Intuitive Comprehension. *A spell invented by Donovan Tailor, when he was a priest of Sytira,* Lydia recalled. *Awkward to be using one of his spells, now that I might be working against him. I suppose the sorcerers of old must have run into that type of problem all the time, though, especially in the rebellions against Xixis.*

Constructing spells was one of Lydia's specialties. She had studied the eastern method of Dominion Sorcery, better known as "Velryan Battle Sorcery". That style of magic utilized incantations, a series of words that were spoken aloud to focus the mind on the intended effect. The words themselves were irrelevant – the sorcerer simply used them to quickly force their mind into the right state. From there, the body would attempt to utilize the spells and Keys the sorcerer had spoken of by drawing on the appropriate dominions.

Spells could be categorized in a number of different ways, but Velryan Battle Sorcerers split them into fundamental spells and complex spells. Fundamental spells created basic effects that only drew from a single section of a single dominion. A simple burst of heat from the flame dominion or a barrier from the Dominion of Protection fell into this category. Complex spells were fundamental spells that had been augmented through the use of Keys – sorcerous fragments that could not be used on their own, but could be added to fundamental spells to change their function. A Flame Key could be added to a barrier spell to make it more potent against fire, or a Wall Key could be added to change the spell's shape.

The Comprehensive Barrier's function was relatively simple – it would draw from the Dominion of Protection to block attacks, and if the attacks were sorcerous in nature, the Key she used from the Dominion of Knowledge would immediately inform her of the composition of the spell. Her mind would interpret this information as readable text in her vision, similar to how her other identifying spells functioned. Not only did this allow her to analyze the spells of her enemies for developing countermeasures, the knowledge she gained was potentially sufficient to allow her to try to cast the spells herself – if her connections to the relevant dominions were strong enough.

Increasing strength at sorcery worked much like exercising a muscle – it required constant practice, but attempting to do too much at once could strain the sorcerer, potentially causing temporary or permanent damage.

Where most sorcerers struggled to maintain their conditioning with one dominion, Lydia actively practiced with five – improving her power at each gradually over time.

The barrier was one of Lydia's favorite spells, and she used it at least once per day in spite of the fatigue it caused her. In her sparring practices at the Citadel of Blades, Lydia had managed to train to block as many as three attacks with a single use of the barrier. Now, two years later, she expected that she could block at least twice that – assuming the spells were of a similar magnitude to what she was used to. More powerful spells – or physical attacks with greater force – would weaken the barrier more easily.

With the reassuring tingle of the barrier against her skin, Lydia walked the rest of the way to Morella's door and knocked politely. Silence followed for several moments, but Lydia waited patiently, and the door swung open after a modest period of trepidation.

Morella stood in the doorway, with Sethridge looming just beyond her. Morella was wearing a simple green dress, but Sethridge was in his formal robes.

"Oh, Lydia, come in," Morella said, giving an uncharacteristic smile.

Calling me Lydia now? That's not that unusual, but she was very formal in the note.

"Thank you," Lydia said, stepping inside. Morella closed the door behind her immediately and beckoned Lydia toward one of three empty chairs at a nearby table. A quick glance told Lydia that nothing in the room seemed overtly out of place – Morella's bookshelves were a bit more bare than usual, but that probably just meant she had taken out a few books and put them in another room for research.

Lydia took the seat nearest to the door and Sethridge silently moved to sit across from her.

"Can I get you anything? Tea?" Morella asked, wandering to the archway that marked the entrance to her bedroom. Morella had been serving Orlyn for several years, and Lydia knew that Morella's quarters were more extensive than her own – she had three full-sized rooms, as well as her own private water closet.

"No, thank you, I just came from dinner," Lydia explained, resting her hands on the table.

"We should get on with this, Morella. This is important business," Sethridge said.

"There's no need to be rude about it," Morella insisted, taking the third seat. "Lydia, the prisoner is missing."

Lydia sat up straighter in her chair, attempting to look startled. Fortunately, she had prepared for this. "What?"

"He disappeared last night. Do you know anything about it?" Sethridge leaned toward her, his expression cold.

Lydia shook her head. "Uh, no. I checked the sword, but it was protected somehow, like Veruden said. After that, I ran into Istavan and spent some time talking to him."

"Istavan? Isn't he supposed to be gone right now?" Morella turned to Sethridge, who simply shrugged.

"Was Veruden with you?" Sethridge asked, folding his arms.

Uh, resh. Did Veruden say he was with me? "No, I don't remember seeing him after our meeting. Do you think he was involved?"

She hoped she didn't just get Veruden in trouble – he was a sweet kid.

"Stop interrogating the poor girl, you're making her nervous." Morella waved a hand dismissively.

Poor girl? Lydia's lip twitched. *I'm not some starry-eyed apprentice. I'm just as high ranking as she is. Bah. Am I really acting nervous?*

Lydia noticed that she was tapping her foot, but she couldn't have been doing that for more than a few moments. She didn't realize she was giving any other tells.

Briefly, she considered the idea that lying to these people might actually bother her on some level – but she dismissed it.

Two years of working together did not make the other sorcerers her friends. Her loyalty, she assured herself, was to Velthryn and to her gods.

"Veruden told us at the meeting that he had already visited the prisoner and checked the sword. Captain Randall says that no one else came to take the key after Veruden's visit – he didn't discover that the prisoner was missing until he went to deliver a meal in the morning."

Lydia nodded slowly. "You think that since Veruden is a travel sorcerer, he might have been able to teleport inside the room, since he had already been inside there earlier. That would remove the need for a key."

"It's one possibility we're considering." Morella scratched a nail absently across the surface of the table. "Personally, I think it's more likely he simply escaped on his own. The chains were broken."

"Chains?" Lydia asked. She had never been inside the Adellan Room previously, so the question would help divert suspicion.

"He was chained to the wall, but those chains were shattered. Did Istavan say why he was back early?" Sethridge furrowed his brow.

Lydia shook her head. "No. He didn't want to talk much. I don't think he intended for me to know he was back."

"We need this resolved before Myros arrives. My last message said he'd be here in about six days. I know you are both busy, but it would be better for all of us if we resolve this on our own," Sethridge pointed out.

"Of course." Lydia nodded. "Do we have any other leads?"

"The sword is also missing," Morella added.

Lydia turned to stare at Morella blankly for a moment. "Well...That's bad, but at least it serves to confirm that the weapon was actually important."

Sethridge nodded. "Do you have any spells that could track the weapon?"

Lydia furrowed her brow, actually considering the question. "Not exactly. I do have a tracking spell, but it requires something directly connected to the object to use as a focus. A piece of metal from the blade, for example, or a shaving from the leather of the scabbard. I didn't think to get a sample while I was there. Did either of you collect one?"

The other sorcerers both shook their heads.

"I fear I have no way of tracing the sword, in that case."

It occurred to Lydia a moment later that Veruden's burn might actually have a sufficient lingering amount of dominion essence from the sword to be used as a focus for her tracking spell, but she didn't correct her earlier statement.

And if I wanted to track Taelien, I could try to use the chains, she realized. *He used a dominion bond to manipulate them — that's almost guaranteed to have left some of his essence.*

Normal dominion sorcery allowed a sorcerer to draw energy from a dominion through the use of spells and keys, and then briefly manipulate that energy within the parameters of a spell. A rarer form of sorcery, core sorcery, allowed for the manipulation of raw materials that already existed in the world — such as changing mud into stone or raising the temperature of water.

In both cases, a sorcerer needed to learn how to interact with the relevant dominions — an arduous process that some sorcerers spent their entire lives perfecting. A dominion bond represented a powerful, permanent connection to a specific dominion. Such a bond could amplify sorcery for that dominion, and make core sorcery for materials of that dominion much easier to perform.

Rethri established a bond to a specific dominion as part of their coming of age ritual — but for humans, attempting to emulate that ritual had proven disastrous and often fatal. Most human bodies were simply not capable of handling the intensity of the constant flow of energy that a dominion bond created.

Apparently, Taelien's body was.

"That's unfortunate. Perhaps we can find something for you to use to track the sword later. In the meantime, I'd like to discern his motives for being here." Sethridge leaned back in his chair, closing his eyes.

"It should be obvious, dear," Morella turned toward Sethridge, her tone just as patronizing as it had been to Lydia. It almost made Lydia smile. "We capture a follower of the Tae'os Pantheon wielding a holy relic of their religion. Obviously, we panic a bit, calling one of our gods to investigate – which we have done. Myros should be here within less than a week. Perhaps they counted on it being Myros, knowing he would be the most accessible, and that he would order a severe punishment for the prisoner. Permanent imprisonment, at least, or execution."

"And the followers of Tae'os, believing one of their chosen had been imprisoned or executed by our government, rise up against us?" Sethridge finished, lacking conviction. "I think not."

Morella shook her head. "Not the people here, of course. Velthryn, once they get word. Someone wants us to start a war."

Sethridge sighed. "If the followers of the Tae'os Pantheon wanted a war, why go through such an unnecessarily complicated process?"

"I never said anything about the followers of Tae'os being the ones who wanted the war." Morella smirked.

"You think that a third group is orchestrating this." Lydia nodded. *Well, that explanation is certainly convenient for me.* "Valeria or Selyr, perhaps, hoping to take advantage of the war to expand their own territory?"

Sethridge nodded slowly, his lips tightly pursed. "Possible. Our power has been expanding rapidly. I suppose even those leaf-lovers in Liadra might see us as a growing threat to be quashed. It seems too simple, however."

"Simple can be effective," Lydia pointed out. "If it looks like we're executing a symbol of the Tae'os faith, it's hard to believe they wouldn't respond to that."

"In that case, it's best not to give them what they want. We should recapture the man, but simply keep him prisoner, rather than have him executed." Sethridge steepled his fingers.

"I'm not sure Myros will agree to that." Morella frowned. "But we can try to convince him. The sooner we retrieve the prisoner, the easier that will be."

"And how will we ensure he doesn't escape a second time?" Lydia asked, trying to come across as if she was contributing their planning.

Sethridge shrugged. "Sorcery typically requires a tongue."

Taelien's doesn't — his style of casting is more similar to Jonan's. And he had access to a dominion I had never seen before. A second bond, stronger than his bond to metal. She still hadn't quite sorted out what it was.

"Yes, let's cut out his tongue. That's not going to antagonize anyone," Morella said, her voice dripping with acid.

"I take your point," Sethridge rolled his eyes. "Fine, fine. We'll just use rope next time, and put guards in his room. Sorcery does not confer invincibility."

"All right. I'll see if I can figure out another spell I can use to track him or the sword. If the two of you find any clues about him, please let me know immediately." Lydia stood up, nodding to each of the other sorcerers. "I will inform you if I discover anything."

"Very well, then, Scryer. I wish you Rialla's luck," Sethridge said, a mild smile twisting his lips. His smile was twice as unsettling as his accusations had been.

"I will pray that I do not need it," Lydia replied.

They were the truest words she had spoken in nearly a day.

The sorceress made a cursory effort to search the palace, including visiting Captain Randall to ask basic questions about the prisoner. She also tried to determine Istavan's current location, but it seemed like no one had encountered him since "Istavan" left with Lydia the night before.

Interesting. Seems like Istavan is up to something of his own. She wasn't quite sure if that would be beneficial to her yet. If Istavan had gone to the others and claimed that she had attacked him, at least she could have dealt with that confrontation directly. His absence saved her trouble for the moment, but she knew it could prove a greater problem later.

With that in mind, she checked the armory for any clues about what might have happened to Istavan after their battle. The weapons and items inside were sorted neatly — all signs of the fight had been removed, and she found no traces of additional sorcery.

I'll need to investigate this more later, she considered, *but for now, I have more pressing matters to attend to.*

Lydia knocked soundly on the door to Jonan's borrowed home. Her left hand adjusted her scabbard, her right hand drifting to the hilt to prepare to draw – just in case she was wandering into a trap.

The door swung open, revealing a somewhat disheveled looking Jonan on the other side. "It's late," he mumbled. He waved his hand in a loose gesture of welcome. "Come in."

Lydia didn't release the grip on her sword until after Jonan had moved out of the way, giving her a better view of the room. Even then, she reminded herself that he could have been hiding any number of invisible attackers. "Dominion of Knowledge, illuminate the hidden," she said as she stepped inside. When no assassins manifested, she nodded to herself and released her grip on the weapon.

"Not very trusting, are you?" Jonan remarked. "Close the door, if you wouldn't mind."

Lydia shrugged at his comment, moving and closing the door, and then noting a lock and turning it into position. "You shouldn't be, either. When you opened the door, it could have been anyone on the other side."

"I looked through the door before I opened it," he said, tapping on his glasses meaningfully.

"You have a spell for that?" Lydia perked up in spite of herself. Seeing through objects would be a tremendously useful skill to have.

"Sure," Jonan said. "It's just a different application of the same spell that makes me invisible, really."

Lydia raised an eyebrow dubiously. "That should have made the door invisible to me as well, then, unless you added some sort of key to it."

"Key? Ptah. You Velryan sorcerers are so inflexible. Always trying to codify things that are easily mutable," Jonan remarked with a grin.

Lydia folded her arms. "Incantations and keys allow for greater precision. They're tools for conceptualizing and memorizing things that are difficult to break down into component parts at the time when a spell is cast."

"Less like tools, more like crutches," Jonan said with a half-shrug.

"That attitude is why Kesites make great assassins, but Velryans win wars," Lydia shot back, pushing up her own glasses.

"Oh, which wars exactly? Never mind – that's not important," Jonan said, suddenly shaking his head.

"You're right," Lydia said. She added abruptly, "I want you to show me that spell, though. Would you be willing to cast it on me?"

"Why?" Jonan said, quirking a brow. "You won't perceive any difference."

Lydia tapped on her left arm. "I'm a sorcerer, too, you know. I have my ways. And don't try to cast something else – I'll know."

"Ahh," Jonan said, nodding in acknowledgement. "A knowledge sorceress, yes. Of course you'd want me to cast it on you. Very well."

And, with a nonchalant wave of Jonan's hand, Lydia was bombarded.

Eyes close. Erase target in mind. Sustain image; target self. Open eyes.

Her Comprehensive Barrier spell had been triggered, as she knew it would be – but the results were far from typical. Usually, she was presented with the name of the dominion of the spell, the name of the spell, and any keys that were used to modify the effect. It seemed that Jonan's method of sorcery was so distinct from her own that the Dominion of Knowledge itself reacted – and stored the information – differently. Perhaps what she was seeing was a transcription of Jonan's own thoughts – conscious or unconscious – as he had cast the spell. She had no way of knowing.

She did note immediately, however, that a gesture with a hand was not one of the steps. Was that just a dismissive gesture and not part of the spell itself? Or was it a method that Jonan used to focus, similar to her own incantations?

She would ask another time, if at all. For the moment, she preferred to give Jonan as little information on what she had gathered as possible.

"Huh," she said.

"Huh," Jonan replied in kind. "That's never happened."

Lydia tilted her head to the side. "What's never happened?"

"You're not invisible – the spell didn't work." Jonan said. His eyes brightened after a moment. "Protective sorcery?"

Lydia nodded.

"Fascinating. I've never seen protective sorcery that can block a Sight spell before. It's unintuitive that it could even be possible – my spell should be affecting my senses, rather than actually changing you in any way."

"Perhaps it prevented your spell from even targeting me properly," Lydia speculated aloud. She was equally intrigued – she had expected the spell to be blocked, but that was without a full knowledge of how it worked.

Now that she had comprehended his methodology for casting the spell, a few moments of consideration gave her something of an answer – his second step was "erasing" the target mentally. *That's the problem – he's unintentionally hiding the target from himself, rather than making himself unable to perceive the target. I could tell him that, but if I help him improve his methods too much, he might end up erasing me later – in a more permanent sense. Hrm.*

This process had told her something important above and beyond the fundamentals of the spell itself – Jonan's style of casting was alarmingly different from how she had been taught. She knew that the western school of sorcery had a different methodology – she had been taught all about it in her earliest classes. "Assassin's sorcery", as the students called it, was ridiculed for its inefficiency, informality, and ineffectiveness.

She doubted any of the students – or any of the teachers – had met someone like Jonan. His level of ability to manipulate the parameters of a single spell helped put the mocked nickname of his school into context.

Assassin's sorcery. Lydia wondered if, perhaps, she had underestimated what it meant to be an assassin.

"Hungry?" Jonan asked.

Lydia blinked, startled out of her reverie. "No, not really, thank you."

"Well, just come sit with me, then," he gestured to a chair by the table. "We have a great deal to discuss."

Jonan made his way to the table, and Lydia followed, her head still swimming with the memory of foreign thoughts.

Lydia sat a moment after Jonan did, a consideration forcing itself to the forefront of her mind. "Where's Taelien?"

"A good question," Jonan remarked, stabbing a bite of meat on the table with his fork. "Bodily, he's up in the guest bedroom. Mentally, I'm not really clear on that."

The sorceress raised an eyebrow. "What do you mean?"

"We had, um, a bit of an incident while we were investigating the bank," Jonan started, fidgeting with the food on his fork. "To trim the epic ballad to a manageable length, Taelien ended up punching an Esharen to death and we fled with great haste."

Lydia furrowed her brow so deeply that her glasses slid half an inch down her nose. "...What?"

Jonan shrugged. "It did take him several punches. To elaborate briefly, we actually fled with the unconscious Esharen draped over our shoulders – very awkward – but it expired quickly upon our arrival here. He's been upstairs moping ever since."

In an effort to collect herself, Lydia straightened her glasses and sat up in her chair. *An Esharen this far east? That can't be a good sign.* She had heard that some scant few Esharen had escaped the fall of their capital city, but any sane survivor would not have ventured anywhere close to human territory. *Which means someone probably hunted this one down intentionally and brought it here.*

"One of the founding principles of your order involved hunting the Esharen," Lydia noted. "What does it say to you that one of them was in Orlyn?"

"As a point of note, I'm not actually a member of the Order of Vaelien. I simply work with them. That said, this was once an Esharen city, as I'm sure you know. It's plausible that there could be Esharen still living somewhere in the area. That said, I find it more likely that the Esharen we found was...imported. We discovered the creature imprisoned in a ritual barrier utilizing a type of sorcery I did not recognize – and I assure you, I recognize many types of sorcery."

Lydia quirked a brow at that. "What did it look like? Can you describe it?"

"I can do better," Jonan grinned. He reached into a pouch on his left hip and retrieved a mirror, sliding it across the table to her. After that, he finally took a bite of the meat on his fork while Lydia picked up the mirror.

The image that stared back from the glass was not her face, but the body of an obsidian-scaled beast, encircled by arcane markings.

"Huh." Lydia held the mirror closer to her face, squinting at the markings, but they were unrecognizable. Not due to the small size of the image, she recognized to her chagrin – they were simply foreign. "Neat trick with the mirrors."

Jonan simply nodded, continuing to eat while she set the mirror down.

It's more than a neat trick, she realized. *It's a core element of his strategy, and he's handed it to me without asking for anything in exchange. I've been cooperating very poorly by comparison, treating both Jonan and Taelien like threats rather than allies. I made my choice the moment I broke Taelien out. I need to commit to that.*

"And, um, about that spell you cast on me before," Lydia said with a hint of hesitation.

"Hm?" Jonan looked up, still chewing.

"The spell I used to block your illusion – well, it also gives me information about any spells that it stops. The reason your spell didn't work was because of how you broke it down into steps – you tried to 'erase' my image from your mind. I imagine you thought it was just like putting a dark lens over your eyes, but it was really more like throwing a blanket over me so you couldn't see me. That's why it didn't work," Lydia rattled off rapidly, unable to stop herself once she had started.

Jonan blinked. "Amazing! Your spell read my intent? That's – that's just incredible." He set his fork down and wrung his hands at her, grinning fiercely. "Do you realize how significant that is? People have been searching for a way to read minds with sorcery for centuries!"

That wasn't precisely – "The spell was not reading your mind, it was simply translating the portion of your intent that manipulated your sorcery into a format that I could comprehend."

Jonan shook his head, still grinning. "No, no, it doesn't matter. It's a foundation, Lydia. Here, is your spell still operating?"

Lydia nodded, sitting back a bit further, uneasy. "What are you thinking?"

"We should experiment! Here." Jonan flicked a finger at her, and a rainbow-colored beam shot out, striking her even as she pushed herself backward to dodge.

Shiny beam of colors! Her defensive spell reported in an oddly bright display of text across her vision. Lydia landed on the floor a moment later, her attempt to evade the assault having thrown her from her chair. She winced as her hands caught most of her weight, but the fall was short enough that the pain was merely jarring, not bone-shattering.

"Oh, gods, I'm sorry!" Jonan pushed himself out of his own chair, running around the table to offer her a hand.

"Never do that again," Lydia said, grabbing his wrist and hauling herself to her feet. She laughed suddenly, startling even herself. "But that was kind of funny."

The spectacled sorcerer chuckled lightly in reply. "I really am sorry about that," he said. "Are you okay?"

"Yeah, I'm fine. Just warn me a little better before you try to 'experiment'," Lydia chided him. "But it wasn't a bad idea. I'll admit that

I'm used to stopping attacks with this spell, not other types of sorcery. And even then, my sparring partners were always battle sorcerers – and their spells were, if you'll forgive me, much more structured."

Jonan nodded while he straightened Lydia's fallen chair. "It's not that all my spells are unstructured, but with practice, I've learned to create simple effects and manipulate them almost instantly. With greater pre-planning, I can accomplish broader effects, much like I'm sure your sorcerers do. The mirrors are a good example of that."

"And that thing you just did, the ray of light -," Lydia began.

"Just an illusion, that's all," Jonan explained.

"But an illusion real enough to look like an offensive spell, albeit a strange one. And you had never cast that spell before?" Lydia asked.

Jonan scratched his chin. "Well, not in the sense that I've made a multi-colored beam like that before. But it's really just an image creation spell – the same one I use all the time – being manipulated in a specific way."

"Fascinating," Lydia said. "What do you call the spell?"

"Create image," Jonan replied, nodding sagely.

"That's not very creative."

"The creative part comes after I cast it."

"Ah, yes, shiny beam of colors."

Jonan blinked again. "You got that from blocking the spell?"

Lydia simply nodded.

"Wow," he replied. "We're going to need to do more testing with this."

Oddly, she agreed with him. *I'd love to learn more about how he manipulates his spells so freely,* Lydia realized. *That could be a tremendous advantage. And an advantage I never would have had access to if I hadn't given him some modicum of trust. Hrm.*

"That was quite interesting," Lydia admitted, "But I should really check on Taelien. Do you know why he's upset?"

Jonan's expression took a dive toward the grave. "He's made it perfectly clear. He wanted to rescue the Esharen from captivity. He killed it instead. He thinks he's some sort of monster now."

"Esharen are the monsters," Lydia replied automatically.

"Right," Jonan agreed, "But he doesn't see it that way. Apparently growing up with the Rethri made him sympathize with non-humans a bit too much."

"Huh," Lydia mumbled, considering. "I'll be careful about what I say, then." She gestured to the mirror, "From what the image looks like, that thing was already injured. Maybe we can pin it on that."

Jonan sighed. "Already tried that. Didn't take. He said, 'Is it any better to kill a man by exploiting his already broken arm?' And I say 'said', because it clearly wasn't a question. If anything, his tone told me that he thought the injuries made it worse."

Because the injuries gave Taelien what he considered to be an unfair advantage, Lydia realized. *The poor child still thinks war is meant to be fair.*

"All right," Lydia said, brushing her bruised hands against her sides. "I'll try a different angle. Once he's feeling better, I'll need to talk to you more about those ritual markings and anything else you found."

"Of course," Jonan said. "Good luck up there."

"Thanks," Lydia replied. *Let's hope I don't need it.*

Lydia knocked softly on the door to the guest bedroom. "Are you awake in there?"

"Yeah," replied Taelien's muted voice.

"Can I come in?" Lydia reflexively brushed her fingers along the hilt of her saber as she waited through several moments of silence.

"I suppose," came the eventual reply. The sorceress raised her hand to turn the door handle and stepped inside, finding Taelien sitting on the guest bed, wearing little more than underwear. She blushed in spite of having seen him in a similar state of undress before, her eyes taking in his other accoutrements – a heavy series of bandages wrapped around his leg, already soaked through with blood.

"Gods," she muttered, closing the distance between them in moments and kneeling at the bedside. A closer inspection showed three distinct trails of blood merging together in the cloth. "Are there more bandages?"

Taelien jerked a thumb at a closet nearby. "You needn't bother. I'll be fine."

Lydia shook her head and rose to go to the closet. She found a broad roll of fresh bandages in the second drawer she searched. Nearby, she found an unlabeled bottle, scissors, and a smaller bottle of "Reed's Finest Whiskey". Apparently, Jonan had been at least somewhat prepared to deal with injuries.

She snipped off a few additional pieces from the roll of bandages with the scissors and returned to Taelien.

"I'm going to change these out for fresh ones," Lydia explained, beginning to undo the wrap around Taelien's leg. *Whoever wrapped this — Jonan, I assume, given Taelien's attitude — did a good job with it. The cuts must be pretty vicious to have soaked through this far.*

The wounds, once exposed, were fairly gruesome. Three nearly parallel cuts stretched half the length of his lower leg. They had been stitched shut and cleaned, but several of the stitches had already snapped, and a trickle of fresh blood was visible near those breaches. "I'm going to need to give you more stitches," Lydia explained.

"Don't bother yourself," Taelien replied, pulling his injured leg away from her hands.

He can't be shy about a needle after having an injury like this, can he? "I'll make it quick. I can put you to sleep, if you'd like."

"No," Taelien said firmly at first. His expression softened after a moment, and he added, "No, I know you're trying to help, but no thought sorcery. I don't like the idea of my mind being altered. You can stitch the wounds if you feel the need, but I do not deserve such attention."

Ah, is that what this is about? Punishing yourself out of guilt? And it'd be dream sorcery, but I suppose that doesn't matter.

"I'll go ask Jonan where the needle and thread are," Lydia said. "In the meantime, apply pressure to the wound to help slow the flow of the blood."

Lydia started to stand up, but Taelien grabbed her arm. "Wait. I mean, please. Sorry for grabbing you," he paused, releasing her arm. "Can you just wrap the wound for now? I don't want to drag Jonan back up here."

Lydia shrugged. "Sure, but I'm just going to have to unwrap it again later."

"That's fine," Taelien supplied. "I just... I can't talk to him right now."

Lydia sat down on the floor, unrolling her fresh bandages and beginning to wrap them around the leg. "Do you want to talk about what happened?"

Taelien looked skyward. "I am not sure."

Lydia began re-wrapping the wound in silence for a time, thinking about how best to approach him.

"Jonan mentioned that you blame yourself for killing an Esharen. He didn't supply me with all the details, but I can only assume you were defending yourself," Lydia offered.

"I was," Taelien replied, "But I wouldn't have had to if I hadn't been meddling in the first place."

Lydia nodded, continuing her ministrations. "I can understand that, but sometimes doing nothing can be far worse."

Taelien leaned over, looming above her. For a moment, it was disconcerting – his hand had felt like iron when he had grabbed her, and if Jonan's story was true, he had beaten an Esharen to death with his bare hands. That meant he could probably just as easily break solid rocks – he could injure her fatally with a single moment of rage. *If I didn't have a sorcerous barrier in place,* Lydia reassured herself. And a glance at Taelien's eyes told her that it was sorrow, not anger, which guided his movements.

"What can be far worse than taking a life?" Taelien asked.

Lydia paused, suddenly more aware of the droplets of Taelien's blood that had splattered across her hands. "Letting people die due to your inaction," Lydia replied.

Taelien tilted his head to the side quizzically. "There is no way to know if the creature would have lived or died if I had not intervened."

"That's precisely the point," Lydia replied, wiping her blood-stained hands on her trousers. "There's no way to know. It could have been tortured to death. At least a death in battle is clean – and you were trying to rescue it, from what Jonan explained. If it failed to cooperate, that can hardly be blamed on you."

"My involvement can be blamed on me," Taelien replied. "I didn't have to go with Jonan at all. And, even later on, I had a choice. Jonan told me to leave the room without freeing the creature – I didn't listen. After I knocked it out, Jonan told me to leave it behind – again, I didn't listen. It had been alive when I picked it up. Maybe I transported it too roughly, and that is why it died. I had choices, and each time, I chose the route that led to the Esharen's demise."

"You made choices that led to the creature's death, true – but not necessarily the only ones that could have. There is no way of knowing if any choice you had made could have saved the creature. And, more than likely, you spared it a fate more horrible than death in any case. Jonan showed me an image of the Esharen in his mirrors. Someone was hurting it deliberately, while it was helpless. You prevented it from facing more of that."

"I would've thought that a follower of one of the Tae'os gods would be more concerned with preserving life than providing an honorable death." There was a hint of accusation in Taelien's tone, but perhaps a layer of confusion as well.

"It's true that followers of Tae'os believe in preserving life as best we can. From what I understand, you did precisely that. You tried to rescue someone from captivity – at great personal risk, no less – and then even tried to carry the creature's body after it attacked you. And badly wounded you, if I am not mistaking the source of these cuts," Lydia pointed out.

Taelien's silence was her only confirmation, but it was sufficient. He was slouched over now, not looking at her work on his leg, but just staring at the floor.

"Let me tell you a story," Lydia offered. "One of my first missions after being made a full paladin was to investigate claims that monsters had appeared in a noble's house in a small town north of Aayara. We were given the location, the name of the family making the claim, and a brief description of what they had seen. There were things that looked like claw marks in the wood, writing out a name – the name of a deceased previous owner of the house – and something that looked like blood. The child apparently said he saw a monster, too, but we didn't have a good description of it."

"They sent four of us – not out of any real concern that there could be some kind of monster, of course. At the time, I assumed we were being sent because three of us were fresh out of training, and this was supposed to be a no-risk mission to get us to know each other. In retrospect, I believe our commander sent four people so we could insist on greater pay for handling the problem."

Taelien had lifted his head now, and he was listening intently. Unfortunately, Lydia felt her own enthusiasm for the story fading – it was getting harder and harder to tell as her emotions began to kick in.

"Our leader, I won't say his name in case you ever meet him, had us head to the town at a leisurely pace. No horses, no hurrying, no marching at night. It was just going to turn out to be one of the neighbors trying to scare the noble out of the town – or extort them to make a 'sacrifice' to the spirit of the previous owner, which the neighbors would collect. A common con, he told us. I never quite believed it was that simple. My gut told me sorcery was involved, but I did not press the issue."

"And he was wrong?" Taelien asked almost silently.

"We arrived in the town six days after being given the assignment. Four days after we could have arrived, if we had taken horses. Two days after the family had been murdered, torn apart by an abomination from the Plane of Dreams," Lydia said somberly.

There were no tears blurring her eyes, but she rubbed at them anyway. It was a common gesture for evoking emotional impact. "I knew, I just knew, that we should have taken the assignment more seriously. If we had rushed, if we had listened – if we had done something – that family might have survived."

"Or you might have died, too," Taelien weakly attempted to reassure her. He even stretched out a hand to put on her shoulder. It didn't comfort her, but she let him keep it there. If he was trying to comfort her, he had something to distract him from his own worries.

"I might have," she admitted. "We all might have. We found the etchings in the wood with the previous owner's name that the messenger had described. The name had been scratched out, and a symbol was carved above it – a rune representing Daesmodin, the Devourer of Souls."

Taelien frowned at the name. Daesmodin was a story that parents told their children to scare them – a creature of nightmares that was impervious to ordinary blades and sorcery. He vaguely remembered a nursery rhyme that was meant to teach children not to wander into the woods on their own. As he grew older and learned about history, he heard theories that the stories about Daesmodin were based on an actual entity – a harvester of nightmares.

Harvesters were a subcategory of gatherers – dangerous entities native to each of the other planes. The function of gatherers was to reclaim essence of their particular dominion and bring it back to their home plane. Thus, a gatherer of dreams collected dreams. Unlike other gatherers, harvesters were known to spread the influence of their dominion broadly before collecting and returning it. A harvester of flame might set an entire forest ablaze before returning the flame to its home plane. Taelien wasn't clear on the reasoning behind the difference in methodology, but if Daesmodin was a harvester of nightmares, it meant that he'd deliberately spread nightmares in order to collect them at a later time.

Like most entities native to other planes, harvesters were vastly more powerful than most mortal sorcerers. They were not unstoppable – stories indicated that the Xixian empire managed to bind several and use them as living siege weapons. Still, if Daesmodin was real, Taelien was glad that Lydia had not had to face him in battle.

"My spells confirmed a lingering aura from the Dominion of Dreams, but there were no beasts present when we arrived – only bodies," Lydia said. "The parents, three children, and two servants," she added more quietly, finally feeling hints of moisture around her eyes.

That hand on her shoulder did feel slightly reassuring now – but something else made her feel more.

Lydia looked up, locking Taelien's eyes in her own. "That's what can happen if you do nothing, Taelien. You're right – I might have died if I had arrived sooner. If Daesmodin really was involved, even four of us would not have stood a chance. But it is more likely that some lesser nightmare was simply invoking his name, or that a sorcerer did the same. And I would have rather tried and failed – tried and died – than failed through inaction."

Taelien nodded. "I am sorry. I have been a burden to you, as well as to Jonan."

That wasn't my point at all.

"My point is that you should not blame yourself for trying to rescue someone," Lydia said. "You mentioned earlier that you were surprised at how easily I seemed to dismiss the taking of a life. Tae'os followers have many precepts, but another one of them is that captivity and torture are a worse fate than death."

Taelien raised his other hand to scratch at his chin thoughtfully. "I hadn't heard that."

"It's one of Eratar's precepts, specifically," Lydia explained. "Each of the seven gods has different precepts. As paladins, we choose a specific member of the pantheon to follow, but we recall the philosophies that are sacred to each of our gods."

"Is that the reason why you rescued me?" Taelien asked.

A good question, Lydia realized. *Is it?*

"No," Lydia replied, putting one of her hands on top of the hand that sat on her shoulder, a hint of a smile crossing her face. "I did it because it seemed like a good idea at the time."

Taelien returned her fraction of a grin with an even weaker version of his own. "I suppose that was my motivation, too."

Lydia removed her hand from his to finish the bandaging, but she could still feel the lingering warmth from his skin. "The things Jonan and I are doing – spying on people, deceiving them – they are not easy. If you continue to work with us, you may be forced to do more...upsetting things."

"I understand." Taelien removed his hand from her shoulder, setting it instead upon the scabbard of his sword hidden amongst the sheets, which she had neglected to notice before. "Your story has given me a new perspective, and I thank you for that. I still believe that I failed that Esharen, but I understand now that inaction will not unmake that failure. I must try harder – push myself harder – to ensure I do not make the same mistake again."

That's not precisely what I was trying to get across from the story. It doesn't sound like you were weak or needed to try harder, but I suppose if this motivates you to push your despair away, at least I've accomplished my goal.

"Your bandages look sound now," Lydia said, wiping her hands on her trousers again. "Will you be well until morning? I have some further business with Jonan, and then I need to return to the palace. I can come back and redo your stitches in the morning."

"I'll be fine," Taelien assured her. He moved a hand to her face, triggering an instinct to pull away, but she realized after a moment that he was just awkwardly trying to give her a sign of affection. It wasn't something she was particularly used to – her family had never been very physical with her.

"All right," Lydia said, standing abruptly. "I will see you in the morning, then." She nodded to him curtly and turned to leave.

"Good night, Lydia," Taelien said as she departed. "And thank you."

She nodded again silently as she left the room, raising a hand to trace the line where he had touched her face.

After a minute of catching her breath on the upper floor, Lydia descended the stairs to find Jonan still eating.

Huh, she realized, *I guess it's only been a few minutes. It certainly felt a lot longer.*

Jonan glanced in her direction. "Manage to cheer him up at all?"

"Not cheer him up, precisely," Lydia admitted. "But I've fired him up a bit, at least."

"Better than I managed to do," Jonan said with a grin. "You sure you don't want any food?"

"Yeah," Lydia said, "Especially after re-bandaging his leg."

"Oh," Jonan said, noticing her hands. "Um, there's a bowl of water in my bedroom near the bed. It's fresh from the well."

Lydia nodded. "Thanks."

She headed to the back where Jonan had shown them his bedchamber during the forced 'tour' of the house when they had first met. *Just yesterday,* she recalled. *Gods, I get involved with strange men too quickly sometimes.*

She took note of how plain the bedchamber was, aside from an elegant rug near the center of the room. The tools of Jonan's assumed trade were laid out in an orderly fashion next to an assembled mirror. *Another of his dominion bonded ones,* she guessed. Three pairs of glasses – one of which had no lenses – sat next to the mirror.

Lydia rinsed her hands with only the slightest suspicion that the bowl might actually contain some sort of acid and returned to sit with Jonan a few moments later.

"Should I empty the bloody water out somewhere?" she inquired, drying her hands on a non-bloodied portion of her pants.

"Don't worry about it, I'll deal with it in the morning," he replied. "How is he doing?"

I'm mildly surprised that you care so much, Lydia realized. *Maybe you're not quite the monster most of the Order of Vaelien are.*

"He's still plenty depressed about killing the Esharen, and I think he will be for a while. I think I've just managed to focus that feeling into motivation to improve, which should be more productive," Lydia explained.

"Maybe," Jonan replied dubiously. "He was plenty motivated before. That was part of the problem."

Lydia shrugged. "I will take a motivated ally over a complacent one at any time."

Jonan snorted, setting down his cup. "Any time, really? That's a line I plan to remind you about later."

Lydia quirked a brow. "That implies a longer-term partnership than I anticipate."

"You underestimate my charms," Jonan gave her an exaggerated wink. Lydia was forced to giggle in spite of herself. The absurdity was more welcome than she realized. "But more realistically, I have already been here for months. I'll wager you have been as well. This will not be a short assignment."

"Our timeframe draws close to an end, I'm afraid," Lydia replied, his last words drawing her back to serious contemplation. "Or, our time with access to Taelien, at least. Myros is definitely on his way, and he'll arrive in less than a week."

"Well," Jonan said, steepling his fingers, "That's bad."

"You found an Esharen in the bank. Did you find anything else of interest?" Lydia asked, leaning forward against the table.

Jonan shook his head swiftly. "Nothing aside from the runes I already showed you. And they're gibberish, so far as I can tell."

"I could try to use a spell to identify them if you took me there," Lydia volunteered, surprising herself. *That's quite a risk.*

"Too much of a risk," Jonan said. "We didn't leave noisily, but there will be evidence of our break-in. The missing Esharen, and the damage to the room besides. I expect the building to be much better guarded, and with the Esharen gone, they may simply remove the runes."

Lydia nodded. "What about the other facilities from your map?"

Jonan considered the question. "I know at least two of the other facilities are connected directly to Tailor. If he's the one making these bizarre runes, there's a good chance we can find them at one of these other places."

"Very well, then perhaps we should investigate one of those next," Lydia offered.

Jonan's expression twisted into a scowl. "Not to be offensive, but my last experience with bringing someone with me ended rather poorly."

Lydia smiled. "Fair enough. You should keep in mind, however, that I am still a court sorceress. I can probably gain access to most of these places simply by asking – or by making a legal claim to investigate, if necessary."

"That's good, and I haven't forgotten that," Jonan explained. "But it's also our best edge. We don't want to use it until we narrow things down further, otherwise we'll dull it to uselessness. The worst thing that could happen right now would be someone catching on to your involvement in our infiltrations – well, the worst thing aside from us all dying horribly, of course."

"There's a middle ground," Lydia pointed out. "I could go to one of these facilities in an official capacity, and you could follow me invisibly. Once I've gotten us inside the building, we could split up and plan to meet back here at a later time. So long as you can maintain your invisibility, there should be nothing to make us look conspicuous."

Jonan took off his glasses, setting them down on the table, and began to rub his temples. "I still feel we may be playing our hand too quickly that way – your presence may trigger an increase in security. Still, with Myros on the way, we do not have the luxury of taking our time. All right. We will try your plan."

Lydia nodded. "Well, then perhaps we should both get some rest, and plan for an eventful tomorrow."

"An eventful tomorrow," Jonan muttered. "Let's hope not."

CHAPTER VI – A CONTEST OF CONCEALMENT

The Aldwyn Alchemical Archives were ostensibly a government-funded alchemical research center. One of Jonan's contacts – Randall Shaw – had indicated that sorcerous research was also conducted there. This wasn't all that suspicious in itself – alchemy was often considered a branch of sorcery. The size of the facility and the small number of researchers with access to it were factors that made it worth investigating, however.

"You're certain this is a good idea?" Jonan asked Lydia, his eyes nervously scanning up and down across her formal violet robes. *I'll bet they don't get visitors of her stature very often. They're going to be bowing and scraping to try to win her favor. That's a great distraction for me, but word of her visit will spread quickly.*

"Of course not." She straightened the pins on her collar, and then leaned down to adjust her sword belt. "Certainty in the face of variables is a sign of insanity."

Jonan sighed. "Right. Off we go, then." He bowed at the waist, concentrating at the mid-point of the bow. *Erase image of self.*

And with that, he vanished.

"Show off," Lydia muttered. "All right, keep your steps quiet, but stay close. I'll hold doors for a couple extra seconds for you, but any longer and it'll look awkward."

"I will endeavor to do as you say, mistress," Jonan replied, mimicking Taelien's voice with a silly look on his face.

"Just walk," Lydia said, her terse tone failing to hide her grin. She started toward the building's entrance, which was just around the next

121

bend. Jonan complied with her instructions, following close behind her.

A pair of guards stood at the entrance of the facility, just as Jonan had noted in previous visits. He had circled the three-story building and found two other entrances, each equally guarded. His efforts to purchase a blueprint for the building had come up dry, so he had drawn his own best guess at the interior layout from studying the windows. He could have achieved a better version by looking through the walls, but that spell required touching them, and he did not want to trigger any defensive sorcery that might have been on the building until he was ready to commit to a full search.

Thus, he had memorized his quickly-sketched informal blueprint and quickly decided that it was mostly useless. The one useful bit of information was the location of a ground-level room with windows broad enough for a person to slip through. They were latched from the inside, making them a poor entrance, but potential emergency exit.

There were windows on multiple upper floor rooms as well, but Jonan didn't like his chances of exiting through them, even with bushes below to "catch" a potential fall.

The guards greeted Lydia, saluting her and exchanging pleasantries. Jonan didn't pay too much attention to what they said – he just followed in her step, concentrating on maintaining his spell.

I'm not here, he reminded himself. *They can't see me.*

After only a few more moments, one of the guards politely opened the door to the building for Lydia – and Jonan rushed past her, still stepping as quietly as possible, to slip inside.

Okay. It's my turn, now.

Jonan made an immediate left turn, aware of every creak in the wooden floor from his footsteps. *Who puts a hardwood floor in a research facility? Honestly, such a waste of money.*

He passed three doors before finding a staircase leading upward, which he immediately moved toward. A man wearing a long white coat rounded a corner nearby and nearly bumped into him, but Jonan managed to flatten himself against the wall and avoid the collision. Several seconds of heavy breathing followed.

Did he hear me move? No? Maybe? A glance at the retreating figure showed no sign of disruption in the man's behavior. *Safe. For now.*

Jonan turned back toward the stairs and found himself staring directly at a violet robed sorceress – and one who was, most definitely, not Lydia. Her eyes were indigo around a black pupil, without a hint of white around the pools of color. Aside from her eyes, she looked completely human.

Rethri, Jonan realized, his heart skipping a beat. She seemed to stare straight back at him for a moment before she drifted past him wordlessly, her gaze still etched into his mind. He forced himself to note some of her other characteristics – tanned skin and wavy brown hair - in case he needed to describe her later.

Did she just see me? If so, why didn't she react?

And why is a Rethri wearing the robes of a court sorcerer?

Jonan slowly made his way up the stairs, still trapped in thought. *There are only supposed to be five court sorcerers – three human men, two human women. Could a Rethri be escaping at this very moment, wearing stolen robes?*

He briefly debated following her – after all, finding the Rethri was one of his primary goals – but the risk was too great. If the Rethri really was a court sorceress, there was a good chance she had trained with Lydia – and that meant she might have the same spells for detecting invisible people that Lydia did. He was safest as far away from her as possible.

Vaelien's breath. I'm in a terrible position here. I need to move.

He found an open door at the top of the stairs and slipped through it, glancing to both sides before emerging into the unoccupied hallway. The floors were tile here, and the white-painted walls were adorned with decorative weapons and pieces of armor.

Fancy, Jonan thought. *Odd to make an upper floor the ostentatious one. But it's probably not relevant to what I'm looking for, unless there's a very sinister interior designer involved.*

Shaking his head, Jonan started out down the hallway to the left of the stairs. There were several doors, each conveniently marked with a plaque indicating their contents. He passed "Wet Storage" and "Workshop 4" before pausing at "Filing".

That could be promising, Jonan considered. *If they keep their research notes in here, I could potentially find something about tests on the Rethri. Or, perhaps, they might have a list of the personnel at the facility.*

After a moment of internal debate, he pressed on. *Digging through documents could take hours. I need to find something now.*

He passed a door labeled "Waiting" and reached another stairwell – this one leading both up and down - and then turned to check the opposite end of the hall. He passed "Dry Storage", "Workshop 2", "Workshop 3", and "Lounge" before turning a corner. Ahead, he saw a grand pair of double doors – unlabeled – and a tall man with graying hair in the process of unlocking them.

Jonan fell into step behind the man, following him into the room as it opened.

The room was filled with beds. Half a dozen beds, with privacy curtains separating them, like in a hospital. The faint sound of coughing from one of the beds drew Jonan's attention, and he realized after a moment they were all inhabited – and by children.

Probably sick children, he realized after taking a step closer. They were all dressed in simple robes and covered in heavy blankets. The gray haired man quietly closed the door behind the pair of them – *oops, that's bad* – and went to sit by the side of one of the children.

"You'll be better soon," the older man said to the child. There was no reply – after taking a step closer, Jonan realized the child's eyes were closed. The child looked to be about eight years old, and he had odd rings of blisters around his eyes. Jonan lifted a mirror to reflect the image of the child, tapping the surface.

Preserve, he told the mirror, and silently tucked it away.

So, this room isn't just like a hospital – it is a hospital. As Jonan softly stepped around the room, he noted three of the other children with similar marks around their eyes – but two of them with no visible signs of illness. The child who had coughed was one of the ones without any marks, however, indicating that there might be some other sign of illness he could not easily perceive.

What kind of sickness causes blisters around the eyes? It doesn't look like shingles or Soren's disease. Jonan searched his memories, but he could not recall any disease that fit the description. *The patterns of the blisters look almost circular. Could someone be burning them intentionally?* Jonan grimaced at the thought.

A possibility, but not the only one. I certainly don't know every disease out there. And if this is a research facility, it stands to reason that they could be looking for cures to obscure diseases.

Jonan turned toward the older man, scanning his collar for signs of the pins that indicated a court sorcerer. He did not find any, but that didn't necessarily mean anything. His vision was beginning to blur, making it difficult to make out any details of the man's appearance.

This is intriguing, but not what I'm looking for. I need to get out of here. Jonan glanced around the room. There were multiple closed windows, but only the double doors leading back into the main structure.

Unwilling to chance the windows, Jonan inched back toward the door. A loud knock on the wood sent him stumbling backward, and he barely managed to catch himself from falling.

"Sir, there's a court sorceress here. She's asking a lot of questions, I think you might want to come down," came a female voice from the other side.

The older man shook his head, touching the sleeping child on the forehead – Jonan winced at that, hoping the disease was not communicable – and stood up with a groan.

"Fine," the gray haired man said softly, probably too softly for the speaker on the other side to hear him. With deliberate steps, he made his way to the door and opened it.

The Rethri sorceress was on the other side.

Of course she was.

Jonan froze, uncertain if he should try to slip past in the few moments it was open. He hesitated too long, the door closing, the Rethri's eyes once again flickering in his mind.

Creepy sorceress is following me. That can't be a coincidence. I am most likely doomed.

Jonan waited in the room for several more minutes, pacing closer to the unconscious children and inspecting the remainder of the chamber. He found a few books sitting on chairs or tables next to the children, but they were all on various medical subjects. None of the children looked malnourished, but they were all pale-skinned, and most of them had ragged breathing.

Odd that none of them woke up when that man – the doctor, maybe – came in. Maybe they're using potions or sorcery to keep the children asleep.

Before inspecting the children further, Jonan reached into his pouch and removed one of his mirrors. He ran a finger across the surface, attuning it to transmit to another mirror, and found a good vantage point to leave it on a table across from the entrance door. The chamber was too large for one mirror to visualize the entire room, but if it faced the door he could monitor who was coming or going.

Minutes passed while Jonan considered when it would be best to leave the chamber. As his mind whirled with possibilities, he realized that he had made a blind assumption – and reached into his pouch for a pair of gloves.

With the utmost hesitation, Jonan used his gloved fingers to open an eye of one of the sleeping children – and stepped back when he saw a pale orb of blue surrounding black, with no sclera at all.

Oh, gods, I've been so stupid, Jonan chastised himself. *The children are Rethri. Or, at least some of them are.*

He briefly considered opening the eye again and using a mirror to record the picture, but the door to the room began to open before he had a chance.

And then the room went black, the light from the nearby windows utterly annihilated.

Jonan instinctively tapped the right side of his head, triggering his spell to see in the dark. It gave him nothing but mere outlines – whatever spell was starving the place of light was exceptionally thorough.

He did, however, see a woman – her body seemingly formed from something darker than the blackness of the room – seeping in the now-open doorway.

"I know you are here," she said aloud, her voice like honey tinged with venom. She drew something from within her robes – a knife, maybe – and stood to block the doorway. "Show yourself, sorcerer. I would rather speak than fight."

Sure you would. Jonan's mind raced, evaluating possibilities. *If these are Rethri children, are they Donovan's prisoners? Or the children of the prisoners, perhaps? I don't remember any reports about missing children.*

I'm going to regret this.

"I'll confirm my presence," Jonan said aloud, maintaining his concentration to continue his invisibility spell. "But I'd rather not show myself. I assume you can see through your own shadows, so it's only fair."

The Rethri woman turned toward the sound of his voice, flipping over the object in her hand.

Yep, definitely a dagger. And she's prepping a throw. He took a quick step to the side, putting himself behind one of the privacy curtains. There was no child in the bed behind that particular curtain, but he hoped she wouldn't realize that. If she was Rethri, he doubted she'd be willing to chance a throw at him while he was potentially standing over a Rethri child.

"If you hurt the child, I will kill you slowly over the course of centuries," the woman said in a warning tone.

"Peace," Jonan said, raising his hands above the curtain. He still wasn't sure if she could see him or not, but he was starting to suspect some middle-ground – much like he had been able to see her outline in the dark. "I am not here to hurt anyone."

"Then why are you here?" She sounded incredulous, slightly shifting her stance.

Well, hrm. Now that I've made the mistake of talking, I suppose I need to make another one. "I'm here investigating reports that Rethri have been kidnapped."

The shadow-woman folded her arms. "And why would you care about such a thing?"

Well, I work for a Rethri god, but I'm certainly not going to tell you that. "My organization is concerned that one of the factions in this city might be working against the Rethri. This would be disadvantageous for us as well."

"These children are afflicted by a plague. We have been attempting to research a cure," the woman offered in a strangely sad tone.

"I don't think that's true," Jonan risked. "The burns around their eyes are too regular. And the man who was just in here touched one of them on the head – you don't do that with a plague victim. And one locked door is hardly enough security-"

"You seem to be here out of concern, not malice. Drop your spell and surrender. I will make sure you are treated fairly." He heard her footsteps approaching the curtain, causing Jonan to awkwardly reach for his own dagger.

What am I doing? I can't fight her.

He bolted instead.

The woman's approach had taken her just out of the doorway – and that was all the space he needed. While she advanced to react to the sound of his steps, he raced around her. Her arm shot out as he approached, but he waved a hand, creating an image of the dawnfire in front of her. The Rethri reeled back, apparently blinded by the trick, and he rushed down the corridor.

Her footsteps sounded only an instant behind him.

Resh, I was hoping that spell would hold her longer.

There was visible light once Jonan emerged into the corridor –

apparently, her darkness spell only covered the room itself. The daylight from the windows was only momentarily disorienting, but it revealed that his vision was blurred to near-uselessness. Maintaining his invisibility spell for so long had taken a significant toll on his sight, and the spell for seeing in the dark had only made it worse.

"Guards! We have an intruder!" the woman shouted.

Something grabbed his leg, and as he fell forward, he realized that he was being dragged down to the floor by his own shadow.

He hit the ground hard, rolling awkwardly as the glue-like pull of his shadow dragged him against the floor. No illusion of light could vanquish the shadow – it would still be there even if he could not see it.

And so, with great hesitation, Jonan conjured flame.

A blast of fire with the heat of a furnace melted the tiles beneath his hand, the incendiary burst momentarily scattering his shadow. He felt a chill as the heat from casting his spell left the body, but the grip of the shadow waned from iron to elastic, allowing him to break free with a burst of momentum.

"Eshav!" the Rethri woman called. It was a popular Liadran expletive, and Jonan grinned in spite of himself. He loved winning.

Jonan half-ran, half-stumbled his way back to the stairway, which came up on him much faster at a running pace. A hand caught his shoulder just as he reached the stairs, and he spun, a ball of fire forming in his hand.

The Rethri woman, her features still entirely wrapped in shadow, stood unarmed behind him. Jonan hissed as his glove caught fire and hurled his sphere of flame into the floor. His will forced the sphere to combust, the explosion hurling the pair apart. Jonan slammed into the wall next to the stairs, his eyes swimming, his body convulsing from the sudden expenditure of too much heat.

Without so much as a moment of hesitation, the shadow-wrapped Rethri bounded back to her feet. The darkness around her seemed to have absorbed the detonation of his spell harmlessly – unlike his shadow, her shroud had not dissipated at the touch of flame.

She loomed over him now, but Jonan's head was swimming, and it took all his will just to push himself into a sitting position.

"I was careless to expect that your illusions meant you would be harmless," the Rethri woman said. "But you chose not to hit me directly with your fire, when you easily could have."

Jonan lifted a hand to the back of his head, feeling something wet. Blood, probably. *Great.* "Yeah, I don't always make the best decisions."

"Neither do I," she said, turning around. "Your invisibility spell is down. You will need to recast it before you leave. Never come here again."

She seemed to glide along the floor as she left, making no sound that he could recognize. He felt a measure of gratitude that she had chosen to leave, though it was hard to feel too positive when his head felt like it was about ready to combust.

Gods, I need to not do that again.

He reached into his pouch, withdrawing his glasses kit. After a few moments of fumbling, he opened it to produce a heavier pair, tucking his current glasses inside. The heavier glasses eased the blur of his vision, and he waved a hand to renew his invisibility.

The world swam around him again, but he couldn't tell how much of that came from the over-expenditure of sorcery and how much of it came from his head injury. *I'll need to get that looked at,* he noted, half-consciously staggering to the stairs. He was forced to awkwardly dodge a handful of guards as they rushed the stairway, apparently reacting to the woman's earlier call.

Jonan's head pulsed with agony as he made his way to exit from the same entrance he had entered, finding an opportunity to sneak out the door as a concerned looking man shouldered it open to leave. He neither saw nor heard any sign of Lydia – but he hadn't planned to. And right now, he barely had the strength to shiver his way back home on his own.

Jonan woke in a bed he had never slept in before. His eyes cracked open, showing him only a vaguely room-shaped blur. A heavy layer of blankets entombed him, and he brushed them aside, hands searching for glasses.

A red-crowned blur loomed over him a moment later. Startled, Jonan pushed himself backward and upright.

"Looking for these?" came an amused voice from the crimson blur. A pale blur – a hand, he realized, as it approached – offered him an object. *Glasses.* He snagged them out of the hand greedily, donning the spectacles in an instant.

Lydia formed in front of him, and his memories cleared somewhat along with his vision. He was in his home – in his false bedchamber, the one above his real one. He had managed to stumble this far on his own – Lydia must have found him shortly thereafter.

"Thank you," he managed to mumble. A shiver ran through him, and he pulled the pile of blankets back atop him. Lydia withdrew from her looming, but only to take a seat at a nearby chair. He tilted his head toward her, noting that she was carrying a half-closed book in her off-hand, a stray finger marking her place within the pages. "How long have I been out?"

"Just about an hour." Lydia flipped the book back open, looked at something, and then closed it completely and set it aside. "If you keep shivering like that, I'm going to need to take you to the palace for treatment."

"Oh, that would end well," Jonan mumbled.

"I see your sense of humor is uninjured, at least. How about the rest of you?" Lydia leaned forward in her chair.

"What, you didn't check?" Jonan lifted his blankets and glanced downward half-heartedly. "The important bits seem to be there."

"I didn't want to presume," she replied with just a hint of laughter in her tone. "Did you find anything interesting?"

Jonan looked back at the sorceress. "Under the blankets, or at the research facility?"

Lydia folded her arms. "At the research facility."

"Ah, it's all business with you. Well, yes, actually. In both places. At the research facility, I discovered something rather important – there's a room on the second floor filled with Rethri children. They appear to be unconscious, perhaps through sorcerous means. The children have some kind of burns or unusual markings around their eyes."

"And under the blankets?" Lydia leaned forward a hint further.

"Um, what?" Jonan stammered.

"What did you find that was so interesting under the blankets?" She grinned, adjusting her glasses.

Jonan pulled back instinctively as Lydia leaned over, causing her to laugh.

"You tell me I'm all business, and then when I play along, you don't know what to do with yourself," Lydia pointed out.

"I was just startled, is all. Let me start over. 'You'd really have to see it to believe it.'"

"Better," she replied, her grin transcending into smirk. "But you need more conviction. Anyway, business. Rethri with strange marks around their eyes."

"Right, business." Jonan let out a sigh of relief. *What a strange woman.* "The markings were in a circular shape. I think they were deliberate, given that Rethri eyes are tied to their Dominions."

Lydia's expression shifted into a glower. "Tell me more about these marks."

"Not much to say, I'm afraid. They looked like blisters, possibly from burns. They were in a roughly circular shape."

"Did they look like letters?"

I wish I knew. "None that I could identify, but if this was done through some kind of branding process, blisters and scabs could easily conceal the original shape of the markings."

Lydia glanced away from him, her expression grim. "Sounds like they could be the same type of markings that you found around the esharen."

"Potentially," he admitted. "I thought of that, but it was too hard to tell."

"Did you check several different people to see if the marks on any of them were easier to identify?"

I probably should have prioritized that, he considered, *but I had other things on my mind.*

"I didn't get a chance to do much poking around. Someone discovered me in the room – in spite of my invisibility. I promise, I wasn't making a lot of noise, either. She was a Rethri woman – wearing the robes of a court sorceress."

Lydia sat up straight in her chair. "A Rethri woman? What did she look like?"

"Looked like she was about your age, indigo eyes, brown hair, skin was about as dark as mine," he explained.

Lydia steepled her fingers, then rested her chin on them. "We have a problem. That wasn't a court sorceress."

Jonan quirked a brow. "Oh?"

"There's no court sorceress that fits that description. I'm fairly sure you've just described Vorain, the fourth god of Orlyn."

Jonan shivered, and he couldn't be sure if it was due to the cold that lingered in his veins. "Well," he considered, "That complicates things. But at least she wasn't trying to kill me."

Lydia quirked a brow. "What happened when she discovered you?"

"I should mention that she passed me once earlier, on the way to the room – and I didn't think she noticed me at the time. I followed an older human man into the room with the Rethri, and then she got his attention and led him outside. That was when she came in and found me. She told me she knew I was there, and she wanted to talk."

"What did she want to talk about?" Lydia cracked her fingers, leaning forward again.

"She wanted me to surrender. I told her I was there looking to find kidnapped Rethri. She told me the kids I had found were not captured – they were plague victims that were being treated. I insisted that they probably weren't, given how regular the burns were around their eyes. That was most likely a mistake," he continued, noting that Lydia was leaning closer, apparently transfixed by his story.

"So, the sorceress – or goddess, if you prefer – blocked the doorway. She wanted me to appear, and to surrender. I think she really did want to protect those children. I refused, of course. I was forced to dazzle her with some astounding spellwork – it really was quite impressive, you should have been there – and flee the area."

Lydia closed her eyes after that, apparently contemplating in silence for a moment.

"I'd show you the spells I used, but I'm afraid I'm a bit too shivery at the moment. And also half-blind." The world around him was sharper with his glasses on, but anything more than a few paces past Lydia was still barely recognizable.

"That's fine," Lydia said absently, waving a hand with a dismissive gesture. And then she went quiet again.

I guess she needs a moment. He sat up, taking a moment to consider for himself. His head swam in the opposite direction, reminding him of his brief head-to-wall collision. *That's going to be irritating for a while.*

Okay, what do I know?

Rethri woman is apparently not a sorceress. She's a goddess, or whatever passes for one around here. There's something that feels off about that.

Several things, actually. Let's break this down. Rethri were supposed to be kidnapped. There are Rethri here, but at least one of them appears to be operating of her own free will. She could have been coerced, but I have no evidence of that. She's probably been here for quite a while, if she's a 'goddess'. I think I remember hearing the most recent god of theirs is Myros, and even he has been around a few years.

"I can tell you're thinking, and that's fine – but help me out with one quick question. What was it about my description that said 'Vorain' to you?" Jonan scratched at his chin, trying to piece things together in his aching mind.

"Around five years ago, a court sorceress named Vorain was raised to 'godhood' by Edon. Vorain was the first new god of the city after Edon claimed the queen regent was divine about ten years back. She had brown hair – I'm not sure about the skin. The stories say that her eyes turned indigo after she became a goddess."

"Turned indigo?" Jonan muttered.

"Yeah," Lydia replied. "That's one of the things I've been thinking about. You saw her for the first time and immediately made the natural assumption that she was Rethri, since she has indigo eyes and no sclera. I should have pieced this connection together the moment you mentioned Rethri were missing, but someone's eyes changing after they become a 'god' isn't exactly typical. We just know so little about the real gods that I initially thought it was just one more piece of silly local propaganda."

Jonan considered the implication. *Could Vorain be human, but with Rethri-like eyes? Gods, is that what they're doing to the children? Are they somehow stealing whatever essence makes Rethri eyes different from ours? If the eye color difference is somehow connected with whatever gives Rethri their extended lifespan...*

"You shouldn't blame yourself for not considering every possible fact immediately. I tried to research this place, and I clearly haven't picked up as much of the local culture as you have – even key facts like the origin stories of their gods." Jonan adjusted his position in the bed, turning onto his side to look directly at Lydia.

She nodded, acknowledging his remark. "You're right, of course. No one can take every piece of data that they've collected in a lifetime into account all at once. I still feel like I should have noticed something was wrong about those eyes, but now we have the clue at least, so we can investigate it."

Jonan nodded. "It's still possible she really is Rethri – maybe she just was concealing her natural eye color before. I saw her use shadow sorcery, at the very least – and she could see through my sight sorcery. If she's a sight sorceress herself, she could easily change the appearance of her eyes."

"Or she could have been human this whole time, and decided at a certain point to make her eyes look like Rethri eyes," Lydia pointed out. "Perhaps to convince Rethri to trust her."

Jonan pondered that. "Do you think she could have been the one who convinced the Rethri to come to this city?" He shook his head. "She really sounded like she thought these children were being protected here. She could have attacked me immediately – or called for guards – and she chose to talk."

"Maybe she knew that if you had gotten this far in your research, you weren't alone – and she was feeding you a false lead. Either to throw off your search, or to lay a trap." Lydia stretched suddenly, standing up. "That's what I would do in her place."

Jonan scoffed at that. "That'd be playing an awfully long con. You'd really do something like that?"

Lydia looked down at him, shaking her head. "I've been a court sorceress of Orlyn for two years."

"Point taken," he replied with a nod. "Okay, so maybe she's crazy devious like you apparently are. We can consider that. It's also possible that she's been deceived herself – or blackmailed, maybe."

"That sounds like a stretch. It sounds like you want to believe her," Lydia pointed out.

You're not wrong. But she seemed so...sincere. "Maybe," he said hesitantly, "But that older man I saw. She was very polite to him, like she reported to him. If she's a goddess, that doesn't really make any sense."

"What did he look like?" Lydia asked.

"Maybe an inch or two taller than Taelien, short gray hair, white tunic, no spectacles," Jonan rattled off. "I didn't catch a lot of other details."

"That's fine, I know who you're talking about. I met him – that's Raymond Lorel, the facility's director. He rattled off all sorts of things to me about what they are supposedly researching there. He didn't mention anything medical, nor about children. He gave me a very guided tour of the building. Showed me some alchemical labs, nothing too impressive. I think the tour was designed to bore me into wanting to leave. The important part is that he didn't look like Edon," Lydia explained.

"Hrm." *Well, that throws a hole in the most obvious explanation.* "You said you've met Edon before. Was there no resemblance? Could it be the same man, but perhaps bereft of illusion magic to make him appear younger?"

"Not a bad thought," Lydia admitted, pushing up against the wall in another stretching exercise. "No, they didn't look all that similar, but an illusion can conceal more than age. As I'm sure you know already, given your occupation. So, yes, they could be the same person."

"And I take it you didn't have a chance to check him with knowledge sorcery?"

"No," Lydia scoffed. "That's normally considered rude."

Jonan chuckled softly. "That didn't stop you from using it on me."

"There were somewhat different circumstances behind that," she said, turning around with a half-smirk. "But you have a point. Please forgive me for dispelling your invisibility, capturing you, and interrogating you a little."

"I think I can find it in my heart to forgive you." Jonan rolled his eyes. "Still, if you can find the justification, you should be rude to that man, too. You can apologize to him later."

Lydia shrugged. "I'll consider it, but Raymond is a well-established scholar, and he's got quite a bit of financial backing. He has powerful friends that we wouldn't want to drag into this."

"Those friends may already be 'into this', if having a goddess on a leash is any indication," Jonan pointed out.

"I most sincerely doubt that he keeps her on a leash. That would be even ruder than using knowledge sorcery on someone without permission."

Jonan sighed. "I see your point. If she does work for him in some capacity, it's probably not out of any actual subservience – unless he's Edon, of course. Or Myros, but that seems unlikely, given that Myros is supposed to be younger."

"Yes, Myros is only supposed to be around our age. He was a talented member of the Queensguard, and he was apparently raised to divinity for defending her against a 'rival god from another land'. An interesting story, but yes, I agree, Raymond does not fit Myros' description. It's possible that Raymond could be blackmailing Vorain somehow, as you mentioned earlier."

"I don't think I said blackmail." Jonan rubbed at his temples. "But maybe I did. It's hard to think with the walls spinning so quickly. I think I need a break from this."

"Well, we've covered a lot of ground in this discussion already.

You've gathered some excellent information. I think you can take a break while we consider all this. Are you feeling well enough to go back to sleep?" Lydia asked.

Jonan shrugged his left shoulder. "I could try. I'm still feeling awfully cold."

"Sorcery exhaustion," Lydia said matter-of-factly. "I was worried at first, but if you can hold a conversation with this little difficulty, you shouldn't need any medical help."

"It'd be much easier to keep warm with some company, though," Jonan pointed out.

"I'll see if Taelien is up," she said in the same tone, walking toward the door.

"I meant you, actually."

"I'm a Paladin of Sytira," Lydia said, shaking her head as she opened the door to leave the bedchamber.

Jonan turned to follow her with his gaze, quirking a brow. "Does that mean you have to be celibate or pure or something?"

"No," she replied with a wry grin, "It means I have refined tastes."

"I'm plenty refined," Jonan insisted. "Like aged coffee."

Lydia narrowed her eyes. "I'm not sure you're supposed to age coffee."

"Oh," Jonan said, giving a dejected look downward, toward his bedsheets. "My whole life has been a lie."

Lydia's laugh was beautiful, like a...hummingbird making a beautiful sound. Jonan never was very good with analogies.

"Good night, Jonan," Lydia offered, a flash of humor still present in her voice. She closed the door behind her.

"Good night, Lydia," he replied.

It really is cold in these sheets by myself.

Jonan shivered.

CHAPTER VII – INEFFICIENT INVESTMENTS OF EFFORT

Focus.

Taelien pressed two fingers of his left hand against the third runestone from the top of his unsheathed sword. The four runes beneath it glowed brightly with azure light, but the rune he touched – along with the two above it – remained unlit.

His right hand gripped tightly around the hilt, holding the sword secure and ensuring the shimmering waves of colorless force that extended a hand's breadth outward from the blade did not come into contact with anything else. He knew from experience what the consequences would be if that devastating aura met any form of solid material.

It's been two years. I should be able to do this.

As he concentrated, Taelien felt the sword's inexorable pull against his strength. Beads of sweat coalesced on his forehead, the hilt seemingly growing heavier with each passing moment.

Sae'kes, heed my call. Use my strength to focus your own. Let your outer edge meet with the blade within.

For just an instant, he thought he saw a hint of light flicker within the gray of the unlit rune of Eratar – just as Lydia swung open the door to the room, shattering his concentration.

The fourth lit rune – signifying Koranir – flickered and died, followed by the rune of Xerasilis after it. The rippling waves of force around the blade began to spread, and Taelien snatched up his scabbard from his left side, quickly – and carefully – jamming the blade within.

Lydia stared at him blankly for a moment, something unfamiliar in her expression. Awe, perhaps?

"Is that...you can actually draw the blade?" Lydia's eyes focused on the now-filled scabbard, her tone of voice matching her expression.

Taelien nodded. "Of course. I thought I had made that clear before. That's hardly the difficult part." He tried not to let his bitterness sink into his words, but it was a paltry effort at bet.

"Gods, Taelien... I knew there was a chance, but it's different to actually see it. That's the Sae'kes, the real thing. And you can use it." Lydia took a step forward, tilting her head down, as if it could give her a better look at the sword within the scabbard.

"Not exactly." He ran his fingers along the metal rim of the scabbard. "Taking it out of the sheath is one thing. There's nothing special about that – I just use metal sorcery to seal the metal part of the scabbard against the blade when I'm not using it. When I want to draw the sword, I reverse the process."

He tapped his fingers against the cross guard, grimacing. "Being able to wield in battle it is another problem entirely. It's been twelve years since my parents let me pick up the sword for the first time. I still can't ignite more than four of the runes."

Lydia snagged a chair from near the door – the same one she had used when she had guarded it earlier – and sat down. "Why does that matter? What does igniting those runes do?"

Taelien shrugged his shoulders. "You saw the aura around the blade, I assume?"

Lydia nodded.

"So far as I can tell, the runestones on the blade exist to condense that aura. The more of them are lit, the more the aura tightens around the blade. Presumably, with all of the runes lit, the aura would be flush against the blade itself. The problem is that the stones appear to require an external source of essence to operate. That means I need to feed my strength into the weapon to make them work."

Taelien ran his fingers across the leather of the scabbard. "So far as I can tell, this scabbard is the only thing that can resist being cut by that aura around the sword. It seems to have been designed to contain the weapon. Anything else – stone, metal, flesh – that touches the aura is torn apart."

"You seemed to have some of the runes under control when I

walked in," Lydia said, gesturing at the weapon.

"Some," he said sadly, "Is insufficient. When I swing the sword with any of the runes unlit, the aura around it whips forward, separating from the sword. The more runes I've managed to ignite, the closer the aura stays to the blade – but even with four runes lit, the most I've been able to manage, the force can extend out more than half the length and width of the blade itself. That's too large to control effectively, especially if I have any allies on the field."

Lydia pursed her lips. "It sounds like you've had bad experiences with it before."

Taelien shook his head. "Only damaged a few objects so far, fortunately. Erik Tarren gave my parents clear instructions that I was never to use it until I could control all seven runes. As a result, my parents didn't even let me draw it until I was eight, and even then, they barely let me move it. As a child, this was awfully disappointing, but as I've grown older I've seen the wisdom in restraint. The sword is worthless until I can control it. And at this rate, that might be another ten years. Assuming I am still making any progress at all."

Lydia sat up, her expression contemplative. "Sounds like a worthwhile investment to me."

Taelien sighed. "Sure, if I want to be able to murder people with relentless efficiency in the future, I see it as a great investment."

"That sword isn't about murdering people, Taelien," she chastised him. "It's a symbol of the Tae'os Pantheon, and their protection of the mortal races. It's a sword for shielding others against monsters."

"Then why," Taelien asked, "Does it have no apparent function other than cutting things apart?"

Lydia folded her arms across her chest, glowering slightly. "It's very likely that you simply do not know how to use it properly yet. Perhaps other powers will manifest when you are able to ignite the seventh rune. Perhaps it is a test to see if the wielder has sufficient force of will to keep the weapon's destructive powers at bay. Anyone who simply uses the sword to kill would be unworthy of its other abilities."

"That sounds like a nice story, but it is only speculation. It seems much more plausible that the sword simply wasn't made for me – or any mortal – to use. If igniting the runes requires essence, it might be that whoever it was built for – the god of swords, if your stories are true – had so much more essence than I do that using it properly was trivial for him," Taelien offered.

"Perhaps, but your explanation is not mutually exclusive with mine. And there are other possibilities as well. Have you found any way to determine what the composition of that aura is?"

Taelien shook his head. "No. My mother was proficient at knowledge sorcery, but any spell she used on the sword appeared to be blocked. She said the aura looks like motion sorcery, but it's persistent, which motion sorcery is not. She was able to identify the scabbard, however – that's just utilizing powerful protection sorcery. She had never seen protection sorcery on the same scale before, but that's all it is."

"Interesting," Lydia replied, raising a hand to adjust her glasses. "Very interesting."

What's so interesting about that? It's just protection sorcery...why would that...

"Ah, are you a protection sorcerer yourself?" Taelien guessed. *That would explain how she survived that spell Istavan cast at me earlier,* he realized.

Lydia nodded absently. "Yes. I was wondering if I could use that to help you – maybe find a way to contain the aura even when it isn't sheathed."

Taelien felt a sudden surge of hope. "Really? I wouldn't have expected you to be willing to help, if you think it is some sort of divine test."

She waved a hand dismissively. "That was just one possibility. And even if it is a test, I'm a Sytiran. We solve tests through ingenuity."

"How'd you get involved with the Paladins of Tae'os, anyway?"

Lydia took a breath. "One night when I was young, I woke to the smell of burning wood. I rushed to my youngest brother's room – Dyson was just a baby at the time. By the time I found him, the whole house was in flames. I didn't know any protection sorcery back then. I panicked and screamed. My parents didn't come for me – a stranger did. I remember hearing him shouting something – a prayer to Xerasilis, I realized later - and bursting into the room, choking and scorched. He carried us both out of the house."

"He was already badly burned when we emerged. He could barely stand, but the first thing he did was ask if anyone else was still inside. I saw my parents outside, but not my other brother or my sister. I told him I thought there were still two other children within. Even as the flames burned hotter, he went back inside, chanting to the god of flames to stand aside."

Lydia looked down, shaking her head. "I had been wrong about Edwin – he was already outside. After the stranger rescued my sister, he stayed inside to try to find Edwin..."

"Did he survive?" Taelien asked.

"Only just. His partner arrived in time to drag him out of the wreckage and get him to a hospital. He was comatose for months, and a beam had crushed his leg. He'll never fight again. He will be lucky if he can ever walk." Lydia tightened her jaw. "And it was my fault."

"He was a Paladin of Xerasilis, then?"

"Lysandri, actually. Paladins of Tae'os pray to all seven of our gods when the situation is appropriate. He was still comatose when I learned who he was. Calor was a complete stranger, and he had risked his life to save us, while my parents had stood aside in fear. He was my hero. He is still my hero. I will never be worth what he did for me."

"When Istavan was attacking me, you stepped right in front of his spell without any hesitation," Taelien pointed out. "You defended a complete stranger."

She shook her head. "It's not the same. The risk was minimal – I knew protection sorcery to keep me safe. And you might have been a stranger, but I suspected you were related to one of my gods."

"You can justify it all you want, but it was heroic from my standpoint. Thank you," he said. "I can see why you joined the paladins, then. Why'd you choose Sytira?"

Lydia tilted her head to the side. "What do you mean?"

The swordsman shrugged at her. "I've never understood why people pick one god or another to worship. Especially you Tae'os followers – if you worship seven gods, how do you pick one to focus on? I would have expected you to pick Lysandri if that's who your rescuer worshipped."

Lydia steepled her fingers, laying her hands in her lap. "Well, for one thing, my compatibility tests indicated that the best fit for me would be with Eratar or Sytira."

Taelien quirked a brow dubiously. "Compatibility tests?"

"They're much like the sorcery aptitude tests you took as a child, I assume. We don't just take anyone who wants to pick up a sword. Applicants are tested to see if they qualify, and if they pass, the tests indicate where they would be the most appropriate...but I have a feeling you were looking for a more emotional answer," she noted, apparently examining his expression.

Taelien cracked his knuckles. "I was expecting one, at least. Do you really worship someone just because your superiors told you to?"

Lydia shook her head. "No, I suppose not. I suspected I would choose Sytira long before I took the tests. She's the patron of scholars, and I've had my nose in a book since I started to recognize letters. All the Tae'os gods have their value, but Sytira gives us knowledge. To me, that's the greatest gift anyone – divine or otherwise – can offer."

That does seem to suit you.

Taelien stood and knelt in front of Lydia, putting a hand on her knee. "Well, knowledge about this sword would be a great gift indeed. I've had this supposed inheritance – this burden – for as long as I can remember. I'd be very grateful for anything you could do to help me use it."

Lydia sat up a little straighter in her chair, but she didn't flinch away from him. "Let's not get too carried away. I'll try to think of something, but it's going to require research. And I'm going to have to bombard you with a lot of questions."

Taelien nodded vehemently. "Yes, I am fine with that. Thank you."

She nodded, patting his hand. "Not a problem. In the meantime, I have another question for you."

"Oh? Ask away, then."

"You mentioned coming to the city to meet Erik Tarren. I was very skeptical about that at first, but having seen that you can actually draw the weapon, I'm beginning to wonder if exploring that angle may have some merit. Did your parents tell you why Erik Tarren left you with them?"

"He was in danger, and my parents got the impression that my birth parents had also been in danger," he said, standing up. "They had been friends of Erik years before, and apparently Erik didn't think his enemies would be able to find me with them. He didn't tell them who my real parents were."

"But he told them the city he was planning to go to? Seems like a poor idea, if he was fleeing from some sort of danger." The sorceress ran a hand across her hair, narrowing her eyes.

"I suppose he didn't think anyone would try to go after my parents for information about him. He hadn't seen them for years when he showed up with me. Anyway, I suppose it's possible Erik Tarren was alive twenty years ago, but is not today. He certainly could have moved to a different city by now. But it is the best information I have."

"I suppose if anyone would know about a wielder of the Sae'kes, it would be Erik Tarren," Lydia mused.

Taelien began to pace around the room, but glanced back toward Lydia. "Do you know something about him? I mean, you and Jonan both knew his reputation as a scholar, but something more specific?"

Lydia nodded. "Specifically, he's well known for writing treatises on sorcerous theory. He's one of the foremost authorities on broad-scale sorcery, especially the applications of sorcery in warfare. He personally engineered the spell that resulted in the fall of Xixis."

"That's very impressive."

"It is, but I'm sure it did make him a host of enemies. And his political views were never very popular in Velthryn." She paused, a half-frown crossing her face. "I have a bit of a personal interest in him as well. I never knew my real father. He left few things of value behind when he left my mother – myself in her belly being one of them, a book by Erik Tarren being another."

Taelien paused in his step, turning to face Lydia completely. A somber expression fell across his face. "I'm sorry. I know what it's like growing up without knowing your real father."

Lydia nodded, and then shook her head, as if to dismiss the thought. A smile replaced her half-frown. "It's all right. My mother married another man when I was only three. So, I had a father figure for most of my childhood. The book has always left me with a hint of curiosity, however. Why'd he leave that book, in specific? It was an obscure one, too – 'The Nature of Worlds'."

The sorceress gave a soft smile. "My mother couldn't read, and my father must have known that – did he leave it for me, knowing that my mother was pregnant? I don't know if the author of the book would have any idea about my father's motives, but he's the only hint I have. My mother never told me my real father's name, or even a description."

"I sympathize," Taelien offered. "Maybe we're related."

Lydia gave scoffing laugh at that, pointing at his head. "Given our hair colors, I'd somewhat doubt it."

"Agreed. I'm sure there are many children with stories similar to our own. Still, it's nice to have some common ground."

Lydia nodded in reply. "I feel the same. So, your parents – did they tell you anything about how to find Erik Tarren, aside from the city?"

"Oh, of course. They gave me an address," Taelien explained, rubbing at his still-sweaty forehead with his off hand. "I probably should have mentioned that earlier."

"We haven't exactly had time to hunt him down until now, anyway. Jonan and I have had plenty to do, and you seem to have been getting yourself into enough trouble to keep busy, too." She gestured at his leg. "How's that feeling, anyway?"

"Only the most minor of agony now, thank you. I've been using the sacred sword of your religion as a cane," he said with a wink.

Lydia rolled her eyes. "Just never tell any priests that you did that. They tend to be a little more fervent about the treatment of holy artifacts. Do you need me to redo your stitches?"

He shook his head. "No, Jonan took care of it in the morning. I should be fine."

"Are you sure? Last time he took care of your stitches, they didn't last the night," Lydia pointed out.

"You're overprotective. Comes with the sorcery, I assume." He smiled. "I'll be fine. I have my sacred sword cane to take care of me," he said, tapping the sheath at his side.

"I thought you were just teasing about that."

"Not at all," he replied, smiling. "Want to come with me to look for Erik Tarren?"

Lydia pursed her lips. "Yes, but I really shouldn't be seen with you. It's a fairly significant risk."

He shrugged in response. "I can wear a disguise. Jonan already gave me a cover identity, and I have a tail coat that he rented. I could go buy a hat and some other accoutrements, if you'd feel more comfortable that way."

The sorceress adjusted her glasses, and then looked him up and down. "If you can disguise yourself to my satisfaction, I'll go with you."

"I'll consider that a challenge." Taelien grinned.

Taelien looked ridiculous.

He knew he looked ridiculous, and he seemed to be enjoying it significantly more than Lydia was. His strategy for avoiding notice was being so noticeable that no one would expect that he could be someone that was avoiding the law.

The garb that Jonan had rented was now accompanied by some new additions – a tall hat accentuated with a plume of blue feathers, a half-length black cloak with golden trim, a half-mask that covered the upper portion of his face, and a new form for the Sae'kes that actually made the sword and scabbard resemble a sword cane. He had purchased black dye and re-colored the leather portion of the scabbard, which was the only part that had been consistently recognizable even when he changed the shape of the metal. The dye stank even after several hours of drying, but he felt the effect was worth it.

Lydia could barely look at him without bursting into a fit of giggles, so he decided that his strategy was working.

The Perfect Stranger was a large, single-floor tavern in the Mercantile District. A wooden sign displaying the name over a painted image of a blue eye-mask hung over the entrance, and Taelien could hear the low murmur of the patrons conversing inside as they approached.

Lydia had taken the time to change into "less conspicuous" garb, and thus she was wearing a brown tunic and pants similar to his own. Her insignia of rank were tucked safely into a pouch on her belt, just in case she needed to show them.

And her hair was down. It was a glorious cascade of fire, and he often found his eyes wandering to the sheet of color. He wasn't sure if she had noticed his occasional staring.

"This should be it," Taelien said, pointing a thumb at the building.

Lydia hooked his arm and tugged him toward the entrance. "C'mon, I could use a drink."

Taelien chuckled as they approached the entrance. "You're in an atypically good mood."

"Gotta blend in with the local atmosphere," she said, but the smirk on her face told him that she actually was in a pleasant mood. He wasn't quite clear on why.

Lydia pushed the door open, revealing a room longer than it was wide. At least two dozen customers were seated at various tables, and another half-dozen stood near the bar. Taelien glanced side-to-side, taking in the patrons of the tavern. None of them seemed to give either him or Lydia any undue attention, but he felt somewhat unsettled regardless.

Lydia dragged him toward the front, seeking the bartender as they had planned. When the man behind the bar turned around, she froze.

So did he.

The man was tall, about two or three inches taller than Taelien, and a good bit thicker. His rolled-up sleeves revealed that his bulk came from muscle, the kind of muscle you might see on a blacksmith or a lumberjack – or a soldier. His brown hair and neatly-trimmed goatee were flecked with gray. His eyes focused on Lydia for a moment, scrutinizing, and then he tilted his head to the side.

"What can I get for you two?" he asked, a half-grin cracking across his face.

"A mead for me," Lydia said, snapping out of her momentary paralysis. "And what about you, James?"

She put an odd emphasis on his name, but he got the impression it wasn't directed at him.

"Hrm. One of those 'mead' drinks, too," he said, quirking an eyebrow at Lydia. She shook her head at him.

"Two flagons of mead it is," the bartender said, spinning around to walk to a series of cups and bottles up against the wall.

Taelien glanced at Lydia. "Problem?"

"No," Lydia whispered. "Maybe. Don't worry about it."

Maybe? That's not foreboding or anything.

A cup had appeared in front of Taelien by the time he glanced back toward the bartender.

"Can I get you two anything else?" the man asked.

Lydia picked up her cup, "I think my friend had a question for you."

"Oh?" The bartender turned toward Taelien. "What sort of question?"

Taelien suddenly felt very small. *This is foolish. What are the odds this man knows anything about Erik Tarren? I'm in the wrong place.*

"I, uh, heard I might be able to find Erik Tarren here," Taelien stammered, his hand fumbling for his drink.

The man furrowed his brow. "The scholar? Hrm." He turned toward Lydia. "Might know a thing about that, but it might cost you."

Lydia nodded. "We can pay."

We can? Taelien reached down with his left hand to feel for his coin purse – which, of course, he didn't have. It had been taken along with all of his other belongings when he had been captured, and he had not found anything else along with his sword. He had been borrowing money from Jonan to pay for the additional clothing.

"Come chat with me around back," the man offered, waving a hand toward a door behind the bar, and then opening the door and walking through it.

Lydia grabbed her drink and followed immediately. Taelien took another look around the room, scanning for anyone that looked hostile, but he just saw ordinary-looking customers. The only other people with weapons were a couple soldiers playing some sort of game of darts involving three separate boards near the opposite side of the room.

After a quick glance behind him, Taelien picked up his drink and scuttled after Lydia into the back room.

Once Taelien stepped inside, Taelien scanned the room for threats immediately. Most of what he saw was crates and barrels, presumably containing more alcohol and supplies. A single round, wooden table with a handful of stools around it sat toward the back. Atop it sat a deck of playing cards and a bottle of half-empty alcohol.

There was a long spear leaning against the back wall, behind the table – the wooden shaft well-concealed among the boxes and barrels. It was a simple weapon, but a weapon nonetheless. Taelien took note of its position, but the bartender didn't head toward it – he stepped back closer to the pair of them and shut the door tightly.

"Grab a seat," he said, "And keep your voices low."

Lydia led the way, taking a seat all the way toward the back – facing where they had entered. *A good decision, from a strategic standpoint. I wonder if she chose that position deliberately.*

Taelien sat to her left side, awkwardly adjusting his scabbard and hilt to keep them from knocking into the table.

The bartender walked over toward Lydia a moment later, balling his right hand into a fist. In the moment while Taelien tensed for a fight, the bartender crisply brought the fist to his chest, and then released it. "Surprised to see you here, Lydia. Is he one of ours?"

Lydia made a fist and raised it to her own chest. *It's a salute,* Taelien realized, breathing a sigh of relief. *He must be a paladin, like her.*

"No," Lydia replied, gesturing at Taelien. "But he might be more than that."

"I've heard a few rumors," the man nodded. He turned to Taelien, stretching out a hand. "Sorry for being rude. I'm Gerald Mason."

Taelien clasped the man's hand at the wrist. "Taelien Salaris." The pair gave each other a brief squeeze at the wrist, displaying that they had no hidden weapons in their sleeves, and then released their grips with an exchange of nods.

Lydia glanced over to Taelien. "You never told me that last name before."

"I was your prisoner when we made our introductions. And it isn't my last name, precisely. It is my birth name, whereas Taelien is a title I took as my surname. I don't have a family name, since I was adopted." Taelien took a sip of his drink. *What a strange beverage. Tastes almost like honey.*

"Ah, thought so. You must be the one Byron is all flustered about," Gerald said, raising a hand to his chin.

Lydia raised an eyebrow. "What do you mean?"

Gerald lowered his hand in a quieting gesture. "Keep it down, Hastings. And I can't talk long – Tom'll take over the bar, but he'll come looking for me in a few. Anyway, it's nothing secret – there are posters up around town."

"Posters? You mean like bounties for criminals?" Taelien asked, leaning forward against the table.

"Not wanted posters," Gerald said. "They're a challenge. They say that the 'bearer of the Taelien is challenged to appear in the Court of the Spear', or something along those lines. Basically, the prince is offering the 'Taelien' a chance to fight to prove his innocence of some sort of crime. I thought it was just a prank at first, but the number of posters indicated a real effort. And then after a day or so, I started hearing that some of them have the royal seal on them – forging that is a high crime."

"Yeah, that's talking about this Taelien," Lydia said. "I'm not sure how much else I should say."

Taelien quirked a brow. "Why not? I take it he's one of your fellow p–"

Lydia shoved a finger in Taelien's face. "Never say that word aloud in this city."

Taelien frowned, but he went quiet.

"We're in a closed room, but you're pretty loud, and it's a bad habit to start spouting information that could get someone killed. And yes, he is. But we're not supposed to know about each other," Lydia said.

"Don't be too hard on the lad." Gerald finally took a seat on the opposite side of Lydia. "Look, Salaris – people like Lydia and I are doing work that isn't exactly legal here. We are not supposed to know about others like us, in case we get caught and interrogated. It's a big city, and there aren't many of us – at least I assume there aren't – so we don't run into problems like this very often."

"The more information we share with one another, the more we could potentially give away if one of us is captured," Lydia continued the explanation. "So we're going to be a little vague with each other here."

"Aye, but we can talk a bit." Gerald turned toward Taelien. "Any idea why the crown prince wants you in the arena?"

Taelien glanced at Lydia and she nodded to him. "I was arrested for carrying a symbol of the Tae'os Pantheon when I first arrived in the city. I was imprisoned in a strange cell in the low palace. I'm still not sure on why."

"Calling what you carried a symbol is an understatement. Show him the sword's real form, Taelien." Lydia made an expression of wry amusement.

Taelien nodded, raising the scabbard.

Revert, he commanded the metal.

The metal shell retreated from around the pommel jewel, and the crossguard expanded outward, reforming into a pair of silvery wings. Gerald gawked openly for a moment, and then raised his fist to his chest again. Taelien almost responded before realizing that Gerald was saluting the sword, not him.

"Gods around us...," Gerald muttered. He turned to Lydia. "If he can change the shape, how do you know that form is the real one, and not the other form?"

"It was taken away from him for several hours, and it looked like that – the Sae'kes Taelien – during that time. None of my efforts to identify its functions have succeeded. It has powerful sorcery, and I could not even draw it out of the scabbard myself. Taelien here can draw it, and I've seen him make several of the runes on the surface glow," Lydia rattled off.

"My," Gerald said, "I never thought I'd actually see...Amazing. Would you be willing to show me the blade?"

"It's dangerous," Taelien warned. "I'll just draw it out a little." He stood up, drawing the blade enough to expose the unlit rune of Lissari near the bottom of the blade. To further the demonstration, he took a breath and concentrated, feeling a surge of his essence flood into the weapon. The rune flashed azure, and he snapped the sword back into the sheath.

"Beautiful," Gerald said. "Thank you, I never believed I'd see it with my own eyes."

"So, Taelien walked into the city with the Sae'kes, and someone in a high place – presumably Byron – panicked. Byron's coronation is in a few weeks. It's very plausible that he thought Taelien was sent either to make some sort of political statement, or perhaps to assassinate him during the coronation." Lydia tapped a finger on the table, apparently thinking.

"According to rumors, Myros discovered an armed group – presumably assassins - skulking about the high palace a few months ago. They say that's why the coronation was delayed. I assume the prince and the queen regent are somewhat on edge, given that the new date for the coronation is fast approaching."

Taelien scratched at his chin. "I wasn't hiding the sword, though. I mean, if I showed up in the middle of the coronation and attacked Byron with the Sae'kes, sure, that'd be a pretty serious political statement. But if I was going to do that, wouldn't I have made some effort to conceal the sword when I came into the city?"

Gerald shrugged. "If you're afraid of being killed, you're not necessarily thinking rationally. Besides, even if you're not an assassin, I'm sure having the sword of an outlawed religion in the city at the time of your coronation would be disconcerting. Maybe he's worried about you inciting a rebellion."

"Wouldn't be enough people to do much with that," Lydia noted. "But you're right, Byron probably isn't thinking that way."

"Hrm. Why challenge me openly, then? Wouldn't that just call attention to my presence?"

Lydia rubbed a hand against her left temple. "That depends on how the challenge is structured. Do you know the details, Gerald?"

"Says that if he wins, he'll be given an ambassadorship. Seems like a reasonable tactic – if Taelien loses, he's removed from the picture, either by being killed or imprisoned. If Taelien wins, he's made into a public figure, where Byron can assign people to keep an eye on him."

Taelien nodded. "Thank you for the insight. Why did you invite us into the back when I first asked about Erik Tarren?" Taelien asked.

Gerald folded his arms. "I thought you were a part of the organization that Lydia and I belong to. That's a code name for one of our missions."

Lydia seemed visibly taken aback by that. "Really? You mean there actually...?"

"Oh, Master Tarren isn't actually here," Gerald explained. "Sorry to disappoint you. It's just named after him."

Taelien's shoulders slumped. "My family sent me to find him. They said I should look for him here."

"Are your parents members of my organization?" Gerald asked.

Taelien shook his head. "Not that I am aware of. Not the parents that adopted me, at any rate. Perhaps my biological parents were, but I don't know their names."

The bartender took a breath, shaking his head. "If you're here about Master Tarren, I'm afraid you're about ten years too late. He used to own this tavern. Members of our organization would meet here, and he'd teach them. This was before my time. When he left the city, he left the tavern to a friend, who in turn passed it off to me. I doubt the old man is still around, sad to say. He was ancient."

"It's possible he's still alive, given that he most certainly knew how to extend his life with sorcery," Lydia pointed out. "What's this mission that's named after him? Was he involved in it? Can you tell us anything about the mission that could potentially be relevant to Taelien?"

Yes, anything, please. I need to know.

Gerald scratched at his chin. "There was a battle many years ago between the armies of General Therin of Whitestone and Vyrek Sul, the Emperor of Xixis. During their final battle, Erik Tarren cast a spell that shattered Vyrek Sul's weapon – Cessius, the Staff of Dissonance. He later successfully banished Vyrek Sul to another world. Sul's followers gathered up the pieces of Cessius and hid them away in secret vaults, awaiting their master to return to this world and reclaim his empire."

"I've heard the story, although I heard that Therin was the one that destroyed the staff. Anyway, the details are largely irrelevant." Lydia mentioned.

"This was a Xixian city," Taelien realized. "You think Cessius is here."

"Master Tarren thought a piece of it might be here," Gerald said. "He never found it, though. After he left the city, our organization decided to pick up where he left off. They named the mission in his honor. I don't know where Tarren went after he left here, unfortunately."

Taelien nodded. "Thank you. You've already helped a great deal. More than you know."

Cessius, the Staff of Dissonance. The weapon of the Xixian Emperor. Perhaps I'm meant to help finish Erik Tarren's work.

"Sorry, kid. Finish the drink - it's on me. Maybe it'll help you feel a little better," Gerald offered. "Lydia, I've gotta get back. Pretending you were paying me for information is one thing, but this is taking a little long for that."

Lydia nodded and smiled sadly. "It was good to see you, Gerald. We probably won't be meeting again anytime soon."

"Well, here's hoping we both finish our secret missions soon, so we can go home." Gerald stood up from the table.

"I'll drink to that." Lydia smiled, raising her cup and bumping it against Taelien's. Startled, he spilled an inch of liquid and nearly fell backward, triggering a cascade of laughter from the two paladins.

Paladins.   I'll   never   understand   them. Taelien took a drink and stood to leave. "Gerald, before I go. You said you didn't know where Tarren went, but do you have any idea who might?"

Gerald shook his head. "He didn't tell my predecessor, as far as I'm aware. He was close with some of the leaders of my organization, but I don't think they'd give his location away easily if they had it. Of course, since you're carrying the sword of the gods around, I take it you're actually someone important to us. Maybe someone very important, as Lydia was implying earlier. If I had any advice, I'd say you should talk to someone at the top of my chain of command. Maybe Orin Dyr."

Taelien scratched the back of his head. "I suppose that makes sense. I might do that. Thank you, I am in your debt."

"Don't be forgetting that if you do turn out to be important," Gerald grinned, "And also, you might want to cover that sword back up."

"Ah, right." *Ordinary.* The metal stretched back into its inconspicuous state, and Lydia clenched her jaw as she watched. She still didn't seem to like the idea of modifying her order's sacred symbol.

"I guess we should head home, then," Taelien said.

"Not before I finish my drink," Lydia insisted, elbowing him as they stepped out of the back room. A smile had returned to her face, and Taelien mused that he liked her much better with that expression.

Later that evening, Taelien glanced at a piece of parchment nailed to one of the city's many announcement boards. It read,

In the name of Crown Prince Byron,

The bearer of the Sae'kes Taelien is challenged to fight for the truth of his gods in the Court of the Spear on the Ninth Day of Highwall at the fourth hour after the rising of the dawnfire.

Should the bearer of the Sae'kes Taelien be successful in this challenge, he will be treated as an honored ambassador and granted a boon of his choice.

Taelien smirked, attaching a parchment of his own atop it.

His reply read,

Challenge accepted.

CHAPTER VIII – DEFINITELY A TRAP

"Just so we're both clear, you're aware that this is obviously a trap, right?" Lydia asked, her arms folded across her chest.

Taelien shrugged, leaning back against the wall near the door to Jonan's kitchen. "Sure, but it also presents an opportunity. If I win, I can demand knowledge about the captive Rethri in a public area."

Lydia shook her head. "That's not a good strategy. They could just have the Rethri moved, or even killed. Or just deny knowledge of the situation. You have no proof. And Byron might not even know about the Rethri, anyway."

Jonan walked in, passing Taelien to lay a plate of steaming meat and vegetables in the section of the table.

"How'd you cook that?" Lydia quirked an eyebrow at Jonan.

"Magic," he said, waving his hands in the air in a seemingly meaningless gesture and retreating back into the kitchen for more dishes.

Lydia shook her head, switching back to a more important train of thought. She looked back to Taelien. "If you're going to ask for a boon, don't use it to try to publicly humiliate the local leaders. Do something friendly. Get on the inside. We can do more effective work that way. But that's assuming you can win – which, I'm going to be honest, I don't think is a very good idea to bet on. They have every advantage here; information, territory, numbers. We don't even know what challenge they will present you with. It certainly won't be fair."

Taelien grinned. "That's the type of situation I do best with. Besides, they're not going to want to kill me. I'm too important as a political prisoner, right?"

Lydia quirked a brow at him. "Um, no. Not at this stage. You've already escaped once. They are not likely to take that risk a second time. Moreover, an arena is the perfect place to have you removed – no matter how rigged the match might be, they can claim you died in honorable combat. If anyone tried to retaliate on your behalf, they will look like the villains, at least to the people of this city."

"Well, I suppose I'll just have to make sure not to die, in that case," Taelien tapped the sword at his hip thoughtfully.

He's enjoying this. Is he insane?

Lydia's lip twitched. *Velthryn's fate could hinge on his actions. I can't let him die in there.*

"You need to take this seriously. There's more at risk than your pride, or even your life." Lydia pointed at the Sae'kes on his hip, still disguised by Taelien's metal-altering sorcery. "If Edon gets his hands on that sword – publicly – there's a good chance it will lead to a war with Velthryn."

Taelien scratched at his chin. "You really think an army would march to war over a piece of metal?"

"It's more than that, Taelien. That sword is a symbol of a religion. And one I think you should take a little more seriously, given that there are fair odds you could be a figure in that religion's history if you survive long enough."

Taelien tilted his head to the side. "You don't actually think I'm related to one of your gods, do you?"

Lydia raised two fingers to adjust her glasses. "I don't know, Taelien. But the people of Velthryn need something to believe in – it's been years since one of our gods has appeared in person. Even if you're just a man with a sword, many will see you as a sign. You have a good heart, too. I could see people wanting to follow you."

Taelien leaned back further, resting his head against the wall and looking away from her. "I've led people before. It rarely ends well. If a religion wants to follow me just because I carry a particular weapon, I don't want anything to do with it."

Lydia scoffed. "Don't be so dismissive of an opportunity to help people just because you can't agree with every element of their reasoning. Maybe if you took the time to learn about the Paladins of Tae'os, you'd understand why they'd be willing to follow a symbol."

He turned straight toward her, his blue eyes focusing on her own with a sudden intensity. "Would you follow me, Lydia? Knowing what you know about my heritage, about my doubts?"

Careful, Lydia. Don't be impulsive about this.

"No," she replied. "But I could follow who you could be, if you give yourself a chance to grow."

In truth, Lydia considered, *I would rather be the one leading you. But you don't have to know that.*

Taelien sighed, throwing up his hands. "I think you're making assumptions about who I 'could' be based solely on an item, not my own background or personality. You know practically nothing about me."

"You're wrong. I know you carried a dying Esharen – who had tried to murder you – over your shoulders, trying to rescue him from torture. That speaks much for your character, and for your potential as a symbol. More than the sword. At least to me."

The swordsman looked away from Lydia, slumping his shoulders. "If you're basing your assessment of my personality on one of my greatest failures, I can't imagine you have very high standards."

Lydia pressed her lips together, biting back a sharp response. *He's still grieving,* she reminded herself. "I was talking about your intentions. You took a tremendous risk to try to help someone else. That's commendable. But if you don't like my example, give me a better one. How do you define yourself?"

He glanced back in her direction, but still refused to meet her gaze. "I don't really know. That's a part of why I'm here. People see the sword and assume that I'm some sort of demigod, or that I have the 'makings of a great hero'. I've spent my entire life living in the shadow of a god that I don't even know if I believe in."

Lydia quirked a brow. "I don't want to be cruel, but that explanation sounded like you define yourself by the sword just as much as anyone else does."

Taelien grimaced. "There's some truth to that. That's probably why I hate it so much when other people mention it. I won't have peace of mind until I know who wanted me to have this thing and why."

"And then what? You trade the expectations of the general populace for the expectations of whoever wanted you to have the Sae'kes?" Lydia asked, folding her arms.

Taelien shook his head. "I don't know. You've got a point – maybe I'm the one who's obsessing over the expectations of others. Maybe my past doesn't matter. But I feel like there's a piece of a puzzle missing, and

I can't rest until I find it."

Well, when you put it like that, I can see where you're coming from. Lydia's expression softened. She reached out and patted him on the arm. "Well, I'll keep helping you look for answers. After this is all over, I think you should come with me to Velthryn and see if any of the other paladins have information that could help you track down where the sword came from. In the meantime, try not to be too suicidal."

Taelien raised a hand, leaning his face into it. "I'll take your warning about this tournament seriously. If you really believe that other lives may be at risk, I'll take the necessary steps to ensure I minimize that risk."

Lydia nodded. "Thank you."

"As for later, I don't know if I'm going to want to meet with the rest of the Paladins of Tae'os. I'm doing this to help those Rethri, and I'll try not to start a war in the process. I'm willing to learn more about your paladins, but I won't make you any promises beyond that."

"I wouldn't have it any other way," Lydia smiled. "Being able to make your own choices is one of the tenets of Eratar, in fact. And Sytirans and followers of Eratar both have a strong proclivity toward educating yourself, even if it means doubting elements of your faith."

"Good," he said simply. "For now, I have more important things to educate myself about. If you're right that there is a real danger to my life, I should be gathering as much intelligence as I can about the tournament before I participate in it."

"You keep saying tournament," Lydia pointed out. "This won't be a tournament. It's not going to be a competition with brackets and eliminations; think more along the lines of a 'trial by combat'."

"Hrm. Have you seen anything like this happen before?" Taelien asked.

Lydia nodded. "It's very rare, but occasionally you'll see the Court of the Spear used to settle a dispute between nobles, or a trial where insufficient evidence is available. The accusing party will choose a champion and the terms, and the defending party will have to represent him or herself and accept those terms."

Taelien scratched at his chin, considering. "That doesn't seem very fair if the person being accused isn't a warrior. And if the accuser determines the specific terms as well, doesn't that mean they could offer something absurd?"

"Trial by combat is usually a last resort. The judicial system here is heavily influenced by politics – the priests of Xerasilis would hate it. The short explanation is that judges have nearly unlimited authority, and that trial by combat is one of few options the defense has available if the judge appears to be disposed against them." Lydia took a breath.

"That's essentially the situation you're in. Given how public this is, they have two options. One is to present something that outwardly appears to be fair, and attempt to humiliate you. The second is to put you at an overwhelming disadvantage – like to send you in without a weapon – and claim that the match is disproportionate due to the severity of your crime or your affiliation with the Tae'os Pantheon."

Taelien nodded in understanding. "What do you find more likely?"

Byron won't want to come across as weak, which means he won't do something that makes the challenge look impossible. On the other hand, he also won't want to give Taelien any chance of success.

"If I was in Byron's position, I would make the match look to be somewhat fair on the surface, but put you at a hidden disadvantage. Perhaps he'll have a sorcerer on the outside to interfere, or give your opponent a poisoned weapon," Lydia explained.

"You would do that in his position?" Taelien quirked a brow.

"I didn't mean it quite like that," Lydia sighed. "Essentially, I just mean that from his perspective, that's the best way of accomplishing his goals."

Taelien nodded. "All right. So, to avoid poison, I don't get hit. To avoid outside sorcery, I, hrm, don't get hit?"

Lydia frowned. "I'll talk to the court sorcerers prior to the match and try to determine if there will be outside interference. If there will be, I'll see if there's any way I can warn you in advance or counteract it."

"Thank you," Taelien replied.

"Are you certain you still want to do this?" Lydia asked. "Honestly, I'd advise you against it. You're putting yourself in Edon's power, and once he gets a grip on you, I doubt he'll release it."

Taelien narrowed his eyes. "Then I'll just have to break his hands."

Lydia felt herself smirk in spite of the absurdity of the response. *He's so arrogant. It's almost charming, in a way.*

Jonan finally returned with a stack of dishes, setting them down across the table.

"The kitchen try to eat you or something?" Lydia asked him.

"No, not this time," Jonan winked at her. "It wasn't hungry."

"Well, I am," Taelien said, moving away from the wall to take a seat.

"We'll have to talk about this more," Lydia pointed out. "We only have two days to prepare before the challenge."

"Don't let her scare you, Taelien," Jonan said, taking a seat. "She's just worried about you."

Taelien glanced over to Jonan. "Really? That's not the impression I got at all. I was under the impression she was more worried that I would trigger a catastrophic war."

"I can be worried about both," Lydia said. "But Jonan is right about one thing – you shouldn't worry. You should prepare."

"And let us help," Jonan offered. "I think I have a trick or two you might find useful."

Veruden pushed the plate of garlic-butter potatoes over to Lydia's side of the table. "Hey, we need to talk."

"About what?" Lydia asked, accepting the potatoes and picking at one of them with her fork.

"Someone left me a letter that says it's from that Taelien guy. The prisoner," Veruden explained.

Lydia quirked a brow. "What did it say?"

"Says he wants me to escort him into the arena, and to make sure there aren't any other guards on the way in, since I was nice to him before. He doesn't want to get arrested again. You think it's some kind of trick?"

Lydia shrugged. "Sounds pretty reasonable, actually. I wouldn't feel very comfortable in his position."

"Yeah, neither would I. I'm surprised he's accepting at all." Veruden stared down at his plate. "Do you think he's really some kind of criminal?"

"He was carrying a Tae'osian symbol, Veruden. That's against the law." She jabbed a potato for emphasis.

"I guess. Just seems a little extreme to put him through all this because of a sword."

Lydia smiled. "You've got a good heart, but you're a little too trusting. He wouldn't have that sword without a reason."

Veruden frowned. "What do you think I should do?"

"Hrm. I think it's a good idea to make this match happen, so if you have a way to enable that, it's probably good. Tell him you'll help. I'll come with you, though, and back you up in case he tries anything."

The younger sorcerer nodded solemnly. "Thanks, Lydia. You're the best."

She chuckled. "Don't worry about it. Besides, I've been itching to meet him. Have you heard anything about who he'll be fighting?"

The sorcerer laughed. "More like 'who haven't I heard he'll be fighting'. The rumors are running wild. Korin Matthews, Sophia Beaumont, Edrick Case, Velas Jaldin, maybe even Landen of the Twin Edges."

Lydia nodded, trying to keep her face neutral. It was easier than forcing a smile. *Those are almost all Queensguard,* Lydia realized. *And some of the best. I think I've heard of all of them before – and Velas and Landen are both champion duelists. I've seen Landen fight before, at least. Maybe I can give Taelien some advice if he ends up being the opponent.*

"That's quite a list," Lydia mused. "I wonder who they'll end up picking."

"Rumor has it that Edon will select the champion personally," Veruden told her.

Lydia blinked at that. "Edon is going to be there?"

"That's the word," Veruden grinned. "Exciting, isn't it?"

Lydia nodded, taking a fork of potatoes and chewing fiercely, thinking. *They won't need to have a sorcerer in the stands to interfere,* Lydia realized. *Edon could just do it himself.*

I need to be ready to counter that. But how? If I put a protection spell on Taelien before the match, it'll work on anything – not just Edon's interference. And they'd certainly detect it, and trace the spell back to me. That's no good.

"How's your hand healing?" Lydia asked absently.

Veruden winced. "Healing seems to have slowed down. Guess that ointment wasn't quite the cure-all Sethridge told me it would be."

Lydia nodded. "You have my sympathies. And my thanks, too – if you wouldn't have gotten that burn, I probably would have tinkered with the sword and burned myself."

"Better me than you, then," he smiled. "But if I took a burn for you, you can treat me to a better meal than this sometime."

"Deal." Lydia grinned.

Lydia stood with Veruden near the rear entrance to the arena, both of them wearing their formal robes. She saw Taelien approaching in innocuous peasant garb, but she initially ignored him. Veruden seemed to notice Taelien a few moments later, waving with his bandaged hand.

"That's him," Veruden said.

The sorceress nodded to him, resting a hand on her saber as Taelien approached, trying to look overtly suspicious.

"Thank you for meeting me here," Taelien said, reaching out with his left hand to clasp Veruden's own uninjured hand. Veruden clasped Taelien's hand at the wrist, smiling like he was seeing an old friend.

"Good to see you again," Veruden said, releasing his grip on Taelien's arm after a brief trust-testing squeeze.

"And who is this lovely creature?" Taelien asked, turning toward Lydia.

The sorceress barely resisted rolling her eyes. "Lydia Scryer," she replied, extending a hand.

When he knelt and kissed her hand, she did roll her eyes.

Gods, what a show off.

"It is my earnest pleasure to meet you, miss Scryer," he said.

"Good to meet you. Ready to fight?"

He stood up and nodded. "Naturally." He turned his head toward Veruden. "Have you made the preparations I asked for? I don't feel like walking in here just to get arrested again."

She glanced back and forth between the two men, and then back toward Veruden.

"Don't worry, I've cleared the halls up to the armory. We'll get you geared up, and then watch you from the stands." He paused for a moment, considering. "Didn't bring the sword?"

Taelien quirked a brow. "I thought you still had my sword?"

Not bad, Taelien. Not bad.

Veruden frowned. "I'm not sure on that, honestly. Maybe one of the older sorcerers has it."

Lydia shrugged. "I'm sure you can ask after the match is concluded."

"Yes," Taelien replied. "Of course."

Veruden led the way into the back entrance, and true to his word, the halls were empty of guards. They passed several rooms before stopping at an unlabeled door on the right side of a long hall, which Veruden unlocked with a key. The door was directly across from another hallway. Lydia glanced down the hall, noting an open doorway at the end of it – the entrance to the arena itself.

"There should be everything you could need in here," he said, opening the door.

"Any idea on who he's fighting yet?" Lydia asked, hoping for any last-minute insight.

"What, and spoil the fun?" Veruden said, chuckling. "No, I haven't heard anything. You can bet on the Queensguard, though."

Lydia stepped in the room, holding the door open as she quickly scanned it for enemies. There were no other people inside – no visible ones, at least.

"I need to go tell Edon that he's here," Veruden said. "Uh, Lydia, can you watch him for me?"

"Of course, I won't let him escape," Lydia replied with a grin.

"The match is set to start in half an hour. Someone will come get you when it's time. Good luck."

Veruden raised a hand to his right shoulder, giving Taelien some kind of unfamiliar salute, and then turned to leave.

So far, so good.

Lydia closed the door to the armory as Taelien stepped inside. "Dominion of Knowledge, illuminate the hidden!"

She scanned the room a second time, but nothing had changed. She breathed a sigh of relief, reaching into the pouch at her left side and retrieving a small glass mirror, which she placed on the left side of the room behind a rack of spears.

Retrieving a piece of parchment and a quill, she hastily scribbled a note and pressed it against the surface of the mirror.

At the armory. Clear so far.

She ran a finger across the mirror, following Jonan's instructions to send the message, and then removed the piece of parchment.

"Okay," she said, turning to Taelien, who was busy testing the weight of a sword on the opposite side of the room. "The guards should be here in just under thirty minutes. We have a brief window to plan."

"I think our plan is fairly well-established at this point," Taelien said. "I just need to find a good blade."

"Everything I've heard has indicated you're going up against someone from the Queensguard, which means they will likely be using a sword, a shield, and plate. You're probably best off with either a mace and a shield or a reach weapon, like a spear or a glaive," Lydia advised. She glanced back over at the mirror, seeing a different note showing in the surface now.

Acknowledged. I am in position in the stands, it read.

That was quick. She ran a finger across the mirror in the opposite direction, which would remove the frozen image of her note from Jonan's mirror and switch to showing the room. If they were lucky, Taelien's opponent would come into this armory next – and then Jonan would be able to see the opponent preparing and warn Lydia in advance.

Not that she could do much if Taelien had already left the armory at that point, but if Jonan observed something suspicious – like poison – Lydia knew she might have to take drastic action to save Taelien's life.

"I'm no good with a mace and shield," Taelien confessed. "Your logic is sound, but I think my odds are best with a weapon I am familiar with."

"You should have brought the Sae'kes, then," Lydia pointed out.

Taelien shook his head vehemently. "I thought you were the one who didn't want to risk losing it."

"Sure, but losing your life could be almost as bad," Lydia said with a wry grin.

"I'm flattered that you think I'm worth almost as much as a sword," Taelien said, hefting a different – much longer – sword. It was unadorned, and looked inordinately heavy.

"I think you're worth at least twice as much as that sword," Lydia said, pointing at the one he was carrying. "Just perhaps not quite as much as one that was forged through the collaborative effort of seven gods. I think that's fair."

Taelien shrugged. "I think you underestimate both me and 'ol rusty here." He lowered the sword's tip to the ground, a smirk crossing his face.

Lydia narrowed her eyes. "You can't seriously intend to use that thing. It's huge, unwieldy, and it looks like it's probably not even made of steel."

"Iron," Taelien said, tapping a finger against the pommel. "Good, reliable iron. Heavily used, but unbroken. Someone made good use of this sword once. Seems a shame to let it die on a shelf."

"Now who's getting overly sentimental about swords?" Lydia smirked.

But how does he know all that? Is he speaking figuratively, or is his metal dominion bond really potent enough that he can tell all that information just by touching it?

"From a practical standpoint, a lighter sword isn't going to be able to bust plate. Sure, steel would be superior, but they do not have any heavy steel swords here. I could merge two of them together, but it would be a considerable expenditure of sorcery, and I would be playing my hand early. I would rather my opponents – both in the ring and in the crowd – not have a good idea of my capabilities until after the match begins," Taelien explained.

Lydia nodded. "That's a better explanation than I considered, but do you really think you can incapacitate someone in plate with a sword like that?"

"Easily," Taelien said. "This isn't my first bout in an arena, you know."

"You mentioned you had sword experience, and I saw how you handled yourself with Istavan – but you never mentioned anything about fighting in a ring."

Taelien grinned. "I'm just full of surprises."

"You should at least put on some armor," Lydia pointed out, gesturing at stand where well-maintained leather, chain, and plate armor were stocked.

Taelien shook his head. "No, it'll just slow me down. If I'm fighting against an opponent who is wearing plate and using a shorter weapon than I am, I want to be mobile. I can try to out-distance him."

"How? You're still missing about half a leg." She pointed at his injured leg, and then moved her hands up to her hips to glower at him.

He shook his leg in the air. "Aww, it barely stings at this point. Sure, it'd be bad if someone hit me there, but I don't intend to get hit."

"You're going to be murdered if someone in plate manages to get on top of you, though," Lydia pointed out. "That's quite a risk."

"I know," Taelien grinned. "Keeps things interesting."

Lydia sighed. "It's been nice knowing you. Really."

"Don't look so grim," Taelien put a hand on her shoulder. *He's awfully affectionate*, she realized. *Maybe it's a Rethri thing.* "I have this completely under control."

Nothing to do but to try to believe him at this point.

And possibly try to cheat on his behalf, if necessary.

"We've got some time before the match. Do you want to spar a little?" Lydia offered.

"That sounds like fun," Taelien said, "But I think it's a little too late for that. I do have another idea, though."

He walked back to the weapon rack, picking up the next sword down the line in his left hand, lifting it up and down to test the weight.

"Checking the weight of all the weapons so you can know how much effort you have to put into your parries?" Lydia guessed, intrigued.

"Something like that," Taelien replied. "You'll see soon enough."

"You're going to tease me before you potentially fight to the death?"

"Is there any better time?" Taelien grinned, setting the sword down and picking up the next one.

The Court of the Spear was a colossal coliseum, made in the times of Xixis for teams of slaves to battle to the death. The floor was unforgiving stone, gray tainted with the faded red of blood from days long gone. While the court was still used for trials by combat, such events were rare and sparsely attended.

This crowd packed the stands nearly to overflowing. The rumors of a battle involving a 'demigod' had spread to the far reaches of the city, igniting the local imagination in a way that no simple court battle could.

And, of course, it was a rare opportunity to gaze up on Edon himself – the God of Ascension. Edon stood on a flat, raised platform, overlooking the stands and arena. Even high above, he cast an air of majesty that even Lydia could not refute. His bright blue robes were trimmed with silver, and his brown hair pulled back into an elegant pony tail. On his right hand, he wore a ring inlaid with a transparent crystal that glittered in the dawnfire's light. Only his eyes showed any hint of his age – no gray touched his hair, and only the faintest smile lines marked his face.

King of Orlyn's 'gods', what are you playing at?

Lydia took her seat next to Veruden. The two of them had a box to themselves – one of the benefits of being among the highest ranking officials in the city.

Nearby, Lydia could see several other private boxes. The Queen Regent herself was absent, but her son, the Crown Prince Byron, stood in his own private box, flanked by a half-dozen armed members of the Queensguard. At sixteen, he was easily old enough to rule as king now, but his face still glowed with the exuberance of youth. His flowing purple cloak, trimmed with silver, only added to that image, enshrouding the majority of his slender form like a blanket.

What game are you playing here, young prince?

She had only met the prince twice, and on each occasion, he had asked her intelligent – if uneducated – questions. *"Why is it that some people are born with magic, and others are not?"* he had inquired in one instance, but Sethridge had cut her off before she had a chance to reply. Sethridge's response – that it was the "same reason some people were born as princes" – had been hardly adequate, but she had not been of sufficient ranking to argue with him at the time.

Byron's position in the kingdom was an awkward one, and Lydia felt a twinge of sympathy for him. Orlyn was steadily developing into a theocracy, and his own mother was revered as a goddess – but he was not considered a god. Lydia suspected that was why he had not yet been crowned as king – it would represent a shift in power that would be disadvantageous to the local gods.

The mysterious figures that had been discovered near the prince's room in the palace just prior to his scheduled coronation could have easily been hired by Edon or even the queen regent. An assassination attempt was an excellent excuse for delaying the prince's ascension, and the fact that Myros had been the one to catch the "assassins" made it even more likely that the local gods had arranged the situation for political reasons.

Other nearby boxes were occupied by the high nobility, another group that saw their power waning in the face of the rising power of the Edonate religion. Lydia noted many of their eyes were on Edon, rather than the arena below.

"So, what'd he pick?" Veruden asked.

"Greatsword," Lydia replied, a twinge of distaste in her voice.

Veruden chuckled. "Seems like his type. Wonder how long he'll last down there."

"I wouldn't count him out just yet," Lydia said, surprising herself.

"Really?" Veruden quirked a brow. "I thought we were setting him up to fail."

"Sometimes it's not possible to set up the circumstances of a fight to guarantee one outcome or another," Lydia pointed out.

Veruden nodded. "I hear that. Still, I wouldn't give him very good odds. Oh, look, here he comes."

Taelien strode out into the arena to the sound of ten thousand cheers, his huge, unadorned greatsword leaning against his right shoulder. He still wore simple, unadorned brown clothing without a hint of armor.

He was limping, but just a bit. It might not have been noticeable if Lydia didn't know what to look for. She winced at the sight.

Veruden clapped along with the crowd, laughing at the same time, but Lydia felt her heart tighten in her chest. *Don't get dead, Taelien.*

He seemed to hear her thoughts, looking up from the arena floor in her general direction. She doubted he could see her from the floor below, but he waved — both to her, and to the rest of the crowd, which only caused another surge of cheers.

Lydia adjusted her pouch, slipping it onto her lap, ready to remove the second of the mirrors that Jonan had given her if necessary. She didn't want to use it if she could avoid it — Veruden would undoubtedly notice she was practicing some sort of sorcery, and she wasn't sure she could explain this one away.

She had discussed a number of different contingency plans with Jonan, but she hoped that they wouldn't have to attempt any of them. Every plan had its own risks. The most likely involved Jonan attempting to make Taelien invisible so that he could escape, but Lydia suspected that Edon would have ways of countering invisibility. If he was actually Donovan Tailor, he had been practicing knowledge sorcery before Lydia was born.

The door opened on the other side of the arena, and a figure in heavy plate armor stepped out, carrying a shield and blade, just as she had predicted. The crowd cheered as the knight raised his sword to Edon in salute, and the crowd continued to cheer as another figure followed the first into the arena.

Another armored figure, this one in chain mail, carrying a shield and a mace.

And a third, armored in plate, and carrying a shield and a hand axe.

And a fourth, helmless, carrying a pair of short steel swords, already drawn. He was young, but his unkempt brown hair and untrimmed stubble gave him a rugged look, and the crowd gave another surge of cheers as they recognized him at the same time that Lydia did.

Landen of the Twin Edges, champion duelist. And, Lydia understood as the three other figures fanned out to surround Taelien, *three other members of the Queensguard.*

Gods, Lydia stood up in her chair. *They're going to make him fight four-to-*

one.

The doors to the opposite end of the arena remained open, however, and a fifth figure stepped in to face Taelien directly. With silvery armor etched with golden runes and carrying a spear formed from an unmarred piece of steel metal, there was no mistaking Taelien's final challenger.

Myros, the god of battle, had entered the ring.

The crowd went silent.

He's not supposed to be here yet, Lydia considered, *but there he is. Sytira, forgive me for my arrogance. I should never have let Taelien stay in the city.*

"Challenger," Edon's voice resounded across the area, sounding as clear to Lydia as if he stood directly at her side.

Sound sorcery, Lydia processed absently, her mind too focused on the oncoming battle to worry about Edon's method of projecting his voice.

"You have proven your bravery to answer my call to the arena. You no doubt seek to prove the legitimacy of your gods. We will now test if your might matches your will. You now face several of the greatest warriors of this kingdom. Myros, the god of battle himself, will be the judge of your prowess. If you can survive to the satisfaction of Myros and myself, I will grant you freedom, the rights of an ambassador, and any boon within my power!"

Gods, he's not even trying to make this look fair. He's trying to sell the idea that the reward is worth the risk.

The crowd shouted encouragements, and Taelien made a slashing gesture with his hand. The crowd seemed to understand, going quiet after a moment of murmuring.

Taelien turned to Edon to shout a reply. "And if I defeat them all?"

Lydia looked down at Taelien, eyes widening. *Don't. That's...suicidal.*

The crowd's reaction to this was a mixture of clapping and laughter, and after a moment, Edon waved and silenced them again.

"If you can defeat all of your opponents," Edon said, "I will offer you the chance at a place in my own court."

Taelien gave Edon a formal bow at the waist, and then turned toward Myros. "Well, then. What are we waiting for?"

"The rules are simple," a voice came from Myros' armor, strangely distorted, and seeming to echo from the walls of the arena.

More sound sorcery, Lydia thought. *That could pose a problem – they could make Taelien hear phantom sounds, throwing off his combat reflexes.*

"Dominion of Knowledge, illuminate your sources," Lydia mumbled, scanning the crowd. Veruden glowed brightly to her right, and Taelien and Myros shimmered like stars in daylight. As she scanned the arena, she quickly found Sethridge and Morella glowing in another private box nearby.

And, as she gazed up to the dais where Edon stood, she realized that he was not glowing at all.

No aura of sorcery? Lydia pondered. *Is he shielded somehow? That's going to make it harder to notice if he tries to interfere with the match.* She shook her head, looking back down toward Myros.

"You may begin by engaging whoever you choose. Every two minutes, a new opponent will join the fight. If you can defeat an opponent in less than two minutes, that gives you a chance to rest. If you can survive for ten minutes, you will be deemed successful and given your boon," Myros concluded, planting the Heartlance in the arena floor.

One opponent immediately, one more every two minutes — that means up to five opponents. Even if he survives fighting the others, he's going to have to fight Myros. Maybe if he keeps his distance, he can shave down the amount of time Myros can engage him before the match ends. Assuming they even let the match end.

And Myros has the Heartlance, Orlyn's sacred artifact. They say any wound it inflicts will bleed forever, giving strength to the wielder.

Lydia raised a hand to her chest, not in pain, but in a fist. A salute.

Two minutes of battle against a god. You'd better be what I hope you are, Taelien.

"Sounds great!" Taelien shouted back, his powerful voice nearly inaudible due to the sheer size of the arena.

"Begin!" Edon shouted from above.

Taelien charged straight at Myros.

Oh, no.

Taelien's greatsword sang through the air, the Heartlance lifting to meet it at the last moment. A flurry of rapid slashes sent sparks flying from Taelien's rusted steel as it impacted again and again against Myros' weapon, every strike deflected with the smallest modicum of effort possible.

Lydia leaned over the edge of her box, transfixed by the display. Taelien lashed out from a dozen angles, each strike leading fluidly into the next, only to meet the unrelenting wall of steel each time.

Finally, after a few heartbeats of Taelien's assault, Myros struck back. A simple horizontal swing of the spear slammed into Taelien's weapon, carrying him backward with enough force to take him off his feet, sending him sailing backward twenty feet in the span of a breath. Myros followed instantly, dashing across the arena floor in a blur, spear poised for a killing strike as Taelien landed and began to slide across the stone.

The moment Taelien landed, he was swinging again, deflecting the Heartlance and stepping in closer, his blade touching the air where Myros' helm had been an instant before.

The Heartlance's bottom flew upward, forcing Taelien to side-step to avoid being smashed, and he brought his blade diagonally across toward Myros' gauntleted hand. The god of battle stepped back, avoiding the strike, and then planted the spear back into the stone, pausing.

"Unexpected," the voice said, a whisper that carried across the whole of the arena.

Taelien's reply was too quiet to hear, but it was followed by a flash of his blade toward Myros' right arm.

Myros stepped back, withdrawing the spear, and raised the weapon in something that looked like it might have been a salute.

"Second warrior, engage," Edon shouted.

That couldn't have been two minutes, Lydia considered, watching as the man with the sword and shield circled around behind Taelien to attack.

Taelien, seemingly oblivious, pressed his attack at Myros. A splinter of iron broke free from his blade as it struck the tip of the Heartlance, and Taelien stepped back, barely dodging a thrust aimed at his chest.

As the second warrior approached, Taelien spun and smashed his greatsword directly into the man's shield, causing an ear-ringing vibration and taking a visible chunk out of the wood. Grinning, Taelien danced backward, the Heartlance's point catching him across the right shoulder as he retreated.

Taelien stumbled back a few more steps, his left hand reaching across to press against the wound.

Lydia winced. *It's all over. A wound from the Heartlance will continue to bleed, no matter how much pressure he puts on it.*

With a shout, Taelien's hand glowed red, and even from a distance, Lydia could see a hint of smoke rise from Taelien's arm.

And then he was back on the attack.

Flame sorcery, Lydia realized. *He just burned his own wound shut. By the gods, how is he standing?*

Taelien's sudden resurgence caught the Queensguard defenseless, and Taelien smashed the steel sword right out of the man's hands. A moment later, Taelien was in close, slamming a fist into the man's face, and past him, shoving the plate-armored warrior to the floor.

The Queensguard went down, and Myros gave a nod, spinning the Heartlance and diving forward for another attack.

This time, Taelien winced visibly as the Heartlance connected with his blade, but he gave no ground. Myros grabbed the spear in both hands and forced it directly against Taelien's iron blade, pushing him downward toward the ground.

"Third warrior enters," Edon proclaimed.

And, in the moment of distraction, Taelien swept Myros' leg.

The warrior-god toppled to the ground, rune-etched plate flashing, and swung the Heartlance directly at Taelien's feet. Taelien jumped over the strike, then turned and raced toward the newly-incoming warrior, laying a horizontal slash into the Queensguard's shield.

Lydia glanced at Veruden, noticing for the first time that he was at the edge of the booth, leaning over it along with her. He seemed just as transfixed by the fight as she was – which gave her a window to act. Never taking her eyes off the fight, Lydia sat back in her chair, swiftly removing the mirror, quill, and parchment.

Taelien landed a single glancing blow against the shield, and another against the warrior's left greave. The axe-wielder's counterattacks were too slow, too short-ranged to catch Taelien as he danced backward, readying himself as the god of battle stood back up.

"Fourth warrior enters," Edon proclaimed.

This time, Taelien was the one distracted, gazing upward toward Edon, betrayal evident on his face. *It hasn't been two minutes,* his face seemed to say.

I know, Edon's grin seemed to reply.

Growling, Taelien spun on his feet as the Queensguard with the shield and mace began to advance. Taelien charged – right past the mace-wielder, and toward the Landen of the Twin Edges, the only fighter that still remained on the sidelines.

Landen gave a nod of acknowledgement as Taelien approached, catching Taelien's incoming blade a graceful parry with his left sword, and then trying a counter with the right.

Taelien blocked the riposte easily, taking a step back, and wincing noticeably as he landed heavily on his injured leg. Lydia winced along with him, watching as Landen raised both of his blades into a high stance, practically sitting the blades atop his armored shoulders.

The Lysen Tear stance, Lydia realized. *He's inviting Taelien to take a swing at him, gambling that he can parry anything that goes toward his exposed head, or trade hits if Taelien goes for a lower part of his body. Since Taelien is unarmored, Landen expects that trading blows would be to his advantage.*

Taelien smirked, nodded, and took a swing at Landen's feet. Landen hopped over the strike, swinging downward with both blades. Taelien caught both against the greatsword, then surged forward, shoving Landen back. Landen slashed as he stumbled backward, but his cuts met only open air.

Myros was approaching from Taelien's side, but the swordsman didn't seem to notice. Lydia grit her teeth, pressing closer against the edge. *I can't shield him from here, but maybe if I was a little bit closer...*

Taelien spun away, tapping the flat of his blade against one of Landen's weapons, and then rushed across the arena into an open space, leaving Landen with a perplexed expression.

Taelien's head scanned from side-to-side, taking in his four remaining opponents. Myros made a gesture at the three Queensguards, and they spread out at equal intervals, moving to surround Taelien and approach him at a steady pace.

Taelien planted the tip of his sword against the stone and used his off-hand to beckon for Myros to approach.

Myros didn't take the bait – the four opponents continued to advance as a group, while Lydia snatched one of her pre-written notes and placed it against the mirror.

Plan E, it read.

Myros surged forward, a wave of steel piercing a dozen places as Taelien struggled to dodge. A second and third cut landed against his skin, and Taelien fell backward, a perplexed look on his face as he backed up nearly into the stone wall of the arena.

Taelien gripped his blade tightly, taking flashing strike at Myros' midsection, but the Heartlance was there – and the bladed edge tore Taelien's rusted iron apart.

Left with half a sword, Taelien struggled to parry Myros' next strikes, each seeming to come faster – and harder – than the last.

Finally, the fourth strike dislodged the iron weapon from Taelien's hand.

Myros gave a nod and raised the Heartlance, preparing for a killing strike.

And the Sae'kes descended from the sky like a comet, trailing silver fire.

Taelien caught the still-sheathed blade in his right hand, spinning it in whirlwind of silver light, deflecting the Heartlance and landing a strike against the chain mail on the inside of Myros' right elbow.

Myros took a step back, stunned, as the crowd took a collective breath.

The scabbard of the Sae'kes, lined with metal, was sharpened into a blade. A blade now wet with the blood of a god.

Landen stepped in next, undeterred by Taelien's resurgence, but Taelien parried his strikes easily now, his weapon a blur of untraceable motion. Two, three strikes landed against Landen's plate, but none made a mark – and another Queensguard had stepped in behind Taelien, mace at the ready.

Taelien sidestepped to avoid the mace strike and rushed at Myros, but the god of battle had recovered quickly, and the Heartlance thrust forward to impale the incoming fighter. Taelien slapped the spear aside with the Sae'kes, never stopping his charge – and slapped his left hand against Myros' armor as he rushed past.

Landen's blades shot out of his hands, followed by the blade of the first Queensguard to fall, and the mace and axe of the other guards a moment later. All of them flew directly toward where Taelien had touched Myros' armor.

"What the...?" Veruden muttered, no doubt mirroring the thoughts of near-all the people in the stands.

Magnetism, Lydia realized. *Taelien's feints, each time he clashed against their weapons – he was magnetizing them.*

Myros was a tornado of motion, slamming each of the projectiles with the Heartlance, deflecting them harmlessly. As each weapon was knocked backward, the remaining Queensguard retreated to avoid being hit by their own now-flying weapons.

Orlyn's god of battle was not so easily deterred.

As each weapon boomeranged back toward Myros' now-magnetized armor, Myros smacked them aside seemingly effortlessly, advancing toward Taelien one step at a time.

Taelien fell back toward where he had entered the arena, a look of determination on his features as he leveled the still-sheathed Sae'kes in front of him.

Myros snatched one of Landen's swords out of the air and hurled it at Taelien, who obligingly dodged the strike. Myros charged as Taelien dodged the rebound, bringing the Heartlance downward in a heavy strike, too fast to avoid. Taelien parried, but the strike drove him back toward the ground, and Myros hopped over Taelien's attempt to perform the same sweep that he had before.

The Heartlance tilted upward, catching Taelien under the chin, flattening him against the arena floor with a thump.

Myros did not hesitate, plunging the Heartlance's point toward Taelien, but he rolled to the side. The point grazed Taelien's side and pierced into the ground.

Taelien's hand shot upward, grabbing the Heartlance and pulling it deeper into the ground. Myros grabbed the spear with both hands, lifting it – and Taelien off of the stone.

Taelien released his grip, tapping Myros on the armor with his hand a second time, and then shoved him toward the entrance.

Myros spun toward Taelien, thrusting the Heartlance at Taelien again, but the Sae'kes flickered and deflected the strike.

Then a spear flew out of the entrance hallway, arcing toward Myros armor –

Followed by two dozen other weapons and pieces of armor.

Myros swept the spear in a wide arc, and the entire audience could hear the god's sorcery-amplified curse. Weapons and armor shattered from Myros' strikes, but each piece of shrapnel simply boomeranged back a moment later.

Meanwhile, the magnetism gradually began to pull two of the remaining Queensguard across the arena, the intensity of the force now sufficient to drag them – armor-and-all.

Taelien continued to retreat, his off-hand reaching down to cover the freely-bleeding wound from the Heartlance's last successful strike.

And, Myros continued to spin and deflect each of the weapons, Taelien raised the Sae'kes to throw.

"Enough!" Edon's voice boomed.

The magnetized weapons clattered to the ground, and Lydia gasped as sorcery washed over her, triggering her Comprehensive Barrier.

Eru volis mar sharu taris.

The words were nonsensical to Lydia, but the effect was familiar – too familiar. *Counter Sorcery*, Lydia recognized immediately. *The ability to remove any sorcerous effect. The greatest Gift of Sytira.*

Edon had just invoked what she had only ever known to be the power of Sytira – and with greater effect than she had ever seen.

"No," Lydia muttered. "How?..."

As Lydia watched, even the runes on Myros plate flickered for a moment, as the god of battle looked upward toward Edon.

"The challenger has proven, beyond the doubt, that his might matches his bravery. He will be given a place as an ambassador to our court, and the boon that I have promised."

Taelien nodded, slumping to his knees, catching himself on the Sae'kes. Myros advanced on the fallen warrior, and Lydia gripped her sword, readying herself to vault over the rail – a forty foot drop - if Myros attacked again.

As Myros drew close, the god of battle thrust the Heartlance downward – anchoring it in the stone – and reached down with a gauntleted hand. Taelien clasped the gauntlet, and allowed Myros to haul him to his feet.

The crowd cheered wildly as the pair stood, each raising an arm to acknowledge the city's cries.

Lydia breathed a sigh of relief, releasing her tense grip on the handle at her side.

"Well," Veruden said, looking to her. "That was unexpected."

Lydia found Taelien in the now nearly emptied armory, a medic tending to his wounds. Landen of the Twin Edges was sitting next to him.

The sorceress was still jittery with nervousness. "Plan E" had been one of the contingencies she had hoped to avoid – placing the Sae'kes and Taelien in the same location was gambling at the possibility of losing both. The swordsman had proven to be worthy of the risk, but she still felt the mild echoes of panic at having made such a rash decision.

"Resh, boy, you gave me an embarrassment there," Landen was saying. "People are going to be talking about that fight for years to come."

"Thanks," Taelien said, wincing as the medic plunged a stitching needle deeper back into the skin on his left side. "You've got great speed and reflexes, but my sorcery gave me an unfair advantage."

"That's an understatement," Landen replied. "But you needed it. And if you had to prove something today, gods, you sure proved it."

Landen looked up, seeming to notice Lydia entering. "Ah, court sorceress. You catch all that?"

Lydia nodded. "Great fighting, both of you. Where are you both heading next?"

"Dinner, I think," Landen replied. "Edon wants to meet Taelien at the palace as soon as he's patched up."

"I'd imagine. That was quite a show. Do you two mind if I come along? I'd love to hear more about the fight from your perspectives," she asked.

Landen shrugged. "Up to this guy," he nudged Taelien, triggering another wince. "What do you say, swordsman? You want the sorceress to come to dinner with us?"

"Well, if you put it like that, I don't see any way I can refuse," Taelien said, giving Lydia an exaggerated wink. "Didn't catch either of your names, actually."

"Lydia," the sorceress replied, nodding to Taelien.

"Call me Landen," the other swordsman replied. "What about you? I've only heard them calling you the Taelien – which I guess is true. Reshing showy there. How'd you make it come out of the sky?"

"Trade secret," Taelien replied. "And you can call me Salaris."

CHAPTER IX – DECIEVING SIGHT

Jonan was exhausted and, once again, half-blind as he stumbled into his false bedroom. Maintaining his invisibility over two hours had taken a toll, and casting the spell to cause the Sae'kes to shine like a comet as he hurled it into the arena had added to that burden. He had rushed to a hiding place as soon as he had thrown the sword, abandoning the invisibility spell, but the cost to his sight had still been significant.

Still, he considered with a grin, *it was worth it. I just wish I could have seen Taelien's expression when he saw it falling from the sky. Or Myros expression – that'd have been even better.*

Throwing the sword to Taelien had been Lydia's emergency plan – and one that had proven to be more successful than he had imagined. On one level, he regretted parting with the sword – he could have simply left the city with it and come home to a cascade of promotions when he handed it over. That, however, was not his mission – nor what he cared about.

He locked the bedroom door and slipped the rug off of the secret passage hastily, eager to get to bed. The lack of guests was somewhat disorienting – Taelien and Lydia had been a near-constant presence for the last several days, and he had been getting used to them.

I hope they're alive, Jonan considered. *Lydia is playing a dangerous game, and Taelien isn't playing at all. He's just dangerous. Or in danger. Probably both.*

With a sigh, Jonan opened the passage down to his room. He had only taken the first step downward when he noticed a glint of glass in the wrong place.

Peering down, Jonan scanned the area with blurry eyes. Broken glass.

Everywhere.

Jonan half-stepped, half-jumped back up the stairs, kicking the trap door shut a moment later.

Erase image of self.

He rushed to his false bed, reaching into the pillow case of one of the bottom pillows and withdrawing a sheathed leather dagger. With that in hand, he moved to the cabinet nearby, opening the third drawer from the bottom. Four unlabeled glass bottles sat in the drawer; he grabbed the furthest on the left.

With the vial in his right hand and the sheathed dagger in his left, Jonan moved back to the trap door and pulled it open, hurling the glass vial inside. As the vial shattered, an inky black mist began to spread across the chamber. Jonan slammed the trap door shut, took a step to the side, and drew his dagger.

And then he waited.

Minutes passed, Jonan's heart rattling in his chest. Gritting his teeth, he eventually returned to the cabinet, retrieving the center bottle of the remaining three.

The smoke should have lined anyone inside, making them visible. If they have to breathe, they shouldn't be conscious at this point. Jonan flicked the cap off the top of his newly acquired vial and gulped down the contents.

With the utmost hesitation, he walked back to the trapped door.

Resh. Now or never, I guess. What would Vaelien do in a situation like this? Oh, yeah, he'd grab whoever was inside and pull the sorcery right out of them. Which I, of course, can't do.

I do have a knife, though, he reassured himself. *It's kind of sharp.*

He knelt down and reopened the trap door, the smoke from the room below rising into his chamber. *Hope this counteragent didn't expire, otherwise this is going to be really embarrassing.*

Jonan took a step down the stairs, tapping the right side of his head with a finger. The darkness seemed to flee from his vision, giving him a clear view of the room below as he descended.

The mirrors lining the walls had been smashed very deliberately – perhaps even artistically. One of the mirrors looked to have been sliced apart into over a dozen equally sized pieces, and another remained within the frame, a web-like pattern of cracks spreading across from the exact center.

Some patterns, if they existed, were more difficult to discern at a simple glance – especially given that Jonan was more preoccupied with finding the intruder.

Once, twice, thrice he glanced over the room – even tapping the right side of his head a second time to intensify his vision further. There was no sign of any intruder within the room. Either they were gone, or their invisibility far outstripped Jonan's capabilities at detection.

He did notice another peculiarity, however – an indigo flower, atop a piece of folded parchment that sat undisturbed on his bed. Gritting his teeth, Jonan glanced around the room one more time, debating retreat.

There was a clear path between the pieces of broken glass, leading to his bed. It was deliberate, though he couldn't be sure if it was left for his convenience, or so that the intruder could easily leave.

He walked the rest of the way down the stairs, drawing the dagger from the scabbard as he walked. Every two steps, he paused, jabbing the dagger at the empty air. It wasn't a certain way to find an invisible watcher, but he felt better taking some steps than none at all. His strikes met no resistance.

As he reached the bed, he swept the flower and note onto the floor using the edge of the dagger, and then flung the bed's covers to a side, checking if someone was hiding within them. Again, he found nothing – and an awkward series of probing attacks at the air above his bed proved equally fruitless.

With another glance around the room, Jonan spun and lashed out in all directions, and then ducked and swept up the note in his left hand, rushing back up the stairs to the floor above.

With a swift kick, he closed the trap door, breathing heavily as he slid the rug back atop it.

Well, he considered, *this is bad.*

The mirrors had not only been his primary means of surveillance, but also his method of communicating with his only contact in the city – an ally that presumably worked for the Order of Vaelien. His orders were to report to this ally periodically, and he or she had a mirror that matched one of his, allowing them to send messages through the mirrors.

How did someone find my hidden room? Was I careless?

He sat upon the nearby bed, setting down the dagger, scabbard, and folded note. A grimace crossed his face as he examined the parchment – it was clearly left for him to find, and it could easily be a trap. *Will this explode if I open it?* He had heard of a type of foreign rune sorcery that allowed for such effects; it wasn't all that dissimilar to what he had accomplished with his mirrors.

But the odds of the parchment being deadly were low. *If they wanted to kill me, they wouldn't have to be so flashy about it. They would have just had to wait until I came home and slit my throat.*

He grit his teeth at the thought. *Helpless again. Some things never change, I suppose.*

Jonan shook his head. *Thinking like this is useless. How'd they find me?*

His contact might have been able to accomplish it. With a matched mirror, they might have been able to use some sort of spell to trace the connection between the two. Knowledge sorcery, most likely. *Like what Lydia uses.*

Lydia had been in his home several times, and she had spells for detecting things that were invisible. It wouldn't be too much of a stretch to assume she could also detect enchanted objects – and he had told her about how his mirrors worked. He had even given her a couple of them.

Yes, he considered, Lydia could have found it. *Or my contact has access to someone with a similar skill set. Maybe Lydia is my contact, or working with my contact. But what would her motive be?*

Jonan shook his head. *I'm ignoring my best clue.*

He picked up the note, and, taking a breath, he unfolded it.

Meet me at the corner of Abigail and Morningway in the Commons at six bells after the nightfrost rises. —V

Jonan folded the note back up, grimacing. *Vague note is vague. Maybe that's what the 'V' stands for. Could have given me a description of who to look for, or —*

Jonan remembered the flower. The indigo flower – indigo like a certain Rethri woman's eyes. *Oh, bloody resh. V stands for Vorain. I just got played by a goddess.*

Picking up the dagger, Jonan shoved it back into its sheath. *Tonight, six bells after the nightfrost. That's not enough time to plan. Not enough time for my sight to fully recover – not even close.*

He lay back on his bed, thinking. *She must have followed me here after our fight. I shouldn't have assumed I lost her. Once she found the house, she could have investigated at her leisure. I can't believe I was so careless.*

But she didn't kill me – not when we first met, nor after she discovered my hiding place. She did smash the mirrors, though. Clearly that was meant to send a message.

It could be someone else – the 'V' and the flower could be a ruse. Unlikely, though. No one, aside from Lydia and Taelien, even knows that I encountered Vorain. Unless Vorain told someone, which is also possible, but if this was one of her agents or contacts it's effectively the same as it being her.

It still could be Lydia, trying to scare me somehow. She has sufficient information, but still no motive. Since it's probably not her, maybe I should go to her for help. That could tip me off if she's responsible, too.

But, if the intruder is watching me, going straight to Lydia puts her in terrible danger. They might have already seen me working with Lydia, they might not have. If it really was Vorain that went down there, I can't let her know Lydia is working against Edon — that puts Lydia at too much of a risk.

He sighed. Wish Taelien wasn't at the palace. *After handling one god, I'm pretty sure he could tackle another. I need to get that powerful someday.*

Okay. *Enough self-recrimination. Action time.*

Jonan sat up, contemplating his options and resources. It was time to make a plan.

Jonan sat across the street from Abigail and Morningway, wrapped in a blanket, a half-open bottle of whiskey at his side. An illusion wrapped him tighter than the blanket, producing false stubble, wrinkles, and blemishes on his clothes. He hunched forward, staring at seemingly nothing — but his gaze was firmly fixed on the point where his contact was supposed to arrive. Occasionally, his eyes would dart from left to right, scanning for anyone that approached him.

As he anticipated, most passersby kept their distance from him. Many avoided even looking at him. The smell of whiskey on his breath probably helped — that was real. Not only had he needed a drink, the odor helped add to his disguise. He didn't beg for money or mumble — he didn't want to do anything that might garner him any additional scrutiny.

He wasn't quite sure what constituted six bells after the nightfrost rose — the 'rising of the nightfrost' was a somewhat subjective time. He had decided to arrive about an hour before the dawnfire set, and sat watching the area with temporarily enhanced vision. His vision had recovered only slightly during the intervening hours, and maintaining both the illusion and his sight enhancement was a dangerous prospect. He knew he could cause himself permanent damage by straining his eyes too much, but he saw no better alternative.

The indigo-eyed woman arrived without fanfare about forty minutes after he had. She looked to be alone, and she still wore the violet robes of a court sorceress, dotted at the collar with three of the same spear-marked pins that Lydia wore.

Jonan glanced across her body for weapons, finding none that were obvious. Her voluminous robes could have concealed daggers beneath, perhaps strapped to her legs, or even sheathed inside her boots. From his vantage point, Vorain didn't look like much of a goddess. She shifted from foot-to-foot, glancing around the area as awkwardly as he had, and eventually began to pace.

After a few minutes, he felt somewhat sorry for her.

That girl broke my stuff, he reminded himself. *Don't be too nice.*

Still, he had to admit while he watched her, *she looks very...normal. Even with the indigo eyes.* That normalcy had a certain charm, given the madness he had been dealing with lately.

After a few minutes of pacing, the woman turned and looked as if she was debating leaving. He stood, discarding the blanket – he'd pick it up later – and walked across the street behind her, abandoning his illusion.

She turned around at the sound of his footsteps, taking a step back as she noticed him. Then her eyes flicked to the side of him, catching the discarded blanket, and she cracked a grin.

"Clever, hiding in plain sight. I expected you to be invisible, and I was checking for that." She folded her arms in front of her, her prior signs of nervousness fleeing from her visage.

"I do endeavor to keep things interesting, miss Vorain," Jonan replied, matching with a smirk of his own. "Now, how can I be of service?"

"Well, if that's the question you want to ask, you can leave the city," she replied. "Leave and never come back."

Jonan put his hand to his chest. "I'm wounded. After all you've seen me do, you can't think of a better way to put me to use?"

Vorain frowned. *That's good, keep her off-guard. Keep her guessing.* "You're offering to work for me?"

"I'm willing to entertain the possibility, given your credentials. I admit, I've never worked for a goddess before. It does have a certain appeal."

She beckoned to him. "Walk with me."

Jonan tensed. He had been much more comfortable staying in the same area, which he had already examined thoroughly. A walk could — and probably would — lead him into a trap.

"Of course," he replied, bowing gently at the waist. As he took a step toward her to follow, Vorain turned backward and slipped her left arm around his right, taking it as if she was escorting him to a ball. Jonan blinked furiously.

"We can't be talking about gods and goddesses out here," she said. "Rumors quickly take on legs."

Jonan raised an eyebrow at her phrasing. *Must be a Rethri colloquialism.* "All right, then. Where are we going?"

"You'll see," she assured him. "It isn't far."

"Lovely." He suddenly wished he had brought his dagger. It wasn't much, but it was more reliable than the two potions he had shoved into his pockets. He had left it behind to avoid looking like a threat, but given who he was walking with, he was beginning to regret that.

Vorain was truer to her word than he had expected — she led him to a run-down single story house about a block away. She led him to the door and turned the handle, shoving it open.

The entry room was about the size of Jonan's bedroom and near-empty. A small bed lay near the back wall, and a rickety-looking wooden table sat cross from it. The only other room in evidence was a tiny washroom near the back-left side of the room.

Vorain guided him inside, turning to close the door behind them. The wood of the doorframe was warped, resisting her push, but she eventually managed to slide the door into alignment and shut it.

"What's this?" Jonan inquired, glancing around.

"This," Vorain explained, "Is my home."

Jonan turned and quirked a brow at her silently, awaiting an explanation.

"When I first came to this city, this place was a blessing. I was just a girl, and a desperate one at that. My brother and I shared that bed," she pointed, indicating the bed in the corner, "For three years. I couldn't have afforded even this, but the owner was desperate to get rid of it. It wasn't a great neighborhood, you see."

Jonan nodded. *Must have been pretty desperate to sell to a young Rethri girl. I've only seen a handful of Rethri in this city, and they seem to keep to themselves.* "Why were you and your brother on your own?"

She visibly tensed, her expression souring. *Maybe I asked the wrong question.* "Hope," she explained. "My family had given up on him."

Vorain led Jonan over to the table, and she took a seat on top of it. She patted the side, inviting him to sit next to her. The table looked like it could barely hold even her weight, but he didn't want to offend her, so he gingerly took a seat beside her, trying not to put too much pressure on it. She finally slid her arm out from his, glancing away from him toward the wall.

"About one in every thousand Rethri is born without a functional dominion bond. As I'm sure you know, most Rethri are born with a tie to a specific dominion. You can tell which one by looking in our eyes," she said, pointing at her indigo orbs. "When we come of age, we undergo a ritual that strengthens the bond. This helps stabilize our health and slows our aging process."

Jonan nodded. "I grew up near Liadra, so I'm no stranger to the Rethri bonding process. I've even attended a few bonding ceremonies."

Vorain furrowed her brow. "That's rare. You're one of the Order of Vaelien, then?"

That's a trap of a question if I've ever seen one. "No, but I work with them," he replied, giving her a similar answer to the one he had given Lydia. It wasn't precisely untrue.

She nodded at that, seeming satisfied. "Is that why you were concerned about the children? Is this some sort of Order of Vaelien investigation?"

And an even more dangerous question. "Not precisely. Before I get into that, though, you mentioned that some children are born without a functional dominion bond. I've never heard of that before, and I've been around Rethri my entire life."

"It is a sad subject," Vorain explained, "Because the uvar – that's our word for unbonded – are usually returned to Vaelien immediately after they are born."

"Returned to Vaelien..." Jonan blinked. *Lissari is the giver of life to the Rethri. Vaelien represents preservation, but also death.* "You mean they're killed?"

Vorain nodded. "It is considered a kindness. The uvar never develop properly. In the old days, before they were 'sent back to Vaelien', the uvar usually died within a few years of their birth. Sometimes, extreme measures were taken to protect the children – but they would age rapidly and disproportionately, and no amount of sorcery seemed sufficient to repair the damage."

Things were starting to click together in Jonan's mind. "Your brother was born as an uvar."

The goddess nodded, raising a hand and making a gesture across her eyes. "He was. My mother died birthing him, and my father was crushed. I pleaded with my father to eschew the tradition and spare my brother. Elias – that's my brother – was mother's last legacy. Father didn't see it that way."

"So, you took your brother and ran?" Jonan guessed.

"Yes," Vorain said, resting her hands on her knees. "Yes, that's what I did."

She was brave, Jonan considered. *Saving her brother, abandoning her grieving father. I wonder how different things would be if I had been that brave when...*

"The reason I'm telling you all this," the indigo-eyed girl explained, "Is because I believe you wanted to help those children. I've watched you closely, and I think you're one of few humans I've met that would take a risk for one of my kind."

"And you want my help?" Jonan asked.

She shook her head. "No," she put a hand on his shoulder. "No, I don't need that anymore. But you're sweet to ask. I wanted you to understand that the children are going to be fine now."

Jonan frowned. "How?"

"When I ran from home, I chased a myth – a land where they claimed anyone could become a god. The gods, I believed, had power – the power to do anything. Maybe even save my brother. I was just a child, of course. I had barely gone through my own coming of age ritual when I ran away. I didn't understand the ways of the gods, or even the ways of people."

"Looks like it worked out for you pretty well, goddess," he said, cracking a grin.

She chuckled. "If only that were true. I'm still just Rialla Dianis, a girl trying to take care of her brother. Edon, however, is the type of god I needed. The type of god who cared."

Rialla Dianis? Like House Dianis, or the Dianis Arcane College in Velthryn? That explains some things. "So, you're saying the godhood is a lie, but that the idea behind it is good?"

"No," Vorain shook her head. "I'm saying that I'm not a god, but Edon is. And that he cares about people – more than any of the old gods seem to. He is working to save my brother, and others like him."

Ahh, that's what all this is about. Your brother is one of the kids in that hospital, and you'll do anything to save him.

Jonan considered that for a moment, thinking back. "Is Edon the older man I saw in that hospital? The one who goes by Raymond Lorel?"

Rialla shook her head. "No, but Raymond is a good man. He's the one who took me and my brother in – we had nothing when we first came to this city. Elias was deteriorating, and I had no way to stop it. I tried selling my sorcery skills – it didn't go well. But Raymond heard about me and tracked me down. He's a minor sorcerer himself – just stability sorcery. That minor talent was precisely what Elias needed. Raymond bought us time."

"So, Raymond is one of these court sorcerers I keep hearing about? I didn't see any pins on him," Jonan noted.

"No, he's not a court sorcerer. Just a man with a minor talent. My skills already exceeded his when we met, but I couldn't do anything about my brother, and he could. Raymond did have a few connections with stronger sorcerers – he introduced me to Sethridge. When Sethridge saw what I could do, he hired me immediately. Things got better from there – I met Edon and convinced him to help Raymond with researching Elias' condition," she explained, sounding exhausted.

"If Edon really is a god, why hasn't he fixed the problem already?"

"It doesn't work like that," Vorain explained. "The gods aren't omnipotent, and Edon is weaker than most. He ascended from mortality to godhood, much like the Tae'os gods supposedly did thousands of years ago. Gods learn and grow, just like people do."

"Sure, followers of Vaelien claim that he used to fight the Tae'os Pantheon – all seven of them – all at once. But, what makes this Edon a god, then? I mean, you're Rethri – don't most of you think gods are just powerful sorcerers?" Jonan quirked a brow.

"There is a difference between gods and sorcerers," Vorain explained. "And I've seen it. I've seen what Edon can do, and it's far beyond anything a sorcerer like us could accomplish. If I earn it, he promises he'll teach me someday, when I'm ready to control that level of power. But I have no illusions about that. No one shares that kind of power without a price. He might not ever tell me his secret – but he doesn't have to. He's doing good things with it. He's helping cure the sick. What more could I ask of a god?"

Jonan pondered that for a moment. *Okay, so she's convinced he's legitimate. And, I have to admit, that thing where he disabled all the sorcery in the arena was pretty impressive. But there are other explanations for raw power – that Heartlance that Myros was carrying, for example. Perhaps he's learned how to syphon power off from artifacts to cast spells. That could accomplish something on a similar scale.*

"Would you mind satisfying my curiosity and explaining what types of abilities Edon possesses that convince you he's a deity?" Jonan asked.

"I've seen him demonstrate things to me that are outside of the capabilities of ordinary sorcerers. I'm not going to tell you all about that yet – I still haven't decided you can be trusted," Vorain explained. "I've taken a terrible risk just by having this conversation with you, I hope you understand that."

Jonan nodded. "Sure, you could have just killed me while I was sleeping or something. I appreciate that you didn't. If you're not a god, though, why does he claim that you are?"

Vorain scowled. "I don't like it, but he promised the people of this city that they can become gods with sufficient work. He's had to give clear examples every several years, otherwise people would lose faith in him."

"So, he finds people who are supremely loyal – like yourself – to pose as his newly-ascended gods? That doesn't seem quite as benevolent as you make him out to be," Jonan insisted.

"He doesn't like it, either, but he hasn't perfected the process of making other people into gods just yet. And I think the queen is a real god, too," she said, the last part in a whisper.

Jonan perked up a bit at that. "Queen Regent Tylan? You think she's one, too, but you're not sure?"

That changes things, if it's true. I still don't think any of them are gods, but if he's managed to replicate whatever large-scale sorcery he's using in order to fake his divinity using another person, that means the threat is broader than I anticipated. Maybe he has multiple artifacts, or whatever he's using for a power source. What else could be used to power spells on the scale of what happened in the arena?

"I've said too much already. I suppose I needed someone to confide in, since I've been playing this role for so long. But you should leave, now. Get out of this city. Edon will take care of the children."

"Is Edon Donovan Tailor?" Jonan asked.

She turned to face him, her eyes digging into his. "Where did you get that name?"

Jonan slid back on the table, bumping into the wall. "He was a scholar in Velthryn that talked about people having the potential to become gods. His theories were very similar to what Edon claims to be possible."

"Why does it matter who he was?" She leaned closer to him, and his head began to feel heavy.

Resh, she's not just trying to intimidate me, she's using —

"Donovan Tailor visited Keldris about twenty years ago, offering godhood to King Haldariel. After he left, a group of Rethri disappeared. Edon visited Selyr about seven months ago, and similarly, Rethri disappeared afterward," Jonan rambled, unable to stop himself. He started to turn his head away, realizing what was happening, but she reached up and gripped his chin, turning his eyes back to meet hers.

"Stop trying to turn your head. Tell me more about the Rethri that went missing," she commanded.

Stop. She's controlling — "Over half a dozen Rethri were reported missing after what happened in Keldris. No clear connection between them; some young, some old, some male, some female. They were never found. Edon founded his religion about two years after that. After Edon visited Selyr, more than twenty citizens disappeared."

"There can't be a connection," Vorain muttered. "Why are you here?"

"Mostly to investigate the missing Rethri," he replied, gritting his teeth. "And I really wish you'd stop doing that."

The so-called goddess scowled. "I underestimated you again, but I need these answers. I don't like doing this to you, but it's the only way I can make sure you're telling the truth. I'm sorry. Who do you work for?"

"Vaelien," he replied simply. Vorain blinked, giving him an instant of control. *Blindness,* he thought, twitching a finger toward his face to target himself. Directly touching something was generally a more effective way of ensuring his spells functioned properly, but casting a spell on himself didn't strictly require anything other than concentration.

His vision went black - and Vorain's control faded immediately. He took no move to make this change evident to her, however. He simply kept his eyes open, sightless, and awaited her remaining questions.

"You work directly for Vaelien?" she asked, seeming taken aback.

"No," he replied, "I normally work for the Order of Vaelien as a scribe. I was employed temporarily for this assignment because I'm not actually a member, and the officer who hired me believed that someone from high up in the order might be working with Edon."

"What is the name of the officer that gave you the order to come here and investigate the Rethri?" she asked.

"Edmon Burke," he replied, making up a name.

"Were you sent here alone, or with others?" she inquired.

"Alone," he replied. That was truthful, at least. *I hope she doesn't move too much — if she does, my blindness will quickly become obvious. I'll need to turn my sight back on if I sense her shift too much.*

"Do you have any contacts within the city?" she asked.

"Yes," he replied simply.

"Who are they?"

"I don't have his name. I just send him letters through the mirror. We aren't supposed to know who the other is." Jonan's hand slipped down to his waist, inching its way toward his left pocket and the vial inside. He couldn't tell how obvious it was, since he couldn't even see himself, but he was getting progressively more nervous that he was quickly exhausting his usefulness to the indigo-eyed sorceress.

Vorain went silent. Jonan hesitated, taking a breath. *Is she just trying to think of more questions? Did she move her head?*

Resh it. Vision return.

Vorain was looking away from him, but she didn't seem to notice that his eyes hadn't followed hers. With luck, she had already cancelled her spell.

"You didn't have to do that. I would have answered you honestly," he said, trying to sound even more annoyed than he actually felt.

She shifted her gaze back over to him, but he didn't feel the twinge of her sorcery this time. "I have no way of knowing that for certain. And I needed to know the truth. I'm going to force you to answer one more question, and then you're free to go."

He gripped the vial in his pocket, but his movement was too slow — her eyes had seized him again. *Resh, should have acted while I had a window. I'm always too soft.*

"What did you think he was doing with the Rethri he was taking?" Vorain asked.

"Sacrificing them to extend his life span," Jonan replied.

Vorain gasped audibly, standing and beginning to take a step back.

Her control over Jonan faded as her head moved away. Jonan caught her wrist with his right hand, his left hand still sitting in his pocket, ready to strike.

"Now you answer a question for me. How long ago did Edon start gathering up those unbonded children?" Jonan demanded.

Vorain shook her wrist, breaking Jonan's grip. "Seven months ago," she said quietly. "It was my idea. More people to research, to help my brother – and others like him."

"And I take it you went with him to Selyr and helped him find these children? Maybe even helped convince the parents to send the children along with you?" Jonan guessed.

"He's trying to help them," she insisted, "You're wrong about him. He couldn't be using Rethri for that."

Jonan shrugged. "I didn't know about the unbonded when I came here. I doubt the people in the Order of Vaelien who sent me did, either. They just told me the most likely hypothesis they could come up with. Edon looks too young to be a human of his age, and Rethri have ways of slowing down their aging process. It seemed like a logical conclusion."

"Rethri coming of age rituals don't work on humans," Vorain insisted in a whisper. "It's been tried. Variations have been attempted for centuries."

"Sure. And I assume the 'coming of age' rituals don't work properly on unbonded Rethri, either. Making them more like humans." Jonan pushed himself into a more stable position on the table, musing.

"I admit he could have discovered a ritual that works on humans while trying to cure the unbonded," Vorain said hesitantly, stepping slowly away from Jonan. "That's not wrong. He needs time for his research. Using himself as a test subject for a life-saving ritual is no crime."

"No," Jonan remarked, "But what about the Rethri that disappeared from Keldris, nearly twenty years ago? They could not have been involved in this research. As you said yourself, you only suggested it five years ago."

Vorain folded her arms, looking down at the floor. "You're just trying to trick me. You're an illusionist, I should have suspected this."

"You're the one with the thought sorcery – neat trick, by the way. You can just ask me again with the spell, I'll tell you the same things. I won't resist." It was a gamble – if she asked him certain questions again, it wouldn't end well.

"You're wrong about him," she insisted. "Maybe he recruited some Rethri to help him in the early days, before he ascended. I wouldn't be surprised. As for his apparent age, that could easily be an illusion, like one of yours. Or, of course, he has divine powers now. None of the gods are supposed to age."

That last argument was hard to debate. If she was operating under the idea that Edon was an actual deity, and that deities had a way to stop themselves from aging, he had no way of disputing that premise. He had to undermine one section or the other, or he couldn't make any progress. "You said yourself that different gods have different levels of power. Even if Edon is a god, there's no guarantee that stopping his aging process is one of his abilities."

"I should have considered this before," Vorain mumbled. "I just assumed... Rethri adults don't visibly age, so it didn't seem strange to me."

"Help me find out the truth," Jonan offered. "If he's just trying to help your brother, that's great. I would be pleased to report that back to the Order of Vaelien, in fact, if you would let me." *Should I push further...?* *Yes, now is the time.* "Even if I leave," he risked, "Other members of the Order of Vaelien will come to investigate. If you can help me prove his innocence, I can prevent that."

Vorain turned away from him, presenting a perfect target. He itched to strike, but his hand slipped out of his pocket instead. "Please," he pleaded. "Between the two of us, we can verify the truth behind his claims. And," Jonan risked, "If he is hurting Rethri for his own gains, we can stop him."

Vorain spun on her heels, turning to face him again, her jaw tense with anger. "I may have made a mistake in bringing you here."

Jonan stood up, his expression calm. "No, Rialla. You chose to learn. That is never the wrong choice."

"If this gets my brother killed, you'll be wrong about that," Vorain said. "And you'll be dead."

CHAPTER X – THE VALUE OF A PROMISE

Never, Taelien told himself, *ever cauterize a wound with flame sorcery again.*

Each of his wounds ached, but the salve that the medics had put on his injuries – including the gashes from the Esharen on his leg that had perplexed the healers – had eased the pain from most of them. It had done nothing for his self-inflicted burn.

His concern that the wounds inflicted by the Heartlance would refuse to heal seemed unfounded. The medics had claimed that the salve was blessed by Myros, and that was what stopped the bleeding.

Blessed salves, sure, that sounds convincing.

Still, he was in a pretty good mood, in spite of the pain. He limped alongside Landen and Lydia toward the high palace, a place he had heard of but never visited. A half-dozen guards trailed behind them. Veruden had gone on ahead, claiming he had pressing business of his own to attend to.

"We're heading to Edon's own home," Lydia explained as they walked. "It's a rare honor to be invited there. He used to be more active in the kingdom, but he gradually grew more reclusive as more gods ascended."

"Isn't the palace where the rulers of the city should live?" Taelien asked, leaning heavily on a walking staff as he tried to keep pace with the others.

"Oh, sure, the queen regent is there, too," Lydia added. "I see her out in public more, though, so it's not quite as big of a deal."

"Must be nice to have the queen's ear," Landen remarked.

Taelien quirked a brow at the brown-haired swordsman. "Aren't you one of the Queensguard?"

Landen shrugged. "Sure. Ostensibly, we'd be her bodyguards. Thing is, she's a goddess. She doesn't need guards. If she ever did, she's got Myros. A few of us are always assigned to Byron. The rest of us are mostly just for show."

"I'm sorry to hear that," Taelien replied.

"Oh, it's not so bad. I mean, it certainly makes it easy to be successful at my job, since I don't actually have to do it." He chuckled. "Sometimes it'd be nice to feel necessary, though. Or to have a way to prove myself."

"Is that why you fight in the arena so frequently?" Lydia asked.

"Yeah, more or less." Landen cracked his knuckles as they continued to walk.

"I can understand that. I used to do the same thing. I was a kovasi fighter for years," Taelien explained.

Landen glanced over at him. "Kovasi? Isn't that a Rethri thing?"

"Yes, primarily. I grew up outside of Selyr. Kovasi was the local sport. It's a little different than the type of fight we just had, but many of the same tactics applied."

"Ah, well, I feel a little better knowing it wasn't your first bout," Landen said with a grin. "How's kovasi different?"

"Well, its team based," Taelien explained. "And different kovasi bouts use different territories. There is no clear arena. Essentially, two to four teams of six are sent to different places in the forest, given rough maps and non-lethal weapons, and told to hide a sigil from the opposing teams. To win, one team must gather the sigils of all of the other teams, while retaining their own. Matches would sometimes last several days."

"Wow. Several days out in the Forest of Blades? Isn't that dangerous?" Landen asked.

"Of course," Taelien replied. "That is part of the charm."

"How do spectators watch such a large area?" Lydia asked.

"They don't," Taelien explained. "Judges accompany each of the teams to observe and record. Once the match is completed, the teams reenact key moments in a performance for audiences."

"Like, you play-act things you already did?" Landen asked.

Taelien nodded. "Yes. It is not as difficult as it sounds. Rethri culture places a strong emphasis on honest communication and humility, thus you rarely see anyone wishing to distort the events that occurred."

"Humility, eh? Guess you didn't pick up all the aspects of Rethri culture," Lydia said, nudging him lightly. He winced – even the light touch briefly reignited the pain in his right shoulder.

"Indeed," Taelien muttered, attempting to ignore the pain. "I've always been better at winning."

"Hey, that's it up there," Landen pointed. Taelien's eyes followed his gesture, widening as he traced it to a broad spire piercing high above the city.

Taelien squinted, noticing tiny windows in the structure for the first time. From a longer distance, he had previously assumed it to be a mountain. "People live in there? It looks to be wrought for giants."

"When humans took over Orlyn, they wanted to prove that they could make something more impressive than what they had been forced to build as slaves. Thus, the high palace was built to replace the low palace – which had been the seat of the Xixian prince that ruled here," Lydia explained.

"Huh," Landen said. "I heard Edon made it."

Lydia shook her head vehemently. "No, the high palace long predates Edon's coming to this city. It was made through hard work, not sorcery. That is part of what makes it so impressive."

The trio walked in silence for the next few minutes as they approached the palace grounds. Taelien marveled at the pristine garden they passed through on the way, the cultivated flowers accompanied by statues of each of the four local gods and champions of the days of old. As they finished the journey through the garden, the cobblestone path met with a marble walkway lined with silver-etched stone columns. As Taelien glanced at each of the columns, he could see that the silver was some sort of tiny script, but it was unreadable from the center of the path where he walked. *Such wealth,* Taelien considered. *How many men and women could be fed for what these marvels cost?*

Four soldiers clad in polished mail saluted firmly as the trio approached. They stepped aside as the gate swung open, apparently controlled by some sort of internal mechanism. Lydia took the lead, apparently familiar with the location, while Landen and Taelien trailed behind.

"You come here often?" Landen asked toward Lydia.

"I used to work here," Lydia replied. "When I was first hired as a court sorceress, I stayed here for two months before being reassigned to the lower palace when one of my predecessors retired."

"Ah, that makes sense," Landen replied. "You're lucky, I'd love to have spent that much time here."

Lydia shrugged. "It's not the same when you're working."

The Queensguard gave an understanding nod.

I really need to isolate Lydia so we can discuss a plan, Taelien thought. His injured leg was starting to itch, but he resisted the urge to reach down and scratch at it. *This has gone far beyond what we previously discussed.*

Another group of four guards approached their group moments after they stepped onto the purple carpet of the palace. Their leader wore a gold-etched breastplate, and Landen brought his right hand to his left shoulder in a salute as the man approached.

"Captain," Landen said, freezing in his step.

The leader lazily returned Landen's salute, and then raised his other hand to wipe the sweat off his brow.

"Congratulations," he said, not sounding very congratulatory. "The bunch of you get to come with me. Edon is waiting this way."

Taelien shot Lydia a questioning look, but she only shrugged at him, falling into step behind the new group of guards.

Taelien glanced behind him, noting that not only were the six guards from the arena following them, so were the four that had been positioned at the palace door.

Ten behind us, Taelien considered. *Four in front. And Landen within striking range.*

They passed three more pairs of guards as they marched down softly carpeted halls, but these additional guards didn't join the procession. Taelien wasn't sure if he should be comforted by that fact or not.

As they passed a pair of intersections, Lydia's expression shifted into a slight grimace. Taelien noted a long, spiral staircase on their right side just past the second intersection, which Lydia glanced at as well. Landen's expression seemed cheerful, as if nothing was amiss. That probably meant that either he was unaware of any pending treachery, or he was simply pleased to be a part of it. Neither thought was particularly reassuring.

What are the odds that they know Lydia is working for the Paladins of Tae'os? Taelien considered. *I really shouldn't have accepted Landen's idea to bring her along. Granted, having an extra sword would be handy in my current condition, but I wouldn't want Jonan to have to rescue both of us later. Assuming there would be anything left to rescue.*

The guard captain with the gold-trimmed breastplate led the group to a third intersection, at which point he led the group to the left. Lydia slowed her pace, moving to a position directly at Taelien's right. The others didn't seem to notice.

The front guards paused at a rose-colored door, taking positions to either side of it. "This way," the captain said, knocking twice on the door and stepping to the side of it.

The door opened from within, a tall blonde-haired man standing within, the Heartlance resting comfortably in his left hand. He was wearing a short-sleeved white shirt and gray trousers.

"Ah, please, come in!" he said, sounding jovial, almost boyish.

"Thank you, Lord Myros," Landen said, raising his right hand to his left shoulder and bowing at the waist. Lydia made the same gesture, surprising Taelien for a moment.

Should I do the same? Probably.

He chose not to.

"Thanks," Taelien replied, stepping inside the open door. He gaped at the display of food within – half a dozen chefs bustled around a table set for ten, laying out steaming platters of a dozen exotic dishes. Even from the entrance, Taelien could smell garlic, onion, and the distinct aromas of cooked beef and chicken.

A single figure sat at the head of the table – the one who had stood on the dais above the arena, shouting downward. *Edon.* He somehow managed to look just as tall while seated as he had while looming over the arena – but it was a trick of presence, not of light. Edon seemed to emanate an almost palpable sense of confidence.

The god of ascension motioned for Taelien to come forward, a crystal-inlaid ring on Edon's right hand sparkling brightly, and Taelien approached without hesitation.

"Where should I sit?" Taelien asked, gesturing at the empty chairs surrounding the table.

"You're our guest, sit wherever you'd like," Edon replied.

Taelien walked past another pair of guards that stood on the inside of the doors – noting that these guards were wearing full plate, including helms – and took the seat to Edon's left. It was a position of challenge in Rethri culture – it meant that he could draw his sword directly into an attack. He wasn't sure if Edon caught the meaning behind it; the local culture likely had different standards.

Edon only smiled benevolently, waving for the others to approach. "Please, Landen, Sorceress Lydia, Myros, come join us."

Taelien glanced around, looking for the other combatants, but he could see no sign of them. "Will the other Queensguard be attending?"

"No," Edon replied, "I only invited those who impressed me in the match. And the young sorceress seems to have invited herself," he pointed out. Lydia tilted her head to the side quizzically. "Which also impresses me. You are welcome to stay," he quickly added.

Lydia nodded. "Thank you, Ascended," she replied, bowing and saluting as she had with Myros. Taelien hadn't heard her use that term for Edon before, but he assumed it was probably the man's formal courtly title.

The man with the Heartlance took a seat at Edon's right, directly across from Taelien, just as Taelien had hoped. As Taelien nodded to the blonde man, he noted an oddity when he saw the inside of the spear-bearer's exposed right elbow.

No wound, not even a scar. Even a life sorcerer couldn't heal something so perfectly so fast. Maybe the Heartlance helps him heal faster... But he's a hint too tall, too, even if he's slouching to cover it. This isn't the same Myros I fought in the arena. Still, I'd better act like he is.

Landen sat down next to Taelien, and Lydia next to "Myros". That was mildly awkward – he would have felt better with Lydia at his side – but he admitted it was a good tactic on Lydia's part. If the new Myros took any violent action, Lydia would be close enough to interfere.

"Please," Edon said, "Help yourself to the food. There will be plenty of time to discuss business after we've eaten our fill.

Taelien nodded gratefully, slipping a plate of beef toward him without hesitation. If they wanted to kill him, poisoning the ointment they put on his wounds would have been much more efficient than trying to poison the food for a table with several others.

Seeing Taelien take the lead, the others quickly began to pick at other plates. Chefs came around and left glasses of deep red wine for each guest. *These,* Taelien considered, *would be much more practical to poison. But I don't think they're going to try to off me so soon – it would look too suspicious.*

He took a sip, and it certainly didn't taste like poison. Not that he had much experience to compare it to.

"I have to ask," Taelien began, turning to Edon with a goblet in his hands, "Why the fixation on my presence in the city? I didn't come here

197

to cause any trouble."

"Your capture was a simple misunderstanding," Edon offered. "If I had been apprised of your arrival in the city, I would have offered you diplomatic freedom immediately. Unfortunately, as you are no doubt aware now, we have strict laws against wearing Tae'os-related symbols in public. I sincerely doubt the guards who arrested you had any concept of who they were dealing with."

Taelien nodded. "That makes sense," Taelien replied. "I'm not particularly familiar with the history behind your city. I was just coming here to visit someone. Why do you have such strict laws about Tae'os worship?"

"It usually doesn't come to an arrest," the not-Myros offered. "But we have to be careful not to allow Tae'os followers to propagate the old faith here."

"Why is that?" Landen asked, surprising Taelien. Everyone turned to look at Landen, with Edon seeming to notice the man for the first time. "I mean, they're mostly harmless, aren't they? Believe in life and freedom and such?"

"Some sects have historically been much more violent than others," Edon explained. "But violence is not the primary concern. I cannot tolerate the spread of ignorance in my city. The Tae'os Pantheon may have existed at one point – perhaps they still do. But they are no longer active in the world, and therefore no longer worthy of worship. Their religion misleads people into believing that these gods look after them, guide them, give them strength. That is no longer true."

"The laws are for the protection of the people, Landen," Lydia explained, drawing a half-raised eyebrow from Taelien. "Old god worship prevents people from looking for real, practical solutions to their problems. They might stand over a sick man and pray to Lissari, for example, rather than seeking the aid of a doctor – or of the very real gods of our city."

"I suppose that makes sense, throwing them in irons just seems a bit harsh," Landen replied, jerking a thumb at Taelien. "I heard from Veruden that they put him in chains. In the Adellan Room, no less. Where is Veruden, anyway? Thought he was coming."

Lydia glanced from side to side, frowning, apparently also processing Veruden's unexpected absence.

"Again, it is unfortunate that actions were taken against our honored guest," Edon waved to Taelien, "Without my knowledge or consent. We have no laws that instruct anyone to bind Tae'os followers in chains. Typically, Tae'os-related symbols are simply confiscated, and the followers are educated and sent on their way."

Taelien remembered that someone – maybe Lydia? – had mentioned that Tae'os followers typically weren't treated harshly, and that his case was unusual. And, of course, Lydia had explained that he was going to be executed if he hadn't escaped.

"I take no offense," Taelien said, waving a hand dismissively in the air, turning back to Edon. "I understand that you were not involved in my arrest. That said, I would like to see measures taken to ensure nothing similar happens again."

Edon raised a hand to his chin. "Hrm. Is that what you're asking for as your boon, then? A change in the laws, to protect Tae'os followers from abuse?"

Taelien shook his head. "No, I'll request that as a part of my new position as an ambassador. The boon will come later."

Edon smiled warmly. "Very good. I would hope you wouldn't squander your prize on something as simple as that."

Squander? It would only be squandering the boon because you would not act on it in good faith. If anything, any abuses would simply be more secretive. I'm sure they will be either way, given how public this incident was.

Taelien picked up a cutting knife and began to slice his beef into roughly equally sized pieces, considering. *What should I ask for? What would give me leverage?*

I could ask for the Heartlance, he considered. *It is 'within his power' to give it to me. But I'd risk grave offense. The type of grave offense that would put me in the grave, most likely.*

"You were very open-ended about this 'boon' you offered," Taelien pointed out, still cutting his meat. "What are the exact terms?"

"Ah, an excellent question. The boon must not violate any of our laws, create any kind of threat to the kingdom, or tax our resources in a way that would threaten the lives of the people of the city," Edon explained, leaning forward across the table to pull a plate of bread toward him. The gesture seemed oddly disjointed from his lordly bearing.

"All reasonable restrictions," Taelien said, nodding.

"You can have some time to consider it," Edon offered. "In fact, I would be pleased for you to remain at the high palace as my guest. I believe we could learn a great deal from each other."

Taelien quirked a brow at that. "I am honored by the offer, but I fail to see what knowledge I could offer you. I'm just a swordsman."

Landen and not-Myros both scoffed at that. "You are hardly 'just a swordsman', Taelien. I haven't had a fight like that in ages," the Myros said.

You haven't had a fight like that at all, Taelien thought, but he forced a grin. "You flatter me. I know I could not have won an extended exchange. I was forced to resort to dubious tactics," Taelien offered, trying to sound more humble than he actually felt.

"Dubious or not, they sure worked," Landen said, putting a hand on Taelien's shoulder. "You ever feel like doing a team bout, you come to me first."

Taelien turned and nodded to Landen. "I'd like that, actually. I regret not having a chance to see more of your Lysen Tear style."

Landen nodded. "I'm sure we can set something up in the future."

"Another bout with you in the arena would be certain to draw a great crowd," Edon offered. "You were quite impressive today. We could arrange for you to demonstrate your skills again, perhaps to raise funds for a cause of your choice."

Taelien pondered that. *Another chance for them to try to off me in the ring,* he considered, *but that might be too blatant. Perhaps he just wants to use my reputation to make his city look better. Making me a local champion helps detract from any stories that I was initially mistreated, and it would even help make it look like he's being very reasonable about the Tae'os Pantheon.*

Or, Taelien considered, *it might even look like the Tae'os Pantheon has a presence here. And that it works for, or with, him.*

"I'll have to think about it. Truth be told, I probably need a few days to recover before I make any serious decisions." Taelien laughed, and the others laughed along with him.

"Yeah, you took a bit of a beating there," the Myros said in a friendly tone. "But that's to be expected, given that it was five on one."

"He evened out those odds pretty well, I'd say," Landen groaned. "How'd you do that trick with pulling away all of our swords?"

Edon seemed to turn his gaze more intently toward Taelien in response to Landen's question.

"Trade secret," Taelien replied with a grin. "Maybe I'll teach you someday."

"Don't make promises if you're not going to keep them," Landen replied with a grin.

"Not a promise," Taelien amended, raising his hands in a warding gesture. "Just a possibility. It depends on how long I'm in the city."

"Well, I believe we can all agree that you would be welcome for a long stay," Edon offered, taking a bite of a hunk of brown bread. Still chewing, he turned toward Lydia. "You're awfully quiet, sorceress."

"I am simply overwhelmed in such august company, Ascended," Lydia replied, bowing her head slightly.

"Resh, I don't remember you being so timid when I brought you on as a sorceress," Edon said, waving his bread-carrying hand. "Tell us, what do you think Taelien should ask me for his boon?"

Lydia quirked a brow, turning to Taelien, and then back to Edon. She raised two fingers, pushing up her glasses. "Well, if I was in his position," she said, sounding as if she was pondering aloud, "I would ask you to make me a god."

A broad smile slid across Edon's face. "Ah," he said, setting his bread down. "Now that's more like the sorceress I remember. A brilliant idea, and ambitious. Strictly speaking, it would not violate any of my conditions. Somehow, I doubt it would be to his style-"

"Very well, make me a god," Taelien said. "That is the boon I require."

I was planning to ask for help finding Erik Tarren, but there's a good chance Edon is one of his enemies if Tarren was working with Tae'os followers. This could get me more information, and more power, if it's actually true.

Edon turned to Taelien, tilting his head to the side, chewing for another moment and then swallowing. "Interesting." He paused. "Very interesting. I would not have expected that." Edon glanced to Lydia, and then back to Taelien. "Very well, then. That particular boon has a condition, however."

"You'd really consider that, master?" the Myros asked, shooting a quizzical glance at Edon. Landen seemed to have fallen silent for a change, glancing rapidly between Taelien and Edon.

Edon waved a hand dismissively at the Myros. "I offered him any boon within my capability. Godhood is not simple to obtain, as you already know." He turned to Taelien. "I can't simply snap my fingers and make you a god," he explained. "But I can put you on the path, and offer my help."

"Accepted," Taelien said. "When do we start?"

"As you accurately pointed out, you probably should take some time to rest before doing anything taxing. And, I assure you, the tests of godhood will be taxing." Edon place his elbows on the table, looking straight at Taelien. "There will be considerable danger – both failure and death are possible."

Tests of godhood. That seems like a great time for him to try to get rid of me.

Taelien glanced at Lydia, but her expression was neutral. He looked back to Edon. "I will take some time to prepare for these challenges, then. Perhaps your champions," he indicated Landen and Myros, "Or even your sorceress could help me prepare."

"You will be given all the resources you need," Edon assured him. "But you must understand this – if I help to make you a god, you will be a god of this city. Dedicated to this city, and its protection. Those are my terms."

"I have no objection to that," Taelien replied, turning to Lydia too late to catch the trepidation in her features. A knock sounded on the door a moment later, causing all the people present to turn.

"Open," Edon said, and the door swung open, seemingly of its own accord. A thin, lanky-looking young man stood in the doorway, looking nervous.

"I, um, am so sorry to bother you. The queen – er, Queen Regent Tylan – has requested Lydia," he stammered.

"Go ahead, sorceress," Edon offered. "You can dine with us again another night."

Lydia turned to Edon, putting down her food, and gave him another bow and salute. "Thank you, Ascended. I will look forward to it."

She pushed herself away from the table, giving Taelien one final look, and pleading with her eyes for him to be careful.

I'm always careful, he said with his return glance and a half-grin. *Especially when I'm charging right at my enemies.*

Lydia gave a bow and salute to the Myros, nodded to Landen, and retreated from the room.

CHAPTER XI – NECESSARY PRECAUTIONS

Lydia followed a pair of guards toward the queen regent's sitting room, swallowing her nervousness. She still had her Comprehensive Barrier spell active in case of emergencies, but she was more worried about Taelien's situation than her own. He was isolated now, amongst any number of potential threats – and in spite of his obvious combat prowess, she doubted his chances against Edon and Myros together.

What is he? Lydia pondered as she followed along familiar corridors. *And what do I need to do to protect him?*

Mentioning godhood as a boon had been a gamble – she hadn't expected him to accept. Now, they had placed Edon in an even more precarious position than before. He'd have to deliver his promise to Taelien or find a way to remove the swordsman from the equation quickly and quietly. Like right now, for instance.

The sorceress shook her head, dismissing those foreboding thoughts as she arrived at the door to the queen regent's room. Tylan would have her own agenda, and Lydia didn't have time to worry on Taelien's behalf at the moment.

The guards abandoned her at the door, presumably having only been ordered to escort her that far. Lydia knocked politely. It was hardly her first time visiting the queen regent, but she hadn't been back to the high palace in several months.

"Come in, dear," came Tylan's voice from inside. Lydia twisted the door handle and stepped in, sweeping her sword out of the way to prevent it from knocking against the wood.

The queen regent was sitting in a large chair behind her work desk, inspecting the top of one of the piles of papers on her desk. Her garb was simple gray and white, her face marred by many years of worry lines. If Lydia didn't know the woman, she might have assumed her to be a secretary, rather than the current ruler of the kingdom.

The chamber was simple enough, with broad curtains blocking out the light from the single window and a lit fireplace in the corner providing the only major source of illumination. Three other chairs sat opposite the queen regent, but none of them were currently occupied.

A quick glance from side-to-side told Lydia that there was no one else in the room – at least no one else that was visible. Her instincts told her to check for hidden attackers, but tact overruled her uneasiness. Casting a spell immediately on entering would probably come across as both rude and paranoid.

"Queen Regent," Lydia said politely, bringing her right hand into a salute.

"Close the door behind you," the queen regent said, waving a hand.

Lydia turned and closed the door, feeling even more isolated.

"Come sit down."

Lydia followed the order quickly, taking a seat in the center of the three chairs across from the queen regent. Tylan looked up immediately as Lydia sat, shifting her stacks of paper aside and looking straight at the sorceress.

"I have a task for you, Lydia," Tylan said, steepling her fingers on the table.

Lydia nodded. *An odd time to ask for something, but not that strange, I suppose. She's given me orders before.* "What do you need?"

The queen regent reached to another pile of papers on the table, split the stack, and immediately retrieved a paper from the top. She flipped it around to face Lydia and passed it across the table.

"There's a caravan leaving the city in two hours. They'll be waiting at the address at the top of that page. You're to hand that paper over to the captain of the caravan's guards, Korin Matthews. You'll note my seal at the bottom."

Lydia quickly glanced over the page, noting a wax seal at the bottom with the symbol of a harp. The page instructed that Lydia was to take command over the caravan in the case of attacks by enemy sorcerers. She looked back up at the queen quizzically.

"Problem?" the queen regent asked.

"No, queen regent. Why are you expecting an attack on the caravan by sorcerers?" Lydia rested her hands in her lap, contemplating.

"There have been some peculiar rumors about foreign sorcerers working within the city. Your presence will merely be a precaution," the queen regent said with a soft smile.

Foreign sorcerers? Wait, are those rumors about me? Or Jonan, perhaps?

"May I bring some additional support with me, in that case? Court Sorcerer Veruden, perhaps?"

Tylan shook her head. "That won't be necessary. I'm sure you'll be quite capable of handling any incidents by yourself."

Lydia allowed herself to frown. "And the caravan is leaving in two hours? I'll barely have the time to make it to the gate by then."

"You'd better get running, then. Is there anything else?"

Lydia read over the paper again. "It doesn't say anything about what this caravan is carrying."

"No," the queen regent replied. "It doesn't. There are six wagons. Their cargo is all very valuable. The third wagon from the front is carrying an ambassador from Selyr. The caravan is his. He needs to leave immediately, and he needs to survive the journey to Coldridge. Once you get him there, you can return home. Any trouble should occur before that point."

The sorceress quirked a brow. "Would you mind divulging the source of these 'rumors'? It might help give me some context for making the necessary defensive preparations."

The queen regent waved a hand dismissively. "I have my resources, dear. Just be careful. I wouldn't want anything unfortunate to happen to you."

"Thank you," Lydia said, trying to sound as sincere as possible. *Sometimes I hate this job.*

Lydia pressed a newly-written note against the mirror in her pouch. *Away on queen's business for a few days,* it said. With business attended to, she followed the queen regent's directions to the location of the caravan.

"Korin Matthews?" Lydia inquired, noting a man in front of the caravan wearing a gold-trimmed silver breastplate. He was shorter than most of the Queensguard, but he looked very athletic, and he wore a flanged mace on his left hip.

"That's me," he said, turning around toward her. He looked startled when he faced her, taking a step back. "A sorceress? What can I help you with?"

"Looks like I'm coming along with you for the ride," she said, handing him the wax-sealed letter.

"Huh," he said, reading it over. "I hadn't heard anything about this, but I'm not one to argue with a sorceress. Or the queen, of course. 'Sorcerous support'? What's that mean, precisely?"

She leaned over to whisper to him, "Means we're probably going to be attacked. Possibly by another sorcerer, actually. Keep three eyes open, yeah?"

He leaned back and nodded to her solemnly. "You can count on me, miss sorceress. Let me go tell the other guards."

She snagged his arm as he turned to leave. "Just keep it discreet. I don't want the civilians hearing about it."

Korin raised an eyebrow. "Not sure I see the sense in that."

She leaned in again. "I don't want anyone to panic, and if the sorcerer is among the people within the wagons, I don't want him to know that we're aware he might be attacking us soon."

He nodded solemnly and put a hand on the arm that she had used to seize him. "Not to worry, miss. I'll use the utmost discretion."

"May I inspect the wagons?" Lydia asked.

He shook his head. "Guess you haven't heard yet. Our orders are not to disturb anyone inside those wagons, for any reason. Important ambassadors or some such. Like to keep to themselves."

Ambassadors...And the queen said an ambassador from Selyr... Does she mean Rethri ambassadors?

Oh, gods, are we shipping prisoners?

"No problem," Lydia said brightly. "I'll look forward to working with you and your men."

"Thanks," he said, pulling his arm away. "I need to get back to work."

"One last thing," she said. "Hand that arm back."

He raised an eyebrow quizzically, and then handed his arm back over silently. She took his hand.

"Dominion of Protection, fold against his skin."

A shimmering field of translucent energy enveloped his body for just an instant, and then faded into invisibility.

"Uh, thanks?"

"A precaution, is all. Hopefully it won't turn out to be necessary," Lydia smiled. "Now, let's get this caravan ready to go, shall we?"

Night had fallen before the caravan exited the city gates. They were only about an hour behind schedule, which was good by caravan standards, at least in Lydia's experience. It helped that none of the inhabitants of the five front wagons ever entered or exited their enclosures. Only the people riding in the rear wagon – a few civilians unassociated with the rest of the caravan – came out to finish packing their goods or carouse with the guards.

"Why are there civilians in the last wagon?" Lydia asked.

Korin shrugged. "Until you came by, we weren't aware there was anything unusual about this escort. Although, to be fair, I'm not usually put on caravan guard duty. Lord Esslemont insisted on coming along with us, since he's heading the same direction we are and he wanted protection. I wasn't in a position to argue."

"Why would someone want to leave the city in the middle of the night?" Lydia pondered aloud.

"It's not really that unusual, miss, especially during the warmer months. It's possible they just didn't want to deal with the heat, or perhaps they just had final preparations to make during dawnfire hours."

Lydia nodded. "That might be right. Thanks for the reassurance."

Korin gave her a half-salute and went back to organizing.

The wagon drivers were all members of Korin's guard, which was somewhat unusual, but not unheard of. They seemed well-trained, but nervous – probably because Korin's "trusted few" guards had spread the word of a potential attack to all the others. If the attacker was already traveling with the caravan – a possibility that Lydia had considered – this heightened sense of nervousness might have put the attacker on alert as well. Lydia had judged that warning the guards was worth the risk, but the ambiguity of the situation left a foul taste in her mouth.

She'd need to react, rather than taking the aggressors out in advance. She hated operating that way – though it would hardly be the first time she'd been forced into that situation. She knew to take precautions for the contingencies she was capable of planning for.

"Dominion of Protection, fold against my skin and teach me the secrets of the Dominions that assault you."

Lydia renewed the Comprehensive Barrier that protected her just as the front wagon began to move. The spell sent a tiny tingle along her skin, causing her to shiver for just a moment.

Can't cast too many more of these today or I'm going to be useless for days. Protection spells drew from the body's natural ability to ward off harm. Practicing protection sorcery often ended with Lydia sick in bed or nursing stubborn bruises that appeared from even a mild brush with anything particularly solid.

She'd marched along with the wagons, alongside three regular soldiers and Korin. He'd offered her a place to sit alongside any one of the caravan guards, but she'd declined. Coldridge was a long walk – over a day away, at a caravan's pace – but she didn't trust her perception to be as good while riding. This way, she could periodically walk by each of the wagons to check for disturbances.

The wagons made it out of the city without incident, as she'd expected. She had Korin list out the names of the guards with her, but none of them struck her as particularly suspicious. She'd met a handful of them from work at one of the two palaces, but she didn't know any of them particularly well.

Korin himself seemed friendly enough. His anxiousness faded a bit as they made it into the open air of the wooded trail outside the city, winding toward the north west.

If I was a renegade sorcerer, when would I choose to attack a caravan on the way to Coldridge?

Lydia pondered that question inconclusively, but it led her to a more important one. *Why would someone be attacking this caravan in the first place?*

She let herself fall back to the second to the last wagon, taking a slow pace as she considered her options. *They've been very insistent that no one go inside the other wagons. Someone has to have seen them loaded, though. Maybe I can get one of the guards to talk.*

Then again, if someone along the caravan is going to help coordinate the attack, I don't want to arouse their awareness of my awareness. Hrm.

One of the guards driving the wagon noticed her and gave a little wave. She waved back, giving him a friendly nod, and turned her head back to the road.

If only I could see inside the wagon without going in there.

Like what Jonan did with the door to his house.

I wonder...

She glanced at the door side of the wagon, and then let herself fall behind a little further, out of the sight of any of the guards.

She had no experience at Liadran style sorcery, or at anything involving the Dominion of Sight – but her Comprehensive Barrier had absorbed one of his spells. It gave her an intrinsic understanding of the spell that had been cast, almost as if she had used it herself. She had never attempted to cast a spell based on that data alone before – but now seemed like a good time to try.

First, Lydia had to adjust her Comprehensive Barrier. Her style of barrier would be triggered by any sort of incoming sorcery, regardless of the source. That meant that even spells she attempted to cast on herself would be blocked by it, as long as it was active. Any spell that impacted with the shield would expend some of its energy, regardless of whether or not that spell was harmless. The stronger the spell, the more the barrier would be weakened.

She took a deep breath, visualizing the barrier in her mind, and spoke. "Suppress barrier, face."

Lydia felt a slight tingle across her face as the barrier reshaped, and she knew from experience that she had just created a hole in the barrier. This would both allow the incoming spell to work, and to prevent the barrier from being weakened.

Touching the wall of the wagon, Lydia pictured the spell that Jonan had cast in her mind. *Eyes close. Erase target in mind. Sustain image; target self. Open eyes.*

When she reopened her eyes, nothing had visibly changed. Lydia tensed her jaw in frustration.

What was I expecting? Casting a completely new type of sorcery successfully on my first try?

Hrm. She tapped a finger on the wood absently. *Maybe I can adapt it to work with the Velryan style?*

The sorceress took a deep breath, glancing from side-to-side self-consciously.

Now or never, I guess.

"Dominion of Sight," she muttered, "Erase the image before me, but only for myself."

Lydia's vision blurred – but within the blur, she could see the contents of the wagon. She gaped, both at the success of the spell and the figures inside.

Two Rethri males, adults, reclined against the right wall. They looked awake and aware, and one of them leaned in close to the other, whispering something that Lydia couldn't hear.

On the opposite side were children. Four figures, bundled in blankets, huddled together. Their eyes were closed — she couldn't determine if they were Rethri or human. Upon reflection, she couldn't even tell if they were sleeping or dead; although the blankets wouldn't have made much sense in the latter case.

What am I dealing with here? She had considered the possibility that the missing Rethri were in the wagons, but Jonan's description had only included children. And these adults didn't look to be captive in any way — they were awake, aware, and unencumbered by any sort of chains or shackles.

"Stop the wagons!" came a voice from the front of the line.

Lydia broke into a run, her vision still swimming from her unexpected use of sight sorcery. *Good time to try out a new trick, Lydia. Really.*

She came up behind Korin a few moments later, who stood in the middle of the road, three other guards at his side. He faced off against a figure in violet robes, who stood about ten paces further down the road. It wasn't until Lydia came up to Korin's side that she recognized the bandages on the opposing sorcerer's right hand.

"Lydia?" Veruden's voice called out incredulously. "You're the traitor?"

Lydia quirked a brow at the blur of her friend. "I don't know what you're talking about, Veruden. From this angle, it looks like you're the one barring the path."

Veruden folded his arms in front of him. "The people in those wagons are fugitives. I have orders to return them to the city immediately."

Fugitives? Orders? Oh, resh.

Korin stepped protectively in front of Lydia. "You can let us handle this, miss. He's just one man, sorcerer or not."

Lydia stepped right back in front of Korin. "I don't intend for this to turn into a fight. Veruden, step aside. Let's talk about this. I think we've been set up."

"Maybe you were," Veruden said uncertainly. "I can't step out of the road, sorry, Lydia. My orders were pretty clear."

Time for a gamble, then. "Those aren't fugitives back there. I've met the people in the back – they looked like ordinary civilians. No prison brands, certainly. And the others are supposed to be a Selyran ambassador and his entourage."

"Might just be that you're in the wrong place at the wrong time, then, Lydia. Someone here is trying to sneak prisoners out of the city," he waved a hand at the wagons. "Maybe it's not all the wagons. It'd be smarter for them to come through along with a normal caravan, in fact."

"I'm going to need to see your authorization," Lydia said, folding her arms. Her vision was slowly starting to clear, just sufficiently to make out Veruden's uncertain expression.

"Authorization? What are you babbling about, Scryer? We're both court sorcerers," he waved a hand. "Are you trying to stall for time?"

She shook her head. "Korin, hand over my papers."

"Uh, I don't exactly have them-"

"Get them," Lydia insisted, waving him away. Korin hesitated for just a moment, then nodded and complied. The remaining three guards looked at her uncertainly, but she just raised a warding hand for them to wait.

"I don't see what papers have to do with any of this," Veruden said, taking a step forward.

"My orders," Lydia began, hoping to prevent a bloodbath, "Are from the queen regent herself. With her seal. She asked me – just a couple hours ago, interrupting me in the middle of my meal with Edon and Taelien – to rush here to guard the caravan."

"That doesn't make any sense. Edon ordered me –," he paused, sighing. "Okay, starting to see what you mean about one of us being played."

Lydia nodded. "Give the guard captain a minute to get-"

"Don't need the papers," he said. "I believe you. You said you'd checked one of the wagons, though, not all of them. Only way we can know what's really going in is by checking them all."

Can't disagree with that logic... But the guards were given explicit instructions not to let anyone in the other wagons.

Resh it.

"Yeah," Lydia agreed. "You're right. We check them together. Guards, stand down."

The guards looked from one to another doubtfully, then back to her.

"I'm not sure we're allowed-"

"I'm under the queen regent's authority, remember?" Lydia grinned. "Don't worry, no one is going to blame you if something goes wrong. The responsibility falls on me."

One of the soldiers breathed a sigh of relief about that, but the other two seemed uncertain. They took steps back, away from Veruden, hands on blades.

Veruden walked over to Lydia's side, and the pair of them headed to side of the first wagon. Lydia waved to a pair of guards who were still seated at the coach box, prepared to move the horses at any time.

"Step down and be ready to intercept anyone who attempts to attack us," she ordered the guards. They complied immediately, taking it a step further by drawing the swords at their sides.

"I'll go first," Veruden said, stepping up to the side of the coach and opening the door.

A sword went right through his center a moment later.

Istavan stood in the doorway of the coach, withdrawing his blade with a flourish.

Lydia's sword flashed into her hand, and she reached with her left hand to grab Veruden and steady him – but her hand passed through him. Veruden vanished an instant later.

Istavan stumbled forward as if he had been struck, catching himself on the dirt.

"What in the name of the gods was that about, Istavan?" Lydia demanded, eyes scanning the area for Veruden.

"Should have known this was an ambush," Veruden said from somewhere nearby. The five uncertain guards nearby had their swords drawn, but they didn't seem to know who to point them at. Two of them faced vaguely toward Istavan, while the others looked around with bewildered expressions.

Veruden didn't just teleport, Lydia realized. *Istavan never hit him. He's using sight sorcery!*

"Get Veruden, now!" Istavan rasped, reaching with his empty hand to cover his ribs. "He's here to take the ambassador!"

"Dominion of Knowledge, illuminate the hidden!" Lydia shouted, searching for Veruden. She only caught a vague blur to Istavan's right before a fist slammed into the sorcerer's mask, shattering it to pieces and smashing Istavan toward the dirt.

Veruden appeared above Istavan, a flickering sphere of blue light in his hands, preparing to throw downward.

"No, stop!" Lydia charged at Veruden, swinging the flat of her blade at her friend. He glanced at her just before the blade struck and the sword sailed through him, meeting only empty air. The false image of him flickered and disappeared a moment later.

"He tried to skewer me, Scryer," Veruden's voice said from somewhere on her left. She spun, but she couldn't find him. *Either that sight spell shot my vision too badly for my detection spell to work properly, or he's just that good at invisibility.* Lydia grimaced. *Invisibility and teleportation. And whatever that blue thingy was. Resh. When did Veruden learn at least two more Dominions? And with that degree of proficiency? He's not even using incantations...*

"I need you to stop, Veruden. I don't want to take a side here. We should all talk this out. Guards," she instructed. "Point your swords at that man," she indicated Istavan. "Don't let him move. But if Veruden attacks him again, feel free to stab him, too."

A shockwave blasted Lydia off her feet.

Eru elan lav kor taris, her Comprehensive Barrier reported unhelpfully. The barrier did stop her from feeling the impact as she hit the ground, however, so she was on her feet faster than the guards – who, at a second glance, didn't seem to be getting back up at all.

What the –

Veruden appeared right in front of Lydia, grabbing her sword's hilt and wrenching it out of her hand. The saber spun into the darkness, landing far out of reach. She responded by grabbing his injured hand right hand and squeezing. He groaned and fell to a knee.

"Stop it, Veruden. I don't want to fight you." She emphasized that by squeezing his hand a little harder.

"Going to have to pick a side, even if you don't want to," he muttered through grit teeth.

And then she was clutching air.

Lydia couldn't see him, but she knew where his next move would be. Istavan was still on the ground, shaking his head in disorientation, and none of the guards around him were moving.

The sorceress rushed forward, tackling a flickering blur in the empty air. Lydia met resistance, her lunge catching him in the stomach instead of the shoulder she had been aiming for. Still, she managed to drag him down to the ground with some effort.

That didn't keep him long, however. Veruden was still only half-visible, and he managed to slam an elbow into her ribs, knocking the wind out of her. As she winced, he rolled on top of her. His good hand closed around her throat.

"I don't want to do this. Surrender," Veruden said.

A mailed fist slammed into his cheek, knocking the sorcerer right off of her.

"Got your papers," Korin said, reaching down and wrenching her off the ground with a strong hand. Lydia woozily caught her feet.

Veruden was gone again, and Istavan was still having difficulty standing up. She glanced at Korin dubiously, wondering how he was still standing.

Oh, right. I put a barrier on him before we left. Guess it worked. I should probably refresh that.

"Dominion of Protection-"

Korin went flying, slamming into the side of the wagon. Lydia caught the flicker of his barrier triggering as he collided, but he smashed into it hard, cracking the wooden frame.

Something slammed into Lydia from behind, invisible hands wrapping around her wrists. "Tell me you'll surrender and I'll stop," Veruden's voice said.

She slammed a foot down toward his, but he moved it aside, and she caught only dirt. Through the corner of her eye, she caught Istavan raising his right hand. Veruden must have caught it, too, because he relaxed his grip on her – presumably to try to teleport again.

Not getting away this time, Lydia thought. She grabbed his injured hand again, squeezing hard. "Dominion of Protection, fold against his skin."

"Ignite," Istavan said, a blast of light issuing from his outstretched hand toward Veruden.

Veruden released Lydia, waved a hand, and the incendiary light caught him in the center of the chest. He crumpled to the dirt.

No, Lydia thought, rushing over to Veruden's fallen form. *That shield should have stopped the blast too. His teleport couldn't have been powerful enough to use up the barrier by itself.*

The sorceress rolled him over, revealing a severe burn spreading across Veruden's entire chest. Smoke rose from the charred flesh, and his eyes were sealed shut.

"Clever move, using a shielding spell to prevent him from escaping," Istavan remarked, slowly approaching.

"Don't come any closer," Lydia instructed Istavan in a growl. "I'm still not sure we're on the same side."

Lydia winced as she looked back to Veruden's charred skin. *Resh it. I've never been good at life sorcery.*

"Can you heal him?" Lydia asked, not even bothering to turn toward Istavan.

"I'm not sure why you would even contemplate that, given that he just attempted to kill both of us."

The sorceress glared at Istavan. "You started that, and you're going to give me some answers about that later."

"Interesting. I would think you would be the one owing me answers, given that I last saw you helping a prisoner escape the low place," he said.

He remembers? I'd better play this carefully. "The others haven't filled you in yet? Feh, look, tell me directly if you can heal Veruden or not. I promise I'll fill you in on that prisoner incident after this is dealt with."

"Very well. I will stabilize him, but nothing further," Istavan said.

"Try to kill him and I will end you," Lydia assured him, standing and walking to retrieve her discarded sword.

"I keep my word, Sorceress Scryer. I hope that the same can be said of you."

Istavan bent over Veruden, pressing a hand against the burn. "Mend."

A weave of green, vine-like tendrils extended from Istavan's wrist to Veruden's chest.

Good enough. Lydia turned to check on Korin, but he was already back on his feet, helping one of the other guards stand. The sorceress breathed a sigh of relief. *At least his death won't be on my conscience.*

"Thanks for the save back there," Lydia said, approaching Korin.

"Not a problem. Now, would you mind telling me what the resh is going on here?"

"I'm still sorting that out myself," Lydia admitted.

"Sorceress," Istavan intoned. "You're not going to like this."

Lydia whirled, expecting to see that Veruden had stopped breathing. Instead, Veruden was gone.

"Dominion of Knowledge, illuminate the hidden!" she yelled, searching the area, focusing as deeply as she could. Not even a blur of Veruden was visible.

Resh. He's gone.

Lydia walked slowly to match Istavan's limping pace. It had taken several minutes to get the guards back on their feet, and most of them still looked dazed. One of them had landed at a particularly bad angle and was nursing a broken nose.

Given the unusual circumstances of the encounter, Lydia and Istavan had remained quiet as they helped the guards back to their feet and instructed the wagons to resume their journey. Korin gave a leery glance at Istavan every now and again, but he didn't remark on anything. Once the wagons had resumed their movement, Lydia and Istavan took to the front, walking ahead of the others to scan the road for any more threats.

Istavan's breathing was hoarse, but his face was set with grim determination. Lydia was unused to seeing him without his mask, but he was surprisingly handsome. Like many from Terisgard, he had brown skin and short, curly black hair. She had expected the mask was to conceal some kind of scarring, but no such damage was evident. Perhaps he simply wore the mask to look intimidating or inhuman – it certainly achieved those effects. Even without it, Istavan radiated a strong presence, seeming to loom over everything he observed.

"I will inform the queen that you cooperated," Istavan said, shattering the silence.

She glanced over at him, quirking a brow. "Care to explain that?"

He shivered, showing an uncharacteristic sign of weakness.

He didn't use that much fire sorcery, and it's not really all that cold out, Lydia considered. *Was he already exhausted when he came out here?*

"The queen knew that this caravan would not be allowed to leave the city without a fight. She decided to take the opportunity to see where your loyalties would fall, if tested." He broke into a fit of coughing, covering his mouth with his hand.

Lissari keep you healthy, Lydia thought to herself. She wouldn't dare say it aloud.

"So, this was just a test?" The sorceress shook her head. "People nearly died for a test of loyalty?"

Istavan shook his head, still coughing. After a moment, it passed, and he winced and waved a hand at her in a dismissive gesture. "No, the attack was real," he assured her. "We did not know who it would come from or when, but that was not staged. The 'test' portion was simply that I was instructed not to interfere if you chose to handle the attack by yourself."

Ah, and he would try to eliminate me if I sided with the attackers, Lydia considered. *That does make some level of sense. For a gambling sort, at least.*

"You expected that I would either fight off the attackers or join them. Choosing to investigate the wagons took you off guard," Lydia surmised.

Istavan nodded, straightening his back, as if to compensate for his earlier show of weakness. "Yes. And Veruden proved more dangerous than I could have anticipated."

Lydia folded her hands in front of her. "I'd only ever seen him use travel sorcery before, and even then, a single spell seemed to exhaust him. Could he have been misleading us about his capabilities for years?"

"No," Istavan said simply, pausing to cough again.

That coughing can't be good. Perhaps he used too much life sorcery?

"At a minimum, he was using travel sorcery, either sight or deception to make illusions, whatever knocked out the guards, and a type of blue fire – radiance, maybe?" Lydia mused aloud.

"The spell that knocked out the guards was some kind of powerful sound sorcery," Istavan explained after he recovered from his latest coughing. "It kept my ears ringing for minutes. I couldn't concentrate at all."

"How'd you remain conscious through it? I had a protection spell active," Lydia explained, omitting the odd words she had seen when the Comprehensive Barrier attempted to translate the spell.

It was just like when Edon countered the sorcery in the arena. I think some of the words were even the same. What does that mean? When I comprehended Jonan's spell, it was essentially translating his thoughts to me – could they be thinking in another language? Or a cypher, perhaps?

Istavan chuckled softly, which was slightly jarring. "Before I came out here, I knew there was a possibility I might have to fight you. I asked Morella to cast a spell on me that would force me to remain conscious and aware."

Lydia grimaced. "To counter the sleep spell I used on you last time. I'm sorry about that."

"You still owe me an explanation," he pointed out.

Lydia nodded. "I was pretending to break a prisoner out of the palace to learn who his contacts were. I tried to time it so we wouldn't have any opposition. You weren't supposed to be in the palace. You weren't even supposed to be in the city."

He nodded, smirking slightly. "A miscalculation. I have been working directly – and covertly – for the queen for several months now. To prepare for this very day, in fact. If I had known about your 'pretend' rescue, I would have been glad to help."

She tilted her head to the side. "Really. You have a funny way of trying to be helpful, given that you have a habit of attacking as soon as the door to your room opens."

"Initiative is often necessary in this field of work. Hesitation can be deadly. Waiting would not have improved my odds – either against you and your paladin friend, or with Veruden." He wrapped his arms around himself, looking as if he was struggling to keep warm.

Paladin? What does he think he knows? Lydia glanced back toward the wagons, noting that they were still far enough back that it was unlikely any non-sorcerer could be listening in on their conversation. Her sword was still sheathed on her left side, and she trusted that she was in better shape than Istavan was if she needed to act.

"What were you doing in there with the sword?" Lydia asked.

"I was examining it, of course. I had hoped to break it out of the scabbard. A tool like that blade could have been very useful. Of course, after seeing your friend in the arena, I realize that we did not have a fraction of the information necessary to understand what we were really dealing with." He took a deep breath. "It is difficult to know how to act when faced with only half of what you need to know."

"I do agree. I take it that's your way of asking to trade information?" The itch to draw her steel faded somewhat, but she remained wary. His constant referral to Taelien as her 'friend' was disconcerting at best.

"You have taken a side now, regardless of what you may have wished. It would be in your best interests to solidify your ties to the queen before things escalate further." He clasped his hands in front of him, turning his head to glance downward at her. "Especially given the other allies you've chosen."

"I'm not sure what you mean by that, but I would be willing to agree to trade some information. I won't make any promises of taking a 'side' until I understand what the 'sides' are, however."

"It should be obvious by now, isn't it?" Istavan waved back toward the caravan.

"The queen is moving against Edon," Lydia surmised. "Veruden works for Edon, and you work for the queen."

He nodded. "Very good. And you work for the Paladins of Tae'os."

She paused in her step. "Now, why would you make an assumption like that?"

Her right arm was itching again.

He shook his head, raising his hands. "Peace. The queen has known for quite some time. She has no problem allying with a Paladin of Tae'os – in fact, an alliance with your organization in general would be of mutual benefit at this stage. You needn't make pretenses about the rescue."

Lydia took a deep breath, considering that. *He could be baiting me to admit something he's not sure about. But the logic behind the argument itself is sound – if the queen is starting a civil war against Edon, she's going to need all the allies she can get. Anyone strictly religious is going to side with Edon. If she intends to overthrow him, she needs to demolish the foundation of his power, which is the Edonate religion itself.*

"If, hypothetically speaking, I was a paladin, I still wouldn't be able to pledge any sort of alliance for the organization as a whole," Lydia pointed out. "It would be well beyond my hypothetical authority."

"Of course," Istavan agreed. "But you could carry a message, perhaps. A message that the queen would be more than happy to return Orlyn to being a kingdom under the Tae'os faith, if only the heretic Edon could be removed. If your sword-bearing friend is any indication, it would appear the paladins are already making their own move."

"Eh – I wouldn't assume that," Lydia said hesitantly, resuming walking beside Istavan. "Even I don't know quite what that man is about, in truth. I've been digging at him for days, trying to learn his story, but he's either not a paladin or a spectacular liar."

Istavan pursed his lips. "Truly? You're not lying about that?"

She shook her head. "No reason to at this point. I do know he's dangerous, though. In case that wasn't obvious from his performance in the arena."

"What have you been able to determine about his agenda, in that case?"

Lydia cracked her knuckles. "He seems to be trying to figure out his identity. Claims that he was adopted, and that the sword was left with him. Apparently his adoptive parents told him he could find out something about his heritage in this city."

"Not much to work with. And now Edon has taken an interest in him. He could be used as a tool against us, if we aren't careful," Istavan said, perhaps more to himself than to Lydia.

Interesting usage of the term 'we'. "What's the deal with the caravan? What's so important in these wagons?"

Istavan turned around, gesturing toward the caravan. "Four of those wagons carry former prisoners. We discovered them recently in a hidden facility and liberated them. We believe Edon was using them as some kind of power source to fuel his sorcery."

Now that's interesting. It'd be awfully coincidental timing if they just found out about the Rethri at the same time we did. I've never heard of a way to use people as a power source for sorcery, but the way those children were unconscious, with marks around their eyes... maybe. It doesn't sound impossible.

"So, you think Edon's 'divine' abilities were somehow being drawn from these prisoners?" Lydia asked, only half-rhetorically.

"That would be the theory, yes. He may have more of them, of course – we were only able to liberate the people in one specific facility. It would explain the level of power Edon has been able to demonstrate, as well as his apparent versatility, if he has created a form of sorcery that draws power from other people." Istavan paused, allowing Lydia a moment to consider that.

Everyone has some level of connection with various dominions – that's how we function. Since Rethri tend to have a particularly strong bond to a specific dominion, a person who could draw sorcery from others could have a very potent tool at their disposal. I suppose it might be something like how a person utilizes a dominion bonded item, or maybe a mixture between that and how the Vae'kes can absorb dominion energy directly into themselves.

If the Rethri are his power source, he'd need a way to draw on their power remotely. Something to establish a long-distance connection. Moving them – like what the queen is trying to do – might not even break that connection, depending on what it is.

"Do you have any indication on how he might be drawing on the Rethri's sorcery? When he was above the arena, for example, he did not have any Rethri with him – but he was still capable of casting a broad-reaching spell that removed the sorcery that was active in the arena," Lydia pointed out.

And I also couldn't detect any dominion sorcery on him – which meant he had a way of concealing it, or that whatever he's doing doesn't function in the same way that Dominion Sorcery does.

"When we found the prisoners, there was some sort of writing scratched into their cells. We were not able to translate it, but we believe the writing was the key to how he was drawing on their sorcery." Istavan looked nervous, and he raised a hand to wipe sweat off his forehead.

Sweat? I thought he was cold a moment ago. Well, it probably doesn't matter. That writing seems important – Jonan saw some around the Esharen, too. Could the writing be in the same language or code that the Comprehensive Barrier was showing me?

"All right," Lydia began, "That's all good information. But why is the queen regent moving against Edon? She has one of the highest positions in the kingdom, and she's even considered one of the gods by the Edonates."

"The queen witnessed Edon doing something that shook her to the core. She has not told me what it was, but each time I've asked, I've seen a flicker of fear in her eyes. She is terrified of him – and she believes that if she does not act, she could quickly be replaced." He paused for a moment, and then added. "Having just seen what Veruden was capable of, I believe that I have some suspicions about what she might have been concerned about. He should not have been capable of using those abilities on his own."

Lydia grimaced. *He's right – no one achieves mastery over three new types of sorcery that rapidly. The only way people gain access to new types of sorcery overnight is through Gifts of the gods themselves.*

That was it. That was why the queen was so worried – why Veruden was so powerful.

Edon had learned how to grant the gifts of the gods.

CHAPTER XII – MIRRORS

Three days had passed since Jonan had last heard from Lydia or Taelien. With his mirrors shattered, his sources of information were sparse at best. His vision had recovered substantially, but he still wore the thickest glasses he had available. It was late in the evening and the nightfrost's scant light was barely enough for him to write by, but he didn't want to risk using a dark-seeing spell to make the process more efficient.

I might have damaged my vision permanently again, he mused. *I really need to stop doing that.*

A knock on the front door of his house startled him, and Jonan lifted himself away from his writing desk, instinctively fumbling for a dagger that wasn't there. Shaking his head, he walked to the door.

A tap against the surface made the wood invisible – revealing Vorain standing on the other side.

She was almost inconspicuous, wearing simple traveler's clothes of brown and grey. Only her eyes stood out, and even those gave no indication of her 'divine' status. Large pouches sat on her left and right hips. No weapons were visible on her person, but that didn't mean a thing. Jonan opened the door.

"I've been expecting you," he said, and it wasn't entirely untrue. He did expect her; he just didn't have the faintest idea of when or where she would make an appearance, or if he would survive the first few moments of it. Apparently she had chosen a less than murderous reunion, which was good.

She stepped silently inside, nudging the door shut.

"It's time," she said ominously. "Are you prepared?"

"Um, hrm, give me just a moment." He scampered up the stairs to the former guest bedroom – which was where he had been sleeping for the last few days. Vorain clearly knew that the underground room had been his previous bedchamber, so he hadn't been able to force himself to sleep down there since her last visit. And his fake bedroom didn't seem much better.

Once upstairs, he retrieved a pair of bags – not dissimilar to the ones Vorain was carrying – and attached them to a belt, which he fastened on. In the bags, he carried his last handful of alchemical vials, a pair of still unbroken mirrors, and his mostly useless dagger.

All in all, it wasn't much for infiltrating the lair of a false god, but he'd find a way to get by. He always did.

"Ready now," he called as he half-ran, half-stumbled his way down the stairs.

She looked him up and down. "That was fast."

"Just where, precisely, are we headed?" Jonan asked. "I try to be aware of my odds of survival before I go out at night. And I may need additional supplies."

"The high palace," she said in a half-whispered tone.

He quirked an eyebrow. "Why would you need me in order to get into the high palace? Don't you live there?"

She shook her head. "No. And I could get into the palace itself, of course, but that doesn't mean I could just walk into any room I want – and certainly not without questions being asked. I'm pretty good at concealing myself, but your invisibility is better, and I don't know anyone else who can cast that."

"All right, but that's not really very specific. I should have been clearer. Where, specifically within the palace, are we going? What is our objective? What sort of opposition should we expect to encounter? What path will we be using to leave after we complete our objective?"

The purplish-eyed sorceress leaned back against the wall near the entrance to his borrowed home. She turned her head away from him, gazing toward a particularly normal wall. "We need Edon's notes from his research on the disease my brother is afflicted with. I know where he keeps his research notes, but in spite of my status as a 'goddess', I don't actually have the authority to be in there. There will almost certainly be guards, and probably at least some kind of sorcerous protection."

"Oh, good," Jonan mumbled. "So, all we have to worry about are guards, wards, and possibly gods. Go on."

"You are the one who proposed an alliance," she pointed out. "If you were being insincere-"

"Oh, no, not at all. I just tend to like doing things with better odds of survival, is all. What's our way out?"

"There are windows," the sorceress offered.

"Windows." Jonan forced his eyes shut. "You want us to climb out windows."

Vorain shrugged. "It may not be necessary. My authority will carry us through most situations, and your invisibility spell can handle many others. We may not be detected. But, if we are, the place we are going is only a few floors up."

"Only a few floors up." Am I the only one in this city that isn't some sort of invincible godlike being?

"I, uh, suppose I should go get some rope, then." He did have some rope somewhere – he just hadn't been planning to have to make use of it.

After about five minutes, Jonan turned up a coil of climbing rope, which he had never used. He packed it tightly into one of his pouches, allowing the bundle to stick out just a bit from the top. Vorain quirked a brow at him, but she said nothing.

"I may not be precisely qualified for this kind of work," he mumbled, "But I am as ready as I am going to be."

"Good," she said. "Follow me."

It was deep into the night when they arrived at the gardens before the high palace. Vorain had not shared any further details of her plan, and his efforts to inquire for more details – or even engage in pleasant conversation – had proven largely fruitless.

They were, by Jonan's estimation, nearly in sight of the front gates when she pulled him off of the road into a series of tall hedges.

Well, he considered, *I haven't been dragged off into the bushes by a woman in quite a while. Ever, actually.*

The last thought was somewhat depressing, especially given the context of the situation.

"Hide us," Vorain said simply, "And then follow."

He put a finger on her forehead – which was unnecessary, and her quizzical glance seemed to indicate that she might have known that – and concentrated. *Erase our images, except to each other.*

Since there would be no visible effect of that spell to each other, Jonan added, *make a shimmery thing on us,* creating a shiny distortion that was visible to the pair. Vorain gave an incredulous expression, then shook her head and turned away from him – but not before he caught the slightest hint of a grin on her face.

He grinned in turn, following her toward the palace gates.

Which were closed, of course.

She grabbed his wrist, dragging him forward, between the pair of guards who were chatting at the door. He glanced from side to side, always uncomfortable coming into close proximity with others while he was invisible. He was not soundless, and neither was she.

They reached the door a moment later – and Vorain stepped through it, dragging Jonan behind her.

He felt no resistance as he passed inside the door.

Don't lose the spell inside the door, he thought, briefly panicking. He didn't know precisely what would happen if Vorain's spell dissipated right while he was inside, but he couldn't imagine the results being anything less than horrifying.

After they were through, he took a deep breath, noting that the inside corridors appeared to be both dark and empty – probably on account of the time of night.

That was actually kind of neat, he considered in retrospect. *A kind of travel sorcery, maybe. Hrm. I'll have to figure out how she did that later. And then never do it again.*

She released her grip on his wrist, moving fluidly onward, her steps silent against the carpeted floor. She made a quick glance to each side as they passed intersections, never stopping, never slowing. They reached a stairway leading upward a few scant minutes later, and she stepped onto it. Perhaps it was just his proximity and the comparative quiet, but her first step against the stone seemed to ring in his ears more loudly than it should have.

Jonan followed nervously, a hand creeping into his pocket to wrap around a vial of smoke. It was his first instinct as an escape mechanism if someone saw through the invisibility – the smoke was real, not an illusion, and thus it would still obscure vision even if someone could penetrate his spell.

Where is she leading me, he wondered for the hundredth time. *Another*

Rethri storage area? Somewhere Edon does his research? A trap designed specifically for me, perhaps?

He doubted he was special enough to warrant such treatment, but it was nice to dream from time to time.

They passed three floors on the stairway before stopping at the fourth. The stairway led on, but Vorain stepped off of it into another carpeted hall, which blessedly once again began to muffle the sounds of their footsteps.

Odd how quiet it is here, even considering the hour, Jonan considered. *That also could indicate a trap, but she hasn't reacted to it. Perhaps this location is simply private enough that they don't have many guards active at night.*

Vorain led them past several heavy wooden doors that lined the keep's gray stone walls, seeming focused exclusively on their destination. They passed a patrolling guard, who carried a lit torch in one hand and wore a long sword on his belt. Vorain and Jonan pressed against the wall as they slid past the guard, and he seemed to pay them no notice.

Not entirely abandoned, I guess, Jonan considered. He watched the guard move away from them, noting that the man seemed to be walking very slowly and deliberately. *Could he be expecting to find someone tonight, or is that just how he walks? Or maybe the people here are just very insistent on quiet?*

Vorain led him onward, finally stopping by a door that looked no different from the rest. Jonan noted a keyhole on the door and briefly prayed that Vorain wouldn't drag him through the door to bypass the mechanism.

Instead, she retrieved a key from the pouch on her left side and turned it in the lock. A 'click' indicated that the key had done its work, and she slowly and deliberately turned the knob.

A large room stood beyond the door, a long sofa in the far left corner, opposite a desk and a fantastically large bookshelf. Directly across from their entrance was another door, this one plated in silver and etched with unusual runes.

Similar to the ones around the Esharen, Jonan noted. *Probably some sort of sorcerous protection. We should avoid it.*

And lying on the sofa was a young woman, her eyes closed in apparent slumber. She was mostly covered in multiple layers of wool blankets, and it looked like she was cradling something in her arms beneath the blankets.

Vorain turned and raised a finger to her mouth in the universal gesture of silence, indicating for Jonan to come inside. The pair stepped in and Vorain slowly closed the door behind them.

Jonan glanced back toward the bed with a feeling of trepidation. *Who is that? Where are we?*

A second, more thorough glance around the room took in more details. Only some of the runes on the door were familiar, but at a second glance, he noted a matching symbol on each side that resembled a spear. *That's not a sorcerous rune,* he realized, *but a pictograph representing the Heartlance.*

Looking back at the bookcase, he recognized the markings on the spines of several books he had seen before. A book on the planes by Erik Tarren, a book on the Dominion of Protection by Edrick Theas, even a book on dominion bonds by Blake Hartigan. The first and last were both rare and expensive – the other owner he was aware of was one of the wealthiest people in Selyr.

This is probably Edon's library. And that door on the other side leads to something even more dangerous – maybe his personal bedchamber, or wherever he's holding more of the Rethri. Oh, resh. I should have expected this.

Vorain was heading over to the desk and bookshelf. Jonan followed nervously, glancing back toward the woman in the bed.

Who, he considered, *would be sleeping in Edon's library?*

While her body was mostly covered by blankets, he noted her exceptionally dark hair, which was a stark contrast to her pale skin. *Likely from near Liadra,* he realized. He filed that away for later and moved over to Vorain, who was searching quickly removing and scanning through books on the bookshelf.

Vorain leaned close to him as he approached, whispering in his ear, "Find his research notes."

Oh, sure, that's specific. Jonan was beginning to doubt Vorain's planning ability, and his own wisdom in following along... But Vorain clearly knew something – or, more accurately, many things – that he didn't.

He went to the desk first, finding a stack of papers with a quill and inkwell next to them. Glancing at the top paper, it looked like it was some kind of financial report.

From the Talior and Castle Depository, he realized as he glanced further down the document. *Nothing particularly suspicious about that, but it does confirm his connection with the bank, at least.*

He quickly parsed through the next several papers in the stack before shaking his head and setting them back the way they were. Nothing looked like 'research notes' within that stack, so he moved on to a stack of books that sat next to it.

There were four books in the pile, and a look at the cover of each told him that the first two were histories and the third was one of Erik Tarren's books on dominion sorcery theory. *Could be interesting, but not relevant,* Jonan considered. He paged through them to confirm if the covers hid a different interior, but they all appeared to be what they claimed to be.

The fourth book's cover was blank, and the text inside was gibberish.

Hello, Jonan considered, grinning to himself.

Tesh molain sol ko Eru ravel lares taris, the first line read. A line pointed from the word "Eru" into a nearby margin, with the text "len kor vesu et taris" written aside it.

Not sure if research notes, but interesting, Jonan considered. *It's not in any language I recognize, but it's still using Velthryn letters. Some sort of constructed language or code, then? Interesting. This could be important.*

He poked Vorain in the arm, and she spun around. He gestured down to the open book, and she leaned down, glancing over the page. Her eyes narrowed.

"That might be something. We'll take it, but keep looking," Vorain said.

Jonan shuffled some of the vials out of his left pouch and moved them to the right, slipping them in between the coils of rope, and slipped the mysterious book into the left pouch. It didn't fit properly, and the top stuck out several inches, but it didn't feel like it was going to fall out immediately.

Vorain set down another book on the table and slipped another off the shelf, opening it. "Here," she said quietly, glancing at the top page and then beginning to flip through the pages one at a time.

Jonan nervously glanced backward toward the bed. The girl within had rolled over to her left, and Jonan couldn't see if her eyes were open or closed, but she didn't seem to be moving.

Minutes passed as Vorain read. After the first minute or so, Jonan went to the shelf to grab another book, but Vorain waved a hand for him to stop. She had apparently found what they were looking for.

"Resh," she said out loud. "It's true."

She shoved the book, open to about the mid-point, into Jonan's hands. He glanced at the page.

With their bonds exhausted, the current set of sources are no longer useful. The last batch provided useful output for more than eight years, proving that the second test stage's methods are significantly more efficient. Given the amount of suspicion I generated when gathering the last batch, I will need to revise my acquisition procedures. Raymond's apprentice wants me to look after her brother. That could lead to opportunities to restock, or even expand.

Jonan turned at the sound of shuffling blankets. By the time he had spun around, the young woman was a blur, moving too quickly for his eyes to process. She reappeared in the corner of the room furthest from them, holding the Heartlance in a defensive stance. Wearing only a white nightgown, her body's shape was obvious. She had a soldier's build and a soldier's scars.

And, as he watched, her blue eyes flashed with light and changed to gold. The white around her iris remained – her eyes were human, not Rethri.

What?

Two metal objects flashed past Jonan, but the gold-eyed woman deflected them effortlessly, sending the projectiles to crash into the stone walls.

Vorain shoved the book in Jonan's hands closed, catching his eyes as he glanced toward her. "Run. Take the book and run."

A blade of ice appeared in Vorain's hands and she charged, lashing out at the woman with the Heartlance. The golden eyed warrior parried each strike, breaking pieces of ice off of the weapon, and swept the shaft of the spear into Vorain's ribs. The single strike carried Vorain off her feet, throwing her into the wall hard enough to make an audible crunch.

Vorain crashed to the floor, rolling to avoid a strike from the Heartlance that pierced into the stone wall near where she had knelt a moment before.

Jonan turned and ran, still holding the book. He swept the door open, braving one more glance toward Vorain as he exited the room. Her skin had turned inky black, blending with the dark, but the warrior that faced her stared at her with an unconcerned expression, readying the spear to strike again.

He wasn't quite sure why he cared so much, but he really hoped that Vorain – no, Rialla Dianis – made it out of that room alive. That thought didn't slow his steps, however, as he rushed aimlessly down the hall.

I don't know the layout here at all, he realized. *I'm lost, and also, I'm pretty sure Vorain just used thought sorcery on me again, and she's probably going to die, and resh it all.*

He rounded a corner and nearly slammed directly into a door that was much larger than the others. The wood was framed with gold, and a symbol of a harp was inscribed on a metal plate in the front of the door.

The queen's room, Jonan realized. *She'd better have a window.*

He tried the knob, finding it locked, and grimaced. *Of course it's locked. It's the reshing queen's room.*

This is a bad idea, he told himself, raising his right hand to the lock. Down the hall, he thought he could still hear the sounds of metal striking against something else – possibly Vorain's odd icy weapon.

He called flame, blasting a hole twice the size of his fist in the door, right over the lock. With that obstacle removed, he kicked hard, smashing the door open.

Without pausing a moment, he reached into his pouch and withdrew the rope, accidentally knocking a vial on the floor as he did. It didn't shatter, so he ignored the vial and stepped inside.

The room was grand, opulent, with a titanic bed that dwarfed even the one in Edon's room. An actual harp sat beside it, but neither the bed nor the harp had any user present.

A second glance as Jonan stepped inside told him that the room was – thankfully – currently unoccupied, but he did find one other thing of note. On the opposite end of the room there was a writing desk with neatly folded papers.

Against the wall above the desk was a gold-framed mirror, the metal surrounding it shaped into elegant vines. A familiar mirror, as Jonan had prepared it before he had left Selyr, giving it to his superiors to provide it to his contact.

A piece of parchment was pressed against the mirror, and Jonan approached quickly and snatched it, turning the paper to face him. *Have not received report in days. Need status update. Prisoner walks the Paths of Ascension tomorrow. Need to strike now.*

Oh, resh. My contact is the gods-cursed queen regent of Orlyn.

A loud crash sounded in the hall near the door, and Jonan dropped the paper instantly. There was, fortunately, a window – and a large one. He shoved the window's locking mechanism out of place and flung the shutters wide, and then rushed to attach his rope to the metal frame of the nearby bed.

I really, really hate this part of the job, Jonan considered, tossing the remainder of the rope down the side of the building. After a moment of testing to make sure the rope was secure, he wrapped a length around his waist, tied it securely, and began the climb to dubious freedom.

CHAPTER XIII – PATHS OF ASCENSION

Taelien woke to the faint sound of knocking at the heavy door to his guest bedroom. He grabbed the Sae'kes from within his sheets, sat up, and walked half-unclad to open the door.

A young man in servant's garb stood on the other side. "Um, good day, sir. I am here to bring you to Edon, long may he watch over us, who stands at the Paths of Ascension."

"Sure," Taelien replied, resting the sword at his side. "Give me a few minutes to dress myself."

The servant nodded vehemently, and Taelien closed the door. He didn't understand why the locals seemed to make such a big deal about garb, but he found their embarrassment amusing.

Taelien had spent the last three days recovering, practicing swordplay with Landen, and enjoying the hospitality of the palace. His leg wound from the Esharen was in substantially better shape, but his cauterized burn still ached madly, especially just after he awakened. He rubbed at the flesh around it, but that only made the aching worse.

I probably should be waiting longer before taking such an important test, but if Edon is going to give me the chance today, I can't pass it up. There's no telling when he'll change his mind – or how many new injuries I'll accumulate from any additional surprises in store here.

A few minutes later, Taelien emerged from the room wearing the borrowed clothes that Edon had instructed him to wear on this day. He had a long black tunic trimmed with silver, plain black breaches, and black leather boots with a silver pattern painted on their surface. *Presumably a reference to Aendaryn, the god of swords, since those are his colors. Even here, people associate me with him. I can never seem to escape his shadow.*

Still, he couldn't complain too much. The boots fit surprisingly well, given that the cobbler had only taken his measurements the previous day. *I wonder if these painted symbols are purely decorative, or if I'm walking around wearing some kind of latent sorcerous trap. I suppose I'll find out soon enough.*

Taelien belted on the Sae'kes, spent a few moments adjusting the position of the scabbard, and then another handful of moments debating if he was missing anything. *A secondary weapon would probably be wise.* There were no other weapons he was aware of in his chamber, so he went out to meet with the servant. He'd have to look for a secondary weapon later.

The servant led Taelien down three flights of stairs – which was interesting, given that he was pretty sure he had started out on the third floor – and to a gold-etched wooden door.

"This is the entrance to the Paths of Ascension?" Taelien asked.

"The entrance itself is inside this room, m'lord. I am not permitted to go inside, but Edon should be awaiting you. May the gods watch over you, m'lord." The servant said, bowing deeply. He sounded like he actually meant it.

"Thank you," Taelien said, suppressing a frown. *I hope they're not watching too carefully. If they are, their inaction would disgust me.*

Taelien put a hand on the door handle as the servant scurried away. Taking a deep breath, he pulled the doors open.

The chamber beyond looked to be too large to be inside the palace. It was nearly as long as the arena had been, and that was a grand enough area to seat thousands. The floor was gray stone, with a single broad purple carpet leading straight across the room from where he was standing. Along the carpeted path were titanic marble pillars, reaching skyward toward the ceiling of the keep itself.

That explains the size to some extent, Taelien considered. *This room must occupy space on every level of the keep.* He glanced around to see if there were any entrances along the walls higher up in the room, but he could not find any. He did, however, find Edon.

The so-called god stood at the very end of the path, on the right side of the carpet. He was wearing similar robes to the ones Taelien had seen before, although these were blue trimmed with silver. He wasn't sure if that had any significance – those were Sytira's colors, but it seemed odd for Edon to be wearing them. He was also still wearing the same ring he had been at dinner, and Taelien thought he saw a flicker of some kind of blue light inside it.

Some sort of dominion bonded item, Taelien quickly concluded. *Interesting.*

Across from Edon was Myros – or someone dressed as Myros, at least. The figure was in full armor, including a helmet, and standing on the left side of the path with the Heartlance in hand. A long sword sat on their hip – a new addition. *Interesting. Two weapons indicates a level of preparation for a fight. Are they going to make me fight Myros again? Is that what this is about?*

A grin crossed his face at the thought.

This is the shorter Myros, he noted after a moment. *The one I fought in the arena. I might have an actual fight on my hands.*

Taelien shut the door behind him, taking a casual stride as he walked toward the pair of "gods" waiting for him at the end of the carpet. *They could both attack me at once. That might be a problem. Edon can dispel sorcery, which removes one of my primary advantages. And Myros is both faster and stronger than I am, at least in short bursts. If that's a result of motion sorcery, though, Edon's spell to remove sorcery might counter Myros' physical advantage as well.*

He arrived at the end of the carpet, the pair hushing a conversation as he approached. "So, I'm here. What is this all about?"

"A broad question," Edon said with a fatherly smile. "But I assume you are asking about the tests you'll need to take."

Edon gestured to a series of steps beyond the end of the carpet, which led downward toward another large door. It was massive, at least twenty feet tall, and made of solid metal. Some kind of writing was etched on the surface, but Taelien couldn't recognize it at a distance.

The area in front of the door itself was a circular platform of white marble, a dozen feet below the rest of the room. Six poles carrying lit lanterns were distributed around the ring, illuminating a series of intricate glyphs carved into the floor. *Oh, mysterious runic markings. Those are always fun.*

"That is the entrance to the Paths of Ascension. It is the place where each of us goes to be judged worthy for godhood. Myros, Tylan, Vorain, and I have all walked it, and each of us retrieved something from within. That will be your task."

"I take it I couldn't just cut a piece of rock out of the wall and say I 'retrieved something'?" Taelien smirked at the thought, but it seemed a valid question. There was no reason to strain himself against untold terrors if his instructions were that vague.

Edon shook his head. "No, but a clever thought. I will tell you in honesty that this will be no simple task, and it will not be without danger. The Paths of Ascension proved challenging to each of us, and I trust that you will be no exception. Once inside, you must retrieve an ancient artifact – and it will serve as the source of your power as a newborn god."

Taelien raised an eyebrow. *An artifact? What did that have to do with divinity? Isn't an artifact just another term for a powerful dominion bonded object?*

He stepped forward, getting a closer look at the doors, and finally recognizing the inscriptions. They weren't the strange runes he had found around the Esharen – they were much more familiar. "Xixian," Taelien muttered. "The doors say something about 'until our master returns'. This is a vault, a Xixian vault."

Myros seemed to stiffen at that statement, but Edon just waved a hand dismissively. "You're right, of course. The Paths of Ascension are just a name people of this city gave it after we took it over. The artifacts were wrought with old sorcery, the type that predated human understanding – at least until recently."

"You've figured out what makes them work," Taelien concluded. It made a certain level of sense. "But the people of Xixis took precautions, and their artifacts are well protected."

Edon nodded. "That's the light of it, yes. Even with our extensive study of the first artifacts we found, we've barely brushed the surface of what these objects might be capable of. Myros and I have both made multiple incursions into that place, but each journey carries a real chance of death, even for us. It was designed to ward off anyone other than Vyrek Sul, the Emperor of Xixis, who is supposed to reclaim the treasures inside when he returns. The deeper you go, the greater the treasures within – and the more deadly the traps. Some of the traps even seem to change."

He's essentially admitting that he's not a god. That's...odd. From what I had heard about him, I had expected pulling that truth out of him to be much more of a struggle.

"So, what you're really offering me is a title – that you'll claim I'm a god like you 'are', if I bring you an artifact," Taelien said, narrowing his eyes.

Edon shook his head. "You misunderstand. My offer was earnest – these artifacts have vast power, capabilities that no other living beings today can emulate. Myros and I are gods, Taelien, in every meaningful way. We watch over our citizens, we protect them, and we even give a chosen few our gifts — just as the other 'gods' claim to. I can offer the people of Orlyn anything the older gods can, and I give it freely, without asking for anything in return. Not even worship. I have no priests, no paladins to protect me."

Taelien folded his arms, considering. *Is that what it is to be a god? Just a source of power and protection? Is that what I want for myself? What, exactly, did I think I was asking him for before?*

Did I just want to be more like Aendaryn? More like what people have always expected me to be?

Something about what Edon was saying scratched at the back of his mind — it sounded pretty enough on the surface, but he knew there was something off about it. Something missing.

"You said the traps sometimes change — how is that possible?" Taelien asked.

Edon folded his hands in front of him. "That is the core problem. We don't know. Presumably, something is alive down there."

Alive? Could something have survived down there hundreds of years after the fall of Xixis?

Taelien tensed, his hand unconsciously drifting to the hilt of his sword. He only realized his action when Myros shifted, making the same motion. "What sort of traps are we talking about?"

A booming voice issued from Myros' helmet, no doubt augmented by some kind of sorcery within. "Spears emerge from the walls. One of the rooms fills with cold water. Another has statues that breathe fire."

Edon quirked a brow at Myros. "I hadn't heard about that last one. Something from a recent visit?"

Myros nodded silently.

Edon turned back to Taelien. "Myros visits the Paths much more frequently than I do. On my second visit, whatever controls that place — presumably an ancient Esharen sorcerer — attempted to seal me inside a room. The properties of the stone in the walls inhibit certain types of sorcery, and I barely managed to escape with my life."

A fascinating confession, and another admission of mortal weakness. Oddly, it just makes me more sympathetic to him, though. Perhaps that's part of his strategy.

"Why are you telling me so much about this? I mean, if I live through this, I could tell anyone that you're just using Esharen artifacts to emulate divine power." Taelien shifted in his stance, moving his hand away from his sword.

Edon sighed. "You still don't see, do you? I want you to succeed. I want as many people as possible to succeed in here – and otherwise, in the world as a whole. I want humanity to succeed. You could argue that my claim to godhood is false. You could explain what you've just heard to everyone in the city. What would that accomplish? I am not giving anyone false hope – I can deliver every promise I make. I have the tools to do more for humanity than any god ever has, and as my knowledge grows, my ability to help others expands further. Would you truly wish to undermine that?"

Taelien shook his head. "I suppose not. Your goal seems noble enough, and I respect that. I will say, though, that the people of the city would probably think of you differently if they knew your definition of divinity and the mechanism behind it. I think you know that, too – and that you've been deliberately avoiding making your methodology public. But I won't speak out against you for it, at least not until I've had a chance to learn more. I don't like that you're keeping information from your followers, but I'll give you a chance to see if you're doing more good than harm."

Edon nodded. "Thank you. That's all I can ask. If you survive the vault, I will tell you more about why I have chosen this path, and how my abilities function."

'True' divinity or not, Edon was offering him a chance to test himself against a place of terrible danger for a chance at an artifact. He would have taken that chance without any prior promise of godhood – the challenge itself was a sufficient reward.

"Sounds fun," Taelien concluded. "When do we get started?"

"Are you fully prepared? Do you need any other supplies? Again, I want you to succeed at this," Edon gestured at the door.

Taelien shifted his weight to his right foot, considering. *If there's something alive down there, I'm probably in for a fight. Possibly with another Esharen... I really should ask about that one that was in the bank when I get out of here. Nothing he just explained justifies what was going on there. Resh, he really is a good speaker.*

"I could use an extra sword, actually," Taelien said.

Myros wordlessly drew the long sword and tossed it to Taelien, which snatched by the blade, narrowly avoiding the edge.

"Thanks," he said, nodding to Myros. The armored warrior returned his nod.

"Out of curiosity, why would the bearer of the Sae'kes need another weapon?" Edon asked, tilting his head to the side.

"I try not to use it," Taelien explained, patting the hilt. The sword was in its true form – there was no longer a need to hide it now that everyone had seen it in the arena. "It's too deadly."

Myros nodded in understanding, but Edon furrowed his brow in apparent confusion.

"Well, I suppose I can't begrudge you a second weapon. You may also want to bring a torch – it can get very dark inside, and as I said, something in the walls suppresses some types of sorcery. Especially deep inside."

"Do you want me to bring you a sample of the walls?" Taelien asked with a grin, remembering his earlier joke about bringing a rock as his sign that he had succeeded at the test.

Edon shook his head. "No, we've tried that. Once the rock leaves the paths, it seems to lose whatever property suppresses sorcery. Unfortunate, given how useful that material could be if properly harnessed."

Myros turned and walked to one of the pillars, removing an unlit lantern from a ring on the side. "Here," Myros offered, voice still unnaturally booming from the helmet.

Taelien took the lantern in his left hand, gripping Myros sword in his right. "Thanks. I seem to be out of hands, so I think I'm ready to head inside."

"You're certain? You don't need any further preparations?" Edon asked, sounding nervous.

"Not unless you want to loan me Myros," Taelien said, smirking.

Edon chuckled lightly. After a moment, he muttered, "No. That would be unwise. Last time we sent in two people at once, it did not end well."

Well, that's foreboding. I'll have to ask about that later.

"Then, I think I'm as ready as I'm going to be," Taelien explained. "Wish me luck."

"Good luck," Edon said, sounding sincere.

Myros muttered something that was nearly inaudible in spite of the sound-enhancing helmet. It sounded like, "...keep you healthy."

Taelien nodded to both of the so-called gods, ignited the candle inside his lantern with a stray thought, and strode to the metal doors.

I probably shouldn't waste my strength, Taelien considered *as he pressed his hand against the metal. But I can't resist a chance to show off just a little.*

Open.

A tall rectangle of metal stretched open, making room for Taelien to step inside and revealing a glimmering surface barring the way into a dim chamber beyond. Carefully, he took a step closer and brushed his fingers against the surface of the barrier, bringing back a wet hand a moment later. Thin lines of water began to flow out of the chamber where his fingertips had brushed the surface.

That whole room is underwater, he realized, grimacing. *This is going to be less than fun.*

He glanced back toward Myros and Edon, but they only stared silently down at him from the carpeted area above the rune-etched platform.

It's leaking now, which means maybe I could drain the water out of that entire room eventually – but something tells me Edon wouldn't be happy about that.

Now aware of the water, Taelien pushed a hand deeper inside, testing for any more surprises. The water was cold, but not freezing – he had gone diving in worse conditions near Liadra. Water flowed freely across his arm now, soaking his shirt.

He took a deep breath and stuck his head inside, hoping to glance around and establish the location of an exit, but the interior of the room unlit. Withdrawing briefly, the swordsman took a final deep breath and plunged himself completely inside.

This isn't nearly the kind of fun I was hoping for, Taelien considered as the water chilled his skin. Once inside the doorway, he was forced to fight pressure that pushed outward toward the opening he had created. The casing on his lantern shattered almost immediately, water filling the cage and banishing his only source of light aside from the doorway below.

He planted his feet as best he could against the floor and pushed upward, trying to shove himself above the water level. He raised his sword arm, hoping the blade would collide with the ceiling and give him warning to prevent him from hitting his head.

Taelien's initial push was insufficient to take him to the ceiling, but he resisted the downward pull and continued to swim upward for what felt like minutes. His lungs were burning when he felt his blade impact with something, and he slowed his fervent kicking, his head emerging from the liquid a moment later.

There was barely any room to breathe at the top of the chamber, and still no visible source of light. He considered dropping the lantern, but he hoped that the metal inlay had held the candle in position – if it had, he could still potentially relight it in another room, even without the glass.

Taking several moments just to breathe, Taelien began to feel his way along the ceiling, attempting to find his way toward any sort of alternate exit from the room. He noted that the downward suction appeared to have stopped, and a glance downward showed him only blackness – had his entrance closed?

Edon might have sealed me in here, he realized. *Either to kill me, or maybe just to prevent the water from ruining his pretty purple carpet.*

Or, of course, whatever lives inside here might have shut the way out.

A moment after having that thought, Taelien felt something solid coil around his left leg.

Oh, resh. I had to think about that, didn't I.

The coil yanked, dragging Taelien under the water.

Taelien lashed out with his borrowed sword, striking for whatever had encircled his leg. His attack was impeded by the water's resistance, but he still connected solidly – against something with the consistency of stone. The sword vibrated in his hand, and a second coil wrapped around his right leg, dragging him downward faster.

This is not how I want to die, he told himself.

He swung his sword again, but the strike was equally ineffective. Releasing his grip on the sword, he grit his teeth and reached out for whatever was dragging him downward. His hand felt something smooth and solid, and he felt the Dominion of Stone tingling in the back of his mind. Stone was one of the two prime dominions that connected to metal, but he had never had the talent to properly utilize it.

Now seemed like a good time to start.

Break, he told the stone, but there was no reply.

Fine, if you're going to be like that, we'll do this the hard way. Taelien tightened his grip around the stone tendril and pulled upward. For an instant, he felt his movement downward slow, and he grinned against his pain, releasing the lantern from his other hand.

His left hand joined the right, and he slid them across the stone tendril, seeking a weak point. He couldn't picture the stone as easily in his mind as he could with metal, but he found a crack with his fingers.

You're going to break now, he told the stone, and he heaved with both of his hands.

The tendril snapped, and Taelien surged upward, the second tendril going slack as the first one shattered. Taelien's shoulder bumped something – his lantern, he realized after a moment – as he floated upward, and he snagged it with his off-hand as he made his way back to the surface.

Fortunate I didn't bump into Myros' sword, he realized as his head broke through the water. He took several panting breaths, realizing that whatever had grabbed him – made of stone or not – could probably do it again.

Was that a monster or a trap? More likely the former, given that it went slack when I broke off a piece of it, but how could a monster be made of stone?

He thought back to stories of creatures from the dominions themselves. Could there be a beast native to the Dominion of Stone living in these waters? It seemed unnatural – not only were natives to the dominions rarely found in the mortal world, but it seemed strange that one could survive while immersed in a completely different dominion.

He dismissed his speculation for the moment – he had more important things to consider. He touched the ceiling again, finding protrusions of stone that he could use as hand-holds if something grabbed him again. Slowly, he made his way across the room, with no clear idea of his direction or destination.

As time wore on, he considered lifting his lantern above the water to relight it, but the water level was so high that he doubted he would get more than a few moments of light before it was immersed again. The tax on his body was not worth the brief illumination it would provide – at least for now.

After what felt like at least an hour, his knee bumped into something hard. He winced, but rejoiced at the same time – it was a hard, flat surface. His right hand reached out, finding another wall – hopefully the opposite wall. Once there, he shifted to moving his right hand across the surface, floating along the wall while he searched for any sign of light. Instead, after several minutes, he found a large gap - a rectangular hole, perhaps a few feet high, and above the water line.

Taelien reached into the space, finding it perfectly flat, and apparently empty – at least as far as his arm could reach. Judging that sufficient, he set the lantern inside and steadied himself with his right arm.

Ignite, he instructed the Dominion of Flame, creating a tiny flicker of fire inside the lantern – just sufficient to reveal that the candle was no longer inside.

Oh, this just gets better and better.

Taelien sighed, casting the useless lantern back into the water behind him, and crawled into the stone space.

This would be a really bad time for those spears Myros was talking about to come out of the walls, Taelien considered. *I really need light.*

He considered two options – he could flood the necessary strength into the Sae'kes to make the blue gemstone on the pommel glow, or he could try to maintain a fire with the Dominion of Flame. Either would tax him greatly, but the former would require him to move the sword out in front of him to be of significant use – and he wasn't willing to risk losing the weapon the way he had lost Myros' sword.

Gritting his teeth, Taelien reached out in front of him and called the Dominion of Flame. A warm light formed in his palm, and he shined it against the walls, looking for any holes that looked likely to hold spears. When he found none, he crawled in further, noting that turning around would be impossible in the cramped confines he was pushing himself into. If he had to leave, he'd be forced to push himself backward – which would be an arduous process.

Taelien continued to crawl, finding that the space extended into a long tunnel that arched subtly upward. *I wonder if this is where the water poured into the room from,* Taelien considered. *If so, another torrent of water – or worse – could come down this way at any time.*

Not relishing the thought of being stuck in the tunnel while water washed through it, Taelien crawled his way through as fast as he could. Maintaining the sphere of flame in his hand dried his sleeves, but the chill that came over his body from expending his body heat only made the contrast to his soaking clothes more prominent.

The conjured flame flickered and dimmed as he progressed, seemingly faster than it should have. He drew harder on the dominion, expending more of his own body heat to maintain the necessary illumination to continue. *There's that sorcery suppression they were talking about,* he realized. *It's going to get worse as I get deeper.*

His body was shivering uncontrollably when he caught the sight of another source of light ahead – a green light signifying the exit to the tunnel. He pushed himself forward, extinguishing his own flame immediately, and paused just at the edge of the entrance to the new chamber.

A scythe-like blade of metal swept over the exit of the tunnel, nearly brushing against Taelien's hair.

Really glad I stopped there, Taelien considered, just as a spear flashed from across the room toward where Taelien was still crouched inside the tunnel. His right hand caught the spear just before it smashed into his body, the force of the impact carrying the point of the spear to just in front of his face.

A second later, the scythe swept over the entrance again, smashing the wooden shaft of the spear.

Taelien pondered the amputated spearhead in his hand, flipping it around in his grip. *Xixis apparently took their vaults very seriously.*

A glint of metal signified a second spear launching toward Taelien, but he was ready this time. He hurled his spearhead out of the tunnel, catching the incoming spear head-on and knocking it backward to tumble to the floor. As the scythe swept past a moment later, Taelien kicked off of the floor of the tunnel, launching himself into the room.

Half a dozen steel blades launched from the wall to his right. Without so much as a thought, Taelien ripped the scabbard off his belt, spinning the still-sheathed Sae'kes and deflecting five of the blades, then catching the sixth in his left hand.

He was no longer shivering when he took his next step forward. He was in battle - his body had no more room for weakness.

Another scythe swept out at neck level from the wall behind him, but Taelien caught it on the blade he had snatched out of the air. The scythe's mechanism pushed hard enough to carry Taelien backward, nearly pushing him into the trajectory of the second scythe near the tunnel entrance. Taelien growled, tightening his grip on the trap blade, and felt the metal inside connecting with the scythe.

Every structural weakness within the ancient scythe flashed in his mind, and he swept upward with the Sae'kes' scabbard. The metal lining on the scabbard smashed into the weak point, shattering the scythe apart, and Taelien ducked to avoid the remains of the weapon as it swept by.

For several moments, the only sound was the other scythe sweeping behind him, nearly close enough to draw blood.

"Is that all?" Taelien muttered. "I thought this was supposed to be a challenge."

Discarding the borrowed blade in his left hand, Taelien wrapped his now-broken belt back around his waist. After a few moments, he managed to tie a knot to get it to sit on his waist, and he glanced around the room to try to find the source of the green light.

He found an open doorway about ten feet beyond him, nearly directly across from his tunnel, the green shimmering from somewhere beyond.

Shaking out his wet hair, Taelien stepped forward toward the light.

As he approached, Taelien inspected the chamber beyond. It was much larger than the room he stood within – and in the distance, he could see the glittering of metal objects lined against a wall. Toward the center, directly across from where he stood, was a raised pedestal – and on it was a bright green gemstone, shining with the light that illuminated both rooms.

I think I found what I'm here for, Taelien considered with a smirk. *At least for my first trip.*

It was only after Taelien stepped into the doorway that he saw the chains.

A colossal figure appeared from beyond the pedestal, a wall of shadows and glittering metal, only humanoid in the vaguest of senses. It stood half again Taelien's height, and its body seemed composed of solid darkness, save for long, bladed metal claws on its four front appendages. Its head resembled something that might have been on a huge insect, if the insect had been born in the nightmares of a madman.

A long chain bound the creature around the waist, and that chain was attached directly to the pedestal carrying the gemstone.

Taelien took an involuntary step back. He had heard of creatures like this before – beasts from the Dominion of Shadow itself. They had been bound by the sorcerers of Xixis to be used as weapons in battle, and each one was said to be capable of fighting a hundred men at a time.

He stood before a harvester of shadows, one of the most dangerous creatures of legend.

His hand darted to the hilt of his sword as the creature vanished, appearing right in front of him. The harvester's bladed claws flashed through the air, and Taelien didn't even attempt to parry – the monster was just too large. He stepped backward awkwardly, barely avoiding the strike as it scraped against the stone doorway.

Taelien tensed for another attack, but the creature came no further.

The chains, he realized. The metal chains that were bound around the harvester's waist glittered in the green light, and he realized that they had an inscription – too tiny to read – across the entire surface of each ring. *They prevent it from leaving the room.*

His first instinct was to draw his sword and strike. With the legendary sword of the gods of the Tae'os Pantheon, perhaps he could land a telling blow, even against such a powerful monster. It was bound to the room, which would limit its angles of attack – although he judged that its reach still exceeded his, even with the sword. He would have to be fast.

He released his grip on the sword. *No,* he told himself. *I will not kill another prisoner.*

But neither will I be enough of a fool to let it free.

Taelien charged.

The creature swept its claws at him in a broad strike, just as he had predicted. Taelien dropped and rolled under the strike, pushing himself back to his feet in an instant. He sprinted toward the gem, but the creature reappeared directly in front of him.

Resh. The claws flashed toward him, and his feet were too slow – he had no alternative.

The Sae'kes flashed into his hand, four runes glowing blue on the surface as he parried the strike. Sparks flickered as the claws impacted against the surface, the force of the blow carrying Taelien back several feet. He kept his footing – barely – and stared the harvester down.

To his surprise, the creature paused, lowering its head. A moment later, it opened its maw impossibly wide, revealing a glittering row of teeth as long as Taelien's arm. The harvester made a cackling noise and vanished.

Taelien spun to find the creature immediately, but he didn't parry this time.

Chain, he told the sword.

The blade shifted into a length of gleaming metal chain, and he swept it outward, wrapping it around the incoming claw.

As the claw approached, Taelien jumped backward, merging the Sae'kes chains together into a solid cable and yanking backward. The harvester struggled, pulling Taelien forward with strength that exceeded his own – but that was fine. He didn't need to be stronger than the harvester.

Only the sword did.

As the harvester dragged him in, he launched himself past it, flipping the sword over. *Wings into blades,* he commanded, and the wings of the hilt shifted into dagger-like protrusions. He shoved them straight into the stone floor.

Spread, he commanded, and the daggers embedded in the floor branched outward, creating flat surfaces of metal parallel to the stone.

Taelien danced backward as the creature spun and lashed out with another claw — and then struggled as the new chains from the sword pinned it just out of reach.

The creature emitted a loud, guttural growl, straining against its bonds. Taelien circled around it at a careful distance, with his own chains binding it from moving more than a few feet, and the other set of chains limiting its ability to move away from the pedestal.

Taelien approached the pedestal hastily, only taking a brief glance at the other objects lined against the wall. There were swords, spears, and daggers of metals — and even types of stone — he wasn't even sure he recognized. He noted a golden crown with a ruby set in the center aside some sort of wooden scepter. They were undoubtedly all of great value, but the gem was the most obvious object of value in this room — and the longer he stayed, the more danger he would be exposed to.

It would be a shame not to grab at least a couple more things, he told himself. He found a long sword of a strange red metal that looked like it might fit his scabbard, sheathed it awkwardly, and hooked a silvery dagger into his belt. He didn't trust himself to be able to carry much more through the water.

And, feeling satisfied with his discoveries, he grabbed the green gem with his left hand.

The chains emanating from the pedestal shattered.

Oh, that's —

The creature ripped the Sae'kes out of the floor, snapping the stone apart as it rushed toward him. Taelien managed to draw the red metal sword in time to parry, but the claws pushed past the weapon, ripping into Taelien's left arm. He stumbled back into the pillar, dropping the green gem, and lashing out with a counterstrike.

The harvester batted the red sword aside effortlessly, sweeping a pair of claws toward Taelien's waist level to bisect him.

Noting the length of the claws, Taelien stepped inward, the metal claws clashing against one another as he called the Dominion of Flame around his left hand – and slammed a blazing fist into the harvester's face.

The creature reeled back, emitting a hideous screeching noise as smoke rose from what was presumably a wound. Taelien shuddered at the pain that shot through his injured arm at the impact, but he did not slow his movements. He grasped the metallic cords of the Sae'kes with his left hand, commanding the sword back into a chain.

He stepped forward again, slamming the hilt of the red-bladed sword into the creature's chest as he unraveled the Sae'kes chain from around its claw. After a moment, the sacred blade came free, and he slashed the gleaming blade through the air, sending the creature staggering back to avoid the strike.

That was all the room he needed. He sheathed the red blade and ducked right under another sweeping claw, grabbing the green gemstone, and slammed a shoulder into the harvester as he rose. The creature staggered backward, feeling lighter than its size would have indicated, and he slammed the glowing gemstone straight into the creature's chest. A flash of light nearly blinded Taelien, and another trail of smoke issued from the creature's body as it fell backward.

Taelien shoved past it, prepared to block another strike using the Sae'kes, but it never came. The creature vanished, and after a moment of panic, Taelien realized it had not reappeared within the room.

Good, he told himself. *I don't think I injured it too badly – it should live.*

On one level, he knew it seemed nonsensical to care about the survival of a creature that had just attempted to bisect him...but he needed it to live. He needed to be able to fight without killing.

With the gem in his right hand and the Sae'kes in his left, he strode through the trap room. The claw marks on his left arm burned, and he could feel the Sae'kes drawing at his strength every moment it was drawn – but he didn't care. He had a light source, he had protection, and he knew the way out.

The scythe-like blade guarding the entrance to the tunnel swept in front of him, and he stuck the Sae'kes out. The scythe parted like paper as it impacted with his blade, veering off to strike a stone wall on one of the sides of the room. Taelien smirked as he shivered, climbing into the tunnel.

The next several minutes were agonizing. Brushing up against the wall of the tunnel sent jolts of fresh pain through his injured arm, and every push seemed to threaten to drain away the rest of his remaining strength. The tunnel was angled downward now, at least, which made progress somewhat faster. It was almost refreshing when his hand brushed the surface of the water from the first room – almost.

The chill from the liquid was overwhelming. He shuddered, pushing himself into the water in spite of his growing weariness, and shone the gemstone into the water to find the entrance doors.

He spotted the massive metal doors across the room – so far that he could scarcely believe he had made the swim before – and a second and third set of doors near the bottom of the pool. He ignored the additional doors, groggily swimming using only his legs, his hands still gripped tightly around his sword and gem. The water felt soothing against the burning of his wound, but it nevertheless drained at his strength further. The once-brilliant light of his blade had faded to near invisibility. By the time he reached the opposite wall, he could barely keep his legs moving. He didn't swim downward – he simply held his breath and sank.

When he reached the metal door, his blade flashed outward, carving a gaping hole. Pressure did most of the rest of the work, pushing him against the wall – he simply had to cut the hole wider, and then fit himself through.

He had forgotten how far the top of the door was from the ground.

The water pushed him outside the vault, and Taelien fell more than ten feet before slamming into another pool of water – the water that had collected from the breaches he had created in the barrier after opening the door. The pool barely cushioned his fall, but it prevented him from slamming directly into the stone floor. The impact drove the last air out of his lungs, forcing the glowing stone from his grasp.

For a moment, Taelien was insensate, and then strong arms pulled him from the water.

His vision was a blur at first, and then Myros' helmed head was looming above him. Myros held the green gem in a hand – and stretched it out, placing it in Taelien's hand.

"I think you earned this," came the booming voice.

Taelien gave a weak smile, grasping the gem with what was left of his flagging strength. "Thanks," he managed to stammer before breaking into a series of coughs.

Myros dragged him to his feet, and he barely managed to keep himself from falling back down. *How embarrassing.*

Edon hovered nearby, smiling. "You've done very well, Taelien, just as I had hoped. Now, hand me the gem, and we'll see about giving you godhood, as you deserve."

Taelien wiped the water out of his eyes, and then groggily reached out with his hand, offering the gemstone to Edon. "Here," he said. "Take it."

Edon stepped forward with an outstretched hand, but Myros stepped in between the two of them, raising the Heartlance.

"Don't give it to him yet. He has some questions to answer first," Myros demanded.

What? Taelien shook his head, trying to regain his focus, but he was so tired. With a jolt, he realized he was still clutching the Sae'kes in a death grip in his left hand – and only one rune on the surface was still lit. *Oh, gods.* He fumbled with the new sword in his scabbard, unsheathing it and discarding it onto the floor, and noting that the silver dagger had been lost at some point – presumably during the swim.

He sheathed the Sae'kes immediately thereafter, feeling its drain on his strength cease, but regaining none of the energy it had already stolen from him.

"What's this about, Myros?" Edon asked, his question mirroring Taelien's bleary thoughts. "Is there a problem?"

"There might be," Myros said. "Someone visited me last night. That someone claimed you've been sacrificing Rethri for immortality."

Oh, the Rethri. I knew I was forgetting something important. Guess Jonan or Lydia has been busy.

Edon quirked a brow. "That's quite a claim, and absurd. I do have Rethri guests in the city, as you already know – but they're here of their own volition. Sacrificing people for immortality? That's nonsense."

"See, that's what I thought – until I read the journal they gave me. I didn't read it quite the way they did. I don't think you're doing ritual sacrifices. I think you've been using the Rethri as test subjects for making some kind of dominion bonds, and telling the Rethri it's for their benefit. And you're killing them with your tests." Myros shifted the Heartlance into a combat stance, preparing to strike.

Edon frowned, looking down. "It's not like that," he mumbled. "I never wanted anyone to die. I just need to understand how they work. Without research, without testing, I'll never know enough."

Myros stood a little straighter, and Taelien shuffled the gemstone to his left hand, moving his right to the hilt of the Sae'kes. *This is a really bad time for a fight, at least for me.*

"So, you admit it, then? You've been killing people with your tests?" Myros sounded shocked, perhaps even a bit sad, but it was difficult to judge with the sound-augmentation from the helmet.

"It's more complicated than that," Edon insisted. "I've been testing on people who are already ill. Sometimes, those tests are too strenuous for people in their condition. I had hoped to be able to save everyone, but my progress has been too slow. I've had my failures. I admit that. But I'll figure out how to cure them soon – it will be a net positive on lives. I will save more than I lose."

Myros growled, taking a step forward. "And do these people know you've been risking their lives?"

"The ones who are conscious, yes," Edon replied, shaking his head. "The others were brought by their families. Families that needed hope, and had nowhere else to turn. They needed something miraculous. Divine intervention."

Taelien wearily lifted a hand and pointed at Edon. "That might be true for some, but what about the Esharen you were keeping under the bank?"

Edon spun toward Taelien, raising a clenched fist. "You – you're the one... I should have known. That Esharen, like all Esharen, was a monster. It deserved no better. And I was making valuable progress with my studies on it."

"It," Taelien pointed out, "Was a him. A living, sentient creature – not an object for your studies. If you were really just taking volunteers, I'd think about helping you, even if there were risks. What you were doing to that Esharen wasn't research – it was torture. Taking notes on torture does not make it research."

Myros looked to Taelien, then back to Edon. "You had an Esharen prisoner? And you didn't think that was worth mentioning to the rest of us?"

"You're fixating on the wrong things, Myros. Calm down. I'm sure you don't tell me every little thing that happens in your day. Where would you be if I hadn't found you? Still in Valeria, playing politics with petty nobles? I gave you a part in something greater – a purpose. That's the same thing I'm doing for these test subjects." He was no longer stumbling over his words – he had raised his voice, nearly to yelling.

Myros set the Heartlance against the floor. "You're right about one thing – I wasn't much of anything back at home. You taught me a lot, and I'm grateful for that, I really am. But there's no excuse for torture and taking lives – and if you've been lying about that, I can't trust that you haven't been lying about anything – or everything – else."

"If you're not satisfied with my progress – or my methods – help me. If you turn on me, you're just throwing away all the progress that I made from their sacrifices. Help me, we can finish my research. We can make things better," Edon offered.

"I nearly killed someone last night because of your lies. I nearly killed Taelien a few weeks before – again, because of your lies. I will have no further part in this...and neither will you. You will answer for your crimes," Myros raised the Heartlance. "Surrender now, and I will turn you over to the queen for judgment. Taelien, are you with me?"

Taelien nodded to Myros immediately, plucking the red-bladed sword from the floor and stepping behind Edon. He put the sword at Edon's back.

Edon quirked a brow. "If you were going to try to make a coup, it would have been smarter to do it before Taelien walked the path. Do you really want to do this, Myros?"

"If I had done this before, Taelien wouldn't have had the gem. I've been down there more often than you have – I know how the vault works. I knew he'd find it. And I know what it does," Myros explained.

"Well," Edon said, "That's comforting, that you had a plan, at least. Unfortunately, I must decline to surrender."

Taelien tensed. This wasn't what he wanted, but he was too tired to argue. He was too tired to do much of anything – and he was certainly too tired to fight.

Hope Myros plans to do all the heavy lifting for this one, Taelien considered.

"Now," Myros signaled, shifting to a blur of movement as the Heartlance shot forward.

Edon sidestepped, seeming to know the trajectory of Myros' attack before it occurred, and Taelien was forced to parry the spear himself. He lashed out with the red-bladed sword, but the attack was far too slow. Edon danced to the side, grabbing the Heartlance's shaft and snapping his fingers.

Myros vanished in a flash of blue, leaving the Heartlance in Edon's hands.

"Sad, really. I always liked Myros," Edon spun the spear playfully. "You, I have less of an investment in. And you seem to have made your choice. Eru volar shen taris."

Taelien struggled to raise his sword as a blast of blue-white emerged from Edon's hand, encompassing Taelien's entire body, and his vision went white.

CHAPTER XIV – FORGING DIVINITY

Earlier in the Morning of Taelien's Trial

Lydia and Istavan had escorted the caravan the rest of the way to Coldridge, where they had found Sethridge waiting for them with a second contingent of guards. Istavan and Sethridge seemed unsurprised to see each other, indicating to Lydia that this was part of their plan.

Seems Sethridge has chosen his side, too.

Istavan insisted on staying with Sethridge and escorting the caravan the rest of the way to Selyr to avoid any "further complications". Lydia spent the night in Coldridge, and then headed back to Orlyn on her own.

The sorceress arrived at the city gates after nightfall, so she returned to her own quarters and slept there, heading to Jonan's house the following morning.

Lydia knocked at the door politely, hand resting on the hilt of her sword. Her Comprehensive Barrier was already active, just in case Jonan had decided to change his allegiance in the last few days.

After two minutes without a reply, Lydia knocked again, louder this time.

After another two minutes, she unsheathed her saber and opened the unlocked door.

It was immediately evident that the house had been ransacked. Nothing was where it should have been – and the glassware that had sat on the table near the kitchen had been shattered. This wasn't a robbery – the level of disarray was too deliberate. This was someone sending a message.

"Dominion of Knowledge, illuminate that which is touched by your cousins," Lydia spoke, and a green flicker illuminated the shattered fragments of several scattered pieces of glasswork. The faint signature of dominion sorcery was already fading – breaking the pieces of glass had apparently weakened their bond, which by Jonan's admission was never particularly stable.

"Jonan, are you inside?" She advanced into the building, weapon still drawn. *I could cast another spell to reveal invisible figures, but it's probably not worth giving myself a headache. It's not likely anyone is still present – this place could have been sacked any time in the last few days. If someone wants to attack me, their first attack is going to bounce right off my barrier, and then I'll counterattack as needed.*

She scoured the house, finding more damaged glasswork, and signs that the home had been hastily abandoned. *The food is starting to smell, which is a pretty good indication that Jonan hadn't been here recently. He's too finicky to tolerate anything decomposing in his house.*

There were no signs of blood, no signs of combat – but she did find a rug in his bedroom that seemed slightly out of place. She moved it, checking beneath for any telltale signs of battle, but there was nothing visibly amiss.

Odd, she considered, but she moved the rug back to its proper place and exited the building.

I'll have to get back to the high palace and warn Taelien that Jonan has been discovered. After that, I suppose I'll report to the queen.

A grimace appeared on her face as she walked, deepening with every block. *How was Jonan's location discovered? Is he safe?*

She was about half-way back to the palace when she noted a cloaked and hooded figure walking parallel to her on the opposite side of the street, pacing her. There were plenty of other civilians around, but the hood made the man stand out – it was far too warm of weather for such a thing to be necessary.

Lydia turned left at the next intersection, deviating from the path toward the palace. As she had anticipated, the figure turned as well. She noted the figure's height, build, and finally the glint of glass from the front of his hood before she rolled her eyes and crossed the street to meet him.

"If you're going to follow someone, you might try being a bit more subtle about it, Jonan," she chastised him.

"I am aghast at your accusation," he said, putting his hand to his chest in mock offense. "I am a veritable paragon of subtlety."

"For a moment, I was worried that you might have been killed, but I can see you're just the same as usual," Lydia remarked. She smiled in spite of herself, feeling a hint of her tension dissipate as they continued to walk. She turned again, leading him back in the direction of the high palace.

He slipped his hood down, smiling at her. "You were worried about me? I'm touched. But it'll take more than a couple of goddesses to catch me – not that I minded the attention, given-"

"Goddesses? What happened?" Lydia scanned the streets for anyone that looked even close to as suspicious as Jonan did. The people nearby looked like ordinary civilians on standard business, but that didn't make speaking about complex matters of local politics less dangerous. "And lower your voice."

"As you wish," Jonan whispered, taking a step closer to her and leaning in close. "Vorain paid me a little visit. You saw the evidence of that. I'm fortunate that the broken mirrors are still somewhat functional, otherwise I would never have noticed your arrival."

"Vorain was trying to kill you?" Lydia asked, quirking a brow. "I thought she had let you go previously – what changed?"

"Ah, it wasn't that, precisely. Actually, she wanted my help, so she broke all my things. Women are so complicated, you know? Goddesses are no different, it seems."

Lydia made a face at him at that remark, but he only flashed a grin back at her – one that he must have presumed to be charming, but came across as more obnoxious.

"Continue," she instructed through gritted teeth.

"Well, we had some fun breaking into the high palace, and found a few neat trinkets," he said, reaching into his cloak. Lydia watched him warily, but what he withdrew was just a pair of books.

He leaned close, whispering into her ear in earnest now. "Edon's research notes. Evidence he was experimenting on the Rethri."

Lydia snatched the top book out of his hand. "Ooh, let me see that."

Jonan flinched, shoving the second book back into his robes. "You don't have to be so grabby, I would have been happy to show you the highlights."

"You can't blame me for being a little excited," she pointed out, flipping it open. "This is probably the best lead we've ever found."

Week sixty six. Morella confirms that the procedure to remove the first dominion bond has finally succeeded, although at a great cost – the subject is rapidly deteriorating. I have been attempting to find the correct syntax to renew the bond, but thus far my efforts have met with no success. If I had access to an artifact designed to create a bond, Morella and I could find a solution rapidly, but for now the only possibility is to attempt every possible combination we can think of. If we fail, I fear our subject's life may be forfeit. We must succeed.

"Gods above," Lydia murmured. "This is proof, but it's more than that. It has details about the results of his studies. This could contain the secrets of how he's faking his divine abilities."

"It does contain a few hints of that, yes," Jonan said. "I've only had a chance to skim it, so I'd like that back."

Lydia gave him a sad look. "But – but I wanted to read it."

Jonan folded his arms. "Really? Giving me baby eyes?"

She handed the book back to him, smirking. "You're no fun at all sometimes. Also, I'm sure the queen is going to want to see it. She's already been working to move against Edon, apparently for political reasons."

"Now that's interesting news – but I'm going to have to insist on holding onto it. I went to some fairly substantial work to find that, risking life and so on, and I might have lost a friend in the process. A very beautiful and capable friend, in fact," he said, grabbing the book back from her.

Lydia stepped backward, smirking. "You haven't lost me yet, silly. I'm right here."

"Well, you are quite beautiful and competent, of course, but I happened to be referring to the goddess I was working with. I'm afraid she didn't make it out of the palace," he said with a grimace.

Lydia leaned over, still trying to glance at more of the writing in the book. "What? What happened?"

"Now you're the one that needs to quiet down. We should really find a more discreet place to have this talk. Maybe in Taelien's room – if we hurry, maybe we can catch him before he has to walk the Paths of Ascension."

Lydia quirked a brow. "Is he doing that today?"

"That's the rumor going around the palace," Jonan said with a nod. "Vorain and I broke in last night, found the book, and got caught by another young woman. I didn't recognize her. Dark hair, tall, muscular. She attacked, and Vorain bought me the time to escape. I went out a window, hoping Vorain would catch up to me. She didn't."

"And you haven't heard from her since?" Lydia asked. "And why did she want your help with this in the first place?"

"I put it in her head that Edon was experimenting on her brother – which is almost certainly true. And she knew I had sight sorcery, which is pretty rare, so she strong armed me into helping her investigate. Anyway, I tried to find her today. Swept the prisons, even checked the Adellan room in the low palace, but there's no sign of her. I didn't dare go back into the place with the books, of course. I'm not risking another encounter with that dark-haired girl – she was at least as fast as Vorain, and probably stronger," he concluded, taking a deep breath after rambling his explanation.

Faster than Vorain? That's bad news, if she's working with Edon. But maybe Vorain came out on top in the fight – we have no way of really knowing at this point. And if Vorain won, maybe we can find her and get her to help us at some point.

"All right, let's get to Taelien. He should know about this before he walks the Paths of Ascension. From what I was reading in this book, it sounds like Edon is using artifacts for his experiments, too. Maybe he's using these 'paths' as a trap to get the Sae'kes away from Taelien," Lydia offered.

"Interesting," Jonan mumbled. "You got that all out of looking at one page?"

"I do have an epiphany from time to time," Lydia said with a smile.

"I don't doubt it. You're kind of scary when you think like that, but I think I like it," he said, pulling his robes around him more tightly.

Lydia blinked, not quite sure what to make of that comment. She thought she might be blushing, but fortunately, he wasn't looking in her direction. They continued the rest of the way to the palace in silence.

As they approached the entrance, Jonan finally spoke again. "Should I be making us invisible or something?"

Lydia shook her head. "No need, I'll just tell people you're with me."

He shrugged at that. "I suppose I won't complain about conserving my sight for a bit."

"Good. Now, let me do the talking for a while," she said, adjusting her glasses.

Lydia had no difficulty convincing the guards to let them inside, nor getting directions to Taelien's room. By the time they found it, however, the room was empty.

"That's not a good sign," Lydia muttered.

She turned around, seeing a servant she vaguely recognized walking down the hall. *Same servant who woke me up a few days ago,* she recognized. *He's not wearing his earring this time, but it's definitely him.*

"Young man," she called out, failing to remember his name. "Excuse me!"

He paused, turning around, taking a step back when he saw Lydia. "Oh, um, court sorceress! How can I serve you?"

To her side, Jonan tilted his head to the side, looking perplexed for some reason.

"The man who was in this room – the one they call the Taelien. Have you seen him today?" she asked.

The servant nodded. "Oh, yes, m'lady. He went to the Paths of Ascension about a half hour ago. Would you like me to escort you there?"

She shook her head. "No, that won't be necessary, I know my way about. Thank you, young man. You've been very helpful. I didn't catch your name."

"Stuart, m'lady," he bowed at the waist. "Is there anything else I can assist you with?"

"No, that's quite all right," she said, nodding her head. "Thank you again."

He nodded and turned back around, hastily escaping from sight.

Lydia stepped deeper into Taelien's room, and Jonan shut the door.

"Any of your mirrors in here?" Lydia asked.

Jonan shook his head. "No, I haven't had a chance to plant one. I could right now, if you wanted to keep track of when Taelien returns. I'm afraid my supply is running very low, however."

"No, don't waste one, then. I think we should follow Taelien into the paths and make sure he's safe," Lydia explained.

"That...that would be quite a risk," he stammered. "Could we perhaps wait at the entrance for him to return?"

Not willing to take a risk for Taelien? I can't blame him, I suppose. He's one of Vaelien's servants, after all, not one of us.

Regardless of the justification, she couldn't help but feel slightly disappointed.

"You can wait outside. Can you maintain an invisibility spell on me while I'm outside of your own sight?" Lydia asked.

He grimaced. "For a bit, maybe. That's considerably more difficult – and one of the few places your style of incanted sorcery works better than mine." The admission seemed to pain him, but Lydia found it somewhat comforting. *At least he has one weakness I can keep in mind for if we ever work against each other.*

"Well, as long as you can get me into the paths, I don't think it'll matter. If there are people lying in wait inside the paths, I can always tell them that the queen sent me. The people guarding the entrance to the paths will probably know who should be inside, but once I'm in the door, I should be fine," Lydia decided.

He nodded. "All right. When do you want me to make us invisible? Now?"

She nodded. "If he's already been in there a while, there's no telling what kind of danger he might be in – regardless of whether or not it's actually a trap."

"Are you sure we're adequately prepared for this?" Jonan asked. "If we have to fight Edon – or Myros – or both – how do we handle those contingencies?"

"From my talks with the queen and some of the other sorcerers, I think Edon had two primary power sources. One, I think he was somehow stealing power from the Rethri by manipulating their dominion bonds. Two, he's figured out some way to tap into the sorcery that was used to make some of the most ancient artifacts – like the Heartlance and the Sae'kes."

"Right," Jonan replied. "And he presumably has at least one artifact other than the Heartlance already on-hand. Something tied to the Dominion of Sound – maybe Myros' armor, with all the runes on it?"

"That's a good guess," Lydia admitted. "Edon also wears a ring with a large crystal in it. That could be another artifact."

"Hrm. Only ring I'm aware of that would qualify as an artifact is Hartigan's Star, which has a red gemstone – but I suppose others could certainly exist. The gods made many weapons and jewels that have been lost over time, or so they say," Jonan said, sounding contemplative.

"Well, at least some of the Rethri have been taken care of," Lydia explained. "I should have said this before, but I've been away the last few days escorting some of the Rethri out of the city. On orders from the queen, no less. She's taking overt actions against Edon right now, and I'm not clear on why – the timing can't be coincidental. He sent a sorcerer to stop us, too, which means he's aware that the queen is moving against him," Lydia explained.

"The queen working against Edon should be reassuring me, but it's really not," he shook his head. His expression looked troubled.

"It gets worse, I'm afraid. The sorcerer who attacked us had far more dominions than he should have – as if he was using gifts of the gods."

"Not all that surprising, actually," Jonan replied.

Lydia quirked a brow.

"I read a bit further in that book," Jonan explained. "Most of that research is on dominion bonds. He was trying to figure out new ways to both make and break them. He succeeded at breaking established bonds first, which is odd enough in itself."

"I've heard that Lady Aayara has a way of stealing dominion bonds, but I'm sure you'd know more about that." She gave him a pointed look.

Jonan winced. "Legends indicate that the Vae'kes in general have a way of stealing sorcery from others, yes. Obviously, the Lady of Thieves would be the most famous case, and I do suspect her abilities would extend to moving dominion bonds from someone to herself. That doesn't sound precisely like what Edon was doing, however."

Well, at least he doesn't seem pleased to work for those monsters.

"How can you work for creatures like those? You don't seem like the type of person who would approve of the way the Vae'kes behave. They just take things away from ordinary people – it's directly opposite of what the gods are supposed to do," Lydia said, realizing how harsh her words must have sounded after they came out.

He turned his gaze away from her, a sad look crossing his face. "The order teaches that the Vae'kes only use their power against criminals and threats to the world as a whole. Jacinth assassinates people who are too politically connected for the law to touch them. Aayara steals relics of power from despots and tyrants, turning them over to the Preserver."

His tone softened, and he looked back to her. "Vaelien protects his people. His children are supposed to be an extension of that."

"I note that you say 'supposed to'," she began, but his expression soured. "We can discuss this another time. Thank you for giving me some context on your side of things. What precisely do you think Edon was trying to do, if it's not like how the Vae'kes work?"

"I don't think he ever discovered a way to move a bond directly from one person to another. Rather, he was trying to break bonds on Rethri and replace them with different bonds – like changing a Rethri's bond from flame to stone, for example. He would make attempt after attempt, and someone named Morella would gather information from his tests. She seems like she's his partner in all this. I think she's a former Paladin of Sytira."

Lydia tilted her head to the side. "Morella? A Paladin of Sytira? Why do you say that?"

"There are references about them being together at 'the citadel'. I think they grew up together, and when he was excommunicated, she went with him. From the notes, she seems to have types of sorcery that he doesn't, so he needed her for his research."

Knowledge and memory sorcery, Lydia considered. *Both commonly practiced by paladins and priests of Sytira. I learned the former myself, but never the latter.*

"And this research – you're saying they succeeded?" Lydia asked absently, knowing she had already experienced the answer.

"It seems so. They managed to break bonds first, but wisely he didn't include any details. After that, they struggled for years to try to fix bonds they had broken, and from there, I believe they found a way to make dominion bonds through some new method. A way that works on humans, not just Rethri," he explained. "One of the people he seems to have managed to give new abilities to is a sorcerer named Veruden. That was the man you were sitting with at the arena, correct?"

Lydia nodded. "Yes...that might explain his bandages, actually."

Jonan quirked a brow. "Bandages?"

"Veruden has been wearing bandages on his right hand for at least several days. He claimed it had something to do with trying to teleport the Sae'kes out of its scabbard, but I tried using sorcery on the sword myself, and I never triggered any sort of defenses." She paused for a moment, considering.

"Taelien told me a while back that the only thing keeping the sword in the scabbard was his own metal sorcery. Maybe Veruden hadn't figured out what was locking the sword in place, but he didn't want anyone else experimenting with it, either." She took a breath, adjusting her glasses. "We've been seeing unusual runes in several locations. All around the Esharen, on Myros' armor, and possibly those markings around the eyes of the Rethri children. What if those are dominion marks, like the ones on the Sae'kes? They could be the mechanism by which Edon is giving new sorcery to humans – and Veruden's marks are concealed beneath bandages."

"Hmm," Jonan muttered. "That sounds plausible, but dangerous. I studied reports on attempts to perform the Rethri dominion bonding ritual on humans several years back. The reports concluded that humans naturally excrete excess dominion essence. It's a protective mechanism. If you saturate someone in the power of a particular dominion, they will excrete it as quickly as they can, until their body eventually just breaks down and dies."

Lydia brushed a strand of hair out of her eyes. "A localized mark might function differently. Since dominion marked items are so rare, I've never had a chance to study one for any length of time. It's possible that a dominion mark can contain essence in a specific location, rather than spreading it across the entire body."

"Well, that's just fantastic." Jonan scratched at the stubble on his chin, shaking his head. "In a worst case scenario, that means he could give any person – including himself – access to any or all dominions. We need to think about what might be restricting him, if anything, and any weaknesses this might provide."

"Veruden's bandages – or rather, the flesh beneath them – appeared to physically bother him. It's possible that whatever procedure he uses to make the marks is uncomfortable or damaging."

"The markings around the children's eyes," Jonan half-whispered. "They could have been burned on, like a brand."

"Permanently damaging the skin does seem like it might be necessary for making a dominion mark. That might somewhat limit the rate at which Edon would apply these marks," she noted.

"Good. What else? Resources, perhaps? He'd need planar essence for a specific dominion to make a mark, I assume," Jonan noted.

"Maybe," Lydia said uncertainly. "Or some sort of alternative power source."

"Like the Rethri themselves. Or the artifacts he's been gathering."

Lydia nodded grimly. "Yes. And it's also possible that the dominion saturation that you mentioned earlier could still happen, even with his new method. That might limit the number of marks he'd put on himself, at very least until he's tested the process on others."

"Well, that's a slight comfort, at least. He also might be limited by his vocabulary," Jonan mused.

"Vocabulary? What do you mean?"

"Maybe that's the wrong word for it, but if those runes are dominion marks, they most likely correspond to specific spells or keys. He might need examples of them to make copies," Jonan offered.

Lydia quirked her lips to the right, mentally debating that line of logic. "That implies that there's something intrinsically linking the shape of the runes to some sort of function. As you've pointed out to me yourself, words have no real meaning for casting sorcery – they're just a helpful tool. Why would these runes function differently?"

"That's an excellent question, and one I don't have a good answer to. Maybe it really is the language of the gods," he offered.

"That doesn't explain anything in itself. 'Language of the gods' doesn't automatically mean 'words cause specific effects'," she noted out, pointing at him with a finger to add emphasis.

"Fair," he raised his hands defensively. "I knew it was a bad argument, but I didn't have – okay, better idea. Maybe it's not the shape of the rune that matters, but maybe when the gods made the first dominion marked items, they always put specific spells in specific runes. If it was a language they could read, that could have had a useful function. Looking at an item, they could determine what the function of the object was, and maybe even how to activate it."

"That would mean that in order to learn how to make more marks, he'd need to find existing items with the same marks – and learn how to copy their function," Lydia considered aloud. "Yes, that would explain a great deal about his behavior – and why Veruden wanted to keep the rest of us away from the Sae'kes. He must have realized how valuable the runes on the blade would be for research."

"All right, this is good information – but we still need to go figure out what's happening with Taelien. If we're right, they could be trying to take the sword away from him right now," Jonan concluded.

"Right. Let's go, then. We should try to avoid engaging Edon and anyone else with him in direct combat until we have a better idea of their exact capabilities. For now, I'm going to put a defensive spell on both of us, and we'll try to focus on extracting Taelien and escaping to rendezvous with the queen. You're going to have to wrap your invisibility around us, rather than targeting us directly, otherwise you'll trigger my barrier like you did a while ago. Does that sound like a good plan?"

"Sure," Jonan offered. "It sounds like a great plan. I'll look forward to seeing how it falls apart."

Lydia grinned. "You're cheerful today. Ready to go?"

"As ready as I'm going to be," he muttered.

"Dominion of Protection, fold against my skin and teach me the secrets of the dominions that assault you," Lydia incanted, renewing her own Comprehensive Barrier first. The tingle that spread across her skin lasted longer than usual – a sign that she was exerting herself too much. Still, susceptibility to bruising and sickness was a pleasant alternative compared to the maiming and death that her barriers had prevented. Next, she extended her hand, and Jonan took it.

"Dominion of Protection, fold against his skin."

Jonan's skin shimmered briefly, and then he waved with his off-hand while Lydia grit her teeth at the lingering tingling sensation from her own spells. For a brief, disorienting moment, her own body disappeared – and then his – and then they both reappeared.

"All right, we're invisible, but I've excluded the two of us from the effect. Keep holding my hand, it's easier that way."

She was mildly skeptical about that last part, but his hand was pretty warm and surprisingly soft, so she didn't particularly mind. The sorceress led the way down to the Paths of Ascension.

Lydia had been to the door leading to the chamber in front of the Paths of Ascension before, but she had never actually been inside. A single guard stood at the door – a problem that could have easily been solved with violence, but she had no interest in hurting an innocent.

Even just opening the door would attract his attention, she realized. Grimacing, she inched her way closer to the guard, glancing back at Jonan just before she came close enough to touch the soldier.

Jonan just shrugged at her, so she shook her head and reached out, touching the man's cheek with a hand.

"Sleep."

She felt a tingling sensation in her hand as the Dominion of Dreams surged through her. The guard didn't even have a moment to register alarm – he simply collapsed, and Lydia stepped in to catch him, laying him gently down on the ground. Glancing side-to-side, she detected no other onlookers, and she dragged the guard out of the way of the door.

"Am I still invisible?" she whispered to Jonan. She could have checked with a spell, but she didn't want to tax herself further.

"Yeah," he confirmed. "As long as you stay close, keeping you invisible isn't particularly taxing."

"Can you get him, too?" she asked, indicating the sleeping guard.

Jonan gave her a nervous look. "Sure, as long as I wait right around here."

That's going to be a problem. I could drag him to a side room — he should be asleep for a while — but someone is going to notice his absence eventually. And my sleep spell isn't going to keep him asleep forever. He'll probably raise the alarm as soon as he wakes up.

"I'll drag him into the room with us," Lydia decided. "Make him invisible now, and then you can keep him invisible while I go into the paths."

Jonan nodded, waving a hand. A shimmer of light washed over the surface of the fallen guard's body. Lydia lifted him carefully, straining against the dead weight. "Get the door?"

The scribe inched forward, looking at the door knob like it was a venomous serpent, and hesitantly reached out to touch it. After a moment, he turned the handle and slowly pulled the door open.

The room inside was grand in scale and marvelous in design. Beyond a set of tall pillars, Lydia could just make out a pair of figures on the opposite end of the chamber — Edon and Myros.

Hope they don't hear us.

Lydia lifted the guard and slowly dragged him inside, while Jonan followed a moment later and closed the door quietly behind them. The sorceress laid the guard down to the side of the door, so anyone walking inside wouldn't step directly onto him.

Maybe I should drag him further inside, she considered. *It would take him longer to reach the door and raise an alarm if he has to wake up and run across this huge chamber to get out. On the other hand, he's more likely to wake up prematurely if he's close enough to hear people making noise — and Edon and Myros look like they're talking over there.*

She left the guard where he was, gesturing for Jonan to move up with her. The pair crept forward, and Myros and Edon's voices became clearer as they approached.

"If you'd just let Byron take the throne, maybe Tylan would back down," Myros said, gesticulating with the Heartlance. The voice still boomed out from Myros' helmet with sorcerous amplification, sounding clear even from dozens of feet away. "He's more than old enough, and we both know it."

"Age is irrelevant. The boy tried to have me killed." A deep anger was evident in Edon's tone, and the older man's hands trembled as he turned his head away from Myros.

The armored figure shook his head. "We still have no evidence he hired those men."

"Morella will find something. I am certain of it."

He's talking about those men that were discovered in the palace months ago. Everyone has been assuming they were targeting the prince – but if they were targeting Edon... Well, that certainly explains why Morella has been claiming to have 'more important' things to deal with lately.

"It's been two months. They're long gone. If you try to delay the coronation again, it's just going to look like you're the one trying to hold onto all the power."

Edon shoulders slumped. His response was too faint for Lydia to hear, but she didn't dare to quicken her step to hear more.

"That might be true, but is it worth risking a civil war?" Myros argued.

Lydia was close enough to hear Edon's response this time. "It won't come to that," Edon insisted. "I've already taken precautions."

"I think you underestimate her level of support," Myros countered. "Have you noticed that most people don't even refer to her as 'regent' anymore? She's just the queen to most people."

"Supporting her does not mean supporting the prince," Edon argued. "I have supported her for years – and I continue to. Keeping the prince away from that throne is the best for all of us."

Myros shook his head. "How many delays do you think Byron will tolerate? He's already furious."

The sorceress perked up at that. *Is Edon planning on executing a coup? That would explain why Tylan had the Rethri removed from the city.*

Beyond the pair, Lydia could see a stairway leading downward toward a titanic metal door. Some sort of runes were etched into the surface of the metal, and the base of the door was immersed in a large pool of water.

Resh, how am I going to get down there and open that without attracting any attention?

"It's not about delaying. Tylan will have other things to worry about soon, and she'll eventually see that our current situation is superior to the alternative," Edon replied, folding his arms across his chest. The crystal on his ring flickered brightly as Lydia came closer, and she eyed it warily.

That's definitely some kind of dominion bonded item, but I'd need to get close enough to touch it to figure out specifics.

"I think you're deluding yourself. You can't have it both ways – the queen regent isn't going to be satisfied until her son is crowned. How do you expect to keep her-"

A large hole suddenly appeared near the top of the door, and a flood of water carried a figure – unmistakably Taelien – out into the chamber.

He had a long fall.

Lydia rushed forward, but Myros was faster. The armored figure was a blur, leaving a trail of displaced water that led to the spot where Taelien landed. A moment later, Myros lifted Taelien from the pool, carrying him out to where Myros and Edon had been standing before.

Lydia inched closer, her hand on the hilt of her sword. She was almost in striking range of Edon now, and closing the last few footsteps wouldn't take more than a moment. She glanced at Jonan – he was hovering a dozen yards further away, his expression neutral.

Taelien clutched the Sae'kes tightly in his right hand. Only one azure rune flickered on the surface of the sword, but even that sight filled Lydia with a sense of hope and exultation. *The sword still glows. He's alive.*

She turned her attention to a gemstone that had slipped out of Taelien's hand when he hit the water. She didn't recognize the stone, but dominion bonded gemstones were common in ancient legends. *Could it be a piece of Cessius? That does look like a Xixian structure.*

Taelien managed to push himself to a sitting position, but his arm had been badly mauled, and blood still trailed from several wounds. He glanced at Edon nervously, and then back to Myros.

Myros retrieved the gemstone from the water, examining it for a moment, and then thrusting it toward Taelien.

"I think you earned this," Myros said, and Taelien took the offered stone.

"Thanks," Taelien replied, his expression dubious. He began coughing a moment later, and Lydia had to suppress the urge to step closer to inspect his wounds.

The armor-clad god of battle reached down and hauled Taelien up to his feet. The swordsman looked more than a little unsteady, which was unsurprising, given that he was soaked and still badly bleeding.

Might not need to turn this into a fight after all, Lydia considered. *If they wanted to attack him, they probably would have done so already.*

Edon looked Taelien up and down, grinning. "You've done very well, Taelien, just as I had hoped. Now, hand me the gem, and we'll see about giving you godhood, as you deserve."

Or not. Lydia stepped around behind Edon, putting her hand on the hilt of her sword.

Taelien wiped the water out of his eyes, and then groggily reached out with his hand, offering the gemstone to Edon. "Here," he said. "Take it."

Edon stepped forward with an outstretched hand, but Myros stepped in between the two of them, raising the Heartlance. Lydia looked back toward Jonan, finding him holding a potion bottle of some kind in his hand. He was circling around to a flanking position, and he nodded at her.

"Don't give it to him yet. He has some questions to answer first," Myros demanded. The armored knight was standing in front of Taelien defensively, as if expecting violence to break out at any time.

Taelien unsheathed a second sword, dropping it to the floor, and returned the Sae'kes to its scabbard. Lydia inspected the other sword, noting that it had an unusual red metal blade. *Something from the vault? Probably not worth worrying about right now. Why is he putting the Sae'kes away?*

Is he too exhausted to fight?

Myros continued to argue with Edon, and Lydia glanced over to Jonan. The sorcerer waved back at her, holding some kind of vial in his right hand.

"I nearly killed someone last night because of your lies. I nearly killed Taelien a few weeks before – again, because of your lies. I will have no further part in this...and neither will you. You will answer for your crimes," Myros raised the Heartlance. "Surrender now, and I will turn you over to the queen for judgment. Taelien, are you with me?"

Lydia blinked at that. *That's...surprisingly pragmatic. With Myros on our side, this is going to be a lot easier.*

Taelien glanced at the two figures, and then bent down and picked up the red-bladed sword from the floor and stepped behind Edon. Lydia moved aside, giving Taelien room. He was nearly close enough for her to touch, and she felt the sudden urge to reach out for him, but she restrained herself. Taelien placed the red-bladed sword up against Edon's back.

Edon quirked a brow. "If you were going to try to make a coup, it would have been smarter to do it before Taelien walked the path. Do you really want to do this, Myros?"

"If I had done this before, Taelien wouldn't have had the gem. I've been down there more often than you have – I know how the vault works. I knew he'd find it. And I know what it does," Myros explained.

Please, tell me, Lydia urged Myros silently. She briefly debated reaching down to touch the gem – Taelien was close enough – but she would have to speak aloud to identify it.

"Well," Edon said, "That's comforting, that you had a plan, at least. Unfortunately, I must decline to surrender."

Lydia gripped her sword in both hands, preparing to strike.

"Now," Myros said, raising the Heartlance and surging rapidly forward.

Edon spun away, causing Myros' attack to nearly slam into Taelien. The swordsman looked exhausted, struggling to deflect the accidental spear strike and taking a step back before launching an attack that came too late. A moment later, Edon had a hand on the Heartlance, and he snapped his fingers.

Myros disappeared, the blue flash of some sort of spell effect nearly leaving Lydia blinded. Edon held the Heartlance, smug confidence spreading across his features.

"Sad, really. I always liked Myros," Edon spun the spear playfully. "You, I have less of an investment in. And you seem to have made your choice."

Taelien nodded. "I have."

"Unfortunate," Edon replied, raising his left hand. "Eru volar shen taris."

Lydia stepped in front of Taelien just as a blast of blue-white flame emerged from his hands.

Eru volar shen taris, her comprehensive barrier spell reported. The shield shimmered and cracked around her, the intensity of the single blast shredding the barrier to near uselessness.

She stepped in the moment later, swinging the flat of her blade at Edon's forehead. A barrier, near identical to her own, flashed into existence just before her blade landed, deflecting the strike.

Behind her, Lydia caught a brief glimpse of Taelien desperately waving his hands over a spreading wave of blue flame on his shirt – apparently, her barrier had failed to block the entirety of the blast. He seemed to be attempting to use Flame Sorcery to disperse the fire.

"Interesting," Edon muttered, waving a hand. "Eru volar-"

Lydia struck a second time, but again, the barrier stopped her strike.

"-esu raval taris," Edon finished, waving a hand.

Eru volar esu raval taris, Lydia saw in her mind as she swung a third time. Edon winced as her blade struck the barrier a third time, making a noticeable crack in the shimmering protective field.

That was a spell to break my invisibility, Lydia realized. *And it took down what was left of my barrier.*

Edon slammed the Heartlance into the stone floor, causing golden lines to spread from the impact point upward across the spear. As the glowing lines reached Edon's body, they spread across his hand and into the sleeve of his robe.

That's new, Lydia considered, making a high cut toward his exposed shoulder. Edon raised the spear into the path of her blade and the impact triggered a backlash of force, sending Lydia skidding several feet across the floor.

"Ah," Edon said "Lydia, impeccable timing. I hadn't realized you were back in the city yet. I don't suppose you could convince your friend to surrender?"

Taelien charged straight past Lydia, his clothing no longer aflame. Red metal arced at six angles in rapid succession, only to be met with the Heartlance's steel each time. Taelien somehow held his ground against the sorcerous impact triggered by each parry, but blood still flowed freely from a wound on his right arm, and his chest was ravaged with burns.

Lydia shot a glance toward where she had seen Jonan last, but there was no sign of him. She grit her teeth and stepped forward again, swinging low at Edon's legs to make an opening for Taelien. The swordsman took her cue, flanking to the left and swinging at Edon's shoulder, but Edon simply swept the spear in a half-circle and parried both strikes, knocking both attackers away.

Edon didn't even try to launch any counter attacks — he just calmly raised his spear as Taelien hurled a metal sphere in his direction, knocking the ball aside.

He's faster than he should be, Lydia considered. *He's supposed to be a former priest, not a warrior. Taelien is exhausted and injured, but not sufficiently to account for this difference. The Heartlance must be making him faster, in addition to causing that kinetic impact every time we strike it. Motion sorcery, probably. If I could get it away from him...*

Lydia took a different tactic, swinging the flat of her blade at Edon's hand. He stepped back, sweeping the flat of the spear upward in an attempt to catch her under the chin, but Lydia side-stepped that and drove her blade back downward, making an opening for Taelien to launch an attack of his own.

Taelien took the opening, but not in the way she expected – he rushed forward and slammed his uninjured shoulder straight into Edon, only to bounce off of the sorcerer's barrier. Edon looked momentarily stunned, so Lydia swept her blade into the Heartlance and dragged it downward toward Edon's fingers. The sword connected, but the flickering barrier held, preventing any damage.

Resh, how is he maintaining that barrier through so much abuse?

"Enough of this," Edon said, releasing a hand from the spear to point it at Lydia.

"Dominion of Protection," she rushed to incant, stepping backward as she realized his intent.

"Eru volar-"

"Fold against my skin-"

"...Shen taris," Edon finished. Lydia thought she saw his ring flash for an instant before the blue-white fire consumed her.

CHAPTER XV – UNSHEATHED

The jet of flames washed over Lydia's body while Taelien pounded with futile fervor against the shimmering barrier of energy around Edon, his strikes failing to even make a crack.

When the fire faded, Taelien saw nothing where Lydia had once stood, save the puddle of molten slag that had once been her sword and a pile of bone and ash.

Without a word, Taelien dropped the red-bladed sword.

"I didn't mean for it to come to this," Edon said, sighing and moving the Heartlance back to a defensive posture.

"You are a monster," Taelien muttered.

Edon raised an eyebrow. "Am I? A matter of perspective, I suppose."

Taelien lowered his hand to grip the hilt of the Sae'kes, memories flooding into his mind.

Never use this until you can control all seven runes on the blade, his parents had insisted.

He drew the sword, gritting his teeth. *Lydia blocked his first attack to save me. Just like she did with Istavan – only this time, she didn't have enough left to shield herself afterward.*

Five runes flickered to life across the surface of his blade – Lissari, Lysandri, Xerasilis, Koranir, and finally Eratar.

Close enough.

Taelien lunged forward, and Edon raised the Heartlance, showing a hint of concern for the first time. The Sae'kes flashed silver, smashing into the Heartlance, leaving a deep gouge in the surface of the metal and driving Edon back a step. One of the golden lines faded from the spear.

Edon hissed, drawing his left hand back, looking prepared to cast another spell. Taelien swung again, his blade parting the air and striking the Heartlance a second time, creating a spark of light as the blade cut a chunk of metal out of the shaft of the spear.

"Eru elan lav kor taris," Edon yelled, and a pulsing shockwave emanated from around him, knocking Taelien backward and off his feet.

The swordsman landed several feet away, his head throbbing, his consciousness fading. He could see some sort of faint green structure surrounding him – a barrier? – for a few moments before the green gemstone slipped free from his hand.

I need to get up, he told himself, gritting his teeth. He maintained his grip on the Sae'kes, attempting to push himself to his feet. The runes on his blade were flickering and dying, with only three of them remaining visible. His injured arm screamed in his mind, and his vision swam as he saw Edon pointing his hand toward him, readying for another spell.

"Eru volar shen taris," came a voice – but it wasn't Edon's this time.

A blast of blue-white fire enveloped Edon, emerging from a figure that appeared to his right side, his right hand blazing with fire.

Veruden.

Edon spun toward Veruden, gesturing with his own hand, immediately stopping the tide of flame. The sorcerer seemed uninjured, but the barrier around him was still visible – and Taelien thought he could see tiny cracks in the surface.

"You swore that the other sorcerers would not be harmed." Veruden advanced toward Edon, balling his hands into fists.

"Lydia made her choice." Edon stood up straighter, raising his left hand in a warding gesture. "She attacked me – you saw that."

"You didn't have to kill her!" Veruden raised his bandaged hand, unclenching his fist and pointing his palm at Edon. "Eru volar shen taris!"

Edon didn't even wait for the flames to reach him this time – he just waved a hand in the air, causing the fire to vanish.

Taelien braced himself, gritting his teeth, and made another attempt to push himself to his feet. He managed to regain his footing, but he stumbled backward, nearly falling back to the floor.

"Idiot." Edon shook his head, taking a deep breath. "I gave you everything you have – every opportunity, every power, every gift! I can take them away – I can turn them against you."

Edon clenched his off hand, gritting his teeth, and Veruden's bandaged hand burst into flame again – but this time, the flames spread upward across the sorcerer's body, burning his own flesh.

Veruden screamed, reaching down with his other hand, only to burn that as well.

Taelien steadied himself, focusing on his sword, fighting to reignite the five runes on the surface. They flickered back to life, and he could feel them begin to drain his already flagging strength.

"Not all of them," Veruden yelled, vanishing from where he stood. He reappeared next to Edon a moment later, slamming a blazing fist toward Edon's face. The barrier manifested instantly, broad cracks appearing as it shuddered at the impact of the strike.

Taelien charged.

Edon shoved the Heartlance at Veruden, aiming at the center of his chest. The tip of the Heartlance pierced straight through Veruden's torso, and the sorcerer shuddered at the impact – and then vanished.

The swordsman closed the distance in a few moments, bringing the Sae'kes downward in a diagonal slash aimed for Edon's exposed fingers. The robed sorcerer stepped out of range, releasing his right hand from the spear to level it toward Taelien.

"Eru volar-"

Taelien stepped in close, slamming the wings of his weapon against Edon's barrier. Cracks spread broadly across the surface, but the shield held.

Edon moved his hand to follow Taelien as the swordsman attempted to circle around behind him, continuing his incantation. "Shen taris," the sorcerer finished, a wave of fire emanating from his hand.

This time, Taelien was ready.

His weapon sang in a horizontal slash, the silvery edge catching the flames as they emerged. *Surround,* he commanded the fire. The fan of flames shifted in direction, surging and collecting around the edges of the Sae'kes, forming a whirlwind of incendiary azure.

Taelien grit his teeth, emitting a low growl as his body shivered in complaint. Turning aside the weaker flames that had made it past Lydia's barrier had been difficult enough – manipulating one of Edon's entire spells was beyond anything he had previously attempted.

Runes flickered and died on the flat of his sword – the fifth, then the fourth and third, mere moments thereafter.

His barrier is weak, Taelien considered, taking a step forward. *I could obliterate him.*

Shuddering with effort, Taelien slammed his sword into the ground, burying the vortex of fire in stone. The marble warped and cracked around the encased weapon, the death knell of the sorcerous heat.

Taelien hesitated only a moment before moving to unsheathe the sword from the earth, but that moment was all the time Edon needed. A surge of speed carried the sorcerer forward, the Heartlance aimed for Taelien's chest.

The swordsman reacted quickly, abandoning his blade and stepping backward and to the right, but the spear was too fast, piercing deeply into the flesh near his left shoulder and stopping as it scraped against bone. Taelien screamed, his body shuddering, and grabbed the shaft of the lance with his right hand.

Bend, he commanded the metal shell, gritting his teeth.

The metal gave no reply.

Edon ripped the spear out of Taelien's shoulder, the swords man's own grip failing to restrain the older man's movement. Taelien gave a wistful glance at his own weapon, still stuck in the stone, too far away for him to hope to reach.

Taelien urged his body to move, but succeeded only in falling to his knees. His strength was gone. The blue-robed sorcerer raised his bloodstained spear, preparing for a final strike.

A loud crack sounded behind Edon, and Taelien found himself blinking in confusion as the sorcerer spun around.

"Sleep," came a woman's voice, and Edon collapsed unceremoniously to the ground. The Heartlance flashed blue and vanished.

Lydia stood above Edon, her saber pointed downward at the sorcerer's unmoving form, her gaze evaluating the sight before her.

Taelien fell backward, catching himself on his slightly less maimed right arm, and burst into uncontrollable laughter.

"I saw you die," he managed, sinking the rest of the way to the floor. He shivered uncontrollably, reaching out to grope at the spear wound in his shoulder. "I was...I was sure you had died."

"You saw one of Jonan's very convincing tricks," Lydia corrected, jerking a thumb to her right.

Jonan appeared nearby, grinning, and took a bow. "I'm not much good in most fights, but tricks, yeah, that I can do."

"Lie still," Lydia insisted, walking over to kneel at his side. "You're in pretty bad shape." She winced as she inspected his wound, using her saber to cut off a long section of cloth from the bottom of her robe.

"I...," Taelien began, wincing as Lydia pushed his hand to the side and began to wrap the makeshift bandage around his shoulder wound. "What about Veruden?"

"Also me," Jonan said with a grin. "Veruden was never here. Between reading Edon's notebook and what Lydia told me, I knew enough about him to give a brief performance. I'm fortunate that illusions and teleportation are nearly indistinguishable in the midst of a fight."

Lydia glanced over at Jonan, while still applying pressure to Taelien's injury. "That doesn't explain how you were managing to damage his barrier, though. It looked like you were using Edon's spell against him – how? I've tried using his incantation a dozen times – it doesn't do anything by itself."

"Just another trick, sadly. You reminded me not to try to 'erase' us when I was using the invisibility spell, since it would trigger your barrier. I figured his barrier probably worked similarly, and that an illusion that was designed to 'attack' him would trick the barrier into expending power to defend," Jonan explained, a smug expression on his face.

Taelien turned to Lydia, who was scowling. She didn't look satisfied with Jonan's explanation, but Taelien was far too exhausted to press the issue. He was having a hard time even keeping his eyes open.

Lydia glanced around the room, and then looked back toward Taelien. "Stay with me, Taelien. We're going to get you to a healer. Do you know what Edon did to Myros?"

Taelien shook his head groggily. "No, but it didn't look like his usual attack spell. I assume that was an actual teleportation spell."

"I was thinking that, too. We'll have to-"

The entrance door to the chamber opened. Taelien lifted his head slowly, seeing dozens of soldiers pouring in.

Oh, only a dozen more? Sure, I can handle that. Just as soon as my arm starts working.

Lydia moved away from Taelien, ducking down near Edon's collapsed form. The swordsman blinked, uncertain, but he had enough presence of mind left to renew the pressure on his wound.

A regal figure approached amidst the soldiers, standing tall and wearing a glittering crown.

"Queen Tylan," Lydia said. "You should probably kneel."

It took Taelien a moment to realize that Lydia had been talking to Jonan, not to him. This was good, since his legs didn't seem to currently be listening to his own orders – and certainly not to Lydia's.

The soldiers encircled them quickly and methodically, but kept a distance as the queen regent continued to approach.

"Sorceress Lydia Scryer," the queen regent called out. "You may rise. Care to explain this situation?"

Lydia stood, dusting herself off. "I witnessed this man, who had claimed to be the deity Edon, confess to Myros that he had performed tests on prisoners that resulted in their deaths. A confrontation ensued, in which he cast a spell on Myros. Our guest, Taelien, heroically rushed to Myros' defense. During the conflict, Taelien," she motioned to the injured swordsman, "And I were able to incapacitate the imposter."

Taelien absently noted that Lydia had omitted any mention of Jonan, which he deemed to be a wise decision.

"You have all been very brave," Queen Tylan said, "And you are to be commended. We will investigate the identity of this imposter immediately." She snapped her fingers. "Soldiers, bind that imposter and have him transported to Court Sorcerer Sethridge."

"Taelien is badly injured. May I borrow some of your guards to help carry him to the surgeon?"

"Of course," the queen regent waved a hand to a group of the guards. "You four, assist them."

Four of the armored soldiers approached. Taelien remained wary, but he had to admit, his methods of defending himself were rather limited. "Sword," he mumbled weakly.

"I'll get it," Lydia said, sheathing her saber. She walked past him, kneeling at the base of the Sae'kes and putting a hand on the grip. She waited a moment longer than seemed strictly necessary, and then drew the blade from the granite floor. The sorceress winced in surprise as the blade emerged, bringing a moment of panicked clarity to Taelien's fading senses. Not a single rune remained lit on the weapon.

"In the scabbard, quickly," he urged her. "Don't touch the blade. Don't even put anything near the edges." Lydia was quick to comply, rushing to him and reverently sliding the sword into the sheath. They both breathed a sigh of relief when the blade was secured within.

As the soldiers took positions around Taelien, Lydia retrieved the green gemstone from where it lay on the palace floor and shoved it in a pocket. After a moment, she picked up the red-bladed sword as well, and then moved back to Taelien's side.

"Ready to stand up?" she asked, offering him a hand.

"Not really," he replied blearily, but he took her hand anyway. She pulled him to his feet with surprising strength, catching him when he nearly collapsed onto her. He shivered again, and she pulled him close.

"One of you, put an arm under his other shoulder," Lydia instructed. One of the guards rushed over immediately, and Taelien relaxed when he recognized the man.

"Oh, hey, Landen," Taelien said, smiling weakly and offering the man his injured arm.

"Long day?" Landen gave him a bright smirk, taking Taelien's arm carefully, while Lydia maneuvered around to support him from the other side.

"A little," Taelien admitted.

"Who is this?" the queen asked, gesturing at Jonan.

"My new apprentice," Lydia replied instantly, offering the red-bladed sword toward Jonan. He stood, took the sword, and took up a position at her side.

The queen regent nodded to that, seeming satisfied. "Very well. Come speak to me after you've left the injured men with the surgeon."

Taelien sighed, the idea of Lydia leaving his sight again making him feel more than a little nervous, but he reassured himself that she seemed to have things under control.

This is probably exactly the type of thing the queen wanted, Taelien realized. With Edon incapacitated, *she has no competition for control of the city.*

With that in mind, Taelien allowed Lydia and Landen to carry him out of the chamber and to the surgeon's chambers.

CHAPTER XVI – A FEW KEY EXPLANATIONS

Lydia sat beside Taelien's bed, reading her copy of *The Nature of Worlds*. The familiar pages comforted her, easing the tension in her back that had continued to grow since their confrontation with Edon.

"My everything hurts."

Lydia nearly dropped the book, standing up in her chair and turning toward Taelien. "You're awake!"

"Mm, not so sure about that." Taelien attempted to sit up, but she gently placed a hand on the center of the blanket that covered his chest.

"Slow down. If you sit up too fast, you could tear your stitches," she explained.

Taelien frowned. "Why are you spinning? I mean, it's very impressive, but-"

"We had to force-feed you a couple potions to keep you stable. You had some very serious injuries, especially the spear wound in your shoulder. I made sure a real doctor took care of your injuries, but without the potions, I'm not sure you would have survived."

"Woulda been fine," he insisted groggily. Lydia couldn't help herself from grinning.

"You scared me there. Don't ever do that again, okay?" She moved her hand from his chest to take his hand.

"Okay. What am I not doing again?"

Lydia rolled her eyes. "Getting into a fight with an angry god?"

"Oh. He started it." Taelien raised an arm, pointing accusingly at the air for emphasis.

Actually, I'm pretty sure Myros started it. From your expression, though, I don't think you're totally aware yet. Those potions must have had some sort of intoxicating effect. It's kind of adorable.

She had used identification spells on the liquids before feeding Taelien, of course, but those only served to tell her that the dominions associated with the herbs within – stability and life – were not dangerous. The alcohol-like symptoms might have been from mundane properties in the liquid, or perhaps this was just how Taelien reacted to extreme trauma and blood loss.

"I'm hungry," Taelien pouted.

"Okay, sweet thing. I'll make sure you get something to eat. Take it slow, though."

Taelien nodded in affirmation.

Two days later, Lydia made her way to the queen regent's chambers. Jonan was taking a shift watching over Taelien, but it seemed unlikely to be necessary. The swordsman was still in terrible shape, but he seemed unlikely to expire in her absence.

And that afforded Lydia a moment to finally indulge her sorcery on something other than periodically checking Taelien's condition.

"Dominion of Knowledge, I invoke you," Lydia said, clutching the green gemstone in her pouch as she headed toward queen's chambers.

Help me, appeared in her vision, just for an instant, where her identification results should have. She froze in her step, and the two words were quickly replaced with others.

Dominion of Life.
Dominion of Earth.
Dominion of Nature.
Dominion of Spirits.

Lydia released her grip on the object immediately. *The Dominion of Spirits?* She had heard legends of such a thing, speculation – but this was her first proof it even existed.

Does that mean that this thing is...alive? How could an object be tied to the Dominion of Spirits?

She shook her head. One week with Taelien and now her identification spell never gave her comprehensible results.

I'll try to identify the ring later. I can't risk setting off any defensive spells he might have placed on it while I'm still recovering. She had slipped Edon's ring off his hand when she had knelt next to his unconscious body, and she hadn't had a chance to check it yet. She had, however, noted tiny runes etched into the surface of the metal. For the moment, it was tucked away safely in the pouch on her waist.

Lydia arrived at the door to the queen regent's chambers a few moments later.

She knocked on the door politely, and one of the Queensguard opened it from within a moment later.

"Sorceress," he said, nodding to her politely and stepping outside.

"Thank you," she said, stepping within. The queen regent was seated in a chair near her reading table, her hands folded in her lap. There was no one else inside the room, as far as Lydia could see.

Lydia closed the door behind her.

"You've done very well," the queen regent said. "With that ugly matter dealt with, I can finally have some peace of mind."

"Meaning your son can finally take the throne?" Lydia guessed.

The queen regent nodded. "Precisely. Edon – well, Donovan, as I'm sure you know – approached my husband many years ago about working together to make our city glorious. Donovan wanted resources for his research, and offered powerful sorcery – enough to make a claim at godhood – in exchange. My husband agreed. They had a strong partnership for a time, but my husband passed away a few years later, leaving me and an infant son behind."

"And now that your son is old enough to rule, he posed a threat to Edon's control over the city." Lydia concluded.

"Yes. Edon has gradually been attempting to forge our city into a theocracy. When I was younger, I believed that being called a 'goddess' of the city would help secure the faith of the people in my decisions. As the years have gone on, I realized that I was falling into a trap. By making myself a part of Edon's 'pantheon', I placed myself in an inferior position to him. His influence has been sufficient to delay my son's coronation for several months. I believe that he planned to use your friend, Taelien, as a way to extend his influence even further," the queen regent explained.

The court sorceress nodded. "If the prince took the throne, Edon would have had to contend with a rival for power that was not a part of his divine hierarchy. I assume he probably offered 'divinity' to your son and was refused?"

Tylan shook his head. "No, Byron and Edon have never gotten along. Byron has always suspected that Edon was responsible for my husband's death, but I long ago concluded otherwise. Regardless, Edon never even made the offer. He knew what Byron's answer would have been."

"And so, he needed an alternative – an excuse to keep control. Assassinating Byron might have been an option, but it could have sparked a civil war. When Taelien arrived in the city, he saw an opportunity – start a war with an outside force. With Velthryn, and the followers of the Tae'os Pantheon," Lydia surmised. "With a war raging, he could justify that Byron was too young and inexperienced to take control of the city."

While Lydia spoke that idea aloud, she had a second idea flowing through her mind. Edon seemed to sincerely believe that Byron was trying to have him killed – it was possible that the delay in the coronation was just an attempt to find proof that Byron had hired the assassins. If Edon had obtained that proof, he probably hoped to use that as evidence that the prince could not be trusted with leadership over the city.

The so-called god of ascension clearly had some other plan beyond just presenting evidence of Byron's wrongdoing, but even Myros seemingly hadn't known about the details. Lydia was deeply curious about what those plans were, but she doubted she'd have an opportunity to investigate them any time in the near future.

Edon's plans for Taelien were less certain in the sorceress' mind. There were several possibilities. While she had initially guessed that Edon wanted Taelien to be imprisoned or killed in order to start a war, his more recent actions made that scenario less likely.

It was possible he was legitimately interested in having Taelien as a member of his pantheon - having the current wielder of the Sae'kes working for him might have expanded Edon's personal influence and credibility. Making Taelien one of his false gods might have even served to attract Tae'os followers into joining the Edonate religion.

It was also possible that Edon simply wanted access to the Sae'kes in order to expand his research into dominion marks. If Lydia's suspicions were correct, every artifact Edon gained access to expanded the variety of marks that Edon was able to create.

Finally, it struck Lydia as plausible Edon just wanted more powerful supporters for his own protection – if Byron was sending assassins after him, Edon might have just wanted more people he could trust to defend him against further attempts.

"Yes, you averted that potential war very nicely, my dear. And that is why I brought you here – I know of your allegiances, of course. I would like you to return to Velthryn and assure your paladins and priests that the prince – soon to be king – wants nothing more than peace. The Tae'os religion will be legalized within our city again shortly, and Edon will be tried – and convicted – of conspiracy, kidnapping, treason, and probably murder," the queen concluded.

Lydia stepped forward, bringing her right hand across her chest to her left shoulder in a salute. "I believe we have an accord."

The queen regent waved a hand to dismiss the sorceress. "Good. I will look forward to hearing your organization's reply."

CHAPTER XVII – THE NEXT STEPS

Taelien still hurt in places he hadn't previously realized could experience pain. He remained mostly bedridden, but after the first day – which he had spent almost entirely unconscious – he began taking brief excursions out of the bed to stretch for a few agonizing minutes.

The swordsman had been pleased when he had discovered the Sae'kes hiding beneath his sheets. He knew Lydia must have needed to argue with the doctors to let him keep it there, and he mentally thanked her for the kindness.

Lydia and Jonan had kept a near-constant vigil over him for the first three days of his recovery, and visited frequently even thereafter. After the third day, Landen began to visit, explaining that he had tried earlier but that Lydia had sent him away.

"Paranoid girl, that one," Landen pointed out.

"You haven't even scraped the surface." Taelien sighed.

Landen grinned. "Cute, though. And I think she likes you."

He shook his head. "I think it's more likely she's interested in a version of me that doesn't actually exist, if even that."

Landen nodded sagely. "You'll never know until you ask."

Taelien had fewer visitors after the third day, when it grew progressively more obvious that he was going to survive his injuries. The doctor came in with fresh potions for him to drink and to check his stitches, and a servant with a harp-shaped earring came by with changes of clothes and to empty the chamber pot here and there, but the remainder of his next few days were an excruciating combination of boredom and restlessness.

Every time I get injured, I remind myself not to let it happen again. Still, I remain reckless.

Lydia visited again on the fifth day, taking a seat by his bedside.

"Hey. What have I been missing?"

"Prince Byron is finally getting his coronation in a bit over a week. If you're back on your feet by that point, you can come along with me."

Taelien shuddered deliberately. "I'd better be. I don't think I'll be able to stand more than another day in this bed."

Lydia's warm grin shined down on him. "I keep telling you to be patient. If you keep moving around all the time, you'll just tear your stitches and end up being here longer."

"Patience takes too long," Taelien said dryly. "All right, the prince is going to be king. What's the situation with Edon?"

The sorceress shrugged. "Largely out of my hands at this point. The queen is taking care of the 'investigation' directly."

Taelien quirked a brow. "And you're okay with that?"

Lydia shook her head. "No, but it's not a good time to push. We've had a significant victory – something that could lead toward a long-term peace between Velthryn and Orlyn. I need to report back and work to stabilize that before doing anything else. You should come with me when I leave. I have a clue that might interest you."

Taelien quirked a brow. "A clue?"

Lydia reached into her ever-present pouch, retrieving the familiar glowing-green stone that Taelien had found inside the Paths of Ascension. The swordsman raised an eyebrow at the gem.

"I think there's a good chance it's a piece of Cessius," Lydia explained. "And, after having thought about it, I think the Heartlance might be one, too. I probably should have considered it sooner – if Cessius was broken or disassembled, a piece could easily look like another spear. Or a gem that was inlaid somewhere in the weapon's shaft."

That makes a certain amount of sense. "Have you told-," he stopped himself from giving the other paladin's name, since he couldn't be certain they weren't being watched, "anyone else?"

"Yes," she replied quickly. "And the people I talked to agree with my assessment, but they also will keep looking. In the meantime, I think your best route to gather more information would be to come with me to Velthryn, where we can analyze the gem. We might even be able to use the gem to track down other pieces of Cessius – which Tarren might have in his possession."

"All right, I'll go with you." Taelien sat up in his bed, turning to face Lydia. "But first, tell me more about the Paladins of Tae'os."

EPILOGUE – GREETINGS AND GOODBYES

Five days later, Jonan stood at the city gates. He had hoped to stay long enough for Edon's trial and the coronation, but reporting back to Selyr was a higher priority. He had finished his remaining business in the city, paid his informants for their assistance, and given his final report to his contact through one of his remaining mirrors.

Knowing that his contact was the queen regent, he had briefly considered visiting her in person, but that would have violated his operational parameters. And besides, it was more fun keeping his identity a mystery.

The queen regent had delivered on her side of the plan perfectly – her appearance near the entrance to the Paths of Ascension couldn't have been better timed. He still wasn't certain why the Order of Vaelien had chosen to work with her in the first place, but she had certainly proven to be efficient.

In the distance, Jonan could see Taelien and Lydia approaching, coming to see him off as they had promised. Taelien's left arm and right shoulder were still wrapped in thick bandages, and he walked with a slight limp, but he otherwise seemed cheerful. Lydia was laughing at one of Taelien's jokes, and Jonan felt a very brief pang of jealously at the display.

Bah. I'll probably never see her again, anyway.

He waved with his free hand as they approached, giving the pair as sincere of a smile as he could muster.

"Hey!" Taelien shouted as they came closer, closing the distance quickly and wrapping him in a hug. Jonan returned the embrace awkwardly, pulling away after a moment.

"Um, hey," Jonan stammered. "How's the arm doing?"

"Better, thanks," Taelien said, stepping back to give Lydia room to approach.

Dare I test my luck?

Jonan extended his free hand and Lydia grasped it at the wrist, nodding professionally.

"It was good working with you," she said. "I hope you have a safe journey home."

"Thanks," he said, pulling his hand back and adjusting his glasses. He turned to Taelien. "You know, you could still come with me and visit your family."

He shook his head. "Sounds fun, but Lydia has me convinced that Velthryn is going to treat me a little better than Orlyn did. And I have to admit, I'm pretty curious if they'll be able to figure out why I have this thing." He patted the sword on his hip meaningfully.

"Oh, that reminds me!" Jonan set down his walking staff, undoing his belt and removing a scabbard that carried a long sword. He extended the sheathed weapon toward Taelien. "This is the sword you dropped in the palace. I got a scabbard for it. Consider it a present."

Taelien accepted the sword, holding it up to look at the hilt in the dawnfire's light. "You sure you don't want to keep it? This thing might be valuable. I didn't even recognize the metal."

Jonan shrugged, refastening his belt. "It would just slow me down. I've got a long walk ahead of me, and I pack pretty heavily as it is." He patted his backpack, which was practically overflowing with gear.

"Fair enough," Taelien replied. "Thanks for the present. I'll owe you one, for next time I see you."

Next time. Well, I suppose it's possible I might see you again – your family does live nearby. Her, on the other hand...

"Sounds good," he said, a hint of sadness dripping into his tone. He reached into a pouch on his side, retrieving a flat disc wrapped in cloth.

"And for you, Lydia," he said, offering it to her.

Lydia quirked a brow. "You didn't have to get me something."

She accepted it, removing the cloth to reveal a fine hand mirror. "Hah. I'll make sure I get dressed in front of it every day."

Jonan laughed. "Good. I'll see you both soon enough."

Maintaining the illusion that disguised the Heartlance as a walking stick was a constant strain on his eyes, but nowhere near as difficult as what he had been forced to engage in over the last week. He felt a slight pang of regret that he hadn't managed to sneak away with that fascinating green gemstone as well, but he doubted it could possibly be as valuable as the spear he carried.

Weeks passed in relative calm as Jonan made his way back toward Selyr. As he traveled, he and Lydia would occasionally send notes through their mirrors. He had little of import to tell her, but she gave him useful news.

He read as he walked, drinking in Edon's notes eagerly for more clues about the strange language the sorcerer had utilized for casting his spells. Between scholarly notes, Jonan discovered many more personal passages.

At first, I thought that being robbed of my sorcery was a curse. A punishment from Sytira for daring to speak out against the isolation and selfishness of the Tae'os gods. In truth, retracting my sorcerous abilities may have been the greatest gift she ever bestowed on me, if only accidentally. If she had never done so, I never would have heard the first whispers of divine power, relayed through the simple Intuitive Comprehension spell that I maintained at all times.

The first months were a difficult period of adjustment, a frustrating attempt to wrench anything useful out of those few seemingly meaningless syllables. It was Mora that provided the inspiration I needed to study the fading echoes of my spell in earnest, and for that, she will ever have my gratitude.

Jonan fixated on those particular passages, considering their possible implications. He wished that Tailor had written the exact words that the spell had given to him, but if they were recorded anywhere, Jonan had yet to find them.

Tailor lost the ability to use dominion sorcery years ago and believed Sytira was responsible, but is that the most likely scenario? Sytira isn't known for having the ability to take dominion sorcery away – only the Vae'kes are supposed to be able to do that. Could one of them somehow be responsible for all this?

Unsurprisingly, Donovan Tailor had been found guilty of several crimes. The only surprise was that murder was not among them. That particular crime could not be proven – not without the evidence that Jonan still carried.

"They're going to keep him imprisoned," Jonan explained to his traveling companion, shaking his head.

"That's quite a risk," Vorain replied, turning her bright eyes to glance at his mirror for confirmation. "The new king is too soft."

Vorain still had scrapes and bruises from her confrontation with the strange black-haired girl, but had staunchly refused to tell Jonan exactly what happened after he had escaped. All he knew is that Vorain had somehow talked the other woman down, and that she had gone to check on her brother soon thereafter. Elias was still being cared for by Raymond Lorel, and Vorain apparently trusted the older man enough to leave her brother behind while she traveled for a few weeks.

Jonan shrugged in response to Vorain's assertion. "I think it's a political move. Edon was the foundation of a religion. Executing him would have been almost certain to cause his worshippers to take action."

"More likely than the riots he'll induce when he escapes and proclaims his innocence?"

The scribe waved his hand dismissively. "It'll be hard for him to escape after he dies quietly in a cell."

Vorain quirked a brow. "You think they're going to arrange for that?"

"It's what I'd do," he replied. The memory of a helpless Esharen flashed in his mind.

"Well," she said, "We'll have to see if they're as brutally pragmatic as you are."

"They'd better be. He still has at least two allies out there that we never found," Jonan pointed out.

"Two? Morella and who else?" Vorain asked.

"Veruden," Jonan replied. "From what Lydia tells me, Veruden was badly hurt when she last saw him, but we have no idea what sorts of abilities those strange runes might have given him."

Vorain folded her arms. "Doesn't that mean they have enough information to keep doing what Edon was doing?"

Jonan shook his head. "Maybe. Edon's notes imply that he relied on Morella heavily, so she might have known all the details of the process. That said, the whole kingdom is going to be looking out for them at this point. They might be able to start over somewhere else, but not in Orlyn."

The pair continued their walk silently for a while, before Vorain stopped him by taking his hand.

"Do you really think your order can find a cure for my brother?" She tried to stare into his eyes, but he turned his head away immediately.

"Hey, no need to use the eye tricks. I can't promise anything, but if anyone can help your brother, yeah. Vaelien is a Rethri himself. Not that he's going to act on it personally, but I'm sure there would be a number of talented sorcerers who would be willing to look into it. Especially if I give them a chance to look at all this existing research," Jonan offered.

She released his hand, taking a step away. "Fine," she said simply. "I'm trusting you to take care of it personally," she added after a few more moments.

He nodded once, resuming his walk. "Not a problem."

Weeks later, Jonan finally arrived in Selyr. He rented two rooms at a local tavern, leaving Vorain behind in one of them, and then went to give his report.

When he arrived at Fort Amber, the Order of Vaelien's local headquarters, he was quickly escorted to a private room to wait for a superior officer to arrive. The door closed, leaving him apparently alone in the dark. He sat down on a long bench, nervous that they might send one of the Thornguard to interrogate him.

He waited for a handful of minutes, something itching at the back of his mind, before finally tapping the right side of his head.

A woman was sitting next to him, idly inspecting the walls of the small chamber. Her hair was a sheet of molten gold, brighter than the golden trim on her crimson dress. She looked to be unarmed, but Jonan knew from years of experience that her lack of weaponry was utterly irrelevant.

Instinctively, he slid an inch away from her. She whirled on him immediately, grinning broadly. "You're getting slow, Jonan."

She poked him on the nose, still smiling broadly.

"So, how'd it go?" she asked, gathering her hands under her chin to stare at him.

"I was able to successfully orchestrate the downfall of the target, utilizing a Paladin of Sytira and a swordsman as resources," he explained, attempting to keep himself calm.

Being near one of the Vae'kes always made his skin crawl – and she was the worst of them. She could kill him as easily as she smiled.

The woman steepled her fingers. "And what were you able to ascertain about his identity and motives?"

The sight sorcerer set his hands on the bench, gripping tightly against the wood to ease his tension. "As my initial reports indicated, I determined his identity to be Donovan Tailor, a former priest of Sytira. After being expelled from the priesthood, he traveled to Selyr, at which point he was somehow robbed of his ability to cast dominion sorcery. I don't know how-"

"Speculate," she instructed him, waving a hand.

Jonan tightened his jaw. "Donovan believed that his sorcery had been taken away by Sytira, who was punishing him for preaching that any mortal could ascend to godhood."

"And do you believe that?" she inquired, her eyes fluttering.

"It's a possibility," he began, sensing her gaze weighing more heavily upon him, "But he ignored a much more plausible explanation. Selyr is one of Vaelien's cities, and a Vae'kes could have been responsible."

The woman grinned brightly at him. "Continue."

"He felt it the moment his sorcery was taken from him. He didn't see or hear anyone, but he was under the effects of one of his spells, something called Intuitive Comprehension."

The Vae'kes made a 'hmmm' sound, tapping her fingers on the bench.

"The spell identified the effect that was taking his sorcery, but the words it showed him initially appeared to be gibberish. He wrote them down, determined to learn how his sorcery had been stolen and reverse the process. He shared that information with a friend, a Paladin of Sytira, and they worked together to attempt to find a solution."

"Difficult business, replacing lost sorcery," the Vae'kes noted. "Like trying to sew on a new limb."

Jonan nodded at that. "The Paladin of Sytira hadn't lost her sorcerous abilities, which involved knowledge and memory. The pair of them speculated that if they could determine how his sorcerous abilities had been removed, they could find a way to reverse the process. Not only to give his sorcery back, but potentially to give them – or others – access to new types of sorcery."

The blonde haired woman fidgeted in her seat, frowning. "Is that all? I thought you were going to tell me something interesting, Jonan."

Jonan flinched. "Well, he does seem to have eventually succeeded."

The Vae'kes tilted her head to the side. "How?"

Jonan adjusted his glasses, unsure of how much to say. If the Vae'kes learned the secrets that Donovan had used, his chance of executing his own plans in the future would be drastically diminished.

"Two ways," the scribe began, scraping the necessary words together. "First, he was experimenting on Rethri, figuring out how to adapt their dominion bonds to make use of them on humans. He appears to have found a way to create dominion marks, like the ones found on some of the oldest known dominion bonded objects."

"More interesting, but not entirely unprecedented. Continue."

"He also appeared to have created – or learned – some new kind of sorcery. It involved speaking words in a language I was not familiar with in order to produce specific effects. I believe he was using artifacts as power sources for this type of sorcery, and as such, he was trying to get access to the Sae'kes," Jonan explained, deliberately omitting several details.

"Ooh, the Sae'kes!," she said, clapping her hands together. "Tell me more about that."

Jonan quirked a brow, uncertain.

"A week or two ago, a swordsman entered the city carrying the Sae'kes Taelien. He was immediately arrested and confined. I quickly learned about it from one of my contacts and went to investigate. He was rescued by a Paladin of Sytira, who had been acting as a spy. I found the pair and convinced them to help me work against Edon," he provided.

The woman's expression soured. For an instant, Jonan considered his options for escape, and deemed it impossible.

"And who was this swordsman carrying the Sae'kes?"

"He just called himself Taelien. His physical description matches the legends of the god of swords almost perfectly," Jonan reported hesitantly.

The Vae'kes narrowed her eyes for a second, seeming to burrow into him, and then burst out into sudden laughter.

"Taelien... How fun!" She clasped her hands together. "Did you happen to get a sample of this new sorcery that Edon was using, or perhaps one of the new dominion marks he was making?"

A sample of a dominion mark? Well, Rialla almost undoubtedly has at least one, given the stories about her eye colors changing. At a minimum, her dominion bond has been altered somehow.

"No, my lady," he said with the utmost hesitation. "I did, however, witness him cast spells in that language, and I could write down the words he used," he offered.

A few words would probably won't be enough for her to do anything. I can't let her find the books — she might be able to figure out the whole language from them. And, if my suspicions are correct, Edon was learning different words from studying different artifacts. If she discovered a way to use that type of sorcery with Hartigan's Star...

"Yes, do that. Thank you, Jonan. Now, where is the Heartlance?"

He hadn't told anyone about the Heartlance.

"It's in my room at the nearby tavern," he grudgingly admitted.

"Oh, with that girl? Who is she, by the way?" The Vae'kes gave him what he imagined was intended to be a 'friendly' nudge.

"One of their fake gods," Jonan explained. *This just gets worse and worse.* "Called herself Vorain in the city. I managed to turn her against Edon, and now I believe she will be a valuable resource for us. She said her real name is Rialla Dianis."

The youthful-looking woman reeled back at that, visibly disturbed. "Rialla Dianis? No, her eye color is wrong," she muttered, probably more to herself than to him.

Jonan frowned. *How does she know Rialla? I suppose House Dianis is famous, but I didn't realize she was personally all that well-known.*

"I suppose she could have been lying about that," he offered.

The Vae'kes leaned back toward him, forcing a bright grin. "Of course she was. You've told me everything you need to for the moment. You'll be well rewarded for going outside of your mission parameters to retrieve something so valuable," she reported in a neutral tone. She leaned in close, whispering in his ear. "Bring it to me."

"Yes, Lady Aayara," Jonan replied.

Jonan returned to his room at the tavern in a near panic.

The situation is still salvageable, he told himself. *I need to hand over the lance, but she didn't ask for the books. The books are the key.*

He thought back to Donovan's research notes, remembering that even he hadn't been able to figure out the sorcery on his own. He had needed help from Morella, a former Paladin of Sytira — presumably because the paladin had been able to use knowledge sorcery.

Jonan shook his head, reaching into his pouch and retrieving a quill, and inkwell, and a bit of parchment. Setting the objects out on a nearby floor, Jonan began to write.

Dear Lydia,

I've heard Velthryn is beautiful this time of year.
When would be a good time for me to come and visit?
Jonan

THE END

APPENDIX I – DOMINION SORCERY

It is a most unfortunate truth that the average sorcerer never sees the necessary training to begin to comprehend his or her own potential. With the slightest talent, a sorcerer can be turned from a farmer into a devastating weapon or a bastion of hope – with the proper tools and motivation. Among the Rethri, sorcery remains relatively common, but still poorly instructed. Among humanity, it is viewed with hostility and superstition among the residents of small towns and used for parlor tricks in the few vast cities that remain.

This book is intended to teach certain fundamental points of knowledge that every sorcerer should be aware of, but few today are. That being said, the concepts presented here are intended for those that have already unlocked their sorcerous talents. My previous work in this series, *Introductory Dominion Sorcery*, is dedicated to teaching how to establish an initial connection with a dominion and learn to use it. This book will make little sense without that context, or similar knowledge from having learned how to use sorcery from another source.

The Costs of Sorcery

As a sorcerer gains experience, he or she surely will begin to notice the exhaustion that comes with casting too many spells in a short period of time. It is only upon medical examination, however, that we can uncover more specific details of what is occurring – dominion sorcery, in spite of the name and the concept, is powered by the body.

This, of course, may sound contradictory and on the surface appears to defy the very term "dominion sorcery" – but before you discard this tome as the ramblings of an old man, read on.

As the Rethri have known for centuries, sorcery takes a toll on the body – a measurable toll. Unbeknownst to many, however, this "Sorcery Exhaustion" differs considerably based on the specific Dominion that is being utilized. Most people are still trained that, "Sorcery makes you tired," or "Channeling the energies of the planes takes a toll on your body." These statements are both true, but greatly oversimplify the situation. It has been my conclusion, after many years of research, that the body is not simply channeling the energy of the Planes when you cast a spell – it is serving as a catalyst.

Ask a Dominion of Flame sorcerer – if you are lucky enough to know one – how they feel when they have exhausted themselves from using too many fire spells. In every case I have encountered such a sorcerer – and see the collected data section at the end of this tome for examples of some of those brave enough to volunteer their names and proficiency levels – they have explained it as thus, "At first, I begin to feel chills as I cast. As I continue, I grow colder, and my movements grow more sluggish. It requires more and more effort to continue casting spells."

Exhaustion is present, yes, but we see another important element here – a cold splashing across the body. After hearing this description several times, I thought to investigate it with the aid of a medical doctor, and remarkably, the symptoms were not just in the perception of the sorcerer – the body's temperature is physically lowered when a Dominion of Flame sorcerer casts their spells.

This revelation lead to intensive study on the subject matter, and upon further examination, I realized that each Dominion takes a slightly different toll on the body. Water sorcery causes dehydration, whereas life sorcery appears to more generally impact the body, preventing blood from clotting at its normal rate and impeding other necessary bodily functions.

This suggests that each of the prime dominions, at the very least, have a presence within the body – and that their presence is necessary for basic bodily functions. Conversely, some may suggest that it is backlash – that is, the influence of the opposing dominion on the body – that causes these side effects. In either case, the side effects of most prime dominions can be measurably observed.

Below, I have catalogued a list of the Prime Dominions, their uses, and their primary side effects.

Dominion	Function of the Dominion	Side Effects for Using This Dominion
Life	Governs the function of the organs, such as the rate at which the heart beats. Note that this includes the development of new skin. The Dominion of Life does not govern the brain or thought, however. When used by a sorcerer, the Dominion of Life can accelerate the process of healing an injury, sometimes drastically. This often causes side effects, such as preventing a bleeding wound from clotting until it has sufficiently healed. In addition, applying the Dominion of Life to a wound can cause it to heal disproportionately, causing unusual scarring.	Mild use can result in simple pain. Anecdotal evidence suggests the possibility of spontaneous "injuries" appearing on the sorcerer. A sorcerer who overuses the Dominion of Life would gradually suffer from a loss of function in their internal organs. Just casting a few basic spells might temporarily cause pain in the stomach or kidneys with no long-term effects, but overuse of powerful spells could cause a heart attack, liver failure, or infertility.
Death	The Dominion of Death allows the body to stop a process it has already started. For example, the Dominion of Death signals the body to wake up when you	A subject that uses the Dominion of Death would have a delayed response to things the body should force to stop, such as feeling pain. The body might also continue

	have slept for long enough (otherwise you would only wake up you were woken up by an outside source). The Dominion of Death also stops certain other functions when it is appropriate to do so; for example, the Dominion of Death signals the body to stop feeling pain after a certain period of time has elapsed from receiving an injury. When utilized by a sorcerer, the Dominion of Death can stop bodily processes. Some claim it can even be used to trick a corpse into believing it is still alive.	to sweat after leaving a hot environment. Overuse would prevent wounds from clotting or prevent the subject from waking from unconsciousness (i.e. the subject would be comatose).
Shadow	The function of the Dominion of Shadow within the scope of the body is a mystery. Sorcerers who manipulate the Dominion of Shadow claim to be able to hide in plain sight, concealing the presence of their body from eyes and ears.	Studies suggest that sorcerers who practice the Dominion of Shadow have a difficult time recovering from injuries, diseases, etc. An extreme version of this would be hemophilia.
Flame	It is theorized that this Dominion functions	Without the Dominion of Fire, the

	to regulate the body's ability to maintain its own healthy temperature in any environment. When utilized by a sorcerer, the Dominion of Flame can be used to produce sparks of fire.	body's temperature would be more greatly impacted by the environment. For example, the body would lose the ability to sweat and other self-regulating features.
Water	Regulates the level of moisture in the body, including the processing of water in the body and excreting fluids. When wielded by a sorcerer, the Dominion of Water can produce water from the air or flush toxins out of the body of a subject.	A weakened Dominion of Water would cause the body to show symptoms of dehydration, as it can no longer properly process water. The subject would need to drink larger amounts of water to prevent dehydration and their skin might dry out. In extreme cases, this would also prevent the proper flow of blood through the body.
Wind	Controls the lungs and the ability to breathe. When manipulated by a sorcerer, the Dominion of Wind can be used to project blasts of wind, levitate, or breathe in any environment.	Weakness in this Dominion causes slight breathing problems that can be temporary (such as coughing) or chronic (such as asthma). Completely losing this Dominion would prevent the body from breathing.
Stone	Regulates the creation of bone, muscle, cartilage, and bone marrow. When manipulated by	A weakened connection to this Dominion can result in weakened bones and muscles, and eventual

	a sorcerer, the Dominion of Stone can harden the muscles and the skin, making the body more resilient. Experienced Stone Sorcerers can reportedly manipulate actual stone, changing its shape as they desire.	muscle loss and death.
Knowledge	Within the body, the Dominion of Knowledge controls the basic ability to think and process information logically. When wielded by a sorcerer, the Dominion of Knowledge can be used to gather information.	Overuse of the Dominion of Knowledge would cause a loss of reason and logical thinking. This can impede grammar and vocabulary and the ability to perform mathematical computation.
Deception	Within the body, the Dominion of Deception controls the ability to think contextually, and to approximate, etc. When manipulated by a sorcerer, the Dominion of Deception can be used to trick a subject with false sensory information, i.e. illusions.	A weakened Dominion of Deception causes the body to have a difficult time processing things that are abstract, such as creative thoughts, approximate numbers, and contextual dialogue.
Light	The Dominion of Light is used to break down and/or expel that foreign material. Thus, the Dominion of Light is necessary for recovering	A character with a weakened Dominion of Light would have difficulty recovering from poison, infections, and enemy spells.

	from many forms of poison or disease. The Dominion of Light also allows for recovery from foreign dominions introduced into the body. Thus, someone with a powerful Dominion of Light would quickly recover from enemy sorcery. When utilized by a sorcerer, the Dominion of Light can be used to treat poison or disease. It can also utilized offensively by controlling the light to treat anything it touches as "foreign material".	
Stability	The function of the Dominion of Stability on the body is unknown. When utilized by a sorcerer, the Dominion of Stability can extend the duration of a spell that is already in effect on a target.	The side-effects of using the Dominion of Stability are unknown. Unlike most forms of sorcery, using the Dominion of Stability does not appear to noticeably fatigue the caster. Nevertheless, as with any form of sorcery, caution is advised. It is likely that there are side effects, but that they are too difficult to notice.
Motion	Governs muscular movement.	A weakened Dominion of Motion

	When manipulated by a sorcerer, the Dominion of Motion can enhance or diminish the subject's speed. Some claim that the Dominion of Motion can also be used to amplify or nullify the force of a physical movement, such as swinging a hammer.	would initially result in stiffness in the joints and a lack of flexibility. In extreme cases, this could eventually result in paralysis.

Redundancies and Connected Functions

The functions of Dominions in the body are not isolated. Instead, they function as a system, and many of them are interconnected. The Dominion of Death, for instance, works with regulatory Dominions as the function used to stop processes. Similarly, the Dominions of Flame and Water work together to regulate body temperature, while also having other separate functions.

As a result, there is also overlap in the side effects of weaknesses in specific Dominions.

I theorize that the usage of Deep Dominions impacts the body in much the same way, but my research on the subject is still in progress.

-An excerpt from Intermediate Dominion Sorcery by Eric Tarren, one of the most commonly referenced tomes for sorcery research in major cities.

APPENDIX II – NOTABLE PERSONAGES

Visitors to Orlyn

Name	Title	Description
Taelien Salaris	Taelien	A swordsman from the Forest of Blades. Bears the Saekes Taelien.
Lydia Scryer	Court Sorceress	A sorceress specializing in knowledge sorcery.
Jonan Kestrian	Scribe	A "humble scribe" that works for the Order of Vaelien.
Gerald Mason	Paladin of Tae'os	A Paladin of Tae'os working secretly within the city.

The Gods of Orlyn

Name	Title	Description
Edon	God of Ascension	The leader of Orlyn's pantheon.
Tylan	Goddess of Rulership, Queen Regent	The current ruler of the city of Orlyn.
Myros	God of Battle	The patron of soldiers and champion of the gods.
Vorain	Goddess of Shelter	The least known of the gods. She is the patron of the weak and defenseless.

Court Sorcerers of Orlyn

Name	Title	Description
Morella	Court Sorceress	A sorceress specializing in Memory sorcery.
Sethridge	Court Sorcerer	The oldest of the city's sorcerers.
Veruden	Court Sorcerer	A younger sorcerer. Specializes

		in travel sorcery.
Istavan	Court Sorcerer	A masked sorcerer. Specializes in Light and Life sorcery.

Citizens of Orlyn

Name	Title	Description
Raymond Lorel	Head Researcher	An expert in sorcerous research. He is not officially a court sorcerer.
Landen	Queensguard, "Landen of the Twin Edges"	A talented fighter, also known as Landen of the Twin Edges.
Korin Matthews	Queensguard	A member of the Queensguard.
Randall Shaw	Guard Captain	Captain of the guard for the Low Palace.
Stuart	?	A servant.

The Gods of the Tae'os Pantheon

Name	Title	Description
Sytira	Goddess of Knowledge	Among the most powerful of the gods, and patron deity of many scholars and sorcerers.
Aendaryn	God of Blades	Often considered the leader of the Tae'os pantheon. Known for wielding the Sae'kes Taelien, the symbol of the pantheon.
Eratar	God of Travel	Patron deity of merchants, sailors, and travelers.
Koranir	God of Strength	Patron deity of soldiers. Also associated with the Dominion of Stone.
Xerasilis	God of Justice	Patron deity of judges.

		Also associated with the Dominion of Flame.
Lysandri	Goddess of Water	Patron deity of sailors. Frequently associated with self-sacrifice.
Lissari	Goddess of Life	Patron deity of doctors and healers.

The Divinities of Selyr

Name	Title	Description
Vaelien	The Preserver	The principal deity worshipped by the residents of Selyr, as well as the majority of the Forest of Blades. His "children" are called the Vae'kes.
Aayara	The Lady of Thieves	One of the eldest of the Vae'kes, Aayara is considered a demigoddess and commonly worshipped by thieves, lovers, and gamblers.
Jacinth	The Blackstone Assassin	The other eldest of the Vae'kes, Jacinth is a demigod associated with the execution of justice. He is greatly feared outside of the Forest of Blades and rumored to have slain the gods of several other pantheons.

ABOUT THE AUTHOR

Andrew Rowe was once a professional game designer for awesome companies like Blizzard Entertainment, Cryptic Studios, and Obsidian Entertainment. Nowadays, he's writing full time.

When he's not crunching numbers for game balance, he runs live-action role-playing games set in the same universe as his books. In addition, he writes for pen and paper role-playing games.

Aside from game design and writing, Andrew watches a lot of anime, reads a metric ton of fantasy books, and plays every role-playing game he can get his hands on.

Interested in following Andrew's books releases, or discussing them with other people? You can find more info, update, and discussions in a few places online:

Andrew's Blog: https://andrewkrowe.wordpress.com/
Mailing List: https://andrewkrowe.wordpress.com/mailing-list/
Facebook: https://www.facebook.com/Arcane-Ascension-378362729189084/
Reddit: https://www.reddit.com/r/ClimbersCourt/

OTHER BOOKS BY ANDREW ROWE

The War of Broken Mirrors Series
Forging Divinity
Stealing Sorcery
Defying Destiny

Arcane Ascension Series
Sufficiently Advanced Magic
On the Shoulders of Titans
The Torch that Ignites the Stars

Weapons and Wielders Series
Six Sacred Swords
Diamantine
Soulbrand (Coming Soon)

Other Books
How to Defeat a Demon King in Ten Easy Steps

Made in the USA
Columbia, SC
24 April 2021